A STATE OF

DISOBEDIENCE

P9-DMB-874

TOM KRATMAN

BAEN

Copyright © 2003 by Tom Kratman

A Baen Books Original

Baen Publishing Enterprises
P.O. Box 1403
Riverdale, NY 10471
www.baen.com

ISBN: 0-7434-9920-4

Cover art by Stephen Hickman

First paperback printing, August 2005

Distributed by Simon & Schuster
1230 Avenue of the Americas
New York, NY 10020

Library of Congress Cataloging-in-Publication Number:
2003019967

Production & design by Windhaven Press (www.windhaven.com)
Printed in the United States of America

To Hillary, Janet, and Lon

PROLOGUE:

From: *Staring Into the Abyss: A History of the North American Republic in the First Quarter of the 21st Century*, Copyright 2097, Professor Allan Richardson, Yale University Press

As we have seen in the preceding chapter, at no time since 1860 had the United States of America stood as close to civil war as it did a mere eight years after the turn of the century. With unprecedented sharp divisions in political, economic and social philosophy; with a near perfect balance in the electorate, the Congress, and the utterly political Supreme Court; with the growing specter of political failure equating to the levying of criminal charges, conviction and prison, politics—American politics—had become a very dangerous game indeed.

This was brought home to all with the arrest, conviction and imprisonment of former President Thomas Jefferson Gates on charges of corruption, bribe taking, rape, aggravated sexual assault, unnatural acts, abuse of office, misappropriation of funds, and treason, the imprisonment itself leading to the former chief of state's beating, homosexual rape and murder by strangulation after his Secret Service detail was withdrawn by presidential order. It could well be said that no national-level politician could any longer *afford* to lose an election; the consequences had simply become too dire.[1]

No more could one political party or the other afford losing its control of at least one body of the government: Executive, Legislative or Judicial, for without some political or quasi-political safe harbor, some means of countering and stymieing the opposing party, every member of each party faced a similar fate. None were whole; none pure, and all knew it.

Yet, despite this mutual interest in maintaining the balance of power, the rewards of attaining control were simply too great to be forgone. For the Democrats, control—could it but be achieved—would make the revolution begun in the 1930s complete. Control of the economy, control of education, control of the environment (difficult to understand now, with the then-common predictions of ecological disaster proven wrong, but a powerful concern at the time); could all three branches be made to fall to the Democracy, however briefly in theory, the Democrats could so arrange matters that no one and nothing could ever

---

[1] While it is interesting to speculate on the probable alternate future had incoming President Gregory Tavern forgone the opportunity for revenge upon his former rival; under the circumstances, with Gates' malfeasance so plain and well known, in truth, Tavern had little choice.

remove them from power, or alter their vision of America's proper and just future.

For the Republicans, however, the Democratic dream was a nightmare: thought control through linguistic control, micromanagement of the economy by those least suited to economic power, social engineering under the aegis of the most doctrinaire of the social engineers, disarmament of the population and the creation of a police state to rival that of Stalin or Hitler, at least in its scope if not by design in its evil.

Indeed, it could be said that it was precisely the seventy years of open and quasi war with first Hitler, then Stalin, then with the heirs of Stalin that had put the United States in the position in which it found itself at the beginning of the 21st Century.

For, as a wise man of the times had once put it, "You should choose your enemies carefully, because you are going to become just like them."

And so, subtly, too slowly to be perceived, the United States had become—if not "just," then certainly much—like its erstwhile enemies.

Not that there had been great choice in the matter. Faced with totalitarian propaganda, the United States had learned to twist truth in self-defense. Faced with planned economies, economies able to challenge the west only through inflicting deprivations on the workers, the United States had been forced to greater and greater economic control emanating from Washington. Faced with the possibility of armed invasion (though we know now that was never a realistic concern) the central federal government was forced into taking on more and more responsibility under the aegis of national self-defense.

From the national highway system (to move the military to the ports and defense materials to and from the factories) to the school lunch program (to provide educable cannon fodder for the wars and campaigns) to rates and levels of taxation we can today only marvel at (to pay for waging an often hidden conflict by land, sea, air, in space and—through propaganda and strings-attached foreign aid—in the hearts of the uncommitted); each and every spurt of growth in federal power, each Republican-detested centralization of authority, the Republicans had themselves fought for, at a minimum acquiesced in, in the interests of winning the seventy year war.

Yet, less than a generation after the successful closure of that interminable conflict the United States found itself as thoroughly divided into two hostile camps as had been the world previously.

Briefly, things seemed to be on the road to improvement. National political and philosophical differences seemed cast aside one terrible morning in 2001 amidst the shrieks of thousands of bombed, battered, burning victims of a vicious terrorist attack that threw all awry.

With the screams of the dying in their ears, the vision of the flames seared onto their eyes, no one, not Republican, not Democrat, not the man or woman on the streets resisted for a moment the most severe curtailing of civil liberties in the history of the Republic. Thus when, seven years later, the United States emerged victorious from what was known in some circles as "The Arab War," in some as "The Moslem War," in most as "The War against Terror," not only were all the previous differences found to be still largely intact, the mechanisms of control had been much improved and enhanced.

Worse, as it had been in 1860, the balance was near perfect . . . and perfectly precarious. The slightest shift left or right could tumble the entire shaky edifice into ruin, even into civil war.

Fortunately, at that time the right person, the right woman, appeared at hand.

CHAPTER ONE

From the transcript at trial:
Commonwealth of Virginia v. Alvin Scheer

DIRECT EXAMINATION
BY MR. STENNINGS:

Q. Sir, Please state your name for the Judge.

A. Scheer, Your Honor, sir. Alvin G. Scheer.

Q. And where do you live, Mr. Scheer?

A. Well, the past several months, at least, I've been living, if you could call it that, at the Fairfax County Jail. Before that? I lived in Texas, little town called White Deer, not too far from Amarillo.

Q. Mr. Scheer, please tell the judge your story.

A. Yes, sir. Your honor, I understand from Mr. Stennings I need to tell y'all everything. I don't mind. But where to begin?

   If it 'tweren't the worst of times; surely 'twern't the best, neither.

   Heard something like that once on an old

movie on TV. "Best and worst." Might maybe have come out of a book. Don't rightly know. I ain't no educated man. Always been just a simple working man . . . "simple"— that's me. Not sophisticated, you know. Not like them folks over in Washington, the ones that got all the answers to everything.

I watch 'em. I watch 'em on TV. Got an answer for everything. It used not be so bad; I remember. Used to be a man could rightly expect a job, a wage to support his family and himself, taxes that didn't eat him alive. Nope, surely 'twern't the best.

Lotsa folks turned to religion . . .

Washington, DC

"Willi! Willi! *Willi!* WILLI!"

The sound grew. Louder and louder the crowd chanted as their goddess ascended the stage to the podium. The chant's force caused dust to spring up from little unseen corners of the auditorium. It assaulted the ears. It overwhelmed the senses. It made the internal organs ripple in a way that was unpleasant to anyone not a devotee of politics.

To Ms. Wilhelmina Rottemeyer, President-Elect of the United States of America, the sound was *orgasm*. Never in her life had a thrusting man entering her body given her such a glorious feeling. To be honest, never in her life had a man made her feel anything but weight, that and—not infrequently—disgust. Her ex-husband had mostly made her feel disgust.

Reaching the podium, Rottemeyer surveyed the

rainbow sea of devoted, ecstatic faces before her. She locked eyes with her lover, her *true* lover, retired—and soon to be recalled and promoted—Army Lieutenant General Caroline McCreavy. McReavy smiled warmly. Another small shudder of orgasm swept Rottemeyer's body, though it failed to reach her face.

Lifting both arms up and outward, palms down, Rottemeyer made gentle patting motions. Gradually the sound ebbed. WILLI! *Willi!* Willi! Willi.

She began to speak. "My people. My people. I have just received a telephone call from the President. He concedes the electio—"

Louder even than before, the crowd broke out in a mindless animal shriek of fury and victory. Windows vibrated, threatening to shatter. Rottemeyer vibrated too as she closed her eyes and smiled a sort of Mona Lisa smile, another little orgasm well hidden.

Eyes opened again. The smile grew wider. It grew divine. All gazed—glassy-eyed, slack-jawed—worshipping with hearts full to bursting.

"The way was hard. They" (everyone knew that by "they" Rottemeyer meant the Republicans, the religious right, the antichoice fanatics, the prosperous . . . the people who disagreed with her, in other words) "fought us long and hard trying to steal this election. They tried every low, dirty, sneaky, legalistic trick in the book," said W. Rottemeyer . . . Esquire.

"They even murdered the man who should have been standing here today." *Or at least we made it look that way*, thought W. Rottemeyer, murderess.

"Anything but accept the will of the People!"

The People howled their outrage and their triumph until quelled again by their leader's gentle pats.

"But now the will of the People is made clear to all. Not only do we control the presidency, but with the switchovers and gains in both the House and Senate we control the legislature. With that, we will control the Supreme Court.

"From this day forward the past is swept away. No longer will we tolerate oppression. No more will we accept second place. Never again will the rich oppress the poor. In the new, glorious future we will bring dead white men will finally lose their throttle on progress! My people, the great day is *here!*"

Austin, Texas

"Oh, isn't *this* a great day for the Republic?"

Governor Juanita Montoya-Serasin de Seguin (D, Tx)—she went by her husband's name, Seguin—smiled benignly upon her tall, slender, graying adjutant general. In her size seven dress—not bad for a mother of four strong boys—and with her pretty Mexican peasant-woman face, she radiated maternal warmth and caring. Some said that was what had gotten her elected—"How can you vote against your mother?"

But Juanita was much more than a face. A shrewd politician? Both her rivals and her supporters said so. A woman of principle? There too they agreed, though some of them had, sometimes, disagreed with those principles. Especially did those of her party but not of her state disagree. Juanita was far too conservative to suit the social-democrat core of her party. In point of fact, she was far more conservative than many a northern Republican. Texas had always been a funny place; Texas politics rarely quite matched those of the rest of the country.

"You didn't like Willi's speech, Jack? I thought she did a fine job . . . speaking, that is."

Glaring balefully at his chief (the adjutant general for the State of Texas, like all National Guard officers, took his oath of office to his governor), Major General John Lewis Schmidt answered, "I could care less about the speech, Juani. What scares me . . . terrifies would be more like it . . . is that that . . . that . . . that *woman* has complete control of the federal government for at least the next two years. Worse, she's got dreams and some of them are doozies."

"Dreams? You think?" Juanita laughed. She *knew* that Rottemeyer had big plans for her presidency; big plans for society. Some of those dreams Juanita even agreed with, relatively conservative democrat or not.

Schmidt huffed. "You're just trying to get my goat," he snorted. His sun-worn, leathery face creased in a broad smile. "Still pissed about the pranks your brother and I used to play on you?"

"Oh, that was long ago. Before the war, even."

"Yes," answered Schmidt, dreamily, "it was before the war."

"Incoming!"

Lieutenant Schmidt pressed himself deeper into the muddy earth of the paddy as the air was split by the shattering crump-crump-crump of enemy mortar rounds. The stench of human feces filled his nostrils, causing his stomach to lurch in protest. Scant inches above him jagged, razor sharp pieces of 82-millimeter mortar shell casing whined past like so many giant, malevolent mosquitoes on a homicidal binge.

Around Schmidt a platoon of Vietnamese Rangers— those left alive—cowered under the withering hail. He risked a look around and saw the unit's Vietnamese officer running away, his cast off equipment flying behind him. "Useless dink," he muttered.

A body flopped to the mud next to him. Schmidt tightened his grip on his rifle and began to turn before he heard a calm voice—under the circumstances a remarkably calm voice, "If we can hang on until night we ought to make it, Jack."

The lieutenant smiled. "You mean, sir, of course."

"Sure, Jack . . . I mean, 'sir.'" The speaker scratched his nose with a finger, the middle finger of his left hand.

"Any chance for artillery, Sergeant Montoya?" Schmidt asked, pretending not to have noticed that his subordinate was giving him the universal salute.

"Not a chance. The VC got the radio when they got the radio man."

"Shit!"

"'Shit,'" echoed the stocky little Tex-Mex sergeant. Still with a voice of calm he said, "Not a total loss, though, since that was Lieutenant Dong's excuse for taking off. And we're better off without him. I'm going to get to work on setting up whatever we can of a perimeter." Without another word he crawled off toward a knot of soldiers hiding, poorly, in a little shell crater.

Where does he get it; the courage, the calm? *wondered an admiring Jack Schmidt.*

❖   ❖   ❖

"Jack? JACK?"

Focus returned to the old general's eyes. "Sorry, Juani. I was . . . wandering. Thinking about Jorge. It occurs to me that at the precise moment we were caught in that ambush *your* new president and her ex were calling us murderers and baby killers. Jorge Montoya: a baby killer!"

Dei Gloria Mission, Waco, Texas

"*. . . in nomine Patrii, Filioque et Spiritu Sancti.*"

A very young baby squalled under the Baptismal waters pouring from the vessel in the hands of Father Montoya.

Holding the baby, Elpidia—the diminutive fifteen-year-old mother—looked up at the priest nervously. The Latin words were close enough to the girl's native—albeit poor—Spanish that she sensed the meaning of the words, if not their theological implications. There had been little of God in the girl's short, unholy life. In truth, there had been little of anything good. Drugs, sex, sex for drugs, sex for money to buy drugs; these had been her universe and her faith.

But that had changed. . . .

The slender, tiny, and provocatively clad Mexican prostitute shivered in the cold, windy night of a San Antonio winter. Doing her best to shield her half exposed budding breasts from the wind, the hooker walked past the little gray pornographic bookstore opposite a well-lit used car lot already fronted by several working girls on their nightly patrol. Knowing this was not her area, and the girls already there might object strongly to competition, she continued on her way up Broadway to another area where the streetwalkers gathered.

"Hi Elpi," greeted one of the transvestites standing outside the bright and cheery Wendy's. "Cold night to be dressed for 'work.'"

"No help for it, Susan." Politely, Elpidia used the "girl's" working name. "Got to feed the baby and my man."

Susan nodded her understanding. He (She? It?) likewise was bound as tightly as any slave to the needs, drug needs in both cases, of a derelict.

The girl continued on to the next corner and began her sales pitch. This was a simple procedure; she gave the "look" to every passing car that seemed likely to be holding a man, barring only those that were certain to contain a police officer.

The look? It was something easy to perform, hard to describe, and shared equally by every prostitute who had ever peddled herself on a corner. Part direct stare, part inviting smile, part something subliminal, the "look" advertised her services and prices in a way no other form of advertising could compete with.

Shortly a car pulled over. A quick negotiation session was concluded. Elpidia entered the car, took her money, and proceeded to work.

Half a night and seven autos later, Elpidia was considering calling it a day. Then she reconsidered the beating that was sure to follow if she didn't bring home enough money for her boyfriend's expensive habit and decided on one more try.

She gave the look to a passing Ford Taurus and

was immediately rewarded. The Taurus slowed, turned right, and came to a stop just around the corner. The girl hurried over.

"*Looking for a da . . . ?*" *she asked, then stopped cold, her hooker's false smile suddenly turning to dread as she recognized the clerical collar on the driver as he turned a severe gaze toward her.*

"*How old are you, girl?*"

Elpidia no longer wore the garb of a prostitute. She no longer painted her face, in part, to cover the bruises. Instead, from mission stores she wore clothes that, even though used, still made her look like a real human being rather than some streetwalking piece of meat.

Wrapping the newly baptized baby in a fluffy mission-owned towel, Elpidia clutched it to her breast, patting it dry and whispering soothing motherly sounds. "There, there my little baby. There, there *mi alma, mi corozon.* Hush little Pedro. Mama's here and she'll never let anything bad for you happen."

Father Montoya smiled. He thought, *I might have had a child like this girl. I might have been a grand- father this day.*

The good father turned away from the girl and her baby, turned toward the several dozen people, most of them young people, who made up the population of the mission.

He began, "Today we welcome this child into the warm brotherhood of Christ. We give it, through our Holy Father, a new life, an eternal life. Not for him the never ending death of unbelief, of faithlessness to God."

"But I hasten to add, it is only through the courage of this little boy's young mother that he was allowed to see the light of day at all. For many, too many, young boys and girls the darkness comes before they even are given the chance to see the light. . . ."

Washington, DC

Bright winter light streamed through the windows, bathing the cold stones of the Capitol Building, as Rottemeyer, surrounded by her sycophants and security, entered to address a joint session of Congress.

The Congress she was to address was nearly perfect, her instrument, her tool. It consisted of 535 members, 100 senators and 435 members of the House of Representatives. Not all of either group were present, though the vast majority were. Fifty-five senators were from her own Democratic Party, though three of these were far more Republican than many Republicans. Of the 45 Republicans, three were nominal; "RINOs" they were called, Republican In Name Only. These could be counted on to vote her way about three times in four. Of the members of the House, she had an acceptable, even substantial, majority as well. Never since Franklin Delano Roosevelt held near dictatorial power before and during the Second World War had a President of the United States wielded such overwhelming political force at home. Even the Supreme Court was so evenly balanced—though she hoped to unbalance it very soon—that it was most unlikely to interfere with Rottemeyer's plans in any significant way.

The assembled Congress stood and clapped as she

walked down the aisleway to the rostrum, though the Republicans, most of them, did so out of mere politeness, devoid of enthusiasm.

Senator Ross Goldsmith (Republican, New Mexico) was extremely successful in hiding his enthusiasm. But then, the enthusiasm of the bespectacled, graying, balding old man was so tiny in scope he could have hidden it under a gnat. His hands moved together, rhythmically . . . but they never quite touched.

Standing opposite, Goldsmith's old personal friend and old political enemy, Harry Feldman (Representative, Democrat, New York), noticed Goldsmith's hands, smiled, and redoubled his own efforts.

Goldsmith simply glared as Feldman mouthed the words, "spoilsport."

Reaching the rostrum, Rottemeyer smiled at her Vice-President, Walter Madison Howe, by repute a moderate midwesterner, in fact a purely political animal of little principle. The smile hid her immediate thought, *Reactionary moron.* Turning away, she opened the folder containing her speech. This was a mere formality; she knew it by heart.

"We stand poised on the brink," she began. "We can either go forward, to a new era of peace, progress and prosperity, or backwards to the dark age of old, backwards to the days when women were kept barefoot and pregnant, when blacks were lynched in the streets of the south, backwards to ignorance, want and filth.

"My administration is pledged to work with Congress to go forward, into the future, rather than backwards to the Republican age of deficits, doubt, debt and decline; recession, repossession and retrenchment.

"We *must* go forward into the future . . . and we cannot afford to leave anybody behind in the past.

"We are going to invest in America. We are going to invest in a very large way. No more tax cuts for the rich. No more crimping away social security. Instead we are going to make the rich—and the corporations they control—pay their fair share for the first time. We are going to expand social security to ensure that every American can enjoy a comfortable and secure retirement."

Rottemeyer paused, thinking, *It still amazes me that anyone falls for that "soak the rich" crap. Impossible, of course . . . short of a hundred-percent Gift and Estate tax. The corporations just pass the tax on to consumers like any other sales tax and the truly rich pass their income tax on the same way through demanding higher returns on their investments. And as long as they all do it together the consumer has no choice but to pay. Still, it sounds good and helped get me into the White House. Who cares if it's the truth or not? My job is "divinity," not truth.*

She continued, "The people have spoken clearly of the kind of investment in the future they demand. We are going to a national health care system and we are going to do so very quickly indeed. The people demand and deserve nothing less.

"The people demand and deserve a national public education system that is second to none. They will have it. Among other measures that will be sent to Congress for legislative action is a plan for rigorous testing of schools for quality of education, and national assumption of authority over any schools that fail that test. In short, we will shut down those schools and reopen them under our guidance, funding them directly through bypassing the state bureaucracies."

Senator Goldsmith put his head in his hands, thinking, *Dear God preserve us. This bitch telling all the children what they can think.*

Feldman simply smiled to himself, thinking, *Sure, honey, up to a point. Don't think we'll let you get too far. Don't get too big for your britches.*

"We are also going to put one million new teachers in our classrooms, many of them to go to staff 'Opportunity Academies' to help prepare disadvantaged youths for college. In those academies and in nationally funded and run charter schools.

"We are going to ensure that college education becomes as universal as high school education is today."

Goldsmith asked silently, *Are you going to ensure likewise that that education is as bad as high school education is today? I am sure you will try to. We will stop you if we can.*

"But children need a place to grow up. Another path to investing in America is going to be the creation of more livable communities.

"We hope to work with the states on this matter. We intend to have appointed for each state a federal commissioner who will oversee spending of federal funds within a state. The corruption of the bureaucracy must end.

"Moreover, along with one million new teachers, I intend to see one million new law enforcement officers, *Federal* law enforcement officers, to clean up the streets and make our communities livable again."

Rottemeyer paused briefly to survey the members

of Congress. It was simplicity itself for her to tell friend from foe with no more than a glance at the faces. Republican, and a few Democrat, faces were grim indeed. She locked eyes with Goldsmith, sending the message, *You lose.*

"As the corruption of bureaucracy must end, so must the tyranny of gun-related violence, the violence that murdered the man who should have been standing here today, my late running mate, Senator Palmer. I intend to ask this Congress for an increase in funding for the Bureau of Alcohol, Tobacco and Firearms, said increase to be paid for by a tax, a large tax, on both purchase and possession of these implements of death. This will naturally require registration of firearms to ease collecting the tax.

"Moreover, it seems only reasonable, just and fair that the tax on these hateful implements pay for correcting the natural and predictable results of widespread ownership of firearms. In other words, the tax shall pay for health care to mitigate the wounds and bloodshed these guns cause."

Now this is something where I will support you one hundred percent plus, Willi, thought Feldman, glancing again at Goldsmith.

Over my dead body, Goldsmith returned the glance with a glare.

Oh, grow up, said Feldman's smile.

"This will go a long way toward paying for another cornerstone of this administration's plan: National Universal Health Care. New taxes on another national health menace, cigarettes, will pay for an equally substantial portion.

"The third leg of this program shall be the imposition

of taxes on the great polluters of our environment, heavy industry. In this way we shall protect our environment, preserve the health of our people, and bring ourselves voluntarily into line with the Kyoto Agreements on emissions of greenhouse gasses.

"Lastly, as we march into the future, we must also build from the fragments of our polity one country, one single—unified—people. No more black nor white nor brown nor yellow nor red. No more Texans and New Yorkers and Californians and Indianans. One people. One nation. All united under the leadership of one government!"

Still flushed with the success of her speech to Congress, Rottemeyer met with select members of her Cabinet in the Oval Office.

"It's the expansion of the federal law enforcement capability I have problems with," said her new attorney general, Jesse Vega. "There's a limit on how fast any organization can expand. It's not just a question of funding the money and recruiting the bodies. We've limited training facilities, limited numbers of people trained for upper management, limited number of administrative people to take care of everything from pay to promotions. The U.S. Marshal Service, DEA, FBI and Treasury can only . . ."

"Who said anything about limiting the expansion to only the existing agencies?" demanded Rottemeyer.

"What?" asked Vega, incredulously. "You want to create . . . oh . . . the Surgeon General's Riot Control Police?"

"Tell me why not, Jesse? Does the Surgeon General's office not have an interest in controlling demonstrations that get out of hand at, say, abortion clinics? Do they have a bureaucracy capable of administering an additional force of several hundred or even a thousand? Can they hire people to train the new officers? Yes, to all. So why not?"

Vega stood somewhat dumbly, the effect enhanced by a certain rotundity and a face gone slightly slack from a stroke some years past.

"Well," she continued, contemplatively, "there *has* been a certain amount of expansion of federal law enforcement in places you would not expect. Maybe that's the way to go. I mean, we already *do* have armed turkey inspectors with the Food and Drug Administration, armed agents of the Environmental Protection Agency. Maybe . . ."

"Yes," said Rottemeyer with an air of logical triumph.

Later that night, in a bed in fact chaste, Caroline McCreavy asked, "Willi, I understand your goals and ideals. I even share many of them . . . most of them. But this . . . this . . . creation of a police state. I just don't get it. We don't need this."

Rottemeyer snorted. "Goals I have, love. Ideals? I don't have any ideals. Just ask the Republicans."

"Bu—"

Rottemeyer, interrupting, smiled from where her head rested on a pillow. "All right then. Goals? I believe in power, Caroline. Since I was a helpless little girl and boys were mean to me I have believed in power . . . and sworn to get it. That's my goal.

"And now I have it. And I will never let it go."

"But you have to. In eight years anyway."

Rottemeyer smiled indulgently. "Oh, Caroline, you're so innocent. After these eight years the party will run the country . . . and I will run the party. I will never give it up.

"I'll never give you up, either, Caroline," Rottemeyer added softly.

The other woman smiled back, warmly but with a troubled expression. "Don't tell me you don't have ideals, Willi."

"Ideals," mused the other. "Beliefs. I believe that you can make people better than they are. I believe that people are basically good until the system makes them bad. I believe that there is too much untrammeled economic power in the United States and the world. I believe that if someone has to have power, I can also use it more wisely, more benevolently, than anyone else I know."

"Then why the police state, Willi? And why split it up the way you are planning?"

"I'll split it up because I do not trust power that isn't in my hands. As long as there are fifty law enforcement agencies competing with and suspicious of each other then my power is safe. The police state? A lot of people are not going to like what I think I have to do. And I do not want them able to fight me on it.

"Now come here. . . ."

CHAPTER TWO

From the transcript at trial: Commonwealth of Virginia v. Alvin Scheer

DIRECT EXAMINATION, CONTINUED
BY MR. STENNINGS:

Q. And how did you feel about the President at that time, Mr. Scheer?

A. The President? Sure talked like she meant well. I mean, she was out there in front of the cameras all the time. Checking schools, visiting old folks. Seemed like she really cared, really felt our pain.

I never made much money in life. Used to have to hunt to help feed the family. Couldn't pay the tax on my rifles though, let alone buy the ammunition to hunt with the thing; not at three dollars and fifty cents per round . . . for the tax alone.

When they came and took away my neighbor

after his kids let slip to a teacher that their daddy still had a gun at home? Give him five years for tax evasion? Put his family on welfare? I couldn't face that. So I had to give up one of my two guns. The other? Well, you know by now I buried—

Q. Stop right there, Alvin. The Court doesn't need to hear about any of that.

A. Okay if you say so. Anyway, I never could get the hang of bow hunting.

Q. So you gave up hunting, Mr. Scheer?

A. Well, sure. Though it made it a lot harder to feed my family, like I said. Anyway, sure and some of them new programs did help. When my factory closed, moved down Mexico way . . . trying to run away from the taxes, I reckon . . . and my missus got sick? She could go to the doctor right off, and I didn't have to pay for it. Mind, she had to wait in line for a while, half a day maybe . . . maybe a little more, and the doctor didn't have much time to see her. But he gave her some medicine. And she was okay for a while.

I did get work again, eventually. Didn't make so much as I had been. But they raised the "minimum wage," which seemed to help, a little.

Though, why prices kept going up every time they raised the income tax on the big companies and the rich folks, I don't rightly know.

Weren't for charity, that and welfare food parcels, don't reckon we'd a made it.

Dei Gloria Mission, Waco, Texas

"Sergeant Montoya, post!"

Stripped to the waist, sweating in the sun, despite having a fifty pound sack of government surplus rice over one shoulder, the priest stiffened to attention. The pattern of scar tissue on the priest's abdomen lost color as the skin there stretched.

"Dammit!" he muttered, shoulders slumping again. "How does he keep doing that to me after all these years?"

He turned around and glared into the smiling face of his oldest and best friend. "Why do you *do* that?" An extended finger began to move up to scratch his nose.

"Because I can and because it's funny." Schmidt kept his eyes away from his friend's battle scars.

The priest's middle finger stopped moving. He gave a rueful smile, rubbed it and the index finger of his free hand under his nose and admitted, "I suppose it is at that."

Sack still on his shoulder, Montoya looked around for one in particular of the boys helping him unload the monthly supply run from the 49th Armored Division, Texas National Guard truck—food and truck both courtesy of his friend, Jack Schmidt.

Spotting the boy, the priest shouted, "Miguel, take over here. I am going to have a few words with the general. Elpi, would you bring us a couple of beers from the cellar?"

"Si, Padre," answered the dark skinned, brown-eyed teenager, running to take the sack from Montoya's shoulder. "Come on, Julio. You too, Raul . . . put your backs into it. These men"—he meant the National Guard truck drivers—"don't have all day."

In the cool, dimly lit rectory Montoya and Schmidt sat down on opposite sides of the roughly crafted but sturdy wooden table. The priest took two beers from Elpidia, thanking her. Then he opened both and passed one over to Schmidt. . . .

"Here, drink this, Jack," ordered the sergeant, handing over his own canteen. "Only the best for you."

The lieutenant refused at first, but at his sergeant's insistence took a sip of the tepid, muddy, iodine-tinged water. As he did Montoya glanced down at the red seepage at Schmidt's waist, gift of a mortar fragment ripping across the officer's stomach. Only the bandages Montoya had applied kept the lieutenant's innards from spilling to the ground. It did not look good.

"Not looking too good is it, Jorge?"

"That's 'Sergeant Montoya' to you." The sergeant smiled, hesitated, then continued, "We're down to fourteen men, plus you and me. Ammo's holding out . . . but only because so many of the ones who ran didn't want to carry theirs. What is it, four assaults we've beaten off? No . . . five, I think. They've got to be getting tired of it."

Still on his back, Schmidt nodded weakly before allowing his head to flop to a muddy rest. His practiced eye gauged the setting sun. "It's time, Jorge."

"Time? What time?"

"Time for you to leave me, take what you can save and try to get the hell out of here."

Montoya just snorted for an answer. Then, to change

the subject—admittedly somewhat ineptly, he turned his rifle over and read aloud the serial number, "120857. Good. Still have my own."

"*That's an order, Jorge. Get out and save what you can.*"

"*No.*"

"*Damn you, you wetback! I said get out of here.*"

"*No, Jack,*" answered the sergeant, calmly, as ever. *With determination, as ever.*

"Jack? Are you all right?"

Schmidt collected his wits as quickly as he was able, covering his lapse with a sip and the observation, "Good beer."

"Only the best for you."

"Who was that girl?"

"Just a poor girl who has found her way to Christ."

Under winking stars, Montoya whispered, "It's just you and me and about six of the ARVNs left. They're the best six though: Nguyen, Tri, and their crew."

More unconscious than awake, Schmidt muttered, "Christ," then nodded as if he understood. What was left of a platoon had assembled a rude stretcher out of a poncho and a couple of saplings. On this they proposed to carry off their wounded officer under cover of night.

Montoya spoke a few sentences in reasonably fluent Vietnamese, courtesy of a short course and a long tour, themselves courtesy of the Army. Taking courage from the round eyed Mexican, Corporal Tri grunted his own determined assent in broken English, "We no leave notin' for stinkin' baby killin' Cong."

"So . . ." Schmidt hesitated. "I've got some bad news for you, Jorge. Juanita asked me to tell you. She would have told you herself if you would have a damned phone put in here. I can't use my trucks and busses to transport you and your kids to any more political rallies."

"Political? What political?" the priest demanded. "Murder is murder and there's nothing political about it."

"Come on, Jorge, be serious. There is nothing so political in this entire country as abortion. And with the new rules from Washington, any state that permits any interference is going to get hurt, let alone one that uses an arm of its government . . . which I am."

"Bah. Tell Juanita I am disappointed in her."

"She's doing the best she can, Jorge. Times are tough and getting tougher."

"Not as tough as being twisted around inside your mother and having your brains sucked out through a tube."

Dallas, Texas

Nearly four hundred and fifty people burned candles through the night as Father Montoya led them through prayer and song. Mothers held their babies. Husbands held their wives. All joined in asking for divine intervention to stop what they considered a horrible series of crimes.

Montoya looked with mild disapproval upon a large banner fronting one group of protesters: "We, personally, would object to shooting abortion doctors . . . but we would never want to interfere with somebody else's choice of values. Catholics for Children."

And so Father Flores is heard from again. Montoya walked over to see his fellow priest.

"Don't you think that sign is, maybe, a little—oh—inflammatory, Father?"

Flores' fanatic eyes flashed fire. "Not so inflammatory as what awaits the people who work in that clinic."

"That is God's choice for them, Father, not ours."

A murmur arose among the protesters. Montoya turned about to see a line of armored, shielded and baton wielding riot police forming up the street from the clinic. These were not Dallas police, but the United States Surgeon General's new special troops, specially flown in for their first real test. They were four hundred of Rottemeyer's planned one million new police, raised at the same time and under the same bill that gave her a major expansion of manpower, arms and equipment for the Secret Service's new Presidential Guard, in all but name a personal mechanized brigade.

A loudspeaker blared, "Attention. Attention. In accordance with the Act of Congress for the Prevention and Suppression of 'Emotional Terrorism' you have five minutes to clear away from this clinic. This will be your only warning."

Montoya glanced at his watch, then looked around for Miguel. "Get our people out of here now, Miguel. Hurry."

Miguel just nodded and ran, first to Elpidia where she sat playing with her baby, then to the others. "Father says we have to go now. Hurry."

Before the protesters had a chance to so much as move, long before the mandated five minutes were up, the riot police began their charge. Peaceful dispersal was replaced by panicked, screaming flight.

Undaunted, his flock in danger, Montoya steeled his heart and moved to interpose his own body between them and "police" running amok.

Dei Gloria Mission, Waco, Texas

If anyone among the boys of the Mission held a position of leadership, under the father, it was Miguel Sanchez. Need to rebuild a shed? "Miguel, see to it." "Si, padre." Need to put up a fence? "Miguel, see to it." "Si, Padre. Julio, come on and help me."

Did a field need plowing, a tree need pruning, a boy need "counseling"? "I'll take care of it, Padre."

With the father now lying broken and battered, head bandaged where a policeman's baton had cracked it, much of the day-to-day running of the mission fell to young Miguel, under the guidance of Sister Sofia, the mission's sole nun.

But if anyone, besides the father, held leadership over Miguel, it was not Sister Sofia, but little, thin Elpidia. She had so held since about three days after she and the baby arrived at the Mission.

For her part, Elpidia liked Miguel well enough, as well as she could be expected to like any normal male after the life she had led. But her heart belonged to the priest.

"How old are you girl?"

"Old enough to work," she answered.

Shaking his head slightly, the priest provided his own answer. "Fifteen? Fourteen? Fourteen, I think. This is no life for you, child."

"It is the only one I have, Padre."

"Parents? Family?" he asked.

"None, Padre. Just me and my baby, Pedro, and the man I live with, Marco."

"He sends you out to do this and you still call him a man? We shall see. Get in the car. Where do you live?" asked the priest.

Will overborne, Elpidia entered and gave directions. Following these, the priest drove through narrow back streets and side alleys, past garbage and trash long uncollected. At length the car arrived at the girl's—Shabby? "Shabby" would have to do, though it was much worse than that—apartment.

"Padre, what are you doing?"

"Taking you and your baby to a better life," he answered, without further elaboration. He exited the car, walked around and opened the door for the girl—no one had ever been so polite to her before—and asked, "Which one?" At the girl's hesitantly pointed finger, he ordered, "Lead on. I will follow."

The sound of a squalling baby and the smell of soiled diapers hit them even as the girl opened the apartment's cheap door. There was another smell too, one the priest recognized from days long past.

Sprawled on the couch, a man—Marco—scruffy,

unkempt, filthy, slack faced, smoked a pipe. He looked up as the door opened. "Hope you made some goddamned money tonight, bitch." The man saw the priest as he stepped around to stand beside the girl. "Get the fuck out of my house, old man."

The father ignored the dope smoker. "Get the baby, Elpidia. You might want to gather up its things, too. Neither you nor he will be coming back here."

Doped Marco certainly was. He was not, however, so drugged that he didn't recognize the imminent threat to his livelihood. "You ain't goin' nowhere, you little slut." He stood to bar the way to the baby's unutterably filthy closet. When Elpidia tried to go around him he slapped her to the floor.

Marco was never quite sure, thereafter, how it was that he found himself suspended above the floor, back to the wall and a grip of iron about his throat. He kicked for a little while, his bare, filthy feet impacting on some stone-seeming wall that he knew had not been in the apartment before. With his vision fading, blood pounding in his ears, he dimly heard the priest repeat, "Get the baby, girl."

"Where's Pedro, Elpi?"

"He's sleeping, Miguel."

"Oh. Too bad. I wanted to play with him. Cute little critter."

He looked at Elpidia and said, "You're a good mom." Then he asked, shyly, "Do you think I might make a good father someday? Before he was hurt Padre Jorge told me he had been talking to his friend, Jack, about maybe finding me a decent job with the Guard once I turn eighteen."

"That would be so good for you, Miguel. How is Father?" A tear escaped the girl's eye.

Miguel shook his head angrily. "The same. He can barely walk. But did you see him fight them? It took fifteen of them to beat him to the ground. Fifteen! What a man!" exclaimed Miguel, who had himself once made the mistake of fighting the father. That was the last mistake he had ever made—or wanted to make—where the priest was concerned.

Austin, Texas

What kind of man is this? My very first instance of "hate at first sight," thought the governor of her state's new "Federal Commissioner."

"So you see," droned that worthy, Harold Forsythe, Yale Law '66 and a long-time crony of both Wilhelmina and her ex-husband, "you have got to stop seeing yourselves as separate states. We are all one country and we are all in this together. We can't have Texas going its own way anymore. Take abortion. You have placed some restrictions here that are just intolerable. And so, until those are lifted, Texas can forget about seeing one red cent in federal aid for Medicare or Medicaid. Nor will we permit you to stop funding them at your level. Same for your schools. Nearly half of them have failed Federal certification and no more educational aid is going to them until their entire staff has been reviewed and approved for retention or fired."

"You mean reviewed for political leaning, of course, don't you?" demanded Juanita. "Your entire test was a thinly disguised check of political correctness."

"Well, we can't have unenlightened teachers polluting the minds of America's youth now, can we?" Forsythe smiled smugly.

"And you had better do something about getting a handle on the guns in private hands in this state too. And soon. You are not going to be permitted to give people the right to the implements of death or to deny women the right to do what they choose with their own bodies."

How did we ever let it get this far? wondered Juanita. Then she supplied her own answer. *We let it get this far by letting the federal government take the burden of taxing for us. And now they have more—a lot more—power than the states do because they have so much more money than the states do.*

Dallas, Texas

Guns holstered and concealed, the federal agents poured over the smoking ruins of an abortion clinic torched by fanatics in the night. No note or sign claimed credit for the arson. Nor had anyone been hurt in the blaze.

Special Agent Ron Musashi pondered the lack of evidence. To one of his men he said, "Get me the files on the six leading antiabortion groups in this part of the state."

"Already did it, Chief."

"Good," Musashi complimented. "Who's the most likely candidate?"

"Catholics for Children," came the instant reply. "We suspect them of having torched two other clinics.

Never a shred of proof, though. Professional, you know? Their headquarters is over in Fort Worth."

Fort Worth, Texas

In another life, Ron Musashi would have been happy enough pouring Zyclon B crystals into gas chambers full of Jews. The Rape of Nanking would have been a wonderful vacation. Bayoneting stragglers on the Bataan Death March? Just a pleasant walk in the woods. But for being short of stature—and having the wrong shape of eye— Musashi would have fit right into Himmler's Waffen SS.

Not that he would have enjoyed the killing. All Musashi ever felt from killing was recoil. Though he *did* derive considerable personal satisfaction from a job well done.

This job was made for him. The orders were simple, amazingly so considering they came to him from Washington, DC: "Assume that the occupants found at the headquarters of that terrorist organization known as 'Catholics for Children' are armed and dangerous. Kill or capture them all."

Returning from lunch, Father Flores turned the corner to see an even dozen plain-clothed men—police of some kind, so he assumed, based on the drawn pistols and locked and loaded machine guns—crouching by the main door to his organization.

Unseen by the agents, themselves intent on their mission, Flores ducked back behind the building corner, one eye only watching the event. His heart began pounding wildly as he saw four of the agents draw back a large battering ram then smash it once, twice, three times against the front door.

He heard muffled screams.

The door collapsed inwards, torn off its hinges. Musashi ordered, "Go! Go! Go!" and the first team of four burst over the shattered door and through the empty frame. Inside a woman screamed with fear and shock. Automatically, she reached for her purse.

A gun? The agent who saw her could not take the chance. A burst of submachine-gun fire punched through the woman's body, spinning her in her desk chair while inertia made her head do an imitation of Linda Blair in *The Exorcist*. The woman fell, bloody and torn, to the floor.

As if the initial shots were a signal, the other three agents in the first rush likewise opened fire on the office workers, cutting them down in a welter of gore. Fired. Fired. Fired again. There were no survivors.

When Musashi looked into the woman's purse, he found a cell phone. He left the phone, but added to the purse's contents one small-caliber pistol.

Unseen, Father Flores, olive complexion turning pale, turned and ran; ran for his car, for his life.

CHAPTER THREE

From the transcript at trial: Commonwealth of
Virginia v. Alvin Scheer

DIRECT EXAMINATION, CONTINUED
BY MR. STENNINGS:

Q. So tell the court how it was for you, Alvin, how
it became?

A. Like I said before, life was hard. And it kind of
hurt, you know; me—a man that worked all his
life—having to take welfare parcels and charity
just to feed his family. But pride didn't count for
much. And besides, near everybody in that part
a town was in the same boat, mostly.

Always remember something my daddy used
to say, "Ain't no such thing as a free lunch." The
breakfasts and dinners weren't free neither. They
come with a "social worker" . . . and she done come
every damn week.

First time she come around she stuck her

pointed up little nose into every little nook and cranny in the house. She told my wife—yeah, she'd started feeling poorly again—that if she didn't clean house better she was going to lose her children. Talked down to us, you know, like we were some kind of lower life form. I confess, I kinda lost my temper.

That was a mistake too, no two ways about it. Next week, week after too, we found that our food allotment's been cut. Got cut again the week after that, then again.

Like I said before, I ain't no educated man. Don't mean I'm a dummy though. I swallowed my pride; made my apologies so my family wouldn't starve.

But I never could see the justice in giving that woman that kind a power over us. For a long time, I couldn't see what I could do about it, neither.

Dei Gloria Mission, Waco, Texas

In the dimly lit cloister, Miguel strained to hear the reclined priest's weakly spoken words. Mostly they had to do with things the mission needed done, but that Montoya lacked the strength, in his current condition, to do anything about. " . . . and I want you to do something about the rabbits in the garden, Miguel. I was able to walk—a little—earlier today and I noticed they had been at the new shoots."

Montoya had taught Miguel to shoot—and well—a year earlier. He had, in fact, begun teaching him shortly after having administered Miguel a fairly painful and quite salutary drubbing over a no-longer-to-be-mentioned breach of mission rules. At the time Miguel had thought, *He whips my ass . . . then teaches me how to kill him. What a man!*

Miguel, too, was now rapidly approaching manhood; just as Elpidia had long since reached practical womanhood.

"Father," he asked, hesitantly, "would it be all right if I took Elpidia along, taught her to use the rifle?"

Montoya smiled, knowingly—he had stood in as *"Father" of the bride* on more than one occasion since opening his mission doors. Miguel's interest was plain and, *frankly it would be a good match*. He thought about it briefly and answered, "I think that might be a good thing Miguel. She's had little enough control over her own life so far. Maybe giving her a little . . . what's that word the politicians like to use? Oh, yes, give her a little 'empowerment.' It might be good for her. Yes . . . I think so. Do it."

Miguel felt a little surge of . . . of something. He wasn't quite sure. But this was something he knew how to do—the priest had taught him well—and also something that would give him an excuse to be alone with Elpidia. "Si, Padre. I'll teach her the .22."

"Fine, but you take along the shotgun. Snakes look for rabbit too."

Said Miguel, "Si, Padre. Thank you, Padre," as he took the keys to the father's—which is to say the mission's—meagerly stocked (it held no more than the shotgun, two .22s, and one scoped hunting rifle often used to supplement the mission's food stores) gun rack from Montoya's pale, weak and trembling hand.

Interstate 35, Texas

Musashi still smarted from the intense down-dressing he had suffered at the hands of the United States Attorney General, Jesse Vega, for his failure to get "that damned Catholic fanatic priest, Flores." Vega had not cared in the slightest about the office workers massacred in the Catholics for Children offices, as Musashi had known she would not. But the possibility of someone escaping to tell a story in any way different from the official truth was intolerable. Musashi had no doubts that his orders were to kill the priest, even though Vega had not used the word, nor any that could be construed like it. So he intended to do that.

While one of his agents drove, Musashi studied the map, compared the files on anti-abortion activists, noted the prominence of Father Montoya . . . and came up with "Dei Gloria." He finagled a bit with the GPS cum map display in the car. Finagled some more. A bit more. Then Musashi smiled broadly, the satisfaction and anticipation he felt beaming on his face.

"I think I know where to find our arsonist priest, boys."

Dei Gloria Mission, Waco, Texas

"Father Flores? Can that be you?" asked a startled Sister Sofia of the unkempt—now collarless—Dallas priest. The priest bore the look of a hunted animal.

Breathlessly, Flores demanded, "I've got to see Father Jorge. I must see him, *now*."

"Father Montoya is still very badly injured," Sister Sofia announced, not at all sure but that seeing the condition of his colleague wouldn't hurt the good father's recovery.

"He will see me." Desperately, "He *must* see me."

"Well . . . I don't know . . ."

"What is it, sister?" called a weak voice. A limping and bandaged Father Montoya turned a corner to enter the small Mission vestibule.

"Father Flores?"

Relaxing ever so slightly—he had faith that in a world turned hostile Montoya would never cast him out—Flores sighed and forced a slight grin. "Bless me Father, for I have sinned." Then, more seriously, he said, "I need sanctuary, Jorge. They're after me. They killed all my staff and they want to kill me."

"Killed? Who killed? Sanctuary?" Father Montoya had not yet recovered his full senses from the beating he had received from the riot control police.

"I don't know who it was. But they went into my offices and shot down everyone there like they were dogs." Tears sprung to Flores' eyes. "Jorge, they just massacred everybody."

Montoya forced himself to think clearly; as clearly as he could. "Why?" he asked.

Taking in a deep breath then exhaling forcefully, Flores admitted, "Probably over that abortion clinic that burned down."

"It didn't just burn, did it, Father?"

"You wouldn't ask me to violate the sanctity of the confessional, would you, Father?"

❖   ❖   ❖

"Sight carefully . . . squeeze the trigger," murmured Miguel to little Elpidia. In her sights the unsuspecting rabbit continued placidly munching cabbage from the mission's neatly kept vegetable garden.

Miguel himself cradled the mission's sole shotgun, a semi-auto 12 gauge that looked older than the Priest, not beaten up but rather aged with dignity. There *were* snakes on the Mission grounds, though they were not visible.

Elpidia sighted down the barrel of the other fire-arm, a much newer Ruger 10/22—22 for the caliber, 10 for the number of shots the magazine held when full, which it was. In this case, the magazine held hollow points, much deadlier to a rabbit than round-nosed bullets.

The rabbit looked her way with large innocent eyes. Elpidia closed her own eyes. Her head slumped. "I can't do it," she whispered.

"Yes, you can. You must. He's eating our food."

The girl sighed. Steeling herself, she again took aim at the hapless, albeit greedy, rodent. But it's such a cute bunny.

Montoya shook his head. Unlike lawyers in the same firm, Priests could not share such confidential information. "No, of course not."

"Then all I can tell you is they—the government—murdered my people and are coming to kill me. I need sanctuary."

Montoya was a simple enough priest, no expert in canon law. He knew that sanctuary had once been within the power of a church to grant. He didn't know if it still was and said so.

As Flores was about to speak, the faint but distinctive crack of a rifle sounded.

The shot was audible even at the several hundred yards from the mission's entrance where Musashi and his team waited. Like his agents, Musashi tensed, then relaxed. "Just some kid with a .22," he told his assistants, dismissively. "Let's move in five . . . but slowly and carefully. The file says this is a peaceful group. No forcible entry. The Kevlar T-shirts we're wearing should be more than enough. And, boys . . . we can't afford another major shoot-up. Go easy."

In through the back entrance came Miguel, rabbit in one hand and his other arm around a softly weeping Elpidia. The rabbit, despite the use of hollow points, had not died instantly. Lacking confidence—well, she was new to firearms—Elpidia had aimed center-of-mass. The rifle had cracked; the rabbit—corkscrewing through the air—had given a single, decidedly human-sounding scream, kicked twice and died.

"You have *got* to aim for the head, Elpi," Miguel had shouted. He needn't have raised his voice; the girl was hurt enough as it was.

Miguel had quickly apologized and led her away, shotgun slung and the rabbit—destined for the stewpot—clutched by the ears in Miguel's right hand.

At the rifle shot, Flores stiffened and lost his train of thought, or argument, completely.

"That's just one of my boys taking care of a rabbit problem," calmed Montoya. Continuing, "In any case, though, I don't know enough about canon law and sanctuary to offer them, Father."

"I do not know either, Jorge. I know they will kill me if you do not offer it, though."

"We can't simply kill the priest in the mission," Musashi cautioned his cohorts as they approached the front door. "Too many witnesses and two Catholic groups in as many days would be a bit much, even for the media. We'll just take him and then he will try to escape after seizing a weapon."

"Did you clear those weapons, Miguel?" Montoya demanded, sternly, as the boy-turning-man walked into the foyer with both arms otherwise occupied. It was expressly forbidden to enter the mission with a loaded weapon.

Miguel's mouth dropped open as he tried to stammer out a reply. He *had* been thinking more about Elpidia than the rules for firearms. "Oh, Father, I am sorry. No. I will . . . right away."

"Go outside with them then."

Still leading Elpidia, Miguel began to turn away. They had reached the small, shallow and dark alcove that led to the exit when . . .

Just outside the door, Musashi and his team halted. Though readied, their "knocker" was placed to the ground. Musashi reached up a hardened hand and knocked briskly, twice.

Sister Sofia turned away from the two priests, likewise turned the inside door knob and asked, "Who is—"

She didn't have time to finish as Musashi's assistant pushed her roughly aside.

In burst the agents. "FBI! FBI! Hands in the air," they shouted.

"What is the meaning of this?" Montoya demanded. "This is God's place. You have no right here."

Musashi didn't answer immediately. Scanning the area quickly his eyes came to rest upon a quailing Father Flores. "We're here for him. Stay out of the way and nobody gets hurt."

"I'll get hurt, Jorge," Flores reminded with trembling voice.

Montoya looked at Musashi, measuring him. The agent reminded the priest of certain Viet Cong he had known in the past, however brief such acquaintance may have been. Montoya looked and knew then that Flores did not exaggerate. He was a dead man unless given sanctuary.

"You will take nobody," Montoya announced, interposing himself between Flores and the FBI.

Musashi snorted at the idea of some silly old man trying to gainsay *him* and began to push the obviously injured and ailing priest out of the way. . . .

And found himself, breathless and stunned with his back against the thick adobe of the mission walls. Instinct long honed took over. Musashi's right hand leapt towards his left breast.

In their darkened alcove, Elpidia and Miguel stopped instantly as the main door smashed inward and three strangers entered with shouts and alarm. A fourth remained, faintly perceived, by the mission door. While the girl's hands merely tightened on her

small caliber rifle, the boy instinctively unslung and
drew his shotgun to his shoulder. He took a general
aim, muzzle pointed downwards. Miguel had had
"dealings"—often quite unpleasant ones—with law
enforcement agencies before.

Elpidia stood frozen for long moments as she
watched the priest, the father she had never had, put
his own body between an unshaven, unkempt man
and the one who had announced he was part of the
dreaded FBI. She stood frozen as she watched the
injured father pushed to one side. She stood frozen
as she watched him smash his assailant's back to
the wall. She watched as the FBI agent's right hand
slipped into his suit. She saw, as if in slow motion,
as the butt of a pistol began to emerge.

Screaming an inarticulate "No!" Elpidia unfroze. Her
rifle flew to her shoulder and her finger to the trigger.
If the range was short, the shooter was unpracticed. If
the shooter was unpracticed the rifle had nine bullets
still in the magazine. If the bullets were small caliber
they were each hollow points.

The muzzle of Elpidia's rifle flashed fire.

Though again Elpidia aimed for center of mass, her
first bullet took Musashi in the throat. The soft lead
slug entered just below the Adam's apple. As it met
the resistance of flesh the lead peeled back, expanding
and tearing its way through larynx, meat, blood vessels
and cartilage. Musashi's mouth gaped like a fish. His
body shuddered from shock and pain.

Rifle weaving, Elpidia struck next the agent's right
collar bone, missing the rectangle of light body armor
the agent wore under his suit. Under the bullet's

impact, the bone shattered, casting its own splinters inward along with the fragments of lead.

Musashi groaned and, letting go his pistol, reached both hands up to where his throat spurted crimson.

Elpidia's third shot missed her target's right ear, but her next two punched into and through the agent's face, doing a fair job of scrambling his brain.

The girl's next shot missed completely as an incredible, shocking roar exploded in front of her own face; Miguel's shotgun.

Miguel too, had seen the pistol being drawn. Yet the year-old words of the Father shone clear in his memory: "Do not point a weapon at a man unless you intend to kill him."

Miguel didn't want to kill anybody . . . but understood the priest's unspoken words: "If you do point a firearm at someone, kill him."

He stood frozen, as Elpi had earlier, while her rifle spit its first flame. When he saw the rest of the agents reaching inside their suit jackets—more guns being drawn to kill the girl he loved—he unfroze immediately and lifted the muzzle to point at the nearest of the agents. As if shooting skeet, his finger stroked the trigger. The recoil rocked him backwards, though not nearly so forcefully as the buckshot knocked back the agent who took the blast full in the face. Bones, blood and brain burst, a crimson cloud hanging briefly in the air before decorating the wall.

Miguel recovered from the recoil and swept the muzzle left for his next target. Sweep, stroke, blast, recoil, recover, sweep . . .

The last agent standing exclaimed, "My God they've got guns!" before Miguel's last—hasty—shot tore away half the agent's left leg. He fell outward and, whimpering, began to crawl to safety.

Miguel advanced to finish the job until held in check by Montoya's outstretched arm.

Though shocked by the shotgun's fierce blast, Elpidia recovered quickly . . . as anyone whose life had contained as many hard knocks as hers might have recovered quickly. Her last three shots took Musashi—quite needlessly, he was already dead and his body and mind simply didn't know it yet—in the chest. One was stopped by the body armor, the others just missed and entered the chest cavity, perforating lungs and other otherwise useful organs.

Leaving a trail of blood, the agent's body slid slowly down the wall to come to rest on the bloodstained floor.

Still holding Miguel back, Montoya's eyes swept over the scene: three fresh corpses, three spreading pools of blood. His nose sniffed at the familiar cordite smell. His ears heard the wailing of the lone survivor as he dragged his mutilated body down the neatly kept walkway that led to the mission's door . . . as they heard the retching of Father Flores, spilling his pungent vomit to join the spreading blood.

Montoya sniffed again. Yes, there was something else besides the expected smells. He eyed Flores with a mild distaste, then in charity turned his eyes away.

In the distance, but growing rapidly closer, the priest sensed as much as heard the wailing of police sirens . . . many of them.

CHAPTER FOUR

From the transcript at trial: Commonwealth of
Virginia v. Alvin Scheer

DIRECT EXAMINATION, CONTINUED
BY MR. STENNINGS

Q. So what did you do about it, Alvin?

A. Do? Me? I didn't do a damned thing . . . excuse my
language. Didn't see where there was anything I
could do. Me being a kinda' little fish in a pretty
big pond, and all. I saw on TV where somebody
decided they could do something about it, though.
Quite the thing, it was. News stations didn't hardly
cover anything else for weeks.

Seemed some priest, the Catholic kind, I mean,
well . . . when the government tried to bust into
his church? Done kilt 'em. Most of 'em. Least
that's what the TV said.

There were troops everywhere. Coming off
planes from Washington. Unloading them things

something like tanks but on wheels . . . that was that new "Presidential Guard, Secret Service" group. PGSS they called it. Something in that name rung a bell . . . the name and them black uniforms they wore. But I wasn't sure what. Like I said, I ain't no educated man.

They were landing by helicopter from all over, too. Surrounded the place.

Another funny thing. First few days? There were mostly Texas police surrounding the place. By . . . oh . . . lemme see . . . maybe three days later? Nothing but feds and reporters.

And all the reporters? Well, wasn't too much difference among 'em. All the same story. "Priest was a pervert." "Murderer, too," so they said. "Tax evader." (I says, 'Good for him, if he was.') Weren't but two weeks after the feds took over from the state that the books were comin' out. I didn't read none of 'em, mind you. But I remember seeing the title of one: *Father of Pain*, they called it.

The books came out just about the time everything began to cool down.

Austin, Texas

"Jesus. Jesus! JESUS! what am I going to do, Jack?"

Juanita, agitated beyond measure, paced frantically around the governor's office. "He's my *brother*—I am not going to let him be killed. I . . ." She stopped because she had not the first clue as to how she was going to do anything. When she still had had control of the situation her brother had refused to listen to her and surrender. Now that that control was not oozing but pouring through her fingers?

"What am I going to do, Jack?"

Though he showed it less, Schmidt himself was seething inside. He *knew* that Montoya was not, could not possibly be, guilty of any real crime. "I don't know either, Juani. Jorge is . . . well . . . when he sets his mind on something you just can't change it. I know. I've tried."

Unseen—so he hoped, in the dim, green-filtered light of an early jungle morning, Sergeant Montoya's fingers gently closed the eyes of the last remaining of the ARVN rangers. "Take his soul unto you, O Lord. His name was Tri and like me, he belonged to Your Church." The Vietnamese, wounded in half a dozen places, had added a seventh wound, biting completely through his lower lip to keep silent as he died.

"Leave me, Jorge. Now. Before it is too late."

Montoya ignored his chief. It was light enough to see by now. He removed his helmet and load-bearing equipment, placed his rifle against a tree, and drew out his map and compass, using the compass to orient the map to the ground.

"We're about fifteen hundred meters from the alternate PZ"—the pickup zone . . . *a place where helicopters pick up soldiers. "Since we're overdue, they should be looking for us there. I think we may have lost the VC."*

"Jorge . . . if *you* make it back . . . Tell Juani, would you . . ."

"Don't be silly, Jack. We'll both make it. Besides, she already knows."

"But he and those children don't stand a chance."

Schmidt thought carefully before speaking further. "Ummm . . . Juani. They might stand a better chance than you . . . or anyone . . . might think."

Dei Gloria Mission, Waco, Texas

Muttering, Father Montoya cleared away the detritus of the dank closet until a smallish wooden trunk was revealed. The trunk, footlocker to be precise, was painted green and made of cheap plywood—military issue. He drew the footlocker out into the light then pushed it—after his beating he lacked the strength easily to carry it—across the floor toward a simple wooden chair. The trunk was stenciled—how the letters had faded with the years!—with montoya-s, jorge, ssg, co b, 3rd bn, 5th sfg(a).

The priest fished in his pocket for a set of keys, then sat in front of the trunk and opened the lock; lifted the cover.

A sad smile of days gone by briefly lit Montoya's face. His hands lovingly removed a circle of heavy green cloth. Attached was a small metal device. Montoya read softly, *"De Oppresso Liberi."—to free the oppressed.*

We failed, but at least we tried. The memory drove away a few years and a few injuries.

Gently the priest set the beret on the floor and removed a neatly folded set of starched jungle fatigues, the slash pockets on the jacket's breast surmounted by cloth strips bearing his name and US ARMY. These had no real sentiment attached; he had merely worn them his last day in the army. Boots and load–carrying equipment joined the jungle fatigues.

Beneath these were several boxes of letters; from his sister, from Isabel whom he had once thought to marry, from Jack, too, though those were somewhat more recent.

The letters went atop the fatigues. Montoya stopped and stared at a long, soft, green case.

Austin, Texas

"A chance? What are you talking about?"

Schmidt bit his lip and cocked an eyebrow. "After Jorge was 'wounded' . . . when he got out of the hospital . . . I . . . ah . . . made him a little present.

"Something . . . um . . . special. I doubt he would throw away a present . . . not this kind surely."

The governor's eyes widened. "You didn't?"

Dei Gloria Mission, Waco, Texas

"Old friend," whispered the priest. "Old friend, I have need of you now."

Quivering hands seemed to steady slightly as they took a once familiar grip on a once all-too-familiar implement. Even as his left hand lifted the canvas case, the fingers of the right ran a zipper along the side. Zipper undone, the priest's fingers scooped the rifle's butt from the pocket formed, took a grip and pulled it from the case. A simple twist and the serial number was exposed. Habit long unpracticed still caused the priest to read softly, "120857."

Deciding to take up a rifle again had been difficult for the old priest. His first instinct had been to send Elpidia and Miguel out of the mission, to take the blame for the shootings upon himself. He'd realized quickly that that would never work, certainly not so long as one of the agents had survived. Even if he hadn't stopped Miguel, he had no faith in either Sister Sofia's or Father Flores' ability to withstand rigorous interrogation.

Still he had tried to send the two far away. He had several thousand dollars stashed away; enough, surely, for two nice kids to get a fresh start.

Miguel had been reluctant, but willing. Not for his own sake; he would never desert his priest for that, but for the girl's.

Elpidia had killed the notion. With a will and determination to match even Montoya's, she had simply stated, "No. Never. Not for anything."

Her large, innocent brown eyes flashed fire at the priest's insistence. "I WILL NOT GO!" Would she have stood up so firmly without the careful building of strength of heart and mind under the priest's tutelage? Montoya thought perhaps not.

In any case, naturally, Miguel couldn't leave either. Pride would have forced him to stay if love had not.

With Miguel staying on—again, naturally—none of the other boys would leave either . . . nor the girls.

Even Sister Sofia refused the priest's command. With eyes filled with tears and rabbit-frightened, fast-beating heart she too said, "I stay here."

Resigned, head shaking, the father had limped to his quarters to pray for guidance.

It was difficult to pray, what with the shriek of sirens and the flash of blue lights through the narrow mission windows. If true guidance had come, it had been only in the form of one flash of such light. This, glancing off an icon, had caused the priest's eyes to come to rest on a closet door. A locked door.

"Old friend," he whispered again setting the rifle down and patting it.

Beneath where the rifle had lain rested two bandoleers of ammunition, 140 rounds each of 5.56mm, and seven 20-round magazines, empty. These joined the rifle, the beret, the jungle fatigues, the boots, the web gear.

Beneath all lay a green plastic folder, the Department of the Army crest emblazoned on it. Montoya opened it and began to read, silently:

The Distinguished Service Cross is presented to SSG Jorge Montoya-Serrasin for courage in action above and beyond the call of duty, Qui Nhon province, Republic of Vietnam. . . .

Austin, Texas

Schmidt gave a little bad-boy nod. "Ummm . . . yeah . . . I did. His very own rifle, too. And let me tell you, it was no easy thing getting an M-16 through customs. But a few thousand piastres to an acquaintance in the South Vietnamese foreign ministry . . . a diplomatic pouch . . . and . . ." He shrugged.

"Oh, Jack," Juanita half moaned. "He's gonna get killed." Her shoulders shuddered as tears filled her eyes. "My only brother . . ."

"Then let me go save him now, Juani. Call off the cops and I'll put a cordon around the mission the First Cav Division would think twice about forcing, let alone the FBI."

"It isn't just the FBI, Jack. BATF—well, Treasury including BATF and the IRS—want him for tax evasion . . . the guns . . ."

"Oh, what fucking—pardon my French—absolute bullshit! He's got a church. Church property used for church purposes is *not* taxable."

"You think they care, Jack?"

Washington, DC

Rottemeyer sat at her desk in deep consultation. Around her, at a conference table perpendicular to the desk, sat her wheelchair-bound attorney general, Jesse Vega, and Caroline McCreavy—the President's lover and also the new Chairperson of the Joint Chiefs of Staff. Likewise notable were Rottemeyer's surgeon general, the head of the Treasury Department, and the director of the Federal Bureau of Investigations, Louise Friedberg.

"I don't care about the kids," said Friedberg, furiously. "I don't care about any outmoded, patriarchal Catholic church. I don't care about the governor of some backwards state down by Mexico. They killed my people and I care about that. I care that they end up dead. I want their grandchildren to have nightmares about what comes from fucking with the FBI. I want these people's ghosts to be sorry and afraid."

Wilhelmina stared stonily. She could not, not quite, gainsay the director. After all, it was her Bureau that had uncovered (the irresponsible press said "fabricated" . . . well, they used to say "fabricated," the American press was brave only when they were not pressed) the charges of statutory rape against former Senator Goldsmith. Goldsmith's suicide, following his exposure, show-trial and conviction, had been icing on the cake. Fortunately, the senator had been old and only two federal agents had been required to hold him down and force a pistol into his mouth. Rottemeyer approved of certain necessary actions having as few witnesses as possible.

Goldsmith had only been the first. One by one the Republican members of Congress had been entrapped . . . or for the few—like Goldsmith—who truly were honest and upright . . . simply framed.

Nor had her own party been spared the needed correctional measures. It was to Friedberg and her Bureau that Rottemeyer owed the sudden conversion of Senator Feldman from slightly left of center supporter to ax wielder for the Oval Office. Amazing what the discovery of a previously unsuspected Panamanian bank account could do to political convictions. Or, if not a Panamanian bank account, then any of a number of other crimes could be discovered.

Of course, that was only half the story. In addition to using her Bureau to beat down the opposition it was also necessary, occasionally, to use it to protect the truly worthy . . . which is to say, the politically reliable. The senator from Massachusetts with his penchant for fat teenaged boys, for example; the other with his penchant for thin teenaged girls; for example. The congresswoman from Los Angeles with ties to the Mexican drug cartels, for example. The mayor of the City of Washington, for example, and potentially every one of the pushers, prostitutes and pimps who worked for him.

Yes, Friedberg's loyalty and diligence, as well as that of her Bureau under her direction, deserved special treatment.

"Caroline, can your people take out this damned priest?" asked the President.

McCreavy pondered. She shook her head. "Bad idea, Willi. Posse Comitatus"—the law which forbade using the military for civil law enforcement.

Vega snorted in derision. "Oh, *that*."

McCreavy never had liked Vega, there being a strong suspicion of a previous intimate connection with the President. Still, she was polite. "Not just 'Oh, that.' I can give the orders. I just can't guarantee they will be obeyed. And 'that' would make things potentially much worse."

Rottemeyer's face assumed a puzzled, perplexed look. "I don't understand, Caroline. You've been purging the officer corps for some time now. How many can be left who would not obey your orders?"

"Most," McCreavy admitted with a sigh. "You have to understand these people. The last seventy years have made them good at hiding their thoughts and feelings. Sure I got rid of the stupid ones easily enough; the ones who shot their mouths off once or twice. But most military people have merely kept silent. You might say that they damn our programs and policies by faint praise. I wouldn't trust them to break the law on this."

Rottemeyer felt a momentary flush of indignation— not at McCreavy, no never!—but at the narrow-minded, patriarchal men who ran her armed forces and failed to recognize their place in the world . . . and her own.

"Where do your loyalties lie?" Rottemeyer demanded. "Can't *anyone* here get rid of this fucking priest?"

Still, she was a practical politician. No sense in setting unfortunate precedents. She turned her attention to the Attorney General, Treasury, the Surgeon General and the Bureau. "Jesse, you take charge of this. I want that mission destroyed. BATF will provide some forces, likewise I want a force from the Presidential Guard"—Treasury nodded, both groups fell under his jurisdiction—"and the Hostage Rescue Team"—this set Friedberg to scribbling.

The surgeon general added, spontaneously, "I'll put my security police on alert in case this turns nasty . . ."

Dei Gloria Mission, Waco, Texas

"Maaaaan," whispered Julio. "Whoever thought Padre could look so . . . so . . . nasty?" he asked with more than a touch of admiration and pride.

Miguel turned to look. There, alone in the sun, stood the priest. Atop his head, a green beret. Clothing his body, faded but crisp green fatigues, the clerical collar still visible. Over his shoulders was draped the harness that all boys know to be a warrior's battle equipment.

In his left hand, grasped at the balance firmly but not tightly, was the rifle.

For the first time since his beating the priest had regained the young, vigorous look that belied his years.

He made a motion with his right hand circling over his head. He had used the sign before, to call the boys together. Old habits die hard.

One by one, and by twos and threes, the boys and some few girls began to gather around the priest for their orders.

Austin, Texas

"Just give me the orders, Juani. That's all I ask. Let me save your brother and my friend."

Torn with indecision, demoralized with self-doubt . . . if one had asked an honest answer she would have said "out of my depth" . . . the governor of Texas simply wept.

"Juani . . . I have to do something."

CHAPTER FIVE

From the transcript at trial: Commonwealth of
Virginia v. Alvin Scheer

DIRECT EXAMINATION, CONTINUED
BY MR. STENNINGS:

Q. And when did you get the idea in your head that
maybe something could be done?

A. I guess it was not too long after someone finally
decided to do something, about them kids in the
mission, at least, if not the entire problem. "Cooler
heads prevailed," as they say. We were all plumb
sure that the feds would just go in and kill 'em
all. But we were wrong . . . sort of.

Still and all, one of the folks surrounding the
place—he was one of us, a Texas man, go figure—
decided to give it a try. I don't know what he said
to 'em, both the folks in the mission and the ones
outside. Whatever it was, it seemed to work.

I got myself and my wife up early to watch it on

the TV. Even Daddy came over to see. One lone
man, wearin' one lone star, standin' outside the
mission walls waiting for the kids to come out.

Made me proud, it did.

Course, you couldn't see the man's face or
anything. There must have been a dozen TV
cameras on him, but they were all back where it
was safe and he . . . well, he was up front where
it wasn't.

Qui Nhon Province, Republic of Vietnam, 1966

*"We should be safe here for a while, Jack," Jorge
lied, as he gently laid Schmidt down on the base of
a muddy ditch.*

*Montoya, even carrying Schmidt, reached the PZ
before the helicopters. So, apparently, did the Viet Cong.
So, for that matter, did Sergeant Tri. It was this, seen
as if close up through the lieutenant's binoculars, that
caused the sergeant to whisper, "Christ have mercy."*

*Tri's head was perched atop a red stained pole, his
eyes still closed as Jorge had left them.*

"Wha'? What is it, Jorge?"

*"Nothing, Jack. Nothing. Just relax and wait for
the choppers to come."*

*Montoya searched through his own pouches for
ammunition. Finding a bare three magazines—those
only courtesy of looting the dead, previously—he began
to rummage through Schmidt's own harness.*

*Call it . . . ninety rounds. Five frags—fragmentation
grenades. One claymore. Couple smoke; one colored.
Jack's .45 and twenty-one rounds for that.*

*As he coolly set up the claymore to fire down a likely
trail that led onto the PZ, Montoya began whistling
something, a faintly Arabic sounding tune. "Deguello,"
it was called. It seemed appropriate.*

*As he worked, Montoya heard the sound—indistinct,
faint—of a brace of Hueys.*

Dei Gloria Mission, Waco, Texas

The sound of the helicopter was strange to his
ears. It was straining, so much was obvious. But the
strained pitch was not that of the Hueys with which
the priest was familiar. Perhaps one of those new jobs;
a "Blackhawk," Jack called them.

Montoya strained his eyes against the midnight
gloom. Yes, there it was. A helicopter, some pendu-
lumlike thing swinging underneath.

This was nothing new. Forces had been building
up around the mission for days. Some came by helicopter, some by automobile and truck, some by the
light armored vehicles, LAVs, favored by the PGSS.
Oftentimes the helicopters swung overhead for a view.
So far the priest had refused to open fire on them.
"Let them fire the first shot," he had ordered.

Most of the helicopters had kept high; out of practical range. Curiously, this one did not. With each passing second the priest's grip on his rifle grew tighter,
unseen fingers whitening from the pressure. As the
chopper came over the low mission wall he shifted to
a firing stance. Then he recognized the pendulum, two
big cubes swinging underneath. *A slingload?* Nobody
assaults with a slingload. The rifle lowered.

The helicopter's nose pulled up slightly, raising a cloud of dust and grit. The pitch changed yet again as it settled closer to the ground. The priest saw the crew chief leaning out, watching for the load slung underneath to touch down. When it did the chief put a hand to his throat, said something that would have been unintelligible to anyone not on the same intercom system, and waved to the priest. Montoya waved back.

The helicopter moved forward and lowered itself again, this time until the higher cube touched down. The priest perceived, dimly, some kind of flexible strap falling over the second cube. Then the Blackhawk, black indeed in the moonless night, pulled up and away.

Montoya waved again as he walked forward toward the netted cargo that had been left for him.

He pulled away a letter he had found "hundred-mile-an-hour" taped to the side.

"Dear Jorge," the priest read in the bright oval cast by his flashlight. *"In all the world there is nobody to whom I owe the debts and favors that I owe to you. Please accept these small tokens of my personal esteem in this, your hour of need.*

Sincerely,
Jack

P.S. The ammunition is on the bottom layer of this load; the rifles and such on top. Most of the rest is food, some body armor, gas masks, and some medical supplies.

*There's one radio and half a dozen batteries.
Good luck, friend. I'll do what I can. I am
trying. There's a cell phone in there, one
of those disposable jobs. Give your sister a
call, why don't you."*

Austin, Texas

"Yes, Rodg'—ah . . . mission accomplished? Great.
Great news, friend." With a lighthouse-beam smile,
Schmidt replaced the telephone on its cradle and
returned to the governor's conference table.

"What has you looking so happy?" Juanita
enquired.

"Nothing, Governor," Schmidt answered formally.
"Nothing for you to worry about in any case."

She gave him a look of extreme suspicion, raising
nothing more than a shrug in return. *What have you
done now, Jack?*

Juanita turned her attention to the chief of her
Department of Public Safety and his close cohort,
Jeffrey Nagy, the Senior Captain of the Texas Rangers,
a bejowled and utterly humorless-looking man.

"We're following it, Governor. Company F"—the
Waco-based Ranger company—"has Sergeants Akers
and Guttierez on site twenty-four hours a day."

"Is that Johnson Akers? *The* Johnson Akers?" asked
Schmidt.

Surprisingly, Nagy smiled, his previously humorless
face brightening as the sun brightened the lonesome
Texas prairie; his smile a match for Schmidt's own.
"Yeah . . . him."

"What am I not getting?" Juanita enquired.

PGSS Headquarters, Dei Gloria Mission, Waco, Texas

The tall, thin to the point of emaciated, civilian-dressed man drew no interest from anyone present. His white ten-gallon hat perched back on his head shouted "Yokel!" to everyone present. That he had as open, kind and friendly a face as one might ever hope to see only confirmed the impression.

And indeed, Sergeant Johnson Akers, Texas Rangers, *was* every bit as open and friendly and kind as his face portrayed.

He was also a stone-cold killer; nerveless, unstoppable, impossible-to-intimidate. In all the history of the Texas Rangers and their higher headquarter, the Texas Department of Public Safety, only one man had ever won the Medal of Valor twice.

That man, with his open, gentle, kindly, grandfather's face, sat quietly under his ten-gallon hat, keeping careful track of every federal law enforcement agent, detachment and observer on site . . . and reporting the same to his chief.

What few knew, outside of the Rangers, was that Sergeant Akers had won both medals in the course of saving children.

Sister Sofia sat on a rocking chair surrounded by the twenty-six children of the mission aged twelve and under. (The older ones were either guarding the mission's thick adobe walls, doing necessary work to keep the operation running, or being trained by Father—as best he could under the circumstances—on the dozen rifles and two night vision scopes sent by Schmidt.)

The delivery of two and a half tons of canned and dried food had, to a degree, alleviated Sofia's concerns in the commissary department—though re-hydrating Army "B"-rations had proven problematic to people who had never seen them. Nonetheless, food was food, even if it sometimes crunched when you bit it.

Still, the possibility—she could *not* bring herself to think "probability" let alone "certainty"—of a federal assault on the mission set her stomach to churning and brought tears to her eyes. Her innocent little ones under fire? No. Never. It was unthinkable.

So she led the children in songs, mostly but not entirely of a religious nature, while the elders, in many cases the teenaged parents, stood to and prepared for the worst.

"Now if worst comes to worst and they get over the wall we fall back to the main chapel," Montoya instructed his boys. Miguel looked to the chapel behind him and nodded understanding. He thought, *Father's plan is a good one. From behind the wall only those exposing themselves can shoot at us. And unless they come over in a huge group we will outnumber them. From underneath the central water tank, Julio—who is a better shot than I will ever be—can take care of any tower they might put up to snipe at us. If they use tanks there are the "special" bottles.*

Miguel referred not to flammable Molotov cocktails but to bottles of household ammonia, good for taking out any tank in the world. This was not only true if the tank had an air filtration system, but especially if it had an air filtration system. Ammonia molecules were smaller than oxygen molecules. They would pass through any filter that would pass oxygen through. The bottles were positioned around the mission's adobe wall.

Miguel spared a surreptitious glance at hidden position and emplacements. *The police have no clue about the weapons; all we are letting them see are the old ones we had. We have a chance.*

"Gas!" Montoya announced, half unexpectedly. The boys immediately started fumbling with their cumbersome, clumsy face masks as the priest counted off, "One thousand, two thousand . . ."

Sergeant Akers walked off alone and made a cell phone call directly to the Chief. "Captain Nagy? Boss, there's nearly a thousand feds here. Twelve from the FBI's Hostage Rescue Team. Thirty-seven from BATF. About nineteen from the Department of Justice. A hundred man maintenance and support team for the armored vehicles Fort Hood loaned them. They have about thirty-five cooks with them. Four 'observers' from . . . well, I think they're from Delta. You know, the Special Forces types? Act that way, anyway. Arrogant folks, you know? Then there's two full companies from the Secret Service. Over four hundred in that crew. Plus there are two more companies of riot control troops from the Office of the Surgeon General. Oh . . . and something like twenty-one folks toting guns from the Environmental Protection Agency. No, sir. No, I haven't a clue what EPA thinks they're doing here."

"Yessir. Tell the governor. Forty-eight hours. No more. In forty-eight hours the feds will assault."

Grimly, Akers shut off his own phone, closed the cover, and contemplated a dilemma he had never thought to confront.

Austin, Texas

Nagy sighed. "My man on the ground says forty-eight hours, Governor. Then the feds go in."

"Forty-eight hours," Juanita echoed, faintly.

"Your brother doesn't stand too much of a chance, Governor. They have tanks, armored personnel carriers, two helicopter gunships with Army crews, and some very well-trained specialists."

"Any artillery? Mortars?" asked Schmidt.

"My man didn't see any," Nagy responded. "That would kind of be 'overkill' anyway, wouldn't it?"

"So are tanks. So are gunships."

Juanita shuddered at the image that came unbidden of an armored vehicle crushing her brother's body into the dirt.

Dei Gloria Mission, Waco, Texas

There were in fact only a brace of tanks, those having to be taken from storage where they had languished since the conversion of the Army's First Cavalry Division to a medium force suitable for deployment to and employment in any operation short of real war against a heavily armored enemy. Worse, the tanks had no ammunition suitable for breaching the walls that surrounded the mission.

They did have, however, a number of machine guns suitable for beating down fire when and if the time came for a dismounted team to carry a breaching charge forward. And the defenders had nothing that could penetrate a tank's armor. Moreover, the tanks themselves—seventy tons of moving metal—could breach most walls simply by slamming against them, though this was a tactic much frowned upon by real tankers whose job was largely keeping their tanks running.

Group Commander Sawyers, First Security Group, Presidential Guard Secret Service, patted one of the tanks affectionately.

Austin, Texas

Schmidt saw Juani's involuntary shudder, saw the beginnings of tears forming in her eyes. "Folks. I think we ought to leave the governor alone for a bit."

Juanita shot him a grateful glance. At her nod of agreement the others began to file out of her office. Schmidt lagged behind until all the others had left. Then he quietly closed the door behind them.

Even before they were alone, the governor had folded her arms across her desk, laid her head upon them, and begun to weep quietly.

Schmidt hurried to her side, pulling a chair with him as he went.

Seated beside her, he patted her back affectionately. "Juani, I know how you feel right now. But we have forty-eight hours, no more than that . . . and maybe less. Have you considered calling the President to try to work something out?"

The shaking of the governor's shoulders subsided somewhat. She lifted her head up, wiped a runny nose with a hand, and sniffled, "She won't take my calls, Jack. Her chief of staff said, 'The President is too busy with the crisis.' But that's horse manure. She wants to make an example of Jorge."

"Doesn't she care about the kids in there?" asked an incredulous Schmidt. "Her and all her 'it's for the children' crap?"

Dei Gloria Mission, Waco, Texas

Johnson Akers would do anything to save a kid. He just couldn't help it. He had never been able to help it. Shoot a criminal? Easy. Take a bullet? He'd done that, too. Anything.

"Look, Mister FBI man. Sir, I'm not asking you to risk one of your precious hides getting those kids out. I'll do it."

The senior FBI man on the scene was as arrogant as any federal agent could be expected to be. From his expensively coiffed hair to his Pierre Cardin shoes to the tailored Italian suit in between, he portrayed an image of anal retentiveness difficult to equal. Even the high-fashion Gucci shoulder holster, which his suit successfully failed to hide, reeked of the proper FBI image.

What the man was not, however, was a child killer. His orders left little doubt that the priest was to die. They gave no indication that the kids must as well.

He looked over Akers—from his ten-gallon hat to his string tie to his faded denims and cowboy boots. Something about the old man must have struck a cord. Slowly the agent nodded agreement. "Okay, Sergeant Akers. You can try. I'll pass the word."

"Thank you, sir," said Akers . . . and really seemed to mean the "sir" this time.

"Padre, there's a man at the front gate. Says he's with the Texas Rangers."

"Is he alone, Miguel?"

"Si, Padre. We used a little mirror to check over the wall and around the door. Nobody but him."

With a fatalistic, and yet slightly hopeful, shrug, the priest walked to the gate. "What can I do for you?" he asked.

"Is this Father Montoya?" Akers queried.

"Yes. And you would be?"

"Sergeant Johnson Akers. Texas Rangers. F Company. I've come for the kids if you will let them out, Father."

An old memory tugged at the priest. He hesitated a moment or two, straining to remember. When memory struck, his face split in a wide, happy grin, his decision already made.

"Sure, Sergeant. Can you give me a little time to get them ready? And how do I know it isn't a trick to get the gate open?"

Akers voice was deadly serious. "I don't play games where children's lives are at stake, Padre."

"No. I suppose you don't. Thirty minutes?"

"Thirty minutes will be fine. I'll just wait right here." Akers leaned against the mission wall calmly, struck a match against it, and proceeded to smoke away the time.

"Oh, Sister, wait . . . just a minute . . . please?"

Sofia's face showed how she was torn. "Won't you please go with him, Elpi? You don't have to stay here."

The girl set her own face in grim determination. "I will not leave the padre." Her grim face melted as she hugged her infant son to her breast for what she was certain would be the last time. Tears welling, she very reluctantly passed the boy over to the arms of Sister Sofia.

"Please take good care of him, Sister. Please."

"Hush child. You know I will."

It had not been without difficulty that Montoya had persuaded the sister to leave the mission with the infants. Ultimately, though, his reasoning had prevailed. "Get out of here, Sister. Somebody will have to look out for the little ones."

And so the sister had formed her charges into a column of twos and let young parents like Elpidia bid choking goodbyes.

As the little ones, lamblike, followed the nun to the gate, Elpidia raced to the wall for a last glimpse.

A broadly grinning Akers met Sister Sofia as she began to lead the column of children out the gate. "Sister," he greeted.

Believing that Akers was one with "the enemy," some hundreds of whom were gathered by the operation headquarters to watch the peaceful surrender, the sister halted briefly, looked him over once, then semi-snubbed him.

"I'm Sergeant Akers, Sister. How many children do you have? And how old?"

"I have twenty-six children following me, Sergeant. They range from little Pedro, here; less than a year, up to age twelve."

"Thank you, Sister. Now if you will follow me, please."

"Very well," answered Sofia. Turning her head over her shoulder she called, "Follow me, children."

"Sister?" asked one of the elder ones, Josefina by name. "What's going to happen to us? Once it is over, I mean."

Again the sister stopped, looking mournfully behind her. "I do not know, child." She could never have imagined the years of solitary confinement that lay before her if the FBI was to have its way.

"That nun looks about ready to turn around and go back," announced the spotter of a two man sniper team from the FBI's Hostage Rescue Team.

"What do I do if she does turn around?"

"Drill her," said the spotter to the sniper. "Can't let her take the kids back inside."

"Got it," whispered the sniper, settling his cross hairs on the sister's head, a foot or so above little Pedro's. Pedro was in no danger, however; the sniper was a master.

Crying, "Pedro," softly, Elpidia didn't notice that her rifle was still slung over her shoulder as she climbed the ladder inside the wall for a last glimpse of her son. Parting was more than a mother's heart, even a young mother's . . . perhaps especially a young mother's, could bear.

"Armed target, bearing eleven o'clock," announced the spotter. "Take it."

"On it," said the sniper, making the minute correction to the new target. A slim, long-haired target ascended into his cross hairs. The sniper's trigger finger had already been given the unvoiced command, "fire" when the more conscious part of his mind realized his target was just a young girl.

The sniper flinched in surprise, but not by much. His finger still closed, the rifle still fired, and the recoil still rocked him back.

In the sniper's view, his target—struck by her left shoulder rather than her heart, so much had his flinch accomplished—spun away and fell from view.

As if in slow motion, or in one of those dreams where one seems to move as if through a thickened liquid, Elpidia felt the bullet, heard as much as felt it pass through the complex of bones in her left shoulder, then was forced away from the ladder by the power of the blow. The ground rushed up at her, but also in slow motion. She struck the ground in a cloud of dust raised by the impact of her limp body.

Only a short moment passed before the immediate shock wore off and Elpidia was overwhelmed by the pain of shattered bone and burning bullet track. She screamed.

Miguel had already been running for Elpidia, to stop her, when he heard the bullet crack overhead.

In his view the girl spun, oh so slowly, away from the ladder and collapsed to the ground below.

When he heard her high-pitched, shattering scream Miguel's mind turned half to mush.

Sofia heard the shot, then heard Sergeant Akers' mutter, "Shit," then shout "Down!" before diving himself for a nearby ditch to show the children the way. For a moment only was Sofia frozen. Then she turned and shouted, "Back to the mission, children. Run!"

Sofia did not see Akers draw his pistol. If she had, she would have seen it pointed not at her, but in the general direction of the FBI.

Gathering her skirts around her with one hand, Sofia tried to follow the fleeing boys and girls to the gate. She had nearly made it when the sniper, recovered from his surprise, put a bullet through her panic-filled brain. Little Pedro was flung forward as the sister fell.

"Hit," announced the sniper, softly.

Josefina was already at the gate when she heard the shot. By the time she turned, a fiercely wailing Pedro lay upon the mission walkway. Without hesitation, Josefina ran to pick up the child. With him safely in her arms she sprinted for the greater safety of the gate.

Though the sniper tracked her progress in his scope, he did not fire. There was no point to firing; the other children had already reentered the mission.

As Josefina reached the gate, a hard hand grabbed her clothing and pulled her inside. Then an outraged Father Montoya took a mostly covered kneeling firing position and scanned for targets. Most especially did the father look for whoever had shot Sister Sofia.

"Are you all right, Elpi? Oh, God, please be all right."

Miguel didn't have the training to know that the girl's wound was nonfatal; so far and no farther had the FBI man flinched. But she wasn't talking, she didn't seem conscious, and there was blood all over her side.

Certain the girl was dead, with a wordless cry of utter anguish Miguel began climbing the same ladder from which she had been hurled. With each step upward he muttered, "Motherfuckers. Motherfuckers. Motherfuckers."

"New target. Prior location. Eleven o'clock."

Again the sniper made a minute adjustment. Again, he commanded his finger to tighten. Again the rifle rocked against his shoulder.

"Hit," he announced.

Frustrated beyond words, Montoya saw only a spurt of dust to mark the sniper's position. *Not a chance. They're behind cover from here.* With a sigh of regret he withdrew the rifle from his shoulder, then leaned against the rough-hewn gate to close it. Once it was in place he lowered the bar.

Already some of his people were rushing to the still warm and breathing Elpidia . . . and rapidly cooling Miguel.

CHAPTER SIX

From the transcript at trial: Commonwealth of
Virginia v. Alvin Scheer

DIRECT EXAMINATION, CONTINUED
BY MR. STENNINGS:

Q. Alvin, I know it's hard to remember. It's been
a long time and a lot has happened. But try to
recall and tell the Court how you felt about the
mission.

A. I remember being mad. Really mad. See, it weren't
a fair fight, not at all. Them poor folks in the
mission, young kids most of them, they didn't
stand a chance.

   They made you proud though. Made you think
a little on olden days . . . an' Texas . . . and a whole
bunch of other things that people mostly done
forgot.

   My old pappy come on over to watch my TV
during the assault. He kept whistling something . . .

sounded sort of familiar. I asked him what it was.

He told me, "It's 'Deguello,' boy. The 'throat cut' song. And ain't they a bunch of cutthroats, too?"

MS. CAPUTO: Objection. Hearsay.

MR. STENNINGS: Not offered for the truth of the matter asserted, Your Honor.

THE COURT: Overruled.

Austin, Texas

Schmidt fumed and raged. "Murderers! Butchers! Goddamit, Juani, this has gone far enough!"

Nagy just shook his head while staring at the television. "My man Akers," he announced, "told me your brother's folks did not open fire at all, let alone first, Governor. No matter what GNN may be saying."

"Then what happened?" demanded the governor.

"Akers didn't know; not the whole story. But he was definite that the first shot came from the feds. The second—the one that killed the nun—came from the feds. That the third came from the feds and that there was not a fourth."

"Then what's all that shooting sound they put on the TV?"

Schmidt answered, "They dubbed it in, Juani. Afterwards."

He turned to Nagy, "How'd your man get away?"

"He said there was a ditch by the gate. That he jumped into that and waited for nightfall. Said he wasn't too worried about being shot by the mission folks, but that he wouldn't be too surprised if the feds took a shot at him. Oh, he was in a fine rage ... and Sergeant Akers is *never* angry."

"In a ditch, was he?" Jack mused.

Qui Nhon Province, Republic of Vietnam, 1966

The helicopters had radioed for friends, then proceeded to do whatever they could themselves to help Montoya and Schmidt with their own door guns. It helped, but it wasn't quite enough.

Montoya recited "Ave Maria" as he poked his head and rifle over the wall of the ditch in which he and Jack sheltered. Blam, blam, blam, went the rifle and two of the pair's assailants fell into bleeding, choking, shrieking ruin not fifteen meters from the ditch. A burst of fire drove Jorge's head down again.

Overhead one helicopter made a low pass from Montoya's right. Its left side gunner fired a long burst into the tree line before the pilot pulled his nose up and around to line up for another pass. Jorge saw tracers outline the helicopter even in the bright morning light.

It all seemed futile to the barely conscious, bleeding Schmidt. With a radio between them and the helicopters, the choppers could have cooperated with Montoya, and vice versa. As it was, the shot-up radio being long abandoned, they were each guessing at what the other would do or had seen.

"Jorge!" Schmidt cried as three Viet Cong leapt into the ditch, not far from where he lay.

Montoya turned, attempted to fire only to have his

magazine run dry after the first, missed, round. With an inarticulate shout he drew a knife and charged the VC.

Whatever the guerillas had been expecting to greet them in the ditch, it apparently was not a hundred and fifty pounds of shrieking Mexican fury. They turned and clambered back out again, shouting for help. All except the last got away. That one's escape was halted by Montoya's knife, buried eight inches in his back. He slid face against the earth to the foul dirt below.

Jack reached a sudden decision—sudden, although its nature and implications had been torturing him for days. "Juani, let me roll my division. I've got over three hundred tanks and a like number of other armored vehicles. And they're manned by Texans, Juani. They won't let your brother go down."

Spanish eyes flared. "You want to start a civil war, Jack? We *lost* the last one, remember?"

Schmidt smiled. His multi great-grandfather, the captain, and the governor's, the sergeant, had fought side by side in that lost cause, members of Hood's Texas Brigade. His eyes turned and looked over the governor's bookshelves. He walked over to one and selected from it an old, red leather-bound volume. He checked the index and then opened to a page.

A nod; it was the right page. Schmidt's eyes scanned briefly before he began to read aloud. "'There is no retreat but in submission and slavery. Our chains are forged . . . The war is inevitable—and let it come. I repeat it, sir, let it come.'

"Patrick Henry said that, Governor." Schmidt closed the book slowly, reluctantly.

"Jack, I just don't know."

"Juani," Schmidt persisted, "we won the civil war we had before the one we lost. Maybe you should remember that. Come to think of it, Americans won the civil war before the Texas revolution, too . . . if you'll remember that."

He didn't need to open the book again to say, "'The battle is not to the strong alone. It is to the vigilant, the active, the brave.'"

Dei Gloria Mission, Waco, Texas

The children had kept vigil over the dead; all but Elpidia. She, bandaged, alone and doped to deaden horrifying pain both physical and mental, lay in the mission's tiny infirmary.

Slowly, reluctantly, Father Montoya closed the Bible on the last Mass he ever expected to say on mission grounds. It was a combination Mass and funeral service for Miguel, who lay, eyes closed in eternal slumber, on a table in the chapel. Miguel's body and ruined cranium lay under a black shroud.

Next to Miguel, Sister Sofia slept as soundly.

Father gestured to the corpses. "Why did these two good people die?" he asked rhetorically.

Looking at his charges, Montoya said, "Children, I want to tell you a story. It is of a place that once was and could be again. There was a time when we, here in the United States, did not murder unborn babies. There was a time when people took care of other people—well—and didn't ask the government to spend nearly half the wealth of the country every year in order to take care of people . . . badly.

"There was a time when we were not afraid of the truth here in this country, a time when words meant something real, when they were not just things to be twisted to suit a particular set of politics.

"There was a time when our people were brave and free and strong . . . and honest too, most of them. There was even a time when the faith of our fathers was not considered to be an 'enemy of the state' . . ."

The breeze rifling the priest's hair was warm, unseasonably so for the lateness of the season on the flat Texas prairie. The old, starched jungle fatigue jacket Montoya had removed for mass was again covering his torso, though it was itself covered by an armored vest courtesy of Schmidt.

The priest disdained wearing a helmet.

An even half dozen of the boys sat with Montoya under cover of a low shed. He didn't know if the thermal imagers Jack had told him of would see through the sheet metal roof. Even if they could, he reasoned, they were unlikely to be able to tell the difference between the priest and the boys and the eight or so animals that usually slept here.

Best I could think to do.

Not for the first time the priest wondered, and worried, about the morrow. *Am I doing the right thing? Have I put the kids in the safest place? Can we hold them? Will Jack come riding over the hill to the rescue? Do I want a war?*

On the last point the priest was really rather sure;

he did not want a war. Yet, so it seemed to him, sometimes a fight was the best way to avoid a war. And, looking down the road a few years, he saw a war coming.

"Think the old man in there knows we're coming, sir?" asked his driver of Sawyers.

"Doesn't much matter, does it Ricky? We could walk in armed with rocks and still beat the crap out of them."

"Yes, *sir*," the driver grinned.

"Not much longer now," Sawyers muttered to no one in particular.

Although not directed to him, the driver answered anyway, "We're ready when you are, sir."

We're not, you know. We might have been. If it were not more important to propagandize you kids into the party line than to train you to fight, we might have been.

Sawyers sighed for lost—stolen—opportunities.

"You wanted me, padre?" the boy Julio asked.

"I . . ." the priest hesitated, "I just wanted a few words with you Julio. About Miguel."

"He was my friend, Father; my best friend. They murdered him. In a few hours they will attack and I will have the chance to shoot the people who shot him."

"Julio . . . you will likely never get the man who shot Miguel and Elpidia. That one . . . he was an expert, very special. Not to be risked on something like us. The people who are coming in tomorrow morning are not too different from you. Boys, most of them.

Maybe a little older. Just boys like you though, doing a job they believe in."

Julio raised a skeptical eyebrow. "Are you telling me I shouldn't shoot them then, father?"

"No, son. You'll have to fight; same as me. But when you fight . . . Julio . . . hijo mio . . . remember, good men sometimes fight for bad causes. Try not to hate."

The assault came from the east. With the newly risen sun shining brightly into the eyes of the defenders, Sawyers confirmed his orders and gave the command, "Roll."

The two loaned tanks led the way, driven and manned by hastily familiarized agents of the BATF. Behind the tanks came Sawyers' own two companies, riding safe in their Light Armored Vehicles.

To the south, a crane converted to a tower was raised to provide the Hostage Rescue Team's snipers a clear field of fire down into the Dei Gloria mission compound. Only very close to the south wall—and north and east of some of the buildings—was the team's line of sight blocked.

The team's spotter radioed to headquarters that there was no movement inside the compound.

Montoya felt his heart race as it had not raced in four decades. The tanks made little sound themselves, just the ominous inhuman squeaking of their churning treads. In a way, that was worse than the throatier roar of the tanks in his experience.

There were roars too, those from the LAVs used by the PGSS. Montoya ignored those.

The squeaking of the treads grew in intensity, closer, closer . . .

Chips of adobe and brick flew away from the mission walls in two places as they bulged inward, buckled and crumbled. The tanks had struck them to create a pair of breaches in the adobe for the infantry to pour through.

In further aid of the assault, the tanks had been slightly modified. Their main cannon were partially plugged to allow the projection of CS gas from high pressure dispensers. Fanning back and forth, the tanks spewed a cloud of lachrymatory gas to subdue the defenders.

Montoya already had his mask on, one of those provided by Schmidt in his care package. Montoya's boys likewise had donned theirs with a speed that would have done credit to a regular as soon as they had seen the first white clouds spew from the tanks' muzzles.

With a shout of "follow me," the shout distorted by the mask's "voicemitter," Montoya led a team of three boys forward a few short steps and on to the southernmost of the two breaches. To his left charged four more boys under Miguel's successor, Ramon. All sprinted in a low crouch to avoid possible sniper fire.

The teams reached the undamaged wall between the breaches, then split north and south. Reaching the tanks, the boys threw clear glass bottles full of liquid to impact on the rear hulls and turrets.

✧   ✧   ✧

"What's that, chief?" sniffed the driver of Montoya's target as the first faint whiff of ammonia passed easily through the filtration system and on into the crew and driver compartments.

Before the commander of the vehicle could make an answer the ammonia hit him full strength. It was sudden as an unexpected blow. Eyes streaming, throat closing and choking, gorge rising, he clawed at the hatch over his head, one thought on his mind: *Escape!*

He might have made it out quicker had his gunner not also been trying to crawl through him to escape the overpowering chemical stench.

Montoya calmly shot the driver whose easy escape had been blocked by the tank's cannon, directly overhead. Then the emerging loader took two rounds through the belly before flopping bonelessly back downwards into the tank's bowels. When two heads appeared simultaneously in the commander's hatch he shot them as well, bone and brains and blood flying away. *Father forgive me.*

"Padre, here!" shouted a boy as he passed over a homemade satchel charge. The priest took it with a muttered "thanks," pulled the igniter and leaning around a corner tossed the charge under the tank's right tread. The burning fuse left a curly cue arc of narrow but dense smoke as it corkscrewed through the air.

"Fire in the hole! Fire in the hole! FIRE IN THE HOOOLLE!" shouted the priest as he led and herded his boys back to cover. Even as he himself leapt to safety the charge went off like a kick in the pants, knocking him head over heels to go tumbling along the ground.

Austin, Texas

"That's my boy, Jorge," muttered Schmidt as he, the governor, and her "war cabinet" listened in to reports coming uncensored from the scene. Half the words used were expletives and obscenities.

"Fucking gas isn't working. Motherfuckers took out both tanks . . . Jesus-Fucking-Christ they shot down the crews like dogs . . . Where the fuck are those goddamned helicopters? . . . What in the fuck are the snipers doing? . . . My God . . . they've got guns . . . machine guns . . . Explosives . . . Jesus . . ."

Juanita looked piercingly at Schmidt. "Where . . . where, General, did my brother get machine guns? Where did he get explosives?"

A tiny flicker of a smile. "Jorge always was a resourceful sort, Governor. You know that." Then Schmidt's face lit again in his broadest, brightest flash. "You really want to know? Fine. I gave them to him. I'll be damned if my best friend and your brother was going to be taken without a good fight. They . . . you . . . can do what the hell you want with me. But Jorge Montoya was not going to lack the tools he needed! And can you hear, Juani? Can you hear?" Schmidt pointed at the radio, still sputtering with federal outrage. "He's holding them; beating them."

Softly, "I wish I were there. I wish I were there.

"Do you know why I am not, Governor? Because I still hope to talk some sense into you. I still think that the girl I . . . voted for . . . hasn't got it in her to see her brother cut down by wolves in suits and ties."

Fiercely now, "Let me roll my division, Juani. Send

Nagy there to arrest them, too. Save your brother Juani . . . save those children, Governor."

Juanita's mouth set as if concrete, hard, unyielding. "Do it."

With a triumphant shout, Schmidt headed for the door. "You coming with me, Nagy? We can take my helicopter."

Dei Gloria Mission, Waco, Texas

The press of numbers was too great. It had always been too great. Yet Montoya had hoped that, if he put up a good fight, the feds might just back off to reconsider.

"Dumb bastards don't even know enough to know we're a losing proposition."

"What was that, Father?"

The priest shook his head. "Nothing, Ramon."

The defenders, what were left of them, had been forced back to the chapel. Only Elpidia, wounded and helpless in the small infirmary, the children cowering in the storm shelter, and Julio, waiting for that perfect shot, remained outside of this last ditch. A baker's dozen of the boys and girls of the Mission lay sprawled in death outside, victims of the sniper in his tower, the helicopters overhead, or the near random fire of the PGSS now swarming through the grounds.

That baker's dozen had a slightly larger honor guard of their dead and wounded assailants. Ultimately driven from the breaches by the PGSS, the padre had been helpless to stop the surge of armed inhumanity that had poured into the mission. They hadn't been able to stop it. That hadn't prevented them from bleeding it however.

Even now, from hastily excavated loopholes in the chapel walls, some of the defenders traded shots with their attackers.

Some still fought. Others? The priest's eyes scanned the chapel. Exhausted, was his judgment. He wasted a scornful glance upon Father Flores, cowering under a heavy sacramental alter. Unharmed, unsoiled, but also an unworthy cause to have given his children's lives for, thought Father Jorge.

He looked more carefully; began counting. Eleven of us here. Five wounded; two badly. One of the wounded boys was crying softly, trying to hold his intestines inside. Another, rapidly turning pale with loss of blood, managed to keep silent.

I wonder what happened to Julio.

"In the name of the Father, the Son and the Holy Spirit," whispered Julio as finally, finally, he found the shot for which he had been waiting. It was not a perfect shot. It was not even a particularly good one. But it was a possibility. The first possibility he had had all morning.

The HRT's ad hoc sniper tower had been modified with a steel box at its summit. From that box, sheltered from anything that was not directly in his line of fire, the sniper had poured down shot after shot into the defenders. More than half the mission dead were attributable to that sniper's deadly, accurate fire.

And Julio hadn't been able to do a thing about it. Not a thing. The sniper and his spotter had kept safely back, with a half an inch of steel between them and Julio.

And then, easy targets exhausted, the tower had turned, presenting its half open front face to Julio's scope.

Unseen by the HRT, any potential glare from the scope hidden by a deeply recessed firing position, Julio's breathing paused, his body relaxed, his finger tightened, and his rifle spoke.

The bullet flew straight and true. Before he had the remotest suspicion that he was under fire, the sniper's brains filled the small armored box in which he and his spotter sheltered, covering the spotter with blood and gore.

In the crowded headquarters Friedberg fumed and raged. Bad enough that eight BATF agents were down. Bad enough that some dozens of PGSS were down. But to kill her people? Intolerable. And she would not tolerate it.

"Get me those Army types on the line," she demanded of one of the radio operators.

"Ma'am?" asked the cowed minor functionary; there were a number of "Army types" supporting the operation.

"The gunships, you idiot. About time they earned their pay."

"Yes, ma'am." The operator spoke briefly into a microphone. "Here they are, Ms. Friedberg." The Director of the FBI felt a small satisfaction at seeing the trembling in the hand which offered her the microphone.

"Who is this?" she demanded.

The answer came as if through a "sound blender" . . . the words choppy and distorted. "This is Echo 57. Who is *this*?"

"This is the Director of the FBI." Friedberg waited in vain for a suitably humble response.

"Roger, Director, this is Echo 57. You have traffic this station?" The voice was annoyingly male and had an infuriating lack of humility. There was no noticeable tenor even of respect.

"He means 'Do you have a message?' ma'am."

Friedberg glared at the operator. "I know what he means, you ninny."

"Echo 57, this is the Director. I want you to attack the mission. My people are being hurt and I want it to stop."

There was a barely perceptible pause on the other end, as if the pilots were conferring among themselves. At last came the response, "No can do, Director. Forbidden. Illegal."

Friedberg shrieked frustration. *How dare he?* "Listen to me you nincompoop. I am the Director of the United States Federal Bureau of Investigation. And nothing that I say is legal is illegal. Do you understand?"

"I understand. I will not comply."

"Get me the other pilot."

The operator checked frequencies, but made no changes. He spoke briefly, then announced, "Echo 63, Director."

Friedberg forced a measure of calm into her voice. "Echo 63 this is the Director of the FBI. Echo 57 has refused a lawful order from the President through me. Echo 57 can expect to be prosecuted when this is over. He can also expect to be found guilty, imprisoned, sodomized, and finally audited by the IRS! Now unless you want to join him in prison, I suggest you follow my orders and riddle-That-FUCKING-CAMP!"

"Don't do it, Max."

"Echo 57 this is the Director. Shut up or I'll send you to the worst nightmare of a prison in the federal system! Echo 63 will you comply?"

With an audible sigh, sent through a voice-activated mike, the pilot of the second gunship answered, "Wilco."

A long column of armored vehicles, fourteen tanks in the lead, stretched along Interstate 35, exhausts smoking and treads churning.

"Goddamit, fuck the speed limits. They don't apply to tanks. General Schmidt said 'now' and I want to be there two hours ago." *If only* we hadn't had to send to Fort Hood for main gun rounds, then had to sneak them away from the post. If only. But the general had said "be prepared to fight" . . . and so they had had to stop to arm up.

"Wilco," came from five different senders as the better part of 1st Battalion, 141st Infantry, with pieces of the 1st of the 112th Armor, of the 49th Armored Division roared down the highway.

Sergeant Akers watched from the headquarters as the gunship made another pass on the mission compound, chaingun spitting fury. He had lost count of the number of attack runs it had so far made.

There are kids in there, dammit. Texan kids I swore to defend.

It was hard, so hard. Not to die, no. Hard to break

the rules. Hard to lift his arm against a law enforcement agency. Hard to raise his hand to a woman, even one like Friedberg.

But it's not as hard as standing here watching those kids murdered. Reaching a decision, commending his soul to God, Akers undid the restraining strap on his shoulder holster, thumbed back the hammer, and ensured the safety was off. Then he set those shoulders, and walked into the headquarters.

Akers walked unnoticed—few people ever noticed him, really—to a spot right behind the director. He sighed, still unnoticed, then reached his hand under his jacket. As he did, the kindly expression, the grandfatherly expression, disappeared from his face. What replaced it was something not quite human, let alone grandfatherly.

"The next sound you hear will be your brains hitting the wall unless you call off the gunship, Director. Tell your people to freeze."

Friedberg felt the cold rounded muzzle of the sergeant's pistol pressed against the base of her skull. She felt the warm drizzle of urine begin to run down her legs almost immediately. "Nobody move," she ordered, voice unaccountably and uncharacteristically trembling.

"Call off the helicopter," she told the radio operator, for a change neglecting to insult him.

The operator hesitated. "Now," insisted Johnston Akers, sergeant, two medals of honor.

"Now," echoed the director.

"And I want your agents to drop their weapons and their trousers. Now," insisted the ranger.

"Do it."

❖   ❖   ❖

The gunship made yet another pass. Few buildings still stood undamaged in the compound. From one small one a small person, carrying a rifle, fled. His apparent destination was a large wooden structure, much like a barn. The gunner cut down Julio, then took aim at the building towards which he had been headed.

It was indeed a barn on the outside. But in the center of the floor was a concrete pad with a steel door. It was, in fact, the storm shelter. And under that pad crouched twenty-six children ages six months to twelve years.

The rockets were a mix; white phosphorus, some, and high explosive, others. The explosive shattered the dry wood of the barn. The phosphorus set it alight.

Even as the last salvo of rockets exploded, the WP in lovely art nouveau of flaming arcs, the pilot received the word, "Break off your attack now."

For long hours had the little ones cowered under their shelter while the muffled sounds of furious battle leaked in. Some of these had been enough to shake the structure, setting the younger ones to crying.

"Josefina, make it stop. Please make it stop."

"I can't, Nezi," the older girl said; left on her own as the best choice available since Sister Sofia had been killed. "I'm only twelve."

In time, the sounds of firing abated. Yet Josefina was afraid to venture out. They were safe where they were. Father had said they would be.

But if it got much hotter . . .

❖   ❖   ❖

Montoya heard the chopper approaching. Perhaps, better said, he felt it. He really couldn't hear much of anything. His eardrums had burst from the impact of a flock of 2.75 inch folding fin aerial rockets on the chapel roof.

He tried to move his head to the side. *Oh, God . . . nausea.* His eyes seemed not to want to focus. He forced them, willed them to do so.

Amidst bodies and pieces of bodies, most far too young to have been in that place, at that time, nausea quickened and grew worse. The priest shut his eyes, let nausea wash over him and away. Thought . . . tried to think . . . of something. . . .

The helicopters were distant, their steady wop-wop-wop no louder than the drone of a mosquito. Hands roughly, but no more so than circumstances warranted, pulled Montoya off of Schmidt's body. Montoya opened his eyes; friendly faces, black and brown and white. Round eyes.

"Oh God," he tried to whisper. "See to my lieutenant. I'm fine, I tell you. Check Jack."

"'Jack's' okay, Sergeant. He'll be fine. But let's take a look at you." Busy hands cut away a blood-soaked fatigue jacket, slashed off torn trousers.

"Vug! Stick 'im."

"What happened, Sergeant? How'd you get hit?"

Pain began to ebb as the morphine spread through Montoya's ruined body. He found himself able to answer, if barely. "Grenade. Couldn't get rid of it in time. Had to . . . to . . ."

Montoya felt the calm pat of the medic. "Later, Sergeant. For now, let's get the two of you home."

Opening his eyes, Montoya could actually see the medevac helicopter, though its blade was only a blur. He closed his eyes and gave himself over to the morphia.

Father Jorge still felt the beating blades of the gunship hovering somewhere over the chapel. "Come on, finish it," he whispered.

"Please, God, let it be over soon," prayed Josefina. "Please." All the other children were asleep, or unconscious. It was *so* hot, so unbearably hot in the shelter.

The little girl had tried to open the door, once she understood that it was get out or roast alive. But the door had been jammed tight. It wouldn't budge, not even an inch. She wanted to weep again. *We're trapped here. Oh God, why? Why? What did we ever do to anyone?*

Josefina felt the wall. It was hot, painfully hot, to the touch. With a weak little yelp she drew her hand back, wrapping both arms around the youngest, Elpidia's Pedro. In the girl's arms little Pedro shuddered once, then grew still. "Wake up baby, wake up," she demanded fruitlessly.

"Oh, Elpi, I'm so sorry. I tried. I really tried."

Those were the last articulable words Josefina ever spoke, as heat drove her into unconsciousness and far, far too young a death.

Akers didn't relax even when he heard the first tanks and sirens. Not until he saw his own Texas Rangers enter the room did he even begin to think about anything but keeping the director under his muzzle.

His captain, flanked by a brace of the roughest-looking men in F Company, announced, "Good job, Sergeant. We'll take it from here."

"Sir? Sir, there's two dozen kids in there."

"We know. We'll do what we can. But . . ." and the captain thought of the pillar of smoke rising from the compound.

"Yes, sir." Akers left for a breath of air unpolluted by *federales*.

Once outside Akers stood at the door for a minute. Distantly he heard his captain say, "Ms. Friedberg? You are under arrest for violation of Texas Criminal Code, Sections 19.02 and 19.03. . . ."

The irony of that was lost on Akers for the moment, though he would cherish it into his old age. He was somewhat unsurprised to see tank after tank, track after track pouring into and through the area. He was unsurprised to see scores, hundreds of the President's Elite PGSS and the Surgeon General's special police surrendering as fast as could be.

He was very surprised to see and hear a single blast from one of the Guard's main guns, followed by the near disintegration of a PGSS LAV that had been attempting to escape.

Schmidt had his helicopter set down in the middle of the smoking compound, despite protestations from his chief pilot. Alighting from the bird with two armed guards, he immediately set out for what he instinctively knew would be his friend's last refuge, the chapel.

He announced himself, "Jorge? It's me. Jack. It's over; you can come out now. Jorge?"

No answer. Jack decided to take his chances. Jorge wouldn't shoot him by mistake. Still continuously announcing himself, Schmidt pounded the barred door with his shoulder, only after much effort to be rewarded by a sprung hinge and a—barely open path.

Inside was a scene from a nightmare. Schmidt knew it was because he had had that very nightmare repeatedly of late. Under the altar rested the remains of Father Flores, whom Schmidt recognized only by his vestments. Not far from there lay Father Montoya, bleeding from a score of wounds. Around him and by the walls lay the boys who had followed their priest into death.

Schmidt collapsed to his knees, hung his head, and wept for his dead friend.

Even as the ashes of the mission were cooling, the first book—surreptitiously subsidized by the White House—hit the bookstores: *Father of Pain: The True Story of the Deadly Fanatic Catholic Fundamentalist Cult of Texas*.

INTERLUDE:

From: *Lone Star Rebellion: A Study in Asymmetric Revolutionary Warfare,* Copyright 2078, Colonel Jonathan Hightower, Parameters

From the beginning the governor of Texas was faced with a seemingly insurmountable problem. On the face of it, her state was outnumbered by a factor of about twelve in both economic and population terms. The federal government had de facto, if not de jure, control over the media, thus over what common people thought across the country. That same government was also firmly in the hands of a cabal not merely hostile to Texas and Governor Seguin, but one imbued with a hatred bordering on—in some cases crossing over to—the fanatical. That government also had economic clout never in history equaled, let alone surpassed. And it, with its entire armed force's mustered perhaps twenty to twenty-four times the power of Texas' own National Guard, exclusive of nuclear weapons.

Moreover, the fronts on which this campaign would come to be waged were varied, amorphous and vast. Texas would have to meet—not necessarily defeat but "meet"—the federal government on no less than seven of these "fronts." These were: economic, military, propaganda, legal, domestic political, Texan political and civil disobedience.

Only in the last did Texas have any obvious advantage.

CHAPTER SEVEN

From the transcript at trial: Commonwealth of Virginia v. Alvin Scheer

DIRECT EXAMINATION, CONTINUED
BY MR. STENNINGS:

Q. Keep going, Alvin. Tell the judge what you saw and how you felt about it.

A. I saw the thing on TV. After the fighting was over, you know? When the National Guard and the Department of Public Safety folks started uncovering the bodies? God, it was awful. Poor little charred, shrunken things being lifted up out of that hole in the ground, some alone, some clutching onto one another. One case stuck in my mind; stayed there for weeks. It was a little girl—I think it was a girl but she was so bad it was hard to tell, no hair, clothes turned black—sorta wrapped around what was left of a baby. That one put my wife to throwin' up.

And one old man, looked like my grandfather from what I remember of him, just standing there, crying and crying.

Then the TV cut off and we didn't get no more news about the mission for a while. . . .

Washington, DC

"Shut it off, shut it off for Christ's sake!"

Obediently, Jesse Vega, the Attorney General for the United States, flicked the President's television away from GNN's live coverage of the mission.

Willi Rottemeyer stormed and fumed, drumming a small fist furiously against the top of her ornate desk. "How dare those bastards put this on the air? How dare they?"

Vega put down the remote control and shrugged. "I've already put out the word to shut that broadcast down. And sent a few people to have a little chat with someone in Atlanta who thinks he's important. But there's going to be some fallout from this, Willi. Serious fallout. I think they'll actually try Friedberg. It's Texas, too, so they just might kill her . . . execute her."

Rottemeyer was completely a political animal. Her mind immediately began sorting out the forms in which that "fallout" might materialize. Nearly as quickly she began reviewing plans to limit it. One such plan involved the expression "sacrificial lamb." Then she thought, no, with Friedberg in Texas Ranger custody I need Vega to get through this. Shit! Who would ever have thought that prissy little wetback twat Seguin would have it in her? Bitch!

Rottemeyer hit a button on her intercom. "Get me Governor Seguin on the phone." To Vega she said, "Get me my Cabinet."

Austin, Texas

"It's the President for you, Governor."

Juanita's mouth made a small moue of distaste . . . and not a little outright loathing. She thought briefly before announcing, "Tell the President that 'The governor is busy with the crisis.' I think she'll understand that."

Leaning back in a leather conference chair, Schmidt gave off a loud guffaw. *Now this is the Juani I almost asked to marry me. Would have too, if it weren't for what happened to her brother. Maybe even then, if she hadn't gone into politics. Well, no matter. She picked a good man and I'm glad for it.*

"It isn't funny, Jack," the governor insisted.

Schmidt raised an eyebrow. "On the contrary, Governor, that was the only funny thing about this mess, since it all began."

"Fine then; funny to you. Me? I want to get my hands on that bitch's neck and squeeze til her eyes pop out. What she did to Jorge? What she did to those kids. She's not *my* President anymore either, Jack."

"No?" Schmidt asked, rhetorically. "Well, if we don't do something, and quick, she's going to keep on being our president. And she's not going to stop until she's crushed us like a softboiled egg."

Silently, Juanita nodded. Then she asked, "But what can we do? Secession? Not a chance, Jack. That silly myth that we alone can legally secede? It's just that, a myth, a legend."

"No," Schmidt agreed, a mixture of desire and reluctance clouding his voice. "But we have to do something."

Spanish eyes flashed, dark and determined. "Give Friedberg and her people back? I won't do it. They committed murder of Texans on Texas soil and I am going to see them tried. I am going to think of Jorge and those little kids and I am going to smile when I sign the death warrants."

Juanita sighed. "But I won't have the chance to do that, will I, Jack? Just as you said, she's going to crush us. She's already moved to cut off our side of the story from the rest of the country."

Schmidt buried his nose into shallowly cupped hands; thinking, calculating. Okay . . . secession is out. And even if we could do it, why should we give up a weapon in the enemy's camp? How much good might we get out of a filibustering senator? Maybe quite a bit. And if we did it anyway? The rest of the states would have to either join us and split the country or force us back . . . because they can't tolerate having a democratic majority in both houses forever; which losing Texas' votes would cause.

Hmm. What's left?

Schmidt suddenly stood up and walked to the phone on Juani's desk. Muttering, "There are weapons and then there are weapons," he dialed a number from memory. "Is Stone there?" he demanded. "This is General Schmidt."

"Major Stone? Look, it's like this. You are called up to serve your state at the governor's order. Moreover, pursuant to section seven of the constitution of the State of Texas the Governor has authority to 'call forth the militia to execute the laws of the state, to suppress insurrections, repel invasion, protect the frontier from hostile incursions by Indians and other predatory bands.' It's that 'predatory band' provision that concerns you. So you're called up and all your techno-geeks are called up too, the male ones anyway. Tell the women we'll pay 'em National Guard rates if they volunteer, but we can't make 'em take the deal."

"Calm down, Stone. We're not sending you to the Mexican border. But there are some scenes that the television stations, notably GNN, are refusing to carry. . . . Yes, that's right, from the Mission. I want them going out over the Internet, continuously. Can you do that? . . . Good. Get hopping major." Schmidt hung up the phone.

"What the hell are you doing, Jack?"

"First and second steps, Juani. Seize the moral high ground and blind the bastards. Stone runs one of the major Internet nodes in the country, right here in Austin. Good man, for all that he's a dumb ass tanker in the Guard. We'll get our story out; for a while anyway. And the only way for them to stop us is to cut off communication between Texas and the rest."

"But that's all we can do for now, that and do some planning. I think you need your cabinet on this one, Juani. The cabinet and maybe a few legislators too."

Washington, DC

McCreavy was at something of a loss. Yes, she was Chair of the Joint Chiefs of Staff. Yes, she was an honest-to-God four-star general with the promise from her President of a nearly unique fifth star soon to be forthcoming. Yes, she was very smart, very insightful. "An Intelligence Officer of rare promise." So a general had written of young Second Lieutenant McCreavy.

What she was not, was a combat soldier. Comfortable with maps, with statistical analyses, with reports of doings from across the world; she was most uncomfortable with real conflict and decidedly uncomfortable with real people. "My battalion commander is a posturing simpleton with no better idea of how to lead than to threaten my sergeants with relief to cover her own mistakes and failings." So had a young captain written, many years after the general, and with greater—albeit not complete—truth. The real truth lay somewhere in the middle.

Sadly, the system being the system, the captain's comments never made it into McCreavy's file whereas the general's did.

Still, McCreavy was the best Rottemeyer had in a case like this. And if not so wonderful as the general had made her out to be, neither was she so wretched as the captain's words would indicate.

And she did have a fairly complete military education.

"Militarily we can take them, Willi, but you'll have to pull troops in from all over the country. We might have to abandon some . . . ummm . . . outposts too."

"Outposts?"

McCreavy looked up before answering. "Overseas outposts. We might need them."

Continuing, she said, "Texas has about a division and a bit more. But it's a heavy division. Tanks, infantry fighting vehicles, that sort of thing. We don't really have any forces like that left in the Regular Army or Marines within the United States. Everything was lightened years ago to make them more deployable. Only reason the National Guard still has real tanks is that they are always last in line for new equipment. And we have one heavy corps, really just a big division itself, in central Europe."

"Outposts?" Rottemeyer asked again.

"Peacekeeping," McCreavy answered, simply.

"We can't do that," insisted Rottemeyer's Secretary of State. "The world is in very delicate condition right now and if we were seen to be pulling out . . ." He let the words trail off.

"Worse than that, Willi," chimed in her bald-headed political advisor, John Carroll, speaking in a thick Southern drawl. "A hefty chunk of your support comes from people who want us involved in solving the world's problems. You abandon them; they might abandon you. I can name at least five senators that could turn if you were to pull out of Somalia and Rwanda alone. Then there're the ones who like having an American battalion between Egypt and Israel. Then, too, you've already lost a couple of people over that damned broadcast that idiot Ted let go out."

CIA interrupted. "It's still going out. I was waiting for the right time to mention it."

"*What?* How?" Rottemeyer demanded. "If that fucking Turn . . ."

"No, Willi. Internet," CIA interrupted. "Austin is about third in the country for software and computer design. They have their own node right there. They're making available continuous . . . well, call it what it is . . . propaganda to every home and business computer in America."

"Goddammit this has got to stop!"

CIA shrugged. "We *can* stop it. Interfere with it anyway. All we have to do is cut off telephone service to and from Texas. FCC could do it by tomorrow; next day at the latest."

"Do it," commanded the President.

Somewhat curiously, though at least three members of Rottemeyer's Cabinet had marched in protest over Richard Nixon's having bugged George McGovern's campaign headquarters in 1972, had marched in protest over domestic surveillance being conducted by the CIA, not one thought it remotely inappropriate for CIA to be monitoring internal affairs any longer. They were the personification of perceived morality being a function of whose ox was being gored. Nor did any raise a voice in protest over the President's order to cut communications with a large and populous state.

"Wait," insisted McCreavy. "Can you stop telephone service within Texas? Given the number of cell phones in this country? No? I thought not. Willi, if you cut off external service—land lines and cellular both—we won't have a clue as to what's going on there, we'll lose control of the people we have there, but they'll still be able to plot and plan together. I think you ought to think about this very carefully."

Austin, Texas

The conference room was crowded and smoky; the governor was of the opinion that a man—or woman—ought to be allowed his vices if it helped him work better. She herself didn't smoke. She could easily tolerate those, like her husband, who did.

Schmidt smoked. Under circumstances like these he smoked continuously, big nasty fifty-ring-gauge Churchills. "Well, Governor, militarily I can't promise you much hope. They can't take us quickly, no. But, ultimately, if we're left on our own, they *can* take us. Then we're stuck with guerilla war; always hard on the people. And no guarantee we could win that, if it came to it."

Juanita could tolerate the smoke billowing from Jack's nasty Churchill. She didn't have to like it. And she could see some of her other advisors beginning to turn a pale green. "Could you at least hit the damned filter and the fans I had installed so you could indulge your nasty vice?"

"Huh? Oh sure, Juani," said Schmidt, pushing a button on a rather expensive air filter, turning on a window fan and opening another window a crack for good measure. "Happy now?"

"I'm a long way from happy . . . but it will do. Now what about Fort Hood?" asked the governor.

"I spoke to General Bennigsen, the Third Corps commander. He has heard the tapes of the conversation between Friedberg and the gunships. He's also seen what we pulled out of that storm cellar. He told me he would not obey any orders to use his corps as a police force. But, he also said, if we started shooting he wouldn't have any choice. He will defend his post, he says." Schmidt sounded as if he had a great deal of sympathy for Bennigsen, and the rather miserable set of choices he faced. More than sympathy, there was a tone of admiration and respect for the way he was making those choices.

"So, you are telling me that we don't have much of a military option but neither does Washington?"

"That's about it, Juani. For now. In six months? They could roll right over us. Maybe six weeks if they're willing to disengage from the rest of the world."

Juanita turned to her attorney general, raising one quizzical eyebrow.

The attorney general, David Rothman, was heavyset, dark complexioned, and nattily dressed; a Mormon convert from Judaism. Politically, he was considered to be just a few feet to the right of Attila the Hun, though this was a slight exaggeration. Indeed, his conversion to Mormonism had as much to do with rejection of liberalism as it did with acceptance of Christ.

"We've got two issues, Governor. One is the continuing imprisonment and future trial of Friedberg and her crew. That's the least pressing, though I am sure you can expect the White House to press. The other is . . . well, I think we need to inundate the federal courts with every kind of lawsuit we can imagine; criminal indictments, as well. We need to paralyze them legally, as best we can."

Schmidt snorted loudly; he had little use for lawsuits.

"Quiet, Jack," Juanita waved a hand. "Let him finish. What kind of lawsuits, Dave?"

"Governor, my staff has just begun studying that question. Some preliminary answers, though, include indictments against everyone in the White House, FBI, BATF, EPA and the Surgeon General's office who had anything in the slightest to do with what happened at your brother's mission. Hit them at the same time, personally, with wrongful death suits. Then there's the environmental damage done as a result of the smoke. That's another suit. Your brother's mission was an historic site, too; did you know that? There's another."

"And how many of those suits and indictments will survive the once-over-lightly at the Supreme Court."

"I can't answer that yet, Governor."

Juanita's lieutenant governor interjected a question, "Would it make any difference, really?"

"Would what?" asked Rothman.

"Even if we won all the suits in the world, what makes you think Rottemeyer will pay the slightest attention?"

Rothman didn't need to think about that for long. "Ultimately, she won't, not her. But . . . before she has actually lost them she'll fight them every step of the way. It's just in her nature, I think. She used to be a pretty fair lawyer herself once upon a time. Hated to lose anything, I've heard. And that distraction might help. Will probably help."

The lieutenant governor let his skepticism show plainly. White-haired and bent-shouldered, Dr. Ralph Minden held a Ph.D. in economics. He had been recruited for Juanita's gubernatorial ticket, despite being a Republican, precisely because he was an economist of national standing.

Minden announced, "Won't matter a hill of beans. She's going to cut off funding. She's going to keep taxing. Six months of that and she won't need to invade us, won't need to jail us. There are enough people here dependent on federal handouts that they'll lynch us in the streets long before it comes to that."

"Any way around that?" asked Schmidt. He had always respected the lieutenant governor's opinions.

"Maybe two. One is . . . well . . . why don't we make it illegal for federal income and social security taxes to be withheld in Texas? Won't stop companies whose checks are cut outside of Texas from withholding, mind you. But we are a net profit maker to the federal government in total. Losing revenues on payroll checks cut in Texas will hurt them . . . some anyway."

"What's the other way?" asked Schmidt.

"The Mint?"

"Huh?"

"There are two Federal Mints—divisions of the Bureau of Engraving. One's in DC. The other one? The Western Currency Facility. That's in Fort Worth, just up the road."

Schmidt cocked his head to one side and smiled. "Clever, Doc. You mean we take over the place. Then if they tax us, we just print the equivalent money to cover the tax."

"Yes, General. All of the tax. Plus we can manipulate the money supply if we need to; put a real crunch on the feds. The printing plant in DC just might be able to keep an adequate money supply circulating; half the reason they built a second one here was security and redundancy, after all, not capacity. But they couldn't stand it if we flooded the country with too much money. Holding the mint would send a message they couldn't ignore."

"Won't they just bomb the shit out of the Mint?" asked Schmidt.

Minden paused, then continued. "Right away,

General? Right away and admit they have a revolution on their hands? Right away before they've even tried to take it back whole? Right away before we have a chance to disperse the printing capability? I think not."

Schmidt looked down, thinking hard. Slowly at first, then with growing insistence, a smile forced itself to his face. "You know, Doc. I don't think so either."

Washington, DC

"So what if we don't cut communications with Texas," asked Rottemeyer.

"Can't stop the propaganda coming out of there," announced Carroll, simply.

"But," he added, "maybe we shouldn't worry so much over that. After all, there's propaganda and then there's propaganda."

"Hmm?" queried Rottemeyer.

"Oh, when this all kicked off I contacted a hack writer I know, called National Endowment for the Arts and got him a grant. He's a hack, but he's a good one. *Father of Pain: The True Story of the Deadly Fanatic Catholic Fundamentalist Cult of Texas* will be hitting the book stands day after tomorrow. We'll pin everything from child abuse to drug use to running a prostitution ring on that priest. And we'll get the first dig in. They won't recover so easily from *that*."

"Where did your hack get the information?" asked McCreavy.

Carroll fixed her with a pitying stare.

Cemetery, Dei Gloria Mission, Waco, Texas

Ranks and files of caskets, twenty-six of them undersized, stretched across an open area that was part of the Mission's old Spanish cemetery. Among hundreds of witnesses and participants to the funeral, only a few were related in any way to the victims. Elpidia, seated in a wheelchair—and with her arm and shoulder still plastered—was one of these.

Juanita, her husband, and Schmidt were there, too, of course. In fact, all of Juanita's family that could make it had shown up to bid farewell to their Uncle Jorge. The four boys, Carlos, who worked on Wall Street, Thomas and Roderigo, both still in college, and Mario the youngest and still in high school, stood flanking their mother and father, like an honor guard.

It was her youngest son, Mario—a fine strapping, handsome boy, not too different from his late uncle—who had taken upon himself the duty of pushing Elpidia's wheelchair around . . . that, and offering what comfort he could.

Comforted by Mario or not, Elpidia still wept continuously. All assumed it was for her baby. They were only half right, however. Elpi also wept for her priest and for fallen Miguel, the only men in her miserable life to date who had ever treated her decently for any length of time.

The priest presiding had finished with his portion. The time had come for Juanita to have her say. Tired, and with the fatigue and stress showing on her face from a night spent preparing to speak, she stood. Patting Elpi's good shoulder, Juanita turned then and walked steadily to a podium, her progress followed by the cameras that fed directly to Stone's Internet node and from there to the rest of the world.

Juanita began calmly, "The people who did this, who committed this horrible crime, believe that they have accounted for everything; that they have foreseen *everything*. They think that with their guns they have frightened half of us into submission . . . and with their taxes bribed the rest of us into acquiescence.

"They think that they can get away with anything— murder, mayhem, massacre—by just showing some teeth on a television, promising to steal some more money only so they can give it back . . . after it takes that expensive night on the town in Washington, to be sure . . . and telling us how they *feel* our pain."

Juani's face grew bitter. "'Feel our pain' . . . so they claim. Do they? Did they feel it when they roasted twenty-six of our children alive in a storm shelter? Did they feel it when they blasted a priest of God to bits with their gunships' rockets and machine guns? 'Feel our pain'? They can no more do that than they can feel our rage."

Among the crowd, many began softly to weep, joining their cries to Elpidia's. Schmidt—himself—found the need to wipe his eyes.

"But why not?" Juanita continued. "What have they to fear from us, after all? Haven't they frightened—the half—and bribed the other half?"

Bitterness fell away before rage. "Oh the fools, the fools, the stupid . . . Stupid . . . STUPID and utterly contemptible fools." Juani stopped for breath before continuing. She stepped away to put her hand on her brother's casket. "They have left us our sacred Texan dead. And while Texas, under their yoke, holds these dead, Texas will never be at peace.

"For I have had a vision. And with this vision I speak to those who think themselves my people's masters, and I speak to them in my people's name. Beware, you tyrants in Washington. Beware of the day that is coming. Beware, you sanctimonious hypocrites. Beware of the risen people. Do you think, you tyrants, that law is stronger than life? Do you think, you hypocrites, that your fascist propaganda can outweigh mankind's desire to be free?"

Looking directly into the camera now, face grown red even through her olive complexion, Juanita pronounced the future. "We will try it out with you. We will take back what you have stolen. We will be free."

CHAPTER EIGHT

From the transcript at trial: Commonwealth of Virginia v. Alvin Scheer

DIRECT EXAMINATION, CONTINUED
BY MR. STENNINGS:

Q. And what do you think it was that made your wife ill . . .

MS. CAPUTO: Objection, Your Honor.
This question calls for expert testimony—

MR. STENNINGS: Horse pucky, Your Honor. The Defendant only needs to address what he thought it was at the time and no one is a more credible witness on that than he is.

THE COURT: Overruled. But I caution you, Mr. Stennings, that your client will only be allowed to testify as to his own impressions without the Court taking any note of them as proof, one way or the other.

MR. STENNINGS: Thank you, Judge. Go on, Alvin.

A. Yes, sir. At least, I thought it was the pictures of them kids that set my wife to throwing up. Turns out, it was more than that.

Seems the doctor got it wrong. She had ... well ... I can't pronounce it. Wouldn't even try. But however you pronounce it, she had it and it was killing her.

No, no, I never blamed the doc. I mean, you should have seen him there, wall to wall screaming kids and none of their parents trying to control 'em. Hell, half of 'em were there with nothing more than runny noses but under the new system the doc had to see them, too. All of 'em, or risk losing his license, his job, maybe even going to jail. I heard a rumor once that the government, the feds I mean, was deliberately sending doctors to jail so that they could be put to treating the prisoners. A cost-saving measure, I heard it was. Might have even been true, I don't rightly know.

The wife, she went downhill fast, too. Wasn't but maybe two weeks before she was in the hospital, full time, and ... well, it was awful to see, her just wasting away right in front of me. She held my hand pretty near constantly towards the end, though she never cried. ... Well, I mean sometimes she did cry. But it was for her babies who was going to be left alone in the world.

That wasn't a problem, as it turned out. My folks took the kids in and told me not to worry about 'em.

I was right glad about that, glad and grateful.

'Cause, you see, the very afternoon of my wife's funeral I set me to thinking about what it was that killed my wife. Once I figured it out . . . well, naturally, I went and dug me up that old rifle I'd buried . . . .

MR. STENNINGS: Stop right there, Alvin.

A. No, sir. I don't care who knows. Weren't no one going to kill my woman and get away with it. . . .

Greenville, Texas

"Put your goddamned backs into it, boys. Dig and fill. Dig and fill. The general and the governor are coming and I want you all to make me *proud*."

The speaker, First Sergeant Michael S. ("Iron Mike") Pendergast, of Company A, 144th Infantry, Texas National Guard, smiled blithely to see his men redouble their efforts. Satisfied with that, Pendergast bent again over his own shovel, digging, lifting and sifting sand into bags taken from flood emergency stocks. An irregular stream of dump trucks had been delivering sand to the armory all morning. An even less steady stream had come to disgorge sandbags in their thousands. As piles of filled bags grew, more trucks—these ones army-issue five-tons—were filled to overflowing by other work parties. The men of Company A were moving small mountains of sand.

"Wish to hell we could have some civilians to help us, Top," said one of the men as sand silted around his hands and into the sandbag he held open for the First Sergeant.

The first sergeant glared. "The general said 'no,' Fontaine. So we dig alone. Leastwise, we do until the engineers get here."

"Didn't say we could do anything about it, Top. Just wishin' out loud."

"Just hold the sandbag, Fontaine."

"Yes, First Sergeant," agreed Fontaine meekly as he stretched the mouth of the sandbag in his hand to a fillable size.

From off in the distance, Pendergast heard again the rumble of heavy trucks, heavily laden. "That's my cue," he announced, sticking the shovel blade down into the sand pile. "Take a break, Fontaine."

"Yes, Top."

Buckling on his equipment, Pendergast tucked his helmet under his left arm, sauntered over toward the approaching line of engineer vehicles and waited.

He didn't have long to wait. As the first truck slowed to a halt, a rather splendid looking captain of engineers emerged.

"First Sergeant Pendergast, sir. A Company, 144th Infantry."

The engineer returned Pendergast's salute, answering, "Captain Davis, 176th Engineers. Where can I find your CO, Top?"

"Captain James is in his CP with our battalion S-3, sir. The S-3 is Captain Williams."

"Thanks, Top. My first shirt should be here in a minute or two. You can show him where and how we can help you best."

Washington, DC

Although not ostensibly designed to look down upon the United States, a spy satellite, given the right orbit, was as useful for that in the United States as for anywhere else. Or as useless, some would say. Thus, the head of the National Security Agency could pass on to the Director of Homeland Security satellite photographs and the analyses that accompanied them. Thus could the DHS bring the same to the President.

"There's no doubt, Madam President. None at all. Texas is mobilizing her own military forces. Even expanding them, it seems."

Rottemeyer looked toward McCreavy. "What does that mean to us, Caroline?"

McCreavy consulted her notes before replying. "They have one more or less old-fashioned armored division. Five tank battalions. Four infantry. Four artillery. Three Engineer. The usual support."

Rottemeyer caught on the phrase, "Old-fashioned? That's good for us isn't it?"

Shaking her head ruefully, McCreavy answered, "In this case, no, Willi, it isn't."

"I do not understand."

McCreavy sighed, then went on. "Well . . . let me put it this way. In our entire regular force here in the States, excluding the Marines, we have not a single tank. Nor do we have a single vehicle capable of taking on a tank in a heads-up fight. Not one. Those five tank battalions have more combat power than any one of our divisions. And they could chew even the Marines, who do have tanks, if not that many of them, to bits."

"What about our other states' National Guards?"

"Willi . . . do you trust them? I mean, do you really? You call up the Guard—which does have some other heavy forces—and you might find you're just reinforcing Texas."

Again McCreavy let out a deep sigh. "Willi . . . I am sorry but some of those states, especially those around Texas, *hate* you and everything you stand for. If you push, Louisiana, Oklahoma, New Mexico and Arizona . . . maybe the whole deep south and quite a bit of the Midwest might 'just say no'." Remember that red and blue map from the elections in 2000? Well, imagine the red portion in outright rebellion. It could be that bad. If you push them into it we could face a real war, and we could lose it. I can't answer for that. I won't.

"What I have done, with the Third Corps based at Fort Hood in Texas, is to put them on alert. I have also told them to prepare to withdraw, in case you agree with me that they ought to be withdrawn."

"Withdrawn? Why?"

"Willi, I have spoken with Bennigsen, the commander of Third Corps. He says the propaganda coming out of Texas' governor's office is beginning to have an effect on his entire command. He says his men are 'pissed' at what happened at the mission."

Fort Hood, Texas

Colonel (P) (for the army designated colonels who were selected to become brigadier generals as such; "P" for "promotable") Joseph E. Hanstadt took one final look at his computer monitor, sighed, punched his intercom, and called for his secretary.

"Emily, set me up an appointment with the boss for sometime today, would you?"

Without waiting for an answer, Hanstadt clicked off the intercom then turned back to his computer monitor. He stared blankly at the screen for several minutes, looking at—but no longer quite seeing—scenes of atrocity.

Forcing his eyes away, arising from his desk, Hanstadt clutched his beret in one hand. A grimace of distaste at what he called "this headgear with too many moving parts" briefly clouded his features. Walking around the oversized desk—there were a few benefits to being the Third Corps G-4, or quartermaster—Hanstadt took several steps to reach his office door.

He looked directly at his secretary, whose finger even now pressed the redial button on her own phone, and said, "Emily, if the boss will see me this afternoon that will be fine. If he needs me sooner, or will see me sooner, or you need me, I'll be at the chapel. And I'll leave my cell phone on." Again, Hanstadt grimaced with distaste, this time at the phone attached to his belt under his mottled uniform jacket. I hate those fucking things, he thought.

Hanstadt made a gimme motion at his driver, who obediently reached into his pocket and turned over the keys to the G-4 vehicle. Then, wordlessly, the colonel left the headquarters by the staff door.

The drive to the post chapel was short. Formations of troops passed here and there, marching to their duties. Preoccupied, Hanstadt barely acknowledged their presence.

At the post chapel he parked his Army issue car, a not-too-ancient GM sedan. He could have had a new one—being G-4 had other perks too—but had settled for something a bit more worn in the interests of economy. Others sometimes laughed. That was Hanstadt; skinflint cheap wherever he could save the Army and country he loved a few dollars.

There was neither priest nor minister nor rabbi nor imam at the chapel. Hanstadt entered to a lonely space packed with benches. If not so dreary—being multi-denominational—as a Catholic church might have been, neither was it so bright and airy as a typical Protestant one.

But it was multidenominational. Therefore Hanstadt found padded knee rests—just as if it were Catholic or Anglican—before the altar. He took off his "headgear with too many moving parts," walked forward, knelt before his God, cupped his hands around his face, and began to pray for guidance.

Greenville, Texas

"The guidance is that we have to do it, if it can be done at all, without hurting anybody. Not so much as a scratch."

"Shit, Jimbo," drawled Davis to James. "No way. I mean there's going to be some risk anyway." Davis shook his head repeatedly while staring at the map on the table between them.

"Then I'll have to report to higher that it can't be done. Shit. The general said this was 'important. The most critical mission of all.'" A knock came from the door frame.

"Excuse me, sirs," interjected an eavesdropping Pendergast. "But there's maybe a solution to that problem."

"Go ahead, Top."

Pendergast tucked his thumbs up under his shoulder harness, leaned over, and spit some tobacco juice into a trashcan. "Well . . . you see . . . this here company is made up of about a third cops. Third platoon is nearer to half. Now sure, those guards at the mint in Fort Worth are likely to panic if they see a couple of hundred armed men rolling up on them. If they see heavy armor they will for sure. But cops? Nice friendly cops? In patrol cars? Come to help them out of a bad situation; maybe a bomb threat or something? No way. They'll let us in right quick. And then we have them. And then we bring up the rest of the boys." Pendergast's broad, triumphant smile lit the room, igniting equal smiles in Davis, James and Williams.

Said Williams, "Did I ever mention, First Sergeant, that you have a nasty wicked mind? I admire that. For a truth I do. Why don't you send the boys to pick up their uniforms and squad cars?"

Main Chapel, Fort Hood, Texas

I have worn this uniform so long, Lord, that I do not see how I could ever fit in without it. But I have seen my country change, Lord, in ways that make me not want to wear its uniform any more. Please help me decide. Please.

Deep in prayer, Hanstadt barely startled when he felt the press of a hand on his shoulder. He recognized the press immediately. *Funny how the old bastard can still sneak up on me.*

"Hello, Bob," said Hanstadt, without arising. God outranked even a three-star.

"Emily said I might find you here, Joe."

Hanstadt shrugged. "And so you have. What can I do for you?"

"Joe, you have never been much of a churchgoer. What brings you here now?"

Hanstadt shook his head with a sigh. He had reached a decision but that decision had not come easily, or without regrets. "I'm punching out, Bob. Putting in my papers."

"Retiring? In Heaven's name, why? You have a bright future ahead of you still."

"Retiring or resigning, whatever it takes. I'd prefer to retire."

"Is it this thing that happened at the mission?"

Closing his eyes, Hanstadt rocked his head in affirmation. "It's got to stop somewhere, Bob."

It was now Bennigsen's turn to nod. "Well . . . yes . . . it has. But what can you or I do? We're just old horse soldiers. We do our jobs."

"Not with me, Bob. Never again with me. I have had it."

"But I need you, Joe. We have an order from the chief—"

"That twat!" interjected Hanstadt. "She sucked her way into three stars then ate Rottemeyer to get a fourth."

"Well . . . yes . . . that one," conceded Bennigsen.

"But my orders are to prepare to pull the Corps out of Texas. How the hell am I supposed to do that without my G-4?"

"My shop's got some good people, Bob. Most of 'em will stay."

"And what are you going to do with yourself, Joe?"

Hanstadt grinned broadly. "It does occur that General Schmidt might have a use for my . . . um . . . talents. And, who knows? Maybe someone with a foot in both camps might turn out to be useful to the country."

Western Currency Facility, Bureau of Engraving, Fort Worth, Texas

It was early day with the sun just beginning to peek over the trees in the east. A plainclothed Schmidt and a uniformed Pendergast exchanged bright smiles as a horde of workers almost flew from every entrance to the WCF.

"I knew it would work, sir. One little bomb threat and they are scurrying, guards and all."

"Top, you told them it was an anthrax bomb. That's not little."

The first sergeant shrugged. "So I lied? Fuck 'em . . . sir."

Schmidt said nothing further as he strained his ears for the expected sound. Soon enough—mere minutes, actually—it came; a horde of sirens from every direction. Almost instantly the area around the WCF seemed filled with police cars, forcing their way slowly through the mass of displaced workers.

There were Fort Worth Police; Dallas, too. Along came county sheriffs, a bomb squad, and even a few EMS ambulances. Every vehicle carried members of Company A, 144th Infantry.

Down on the street by the main entrance Captain James—in a borrowed Fort Worth Police uniform— spoke into a microphone in "his" squad car. "Attention. Attention. This is a police emergency. Clear away from the building. Clear away from the building. Uniformed officers will assist you. Report to the nearest uniformed officer. Clear away from the building."

He took a deep breath, a nervous breath—truth be told, and continued. "All Bureau of Engraving security personnel come to this location. We will need you to help control the workers. I repeat, WCF guards report to this location."

While James was speaking two more police cars, one from Dallas and another bearing markings of the sheriff's department for the county, pulled up behind him. Four uniformed officers emerged from each.

Even as the police vehicles rolled to a stop uniformed and a few plainclothed guards from the Mint began gravitating toward James' car. Climbing to the roof, he spoke to them calmly, much more calmly than he felt, while waiting for the rest to arrive.

From over the police radio came the code word "Avalanche," repeated several times: the guards to the side with the rounded extension were under control. James nodded with satisfaction.

"Was anyone left behind in the building?" James asked.

"No, sir," said an elderly, potbellied guard, looking up. "We have procedures for this." The guard looked around, counting heads. "Everyone's here, sir."

James heard the police radio sound, in turn, "Typhoon" and "Hurricane." The guards to the other sides were secured.

"Very good," said James, mostly to himself. His head gave a slight nod in the direction of the eleven "policemen" around him. Instantly eleven guns were drawn from eleven holsters.

"Gentlemen," said James to the assembled guards, "I invite and require you to surrender in the name of liberty, Texas, and—God bless her!—Governor Juanita Seguin."

Three or four guards looked as if they might resist, glaring up at James. Yet, in the main, most of them were as annoyed with Washington as anyone in the state, or perhaps even more so. Glancing around at their fellows who were obviously pleased, those guards who might have resisted decided that discretion was, after all, the better part of valor.

As the guards dropped their pistols, the Fort Worth Bomb Squad, also known as Second Squad, Third Platoon, A Company, entered the building.

Washington, DC

"That bitch has done *what*?"

Vega was as furious as her President. Her rage punctuated every syllable she spoke. "She did it, Willi. Her bastards took over the Western Currency Facility in Fort Worth. And they did it without a shot being fired. Reports are still ... umm ... fragmentary. But there's no doubt they've taken over the building."

McCreavy burst into the Oval Office. "Willi, we have a situation here. Fort Hood, Fort Bliss and even Fort Sam Houston, in San Antonio, are being surrounded by fully armed units of the Texas National Guard. They moved soldiers up in private vehicles while half our troops were leaving for home after their morning physical training. Then they came out, arrested the MPs at the gates and declared the posts closed. Heavy forces are moving up to reinforce the ones who came first."

Vega's cell phone began to ring. She answered it, flashing Rottemeyer a semi-apologetic look. As she listened her face visibly whitened. "My God," was all she could manage to say in return.

As Vega disconnected her phone, she turned uncomprehending eyes at Rottemeyer. "I don't understand, Willi. It isn't supposed to be like this."

"For God's sake *what* has happened, Jesse?"

"They're arresting all of our people down there. Everyone. EPA. Surgeon General's Office. IRS. FBI. U.S. Attorneys. Everyone."

Again Vega's cellphone buzzed. Her face grew yet more ashen. "Willi ... the two senators from Texas ... and they apparently have some support from elsewhere ... have introduced a motion in the Senate to ask the House of Representatives to impeach you."

Austin, Texas

Sweating despite the season, a remarkably animated and excited Nagy spoke into a telephone in the governor's office. "That's right, Captain. I want every federal agent in the state under arrest before tomorrow morning. Every single one of them. No, I don't care about charging them, not yet. Just get them behind some wire. What if some escape? Right . . . good question. Let me think . . . ummm . . . okay, just let them go. The important thing is to restrict their freedom here. If they are in Oklahoma, there's not much they can do in Texas."

All around the office couriers walked briskly to and fro, bringing news of accomplishments, and occasional setbacks. One such placed a file folder in front of the governor. Busy preparing to address the state legislature, the governor simply shrugged and said, "Later."

Outside of the governor's office, the air at the capitol building was tense beyond anything known in the history of Texas since they had fought for independence from Mexico in the 1830s. Even secession in 1861 had not brought with it the sense of sheer imminence that the Seguin government's moves had. Then, like many in the seceding Southlands, Texans had thought their successful secession a "sure thing," an accomplished fact. That illusion had been blasted in the American Civil War. Now, however, few maintained any illusions that reasserting a measure of state sovereignty was more than a forlorn hope. Yet, each man and woman asked themselves, "What else can we do but try?"

Still preparing her speech, the governor continued

to pay little notice to the comings and goings of those around her. An occasional voice called out the name of an arrestee, which name the governor subconsciously filed away.

One name, however, did get her attention. Juanita heard, "San Antonio City Police caught Harold Forsythe trying to get a flight out of the state in company with his 'legal advisor.' Our erstwhile 'Commissioner for the State of Texas' was dressed in drag. 'Kind of tastefully,'" said the arresting officer. At the name, Forsythe, Juanita immediately took notice.

Even as Nagy said, "Put the shark and the Kommissar on the flight," Juanita countermanded, *"That* one, Forsythe, I want brought to me. Before we let him go I want to give him a message."

At that moment Schmidt, returned from Fort Worth by helicopter, burst in. "We've got it, Juani, we've got it."

The room erupted in cheers.

"We took it intact, too. Everything we need for months of operation: presses, paper, ink; the *works*! A bunch of the folks that work there—most of them, in fact—agreed to stay on provided we paid them their regular wage."

Ralph Minden spoke up, "That's a weapon in our hands, Governor. Whatever Washington decides to do, they'll do it with the specters of runaway inflation or economic stagnation looking over their shoulders."

Schmidt added, "It'll pay for a better defense, too, Juani, if and when we actually have to fight."

Juanita shrugged. "We agreed, Jack, that if we fight, we lose. Leaving aside the economic consequences, if Rottemeyer wins, a President who fought and won on her own authority, this country will be in a lockdown like we have never even had nightmares about."

"Sure Juani, we agreed. Even I agree. But if nothing else we have planned works, we'll end up fighting anyway. I'd rather do it better armed than worse."

Juanita didn't answer. She had every intention of ordering her own forces to lay down their arms before it came to fighting if that was the only way to end things short of bloodshed. Of course, she didn't intend to tell anyone that.

"Fine, then," she told Schmidt. "What do you need? Where do you think you can get it? What will it cost? And how will we pay?"

Schmidt, scratching beside his nose, answered, "Well . . . with a federal mint to do our purchasing, I don't see a problem with paying," He grinned. A mint couldn't *counterfeit* the money it printed as a matter of course. "Cost? Hell, we're just starting to figure that out. We've got a fair number of people, tens of thousands really, flocking to join us. A lot of them have guns they buried when Washington started taxing them so heavily. But even there, a lot of them, most really, are non-standard. So I would want at least compatible small arms. I imagine we could buy those almost anywhere and ship them through Mexico."

"All right. When you know what you need, bring it to me and we'll see. And now, if you will forgive me, I have a speech to prepare."

CHAPTER NINE

From the transcript at trial: Commonwealth of Virginia v. Alvin Scheer

DIRECT EXAMINATION, CONTINUED
BY MR. STENNINGS:

Q. Alvin, what did you think about the things Texas started doing after the massacre...

MS. CAPUTO: Objection, Your Honor. That kind of inflammatory language—

MR. STENNINGS: Withdrawn, Judge.

Q. After the mission, Alvin. What did you think about what Texas did after the mission was destroyed?

A. I've got to confess, I was so sheerly tickled when the governor went to the legislature and asked for a law declaring income tax withholding for the feds illegal in the state. Didn't change the withholding, mind you, just sent it straight to the state.

Now, I didn't see the TV when the governor spoke. I was a little busy fixing up my truck, packin' a few things, figurin' out the map and all. Well, I never was too good with a map. So I missed the governor when she came on TV.

But my friends who saw it told me about it. Said the governor used some mighty strong words speakin' to the legislature about federal income tax. "No matter what the Supreme Court may have said, tyranny long endured does not equal law . . . 'Disobedience to tyranny is obedience to God.'" They told me she said that the income tax was illegal from the beginning, never properly made part of the Constitution. Never . . . ratified? Is that the word, Mr. Stennings? Well, if that really was true, I guess that means they were pickin' my pocket every two weeks for most of my life.

The other thing was, she and the legislature said no Texas corporation could pay corporate income tax either. That didn't sit too well with me, the fat cats getting over and all. But my friends said that when the governor explained it, it made sense. See, the corporations never did pay any tax. It was all smoke and mirrors, a sales tax—we were used to that in Texas, of course—pretending to be an income tax. The big corporations? They just raised their prices to cover the tax they paid, plus a little more profit for themselves. So it was just me and folks like me that were payin' the big corporations' income tax. "Obtaining money under false pretenses," the governor said it was. That, and "We aren't going to roll for their scam, anymore, either."

Anyway, the governor's bill passed by a pretty good margin.

Washington, DC

The President's office was bright with the sun, but dark with anger and—more than a little—with despair, frustration and sheer worry. Things were simply not supposed to happen like this; not to her, certainly. Rottemeyer had never in her worst nightmares envisioned the kind of resistance she had generated in Texas, the kind of hatred. She thrived on being loved and worshipped. Indeed, every step of her life had been devoted to purchasing love and worship; albeit generally with other people's money. This change in her fortunes was both unexpected and deeply demoralizing; not least demoralizing to the Cabinet that had had such faith in her.

Privately, Rottemeyer thought of her Cabinet as the "Four F's": "flunkies, flics, flacs and fairies." The first three described, respectively, those who did her job for her, those who arrested those who made her job more difficult, and those who dealt with the press. The last, the "fairies," were scattered about the first three groups, each "fairy" representing cash payment for the unquestioning support given Rottemeyer by much of the extremely influential gay community.

As the herd of "Four F's" droned on, Rottemeyer had rotated her chair around, in seeming contempt for her Cabinet. Still, eyes fixed elsewhere, her ears listened intently to what was being said . . . listened, and didn't like what they heard.

Treasury spoke last and to the President's back. "To my mind, Madam President, the most dangerous things the Texans have done are fiscal. General McCreavy can worry about their having increased their defense forces. I am not worried about that. Ultimately, even she agrees we could handle that problem, if not easily.

"The attorney general fears a breakdown of law and order across the country. That's specious nonsense; sorry. The Texans appear to be doing a fine job of controlling crime within their borders without any federal help. Though, with recent round-ups there, I concede that some Texan criminals are fleeing that state for the other forty-nine.

"The surgeon general's office worries about abortion rights. I think we can safely say that any Texan woman who wants an abortion can easily go to Oklahoma or Louisiana to get one. Women in New York, contrarily, seem safe from being forced to go to Texas to prevent them from having one. They can already not have one, even in New York, if they wish.

"The secretary of state worries about our influence in the world waning when we cannot exercise full power here at home. I submit to you, Madame President, that if we fail to exercise full power at home then to hell with our influence in the world.

"But this nullification of the income tax and other taxes? The grabbing of the Western Currency Facility? These are potentially disastrous."

Rottemeyer swung her chair around. "Explain," she demanded.

Treasury sighed. He knew the President was fully aware of what he was about to say. Yet, still, it had to be stated, and clearly.

"Texas provides something like seven point six percent of federal revenues. A good portion of that goes back to the state, of course, in the form of federal aid. Yet, overall, taxation of Texas and Texans is a profit-making endeavor for the federal government. About a six-cent profit on the dollar. Money from there, other less populated and more conservative states too, goes to paying for social programs all over the rest of the country. Madam President, your continued popularity with the voters depends on those programs."

Around the table heads nodded soberly. Few in Willi's Cabinet had any real illusions that her popularity and power—their own power as well—was, except for a small hard core, anything but bought and paid for through federal largesse. Certainly they had no doubt that it would not survive a significant decrease in federal payouts.

Treasury looked from face to face. Yes, he saw. He had the Cabinet's agreement, by and large. Even the attorney and surgeon generals, State and Interior, agreed.

"We can continue to print money, of course, and write checks that have no tax money to back them. That doesn't matter, per se. Yet the effect of doing so will be increased inflation, indirect taxation if you will. And *that* will also cost influence with the voters."

Rottemeyer scowled, "Can it, Seymour. In about five years. But these are all *leisurely* emergencies. Their consequences can't possibly be felt till this issue is resolved. Plenty of time to head off that problem. Next?"

Treasury tried to go on in that vein. "But Madame President, my predictions—"

"Doesn't matter much what they predict, Willi,"

drawled Carroll. "I can tell you what our time limit is just like that," he said, snapping fingers. "We have until the next congressional elections to settle this problem. Not one day longer."

With this logic Rottemeyer agreed. They had until the next election.

Turning to Carroll, she asked, "Suppose everything Treasury says is true. The increased taxation, the inflation, the shortened revenues; *why* wouldn't the states around Texas side with us to bring that state back into the fold and reduce their own burdens?"

"'Cause they hate our guts, Willi. Simple as that. Did you know that Louisiana, Oklahoma, New Mexico, Alabama and Mississippi have put guards around the houses of the state commissioners you appointed over them? 'To secure their persons,' that's pretty much what those states say. Horseshit! They're under house arrest plain and simple. Arizona's and New Mexico's legislatures went into special session last night to debate nullifying the income tax in those states. I don't think those measures will pass, not yet. But, Willi, they hate us. And if we don't control this thing we're all going to end up with ropes around our necks." Carroll laughed aloud to see three cabinet members unconsciously reach fingers up to massage necks still unstretched.

State consciously removed his fingers from his neck in embarrassment. "There's one way to bring them around, Madam President; a foreign war or crises. That would not only justify any measures we care to take, but would also justify . . . excuse anyway . . . any new taxes or inflation. Moreover, Texas is full of patriotic types, whatever their objections to our philosophy of government. If this crisis were to turn into a disaster . . ."

McCreavy's face grew instantly red and hot. "Are you suggesting we ought to send American troops somewhere to get killed just to turn the Texans' anger away from the President and toward some foreign group?" she asked, furiously.

Rottemeyer made her familiar pat-pat pacifying motion with her hand. "Calm down, Caroline. He's merely pointing out an option."

To State, Rottemeyer said, "Look at the options. See if there is, in fact, some place in the world we need to become engaged in anyway. Look for a place where there is likely to be resistance."

Appalled by the thought of a foreign war, Treasury spoke up again, carefully clipped words still coming out with hesitation. "Madam President"—oh, what the hell, they were old friends—"Willi . . . I know the whole idea is . . . oh . . . say . . . a little 'distasteful' to you. To any of us here, really. But there is something to be said for just letting Texas go. If they'll actually go."

Carroll, whose ancestors had once been forced— most unwillingly—back into the Union, made a spitting sound. "That's the most asinine thing I've ever heard . . . no offense."

"None taken," answered Treasury in a tone that clearly conveyed the message "*asshole.*" "But, again, consider the benefits. Right now we might not survive the next election *with* Texas. But without? Without all those Democrat votes in the House and Senate that may as well be Republican? Without all those individual 'Democrats' voting for a Republican President.

Madame President . . . Willi . . . at least consider letting them go; kicking them out of the Union if they won't toe the line. It would shift the balance of power so far towards our way of thinking that the conservatives would never, never return."

Carroll's voice, in imitation of Treasury's "asshole" tone, countered, "Did you even take history in high school? It is *precisely* because of what it would do to the balance of power in the country that we can't, *can't*, CAN'T let Texas go."

Clasping hands together and rubbing palms, he turned his gaze back to Rottemeyer. "Willi, you don't want to hear this anymore than I want to say it. But the only thing keeping thirty-six other states in the Union is the mere chance that, come next election, they can get rid of us. If Texas goes out, there will go their last chance of getting us out. And so they will leave too. And it won't be like the last time."

Of McCreavy he asked, uncharacteristically using her rank, "General, is there a chance in hell that you can force thirty-six states in the lower forty-eight back into the union with the remaining twelve? Didn't think so. Is there a chance you could keep them from overrunning us?"

McCreavy sighed. She seemed to be doing that a lot lately. "I could defend Hawaii . . . provided we were willing to become part of the Empire of Japan. But you exaggerate the dangers. Surely not more than thirty states would actually join Texas," she added, somewhat sarcastically.

"Okay, thirty," Carroll conceded. "Does that change anything?"

"No."

"Jesus, why did this have to happen to me?" asked Rottemeyer of the room.

The question was rhetorical. Nonetheless, Carroll answered. "Because we moved too fast, Willi."

"Maybe . . . just maybe. But you've already said we have to move fast now . . . and that we don't have any choice about Texas. So we're going to bring it back under control. On my command. Soon.

"In the interim," Rottemeyer continued, "here's what we're going to do. General McCreavy, I want you to pull . . . what was that group? Third Corps?" Seeing McCreavy's nod, she went on, "Pull Third Corps out of Texas and into the surrounding states. Reinforce them with everything we have. You can pull one division out of Germany and any troops we have here in the States. They are to prepare for an invasion . . . no, call it the 'liberation' of Texas. They are not to commence hostilities without my say so. I also am going to at least prepare to take State's advice. I want you to prepare a contingency force for some contingency overseas. Don't argue with me about that, Caroline."

Rottemeyer noted with satisfaction that McCreavy jotted every word down into her notebook and did not argue the point.

Jesse Vega looked up expectantly as Rottemeyer turned her attention towards her. "Yes, Willi?"

"Jesse, I want you to take control of and assemble *all* federal law enforcement personnel and assets in the states around Texas and any that escaped from Texas before they began rounding up our people. I mean *all* of them: BATF, FBI, EPA and the Presidential Guard, Secret Service." Rottemeyer did not much care for using her Guard's common name, PGSS.

"How long will that take?"

McCreavy thought furiously. *In theory we could move fifteen or twenty thousand troops in three days. Theory's shit. In practice double that? Nah, never happen. Double it again and round up to an even two weeks. Then . . . maybe.*

Vega, likewise, contemplated the difficulty of overcoming sheer bureaucratic inertia, cope with interagency rivalry and jealousy, and came up, similarly, with about two weeks . . . maybe.

Exchanging glances, McCreavy and Vega seemed to come to an agreement. They said, almost simultaneously, "About two weeks."

McCreavy then added, "That's just to get the troops—and I mean just the troops and their individual arms—*somewhere* useful. Getting their heavy equipment out of war stocks, bringing it up to speed, issuing it? Madame President, that's going to be another thirty days. Minimum."

Rottemeyer seemed to ignore her. "Can you drum up a propaganda campaign in two weeks? A good one?" she asked Carroll.

"Child's play, Willi." He snorted, disdaining the very notion that *he* might have trouble with something so simple as twisting and distorting the truth.

"Good. Make it child's play. Make it suitable for the 'children' who make up the bulk of our support. I want them clamoring for me to 'do something' . . . to 'save the children.'" The sheer innocence and naivete of many of her supporters brought a smile to her face.

"Now at the end of those two weeks I am going to order you," she said to Vega, "to round up 'dissident, criminal elements' in Arizona, New Mexico, Oklahoma, Kansas, Louisiana, Mississippi, and—especially—Arkansas. I will not be averse if you grab my ex-husband if he happens to be in Arkansas with one of his bimbos. Most particularly do I want you to shut down the irresponsible press that might be against us in those areas. Toss them into prison with the general population. We'll see how they like being made non-anal-retentive.

"At the same time as we begin the round-up, I want the borders with Texas shut down. I mean shut! No food in or out. No manufactured goods, in or out. No telephone service; no mail service. I want that border locked tighter than a drum. If there's a way to stop water from flowing, do that too.

"We'll give them maybe three or four weeks of that, then we'll invade. I don't care how you do it, but be ready by then," she said, with determination, to McCreavy.

After the meeting, McCreavy called aside Treasury to ask what it was he had been trying to make the President see.

The secretary shrugged helplessly. "Oh just this, General. With Texas in control of the Western Currency Facility at Fort Worth, they are able and likely to exacerbate the inflation problem without any help from us. I really do not see where they even have a choice. We can expect them to float their quasi-rebellion on a sea of paper . . . the value of which—until we can change the money format . . . and this will take quite some time—will be subtracted from us."

"Yes, so?" she asked. Economics was never her forte.

"Well between increased taxation and indirect taxation through inflation, we stand a very real chance at some point in time of other states following Texas' lead. And that nobody can really predict. It's almost outside the realm of economics. But you can imagine the spiral that it could cause in the areas least loyal to the President." Treasury meant, of course, "most disloyal." But why add to the tension, after all?

"At some point in time, if this spreads, we will no longer be able, fiscally able, to function as a nation. Certainly not as the kind of nation we in that room envision us as being.

"In particular, the one tax nearly everyone pays is the Social Security tax . . . that and Medicare. Already, we are diverting general revenues to support the Social Security system. Every worker who drops out from paying SSI and Medicare tax makes this burden more insupportable. No, we are not going to have to close down the system. But some economies may have to be introduced. For example we might need an emergency pro tem price freeze on all medical commodities. Nothing bad would happen for a year or two. For that matter we could draft doctors by the battalion and pay them army wages."

McCreavy's face took on a scowl. She knew Willi and her party were not in the business, had never been in the business, of economizing when it cost political power to do so. *Dangerous, dangerous*, whispered a voice in the back of her mind.

"There is some good news," continued Treasury. "It isn't all bad. Take the corporate income tax. Of course anyone in the know has long since realized it's a sales tax on consumers. Many corporations even make a small premium on collecting it, much as they do state sales taxes, although unlike state sales tax this premium is not sanctioned by statute. So the larger corporations are unlikely to relocate to Texas to escape it. But some that are already in Texas will no longer be paying. That's going to hurt too. We'll have to raise the rate on the others a bit . . . meaning more inflation as that higher rate gets passed on. For some marginal industries, though, it just acts like another damned cost. Publishers? The rest of the entertainment industry and all of the support they give our cause? If people are strapped and stop buying their product, the party loses.

"One other troubling thing. The gift and estate tax never brought in more than perhaps two percent of federal revenues directly. Much of that went to collecting the tax itself. Still, much of what the estate tax did not take, it did not take due to clever but expensive lawyering. Thus we managed to obtain quite a lot through income taxation on legal fees. Since Texas has also nullified the gift and estate tax, we expect to see money flowing into Texas to preserve it from estate taxation. This brings it out of our hands and hurts estate planning lawyers who are among the party's biggest supporters and defenders . . . to say nothing of contributors. Lastly, that money could and probably will serve as loans to help keep Texas solvent."

"How long before we begin to feel the effects?" asked McCreavy.

"My people are working on that very question now, General. The problem, again, is that it is not entirely an economic or fiscal issue. Much will depend on people's perceptions. And those my department can neither predict, nor much affect."

Treasury's face took on a somber mien. "Still, I can't help but note that the Great Depression took a matter of days to wreck the economy. This might, or—admittedly—might not, be as bad as that. It's fair to say though, General, that when you invade you had better win quickly."

CHAPTER TEN

From the transcript at trial: Commonwealth of Virginia v. Alvin Scheer

DIRECT EXAMINATION, CONTINUED
BY MR. STENNINGS:

Q. What happened then, Alvin?

A. Well, I left to go east. Good thing I left when I did, too, because they closed the state border down right afterwards.

   I sort of joined up with the big convoy leaving Fort Hood for Oklahoma. There must have been forty or fifty thousand vehicles, all told, what with the Army and all the civilians who decided to get out of the state while they still could. Some of 'em was plainly on the side of the federal government. They were pretty easy to spot: big BMWs and Mercedes cars with bumper stickers saying things like "President Rottemeyer" and such. I think a lot of others just wanted to avoid getting caught up in any fighting. Some looked like they just needed to keep sucking at the Federal tit to survive. They were mostly driving beat up old jalopies.

Couldn't say I really blamed any of 'em very much. Can't say, neither, that I thought much about it one way or the other. Like I told you right off, I got room in me to blame only one person for all the troubles, mine and everyone else's.

Anyway, it took a while to get past the border. Took longer still to fill my gas tank what with all the cars and trucks needing gas, and the Army taking over gas stations. It was nearly three days before I managed to get across Oklahoma and into Kansas.

It was around Oklahoma City that I saw the first riot. Seems some of the locals gathered and went after some of the folks runnin' away from Texas. Next thing I knew, there were people runnin' and screamin'; even some shots bein' fired.

No, I never did know who was shooting. The feds said the local folks. The locals blamed the refugees. The refugees blamed the local police. The local police said it was the feds what done it. And why would local cops lie?

Anyway, I got out of the area in a hurry, I can tell you. I didn't need the police looking too carefully at my truck. Fortunately, with all the diesel fumes from the Army as it passed by, they were mostly occupied trying to keep from chokin' while puttin' down the riot.

Fort Hood, Texas

Amidst clouds of lung-wracking diesel fumes, just as its nose was edging into Oklahoma, the tail end of Third Corps left Fort Hood. The Corps now stood at less than full strength, much less. In a way, Hanstadt was saddened to see how many had taken a variant of the choice he had.

In another way, of course, he was pleased. *Kind of heartwarming to see so many troops who won't fight for that murdering cunt in DC.*

Despite this, Hanstadt waved goodbye—fondly—to those who had decided to stay with the Army. He couldn't blame them, really; couldn't put on any airs of moral superiority. How it might have gone had his retirement not been fairly secure he could not say. Certainly it would have made the decision to throw in his lot with Texas somewhat harder.

Though Washington had never announced the move of the Corps in advance, it was anticipated in all corners. Even now, Hanstadt expected a Texan detachment to show up momentarily to take charge of the post. Most particularly, did he expect the Texans to want the contents of the Ammunition Supply Point, the ASP. There had not been enough trucks, enough willing manpower, or enough time to do more than empty a fraction of the munitions to be found there. Still, he had done what he could to help the Corps commander take whatever could be taken.

That was one way to make sure that none of the rest was destroyed, he thought, not without some degree of mirth.

Hanstadt paused in his reveries at the sound of footsteps padding softly up behind him. He turned to see his driver, Chris Perez, a young man from Long Island, New York who had—somewhat unexpectedly—elected to stay with his old boss.

"Yes, son?"

"Sir, we got a radio call from the MPs who stayed behind and are manning the front gate. There's a Texas National Guard two-star and he wants onto the post."

"Ah. That would be General Schmidt. My compliments to him through the MPs and have them ask him if he would be good enough to join me in the Corps conference room."

"I'll join you in a minute, Chris," Hanstadt said to the driver. "Then you can take me to Headquarters. I need to change, after all."

As he said so, Hanstadt looked around him. Fort Hood seemed so different, now, with the departure of Third Corps. Not merely empty of manpower, it seemed to have been emptied of a certain spirit, in part a fraternal one, as well.

Rio Brazos, Waco, Texas

Shadowing Third Corps north on its way from Fort Hood, through Waco, through Fort Worth, Denton and Gainesville to Oklahoma, followed a platoon of Combat Engineers of the 176th Engineer Battalion under the leadership of their diminutive platoon leader, Jose G. Bernoulli.

Some said "diminutive." To most of his platoon he was "Little Joe." They meant it with affection and respect.

Lieutenant Bernoulli, despite his Italian forebears and the name he bore, considered himself Texan, first and foremost, American—a close second, and Mexican last of all. He never considered himself Italian. So far as he was aware that was just a name that came over with some Neapolitan sutler to a company of Spanish conquistadors.

Bernoulli, a graduate in engineering from Texas A&M, looked over the bridge complex spanning the Brazos and added a few details and an explanatory note or ten to the drawing on the pad of paper before him. Then he tore off the sheet and handed it to one of his squad leaders with the words, "The rest of the platoon and I are heading east to the Trinity River. When you're done prepping these for dropping wait until the demo guard"—the combat unit detailed to secure a facility, usually a bridge, that has been prepared for demolition to prevent an enemy from interfering with that demolition—"shows up and brief the platoon leader or company commander. Leave two men—two *good* men—with them and join us. You'll find us somewhere along the river between"—Bernoulli consulted his map—" . . . hmm . . . Oakwood and Riverside. Questions?"

"Couple, sir," answered the Sergeant.

"Go ahead," said Bernoulli, his face showing—and restraining—a considerable degree of impatience.

"One; do you think it's really going to come to that?"

"Yes," Bernoulli answered, simply.

"Okay . . . then where the hell is *all* the demo we're going to need going to come from?"

"That, Sergeant, I do not know. Maybe General Schmidt has an answer. I, for one, do not."

"Right. All right then, what if I can't find you?"

"Good point, Sergeant. If I haven't seen you by this time tomorrow I'll send someone to the middle of Oakwood to lead you to us. Fair enough?"

"Yes, sir. I'll get on with the job then, sir."

Bernoulli thought briefly and reconsidered. "Hmm. Let me see that sketch."

When the sergeant had returned it, Bernoulli looked it over again, thought a bit more and scratched out one section of the drawing. "Don't prep this section, Sergeant, unless and until I give you the word. We'll try to stretch out what demolitions we have because if the general can't come up with more, a lot more, we just won't have enough."

Fort Hood, Texas

He restrained himself from an impulse to salute that, after decades of habit, had become nearly as ingrained as breathing. "I'm Colonel—retired—Hanstadt, sir," said the now civilian clad man to Schmidt, rather unnecessarily as Schmidt knew Hanstadt from various Corps meetings he had attended over the years.

"Retired?" questioned Schmidt. "Why?"

"Well . . . if I hadn't retired then I could hardly volunteer to become your new G-4, could I, sir?"

Schmidt raised an eyebrow and looked without focusing at some of the decorations on the wall behind Hanstadt. *Be still, my heart. God, could I use a competent G-4.*

"Your forces are slowly, well . . . not so slowly as all that, going up to corps sized. Maybe more . . . no, almost certainly more." Hanstadt added, again quite unnecessarily, "You will need someone a little more experienced than what you have."

God, could I use a competent G-4, thought Schmidt, again, unnecessarily. *And I seem to recall this Hanstadt being very competent indeed.*

"The job is yours. You planned this though, didn't you? What else have you planned?"

Hanstadt didn't answer directly. "Chris, bring the car around. We'll show our new boss what we have planned."

The first place they visited was the main maintenance facility. There Hanstadt was able to show Schmidt not merely machinery, tools and parts, but a large and expert civilian workforce that had not, naturally—being local, accompanied the Corps on its departure.

From the maintenance facility they had driven to some few yards loaded with heavy equipment, row upon orderly row of tanks, other armored vehicles, trucks, construction equipment.

"Somehow, I think the Corps commander, General Bennigsen, wanted you to have these. Certainly he never said a word about either destroying them or taking them with him."

"Why would he do that; want that?"

"A theory? He hopes he doesn't have to fight you and, the more prepared you seem the less likely it is that he will."

"Maybe," said Schmidt, noncommittally.

"Well . . . come to the ASP, sir, and I'll show you why I think so."

That proved a short drive. Once there, Hanstadt led the way into the main office. There, on the wall, was a breakdown, by bunker, by type, by category—training or war reserve stocks—of all the ammunition held there.

It took no special training for Schmidt to grasp all that the wall charts implied. "He left the demo, the mines and the small arms. He took most—not all, but most—of the tank, artillery, and antitank ammunition. I think, maybe you're right. Bennigsen left us what we needed to put on a good show. Funny. Hmm. I wonder if . . ."

The new G-4 answered Schmidt's unasked question. "Yes, sir, Bennigsen took the nukes with him."

Schmidt thought about that, then sighed, "Oh, well. Maybe that's just as well."

"All right, then, Hanstadt; you're the new G-4 and you have your work cut out for you. However, as your first official duty I would like your driver to take me to Post Clothing Sales assuming it's still open."

That too, proved a short ride. And the store was, indeed, open. At clothing sales, Schmidt left Hanstadt and the driver in the car. On his way in he paused briefly to make a telephone call on his cell phone. Though neither of the others knew it, he was calling the governor with a request. When he returned, he opened a small plastic bag and took an even smaller item out of it.

"Here," he said, passing the stars of a brigadier general over to Hanstadt. "You'll need these to deal with my current quartermaster who is something of an arrogant ass, truth to tell."

Speechless, Hanstadt looked at the stars with wonder. "I didn't retire and join you for this."

Schmidt smiled broadly. "If I thought you had, you wouldn't have them."

"I was already on the list for promotion to brigadier general, General," sighed Hanstadt. "I gave that up to join you."

Schmidt was surprised, slightly. He had not known. He said as much.

"No matter," said Hanstadt. "Even if I didn't think you were right, I'd still rather be a BG in the small army of Texas where it means something, at least for a little while, than a two star in the large United States Army . . . where it means less each day."

Again, Schmidt reached into the bag and pulled out a notebook and a pen. These, too, he handed over to Hanstadt. "And now, Brigadier General Hanstadt, let me explain the depths of our problems . . . and of what we have started to do to fix them."

Camp Bullis, Texas

Texas, as did about forty other states, maintained a state owned "defense force." This was purely voluntary; unpaid except when it might be called to state service, scantily equipped and scantily trained. It was the one force available to the governors of those states which had them that the federal government could not legally take control of.

In the case of Texas, now, the seven notional—and, frankly, nominal—brigades of its state defense force had been mobilized and were in the process of expanding at various army camps. One of these, an old installation north of San Antonio, was Camp Bullis.

The old camp had gone through many permutations in the near century of its existence. Established in 1917 and named for a brigadier general prominent in the Indian Wars, Bullis had seen troops off to both World Wars, Korea and Vietnam. It had also seen them return, those who had returned.

Reduced from a high point of thirty-two thousand acres in 1918, the camp now boasted no more than twelve thousand.

Twelve thousand acres, however, was clearly enough for the thousands of new recruits to the Texas Defense Force that assembled there to train under its 1st Brigade—a brigade in name only, further nicknamed the Alamo Guards, and soon to be named the 1st Texas Infantry Division. That twelve thousand acres was enough seemed especially so as these thousands of new recruits had few weapons, none of those being heavy weapons, and boasted little other equipment.

"Weapons and equipment aren't the main problem," lamented the 1st Brigade's commander, Colonel Juan Robles, to no one in particular. "The real problem is that we haven't a *clue*. We're an oversized battalion of quasi military police—old, fat, and undertrained ourselves except maybe as military police."

From a high place where the San Juan Hill scene from the film *The Rough Riders* had been shot in 1926, Robles looked down to a road where a disconsolate "company" of recruits struggled in a herd through the boot-sucking mud. Rather, it would have been boot-sucking if only they had had boots. The Nikes and

Reeboks still shodding most of the men? The mud gulped these down whole.

Robles muttered, "No order, no discipline. No weapons, no equipment, no uniforms. But, worst of all, no leadership and *no* training. We're screwed."

"It's not so bad as all that, Juan"—the State Guard was pretty informal, as Robles' operations officer demonstrated by the use of his commander's first name. "The Adjutant General has already said that he'll send one in ten officers and NCOs by grade to distribute among the State Guard folks. That'll help. And we're starting to get a trickle of volunteers from among the military retirees. Some folks from other states are coming in too. The general even says we'll have some real uniforms soon; weapons too."

Matamoros, Mexico

No uniforms were worn here, though the two Americans carried arms under their light jackets.

Hanstadt listened appreciatively as birds sang in the warm and muggy Mexican morning. Civilian clad and traveling on a civilian United States passport, he waited on the tarmac of the town's still sleepy airport. In his hand was clutched a bag containing several million dollars in new bills from the Western Currency Facility, each one good legal tender anywhere in the world, indistinguishable from other bills printed in the Washington, DC, facility, indistinguishable from bills printed earlier.

Moreover, and the Texans were quite sure Washington knew this, any attempt at undermining confidence in U.S. currency could have disastrous economic consequences as literally hundreds of billions of dollars salted away all over the world, largely by rich people who felt the need for "escape money," came pouring out of the woodwork and into other currencies. The United States had put up with nearly two decades of massive Iranian counterfeiting, and the terrorism that counterfeiting funded, to avoid just such a possibility.

Beside Hanstadt stood his newly commissioned assistant, Lieutenant Christopher Perez of the Texas Guard. In the background were two dozen Mexican workers and drivers with a dozen trucks lined up behind them for the trip to Brownsville. In the foreground, a brace of moderately ancient cargo aircraft awaited unloading. Aboard the aircraft, some hundreds of Chinese-manufactured small arms and tens of thousands of rounds of Chinese-made ammunition.

Hanstadt turned to the chief of the Mexican drivers and workers and commanded, "Unload the planes." To Chris he said, "This will be your job for the near future. Receive, account and pay for what comes here—and remember that that will start including radios, compasses, body armor . . . basically everything almost as soon as I can set up the contracts with the manufacturers and shippers. Then you'll forward it to Fort Sam Houston through Brownsville. You'll need to spot-check a bit for quality. And you had probably better hire the local Mexican Army unit for guards, especially when you have any large quantity of weapons or ammunition stockpiled here or in transit."

"How large are we talking about, sir, total?" asked Perez.

"Schmidt contracted for an even 200,000 rifles, 21,000 machine guns, 12,000 RPG-7 antiarmor weapons, and some really, really impressive amounts of ammunition. Likewise mortars and some heavier antitank systems. That's just what's coming through here. I am told there is a contract for artillery being negotiated even as we speak."

"Negotiated? Negotiated with whom, sir?"

"The Chinese," Hanstadt answered, simply. "All of this material is coming from them."

"Why should the chinks care about Texas?"

"They don't," Hanstadt admitted, "except maybe to wish we would sink into the sea. But they would much, much rather the entire United States sink into the sea . . . and perhaps they see helping Texas—for a handsome profit, mind you, to be sure—as a way to make the United States sink into the sea."

"That's going to happen, too, isn't it, sir? I mean if this thing turns into a no-shit civil war, we are finished as a country and as a power in the world."

As he had before, Hanstadt reflected that his former driver, recently jumped in rank, was by no means stupid. "Well, that's what the Chinese *hope*. But from our point of view, these arms may be the best way to *prevent* a civil war, to buy us time to find some other way."

Austin, Texas

"Nonviolent civil disobedience, Governor—NVCD for short—is the only way you have to win. It is also the only way to win while not destroying the country with a civil war." The speaker, Victor Charlesworth, was an old man now, wrinkled, beginning to stoop, slower in his speech and his movements. There had been a day, though, when he was both young, strong and more than a little handsome. Traces of those looks remained; enough to impress Juanita. When young, those looks—along with a fair talent for acting—had gotten for Charlesworth acting parts as prophets and presidents, generals and geniuses, cardinals and kings.

As a much younger man, Charlesworth had not merely acted the role of kings, he had marched with one. In Selma and Montgomery, Alabama, and in Washington, DC, he had locked arms with the Reverend Doctor Martin Luther King and marched for truth, right, freedom and justice.

He was here, now; in Texas, now; in Austin, now; and in Governor Juanita Seguin's office, now, to help do the same . . . and to teach others.

Right now, he taught the governor.

"It is going to be hard for you, Governor. Hard and dangerous. You are going to have to stand on a lot of balconies. You are going to have to go out and lead your people. You may be shot. You may be arrested. Given the nature and character of the people who are running this country right now, if you are arrested you will probably wish you *had* been shot."

"And . . ." Charlesworth hesitated, for this next advice was possibly tantamount to telling the governor to commit suicide. " . . . and . . . you will have to travel. To open yourself up to being shot. Because Texas, alone, can't win. It can't win a civil war alone, and it can't win alone through NVCD. The states around you, as a minimum, you are going to have to visit, to see, to talk at and to. Other states too, as and when you can."

"Oh, sure," retorted Juanita. "I can just see me talking to Harvard University to sell an antigovernment message. Sure."

"Why not, Governor? I have."

Corpus Christi, Texas

Over the tang of the sea wafted the unpleasant scent of oil seeping up through the ground. Some seabirds swooped down to catch the occasional fish; others dined off scraps and garbage left on the docks. Under Schmidt's feet, the wharf boards creaked and gave slightly.

Reaching a particular boat, shiny, well kept up, smelling slightly of fish sauce, he stopped. "I have to see Mister Minh," Schmidt announced to an alert-looking Vietnamese fisherman.

"Mister Minh no see anybody anymore," answered the Viet. "He too old, too tired."

"He'll see me. We are old 'friends.'"

The fisherman peered intently in Schmidt's face, noted the uniform, noted the rank on the collar, noted the other insignia. Then the fisherman added one plus one plus one and came up with 1964–1972. "I go ask," he answered at length. "You wait here."

When the fisherman returned to the deck and beckoned he said, "Mister Minh . . . ah . . . he say 'okay, come aboard.'"

Walking the plank, then descending into the ship's

bowels, Schmidt followed the fisherman to an aft cabin. They stopped briefly as the fisherman knocked lightly on the cabin door.

"Come in," said an ancient voice in slightly French-accented English.

Entering, Schmidt took in the cabin with a sweeping glance. Much to his surprise, he noticed a crucifix adorning one wall. The ancient Vietnamese man seated at the desk smiled, and explained, "I find the religion of my fathers more comforting with each passing day."

"That is a most unusual sentiment, Colonel Minh," observed Schmidt. "Most unusual for a former political officer of the Ninth Viet Cong Division," he added, somewhat wryly.

"That was long ago; a lifetime of mistakes ago. Why, you were only a lieutenant then . . . and look at you now."

Schmidt nodded. "A lifetime, yes. Long ago, yes. I suppose that's why I never reported your background to the authorities, Colonel, even though I knew you were here. I thought you had paid enough; your revolution betrayed, most of your family killed, yourself forced to flee your own country forever.

"Tell me, how does the idea of fleeing yet again appeal to you?"

"Not much," the old man admitted, his gray and balding head nodding slightly as he did so. "Is that why you have come here? To tell me to leave?"

"No," answered Schmidt. "I came for some advice and possibly a little help."

The old Vietnamese chuckled softly. "Advice? Advice is cheap. In consideration of our . . . mutual . . . yes I suppose it was 'mutual' service, I will even give it for free. Help? Well, I am an old man. I do not think I can be of much help to anyone."

Schmidt looked upward, his jaw shifting slightly to one side. "You might be surprised. But advice will do for now. Tell me, why did my side lose the war and yours win it?"

"Oh, that is easy. We won because we fought you on every possible plane, in every possible way. You lost because you could not fight us the same way. And we only had to win on one plane, in only one way, to win—eventually—on them all.

"Consider, *mon* General, just the scope of the conflict in South Vietnam. Around the peripheries, we employed troops, regulars well trained and fully equipped. You had to match those. This left irregulars more or less free to operate behind your lines, in the bowels of the areas you meant to control, in any case. And, if you had dispersed your troops to root out the irregulars? You would quickly have discovered how long one of your isolated infantry companies could live when attacked by a full Viet Cong or North Vietnamese regiment. The lesson would have been both painful and short."

Schmidt raised a characteristic eyebrow in skepticism.

Minh caught the motion. "You did try, remember? Your side tried at the Chu Phong massif in 1965. You tried at other places. Sometimes that worked reasonably well for you; as when you were able to generate massive artillery and air support for one or two ongoing battles. But multiply the number of possible targets from us from one or two to one or two hundred. Then you could not have given the kind of support on which your side relied so heavily to enough of your people engaged.

"So of course you did not do that. Your regulars and the best of South Vietnam's troops faced ours in the jungles. This led you and the South Vietnamese government to overly expand its army in order to root out the irregulars, the guerillas. But that, in turn, not only made their army diluted and weak, it robbed the south of human talent needed to run and advance their society. In fact, one aspect of this was to make their society so corrupt that decent people joined my side in hordes. And you could not do a thing about it.

"And then, of course there was the terror, especially the singling out of important people in the south to both undermine their society and government further and—and this was *most* important—to cause people to start to worry about the future; their personal future. For you see, even someone who fervently believed in the continued separate existence of the Republic of—South—Vietnam would still 'buy insurance,' would still help us on the side lest his family be targeted."

The former colonel became silent, leaving Schmidt a moment to think. *This is not exactly helpful. We will not be in the position of regulars holding down regular forces so that an insurgency can grow in security. Geometrically, our position is exactly the opposite, with us in the center and the only place for insurgency to grow being behind the wider perimeter, further away from us. Hmm. I wonder if maybe that isn't the same after all.*

"But do you know what really cost you?" asked Minh.

"What really cost you was trying to use soldiers to perform what was essentially a police function, population control. Not only were soldiers much more expensive, but they would never be able to get to know the people of the area they were trying to control. They would also never be able to conduct the kind of investigation that actually might have rooted out our infrastructure. Why, I remember reading a captured copy of your manual on counterinsurgency operations.

"Even today I still marvel that your brightest people could only find a use for police in the short-term supervision of displaced persons while more conventional military operations were going on. This blindness cost your side very badly, mon General."

Schmidt considered. Yes . . . and using the army for the same thing today, here in Texas, will work no better. But then Rottemeyer has lots of police, doesn't she?

Minh continued, "But you did say you wanted my help. Before I say 'no,' why don't you tell me what kind of help it is you need?"

"I need someone who can organize certain kinds of resistance."

"Certain kinds?" Minh raised an eyebrow. "Guerilla resistance?"

"That perhaps, too," answered Schmidt. "But what I really need is someone who can make police work behind the lines a very dangerous thing to be engaged in. I need sabotage. And I might need some terror."

"I see," answered Minh. "Let me think this over carefully."

"While you think, Colonel, think about this: you might never have won your war and lost your country without the influence and actions of Rottemeyer and people like her."

Western Currency Facility, Fort Worth, Texas

"Carefully I said, goddammit! Carefully."

"Yes, First Sergeant," answered a meek Fontaine as he adjusted his hands for a better grip on the piece of a disassembled printer he had very nearly dropped.

Half the printing equipment and supplies, more or less, was staying put in the WCF. The other half was to be forwarded to San Antonio where it could continue to fund Texas even after the federal government took back the WCF.

Everyone, not least among them the facility's defenders, suspected that was just a matter of time.

And so, between fortifying the place, the guardsmen took time out to remove as much as possible of the reason for defending it.

Pendergast shook his head disgustedly and repeated, "Be *careful* with that equipment, Fontaine. The state needs it."

"I promise, Top. I'll be more careful."

Ah well, thought the first sergeant, wandering away. *He's slow and clumsy. But the kid's heart's in the right place.*

Governor's Mansion, Austin, Texas

The governor's son, Mario, sat with his care- and work-worn father in the shade of a square gazebolike structure. Some distance away—out of earshot—walked Elpidia, alone with her thoughts, hands clasped behind her, head down with sadness, circling repeatedly a small fountain and pool.

"I think her heart's in the right place, Mario. She's not a bad girl, not deep down, just a very unfortunate one. But she comes to us with a load of baggage I doubt she will ever be rid of."

"I know, Padre. But she's just so damned beautiful. I find I can think of little else."

"That's your youth speaking, that, and your hormones."

Mario flushed. "Oh, c'mon, Dad. No. Other girls? Girls in general? Sure. Not her. Her I do not think of talking into bed."

Seeing his father's skeptical look, Mario admitted, "Oh all *right*. That, too. But not just that. I think of . . . I want . . . so much more than just that."

"Well, son, she is what we call damaged goods. Not through any fault of her own, no. But even so, the fact remains she has been damaged, and badly. I could not recommend any such girl to you."

CHAPTER ELEVEN

From the transcript at trial: Commonwealth of
Virginia v. Alvin Scheer

DIRECT EXAMINATION, CONTINUED
BY MR. STENNINGS:

Q. How did you pay for the trip, Alvin? Did you
   steal the money?

A. Why no, sir. I ain't no thief. Never have been. I
   cashed in my wife's and my life's savings for the
   trip; all $742 dollars worth. Then pawned whatever
   else I had that was worth anything. Figured that
   was enough for gas and maybe a burger from time
   to time on the way. I planned on sleepin' in my
   truck.

   Drivin' through Missouri, you could see folks
   had a lot a sympathy for what the governor was
   doin'. Except, funny thing, you couldn't have seen
   it on television.

   Nope, weren't nothin' on TV that a fair man

might have called fair. They were still hammerin'
away on that old priest that got killed. But I knew
from what I saw and was told and read before I
left that there weren't but the one survivor, that
little wetback girl. And I never saw her interviewed
for the news I was able to catch when I stopped
for gas, a meal or a beer.

So where they came up with all the stories about
what that priest supposedly done with the kids?
Well, I wonder if they didn't just make it up.

I'm pretty sure they did.

For one thing, I lived in Texas all my life. I
know what a Tex-Mex sounds like, speakin' English
or Spanish. And Puerto Ricans aren't too common
back home. So why do you suppose that of all the
people they interviewed on TV about the mission
and the priest weren't a one of 'em that had a
proper Tex-Mex accent, but a whole bunch of
'em sounded like the Puerto Ricans I'd met? In
particular, they sounded like some Puerto Ricans
I met once who came from New York.

I stopped once, in a small town in Missouri, and
I bought me two papers. One was the local town's;
the other was the *New York Times*. Funniest thing
how the local town's was full of mail from readers,
a good chunk of which was in favor of Texas and
against the feds while the *Times* was nothin' but
hate mail directed at Texas, the governor, and
anything having to do with them.

I didn't know if that was how folks up north
really felt, if it was the news making 'em feel
like that, or if they were maybe . . . pickin' and
choosin' what got into the paper. And if they

were doin' that, I wondered what else they were playin' games with.

Atlanta, Georgia

The head of Global News Network didn't normally have to force himself to think of himself as a "big man." He was not only physically large; he was rich, he was powerful, he was even rather famous around the world. He had grown used to people treating him with a certain respect and deference.

He was shocked.

Somehow, the man had come to believe that Wilhelmina Rottemeyer was a kindred soul; another person whose fondest desires were an end to want, a government that cared, a respecter of the law. And yet, when he had voiced complaints to the White House about what he saw as dangerous abridgments to the First Amendment he was met with scorn.

He was very shocked.

"So you listen here, you stupid bastard," said the unnamed man in the suit with a bulge under the left shoulder, "I don't care about your 'Freedom of the Fucking Press.' The President has said the gloves are off with dealing with assholes like you. She hasn't got time to sugarcoat this crap any more. You will broadcast what you are told to, and only what you are permitted. Is that clear enough even for a moron like you?"

Summoning his courage—the head of the network asked, "And what if I don't?"

The suit picked up the phone from the desk and dialed a number. On the other end someone answered the phone. "This is McCarthy. Put the lady of the house on the phone. She needs to have a little chat with her husband."

"What do you think you are doing? Where the hell did you get my home number?"

The suit just smiled, beneficently, and handed the phone over with the words, "Why don't you ask your pretty new wife what she thinks you should do?"

Whatever the standards of the American press as a whole, the head of Global News was no coward. For himself, he feared essentially nothing. Yet, the color drained from his face as the head of the news agency listened to his near hysterical bride describe what had transpired at their lavish home—the knock, the forcing of the door, the manhandling of her and their young son . . . the slaps . . . her split, puffy lips. When she was finished, he returned the phone to its receiver and said, ashen faced, "I'll play along. Just don't hurt my family."

The suit's smile broadened further. "Well, then, I am glad you are going to be sensible. Not everyone is being so, you know?"

Fort Dix, New Jersey

Most of the major media didn't need the lesson administered to GNN. Leftward leaning already, they were more than happy with Rottemeyer's program. There were some few, however, who did need some sterner measures.

In this former military base turned partial federal prison those who were not being "sensible" came in by twos and threes and tens and twenties. Shorn of hair, and dignity, the dissidents were quickly and efficiently processed into the general population. Fortunately, for them, this was a fairly low security prison. They were spared the very worst that the system had to offer in the way of roommates.

What they had was bad enough, even so.

There was, however, a saving grace. In order to leave, all the assembled newscasters, editors, and writers had to do was sign a paper admitting their complicity in "treasonable activities" and promising to cooperate with federal authorities in the future.

At first, none would. Some few days later, after a particularly nasty homosexual gang rape, a few would. A week later still, and with a regular session of beatings for the recalcitrant, a few more signed and were duly released. Then the heat was turned off in the prison barracks until, as it was announced, the members of the press corps in those barracks decided to cooperate with the authorities.

At that point, the authorities stopped providing physical "corrective measures." There was no need as the freezing nonpolitical prisoners warmed their limbs through strenuous exercise. After that, some of the talking heads would need extensive prosthetic dental work before they could hope to resume their old jobs.

The number of resistors shrank daily thereafter.

Washington, DC

There was a great shuffling of chairs as Rottemeyer and her Cabinet took their places for the daily crisis management conference. Of course, some aspects of the problem were no longer in crisis management mode.

"I always knew the press corps were pussies," mused a highly amused James Carroll. "No offense," he said to Rottemeyer.

"None taken. And how goes 'Project Ogilvie'?"

"Not bad. Not bad at all, really. We are filling the airways and the papers with every nasty, dirty, and underhanded thing we can think of to say about that fucking priest, his goddamned sister, and Texas in general."

"Fine, fine," commented Rottemeyer. "Be sure to pass on to your people how much I appreciate the fine job they are doing."

"I'll do that, of course. But, Willi, this is a labor of love for most of them."

McCreavy, also present, was sickened by the very idea of "Project Ogilvie." To her mind this was nothing less than the destruction of the First Amendment and the rights it guaranteed. She had given most of her life, in large part, to the defense of those rights and others. Now, she could see, all was lost.

But she had also spent too much time in uniform to argue with the boss.

"Willi, I have some bad news. We were hoping that Texas would be too poorly armed to put up much resistance when we roll."

McCreavy paused, contemplating the news she had received, news of tens, possibly hundreds, of thousands of buried rifles, now unearthed and in hostile hands. She considered news of arms shipments through Mexico. She shivered slightly from rumors among the arms dealers of the world of massive shipments of heavy, Chinese-made arms currently in transit.

She decided to speak mostly of more local and immediate matters.

"I have learned, however, that the Third Corps commander, General Bennigsen, left them a great deal of all kinds of war materiel when he and the Corps pulled out. Bennigsen has been relieved of his command and is going to be turned over to the FBI on charges of treason."

"Shit! Fuck!" fumed Rottemeyer, banging her hand against her desk. "What's that do to our plans? Damn it!"

Embarrassed, McCreavy answered, "It's going to make them a lot harder to take down. Worse, Intelligence says they are bringing in enough foreign arms to make them a very tough contender."

"How are they getting the arms, from where?"

"Some of the lighter stuff—rifles, machine guns and such—is coming over the border with Mexico. Apparently they are buying from the Chinese, paying cash to boot."

"Paying cash with money they have printed at *our* currency facility. Bastards! Where else are the weapons coming from?"

"By sea, we think. In fact, a shipment, maybe fifteen or twenty thousand tons worth, is due to go through the Panama Canal sometime next week on its way to Galveston or Corpus Christi."

"Through the Canal?" queried State. "Madam President that *could* give you the foreign crisis you wanted me to investigate creating. General McCreavy, are your forces capable of reoccupying the Panama Canal Zone to stop that shipment?"

"I think we are," answered the general. "But why reoccupy? We can simply blockade Texas' ports or Panama itself."

"But that wouldn't give us the crisis, would it?" pointed out State, reasonably.

"Willi?" pleaded McReavy. "This is simply not smart. What if the Panamanians actually *fight*?"

"Fight with *what*?" asked Carroll. "Bananas? They don't even have an army."

"They do, actually. Some anyway."

"What would it take, Caroline, for you to retake the Canal?"

"I can't say right off the top of my head, Madame President. I can say though, that whatever I use there is something that won't be available here. And why do it when we can blockade Texas' ports? Or maybe we should declare them 'closed,' which makes more sense."

"Sure, Caroline, we'll do that too," answered Rottemeyer. She considered briefly. "Ah to hell with Panama. Wouldn't be enough of a war to do us any good anyway. And with Mexico's border open, the blockade will be incomplete with or without the Canal in our hands."

"In any case, relax. We aren't going to invade another country, not just yet in any case."

Changing the subject Rottemeyer went around the table.

Of Justice she asked, "Are we ready to shut down the Texas Border, Jesse?"

"Excepting their border with Mexico, ninety to ninety-five percent," answered Vega.

"Law enforcement ready to follow the Army in?"

That this was a tougher problem, Vega was loathe to admit. "We have enough . . . initially."

That seemed close enough. Rottemeyer turned away from Vega to the secretary of the treasury. "Are we ready to retake the Western Currency Facility?" she asked of Treasury.

"The Army," a gracious head nod in McCreavy's direction, "has put the better part of a helicopter group at the disposal of the Presidential Guard. They'll go in on your say-so."

"Good. Caroline, after subtracting for what you have scattered around the world, what do you have left for reoccupation of Texas?"

McCreavy mentally pulled out the map she had studied just before coming to this meeting. From the symbols on the map, engraved on her mind, she translated, "Third Infantry Division and most of Second Marine Division are closing on Fort Polk, Louisiana. That's their interim staging area before they move to assembly areas west of Lake Charles, near the Texas border. They'll be joined at Fort Polk by the Second Armored Cavalry . . . though that's really just a big battalion. First Marine Division, minus one brigade, and the Third Armored Cavalry Regiment are assembling in the New Mexican desert west of Fort Bliss, Texas. Along the Texas-Oklahoma border is Third Corps, one armored and two mechanized infantry divisions. Tenth Mountain Division will fly down as we advance to provide backup to the law enforcement agencies. The Air Force is standing by.

"It all just awaits your command," McCreavy concluded.

Good, good; Rottemeyer *liked* it when things awaited her command.

"But there are a few problems, Madame President," continued McCreavy.

"As in?"

"As near as we can tell, Texas has wired every bridge leading into the state for demolition. And they are guarding those bridges, again 'as near as we can tell,' pretty competently. We also have reason to believe that those guards' orders are to blow the bridges at the first sign of our forces."

"So?"

McCreavy suppressed a sigh. It would not do to let presidential ignorance of the military get to her. "So it is not going to be all that quick. A modern division uses up hundreds of tons of supply a day. Those supplies have to go by road and rail, mostly. The farther away from base they get, too, the more they use. Right now, if Texas blows the bridges in, we can get about halfway into the state before we simply run out of gas and have to stop.

"Note, too, the expanded forces the Texans have built up? They are just past lunging range, digging in along a line we probably can't get to all that quickly. Though, mind you, if I didn't have to give up a helicopter group to the PGs then I might be able to grab a bridge or two intact."

"No, Caroline. Nothing is more important than taking the WCF back."

"But Madame President, the Texans will surely have moved half of the printing ability by now."

"It's the symbol of the thing, Caroline."

Carroll cleared his throat. "Speaking of symbols,

Willi, you have a spontaneous demonstration calling for forcible reimposition of law and order on Texas scheduled for about twenty minutes from now. The Marine helicopter is waiting."

Washington, DC

Nothing but the best for the White House; that was the rule. And, if one excepted certain of those elected to sit in the Oval Office, it was a rule that was well followed.

The best, in this case, was a Tandberg 7000 video conferencing system. Though normally the screen was easily split to allow up to thirty-six different participants to be seen on one screen, in this case—in this very private conversation—only two faces appeared in front of Wilhelmina Rottemeyer. And both of those were in the same room, seated side by side. One she recognized easily as the United States Ambassador to Panama—a political appointee rewarded for major campaign contributions. The other she knew from pictures as the president of that country.

"I want you to stop those guns," said Rottemeyer to the President of the Republic of Panama. This was in reference to the shipment of Chinese-built medium artillery contracted for by Schmidt due to pass through the Panama Canal within a few days. "I need not tell you, Mr. President, that the price for failure to do so will be very heavy."

The ambassador winced. Though no career diplomat,

he had still a reasonable sense of tact and deco-
rum.

The foreign president, a man of middle age, middle
paunch, middle complexion, and narrow, beady eyes
did not wince. He knew his, his government's, and
his country's position in the world, that of supplicant
to the United States. He answered. "But of course.
I did not know of it. I will give orders to stop it
immediately."

Austin, Texas

"Telephone, Governor. Someone who calls himself
'Parilla.' Never heard of him."

Juani hesitated, looking at Jack who likewise
expressed his ignorance with a shrug.

"I'll take the call."

"Governor? This is Raul Dario Parilla from Panama. Think of me as an arms dealer, of sorts. My
organization has intercepted the most curious conversation between your President and ours. How?
Oh, let's just say that your embassy here lacks
the very best in video conferencing equipment. I
would like to send something to you by courier.
The . . . umm . . . courier's name will be Patricio.
Can you arrange to pass him through your border
with Mexico?"

Another unrecognized and disembodied voice
answered, in slightly New England accented English,
"I'll be there in forty-eight hours."

Austin, Texas, The Governor's Mansion

Elpi opened the office door and announced, "There are two men here to see you, Governor. A 'Patricio' and a 'Carl.'"

The deeply tanned man with the fierce blue eyes glanced appreciatively at Elpi—a pretty girl was a pretty girl—then shook Schmidt's hand and the Governor's warmly before taking a seat with his assistant in the governor's home office. Though both the men were clad in civilian dress, it was no difficult task for Schmidt to see through that.

"You're soldiers," he announced.

"Yes," admitted the taller of the two, the one who had introduced himself to Elpi as "Patricio." "Rather, we were. Astute of you to notice. Think of us now as being no more than your friendly, neighborhood arms dealers."

"No astuteness necessary. You walk, you stand, you shake hands like soldiers. A blind man could see it. Moreover, you"—an accusatory finger pointed at Patricio—"sound like you're American . . . from the northeast, I think."

The tanned man simply shrugged. "We both are." Then he reached into a briefcase and handed over a video tape. "Watch this. Then we'll talk."

Schmidt fumbled uncertainly with the tape player in Juanita's office until she, herself, came over and fixed it. Then she and Jack watched the video conference between the two presidents in silence.

When the tape was finished, Patricio made a head gesture to his assistant who walked to the VCR and retrieved the tape.

Patricio cleared his throat. "Anyway, that's neither here nor there. I am here to tell you that your heavy weapons shipment from China is going to be stopped."

"Then we're screwed," announced Schmidt, simply.

"Not necessarily," said Patricio. He looked at his assistant, pointedly. The assistant shrugged, it's up to you, boss.

Reaching into his briefcase Patricio pulled out a thin sheaf of paper. This he handed over to his assistant with the question, "How much of this could you make up?"

The assistant flipped through pages, occasionally looking upwards to do an apparent mental inventory.

"Carl, here," explained Patricio, "is our organization . . . ummm . . . you would say 'G-4' or maybe quartermaster. Can you bring your G-4 here, general? Maybe we can help each other."

Schmidt went to the telephone to call his headquarters.

"Well," announced Carl after some reflection, "We do not have exactly the arms these people are going to be losing. But we can make up a fair amount of it. It's going to be lighter stuff, lighter and older, that we can trade you for this."

"Trade?" asked Schmidt.

"Yes," answered Patricio. "You sign over the rights to your heavy Chinese arms to us. We provide you with arms, mostly Russian and Chinese, that we currently hold. Though where you trade us a 122-millimeter gun, you are only going to get an 85-millimeter in return."

"That's piracy," insisted Schmidt.

"No," countered Patricio, "it's business."

CHAPTER TWELVE

From the transcript at trial: Commonwealth of
Virginia v. Alvin Scheer

DIRECT EXAMINATION, CONTINUED
BY MR. STENNINGS:

Q. Did anything happen between Oklahoma and
   Maryland, Alvin?

A. No, sir. Everything was real quiet . . . well, not
   counting that there were a lot of Army trucks on
   the road all headed the way I'd come from.

   It wasn't until I reached Maryland that I saw
   the first anti-Texas demonstrations. I confess, those
   really annoyed me, being Texan and all, myself.
   But I never did nothing about it.

   I decided I'd be better off heading a bit north
   and then comin' down from that direction. That, and
   keeping my mouth shut as much as possible.

   So I went to Baltimore and looked around for a
   job to keep me going for a while. Found one, too,

though I'd had better. Still, I wasn't ever afraid of work, only of not havin' any. So I put up with the stink of the grease and those nasty hamburgers while I settled in and looked around.

One thing I found out right quick: I was not getting anywhere near the White House. Nor any government building, for that matter. Never really thought to see my own country's capital locked down like they was ready for a siege. But that was the simple truth of the matter.

Not that I couldn't get into DC. I could and did. But I couldn't get anywhere with my truck, not anywhere useful. So I got used to public transportation—it really wasn't so bad except for the folks, some of 'em, that you had to ride with. And I did my looking on foot.

But where was I? Oh yeah, I remember. The anti-Texas demonstrations in Baltimore. I actually went and marched in one . . . sort of got curious, you see?

First thing struck me was that somebody in a suit and tie with one of them hand-held loudspeakers had everyone sort of lined up. At the end of the line was another one, a girl this time, passing out money and picket signs. She said, "Fifty dollars now. Another fifty at the end of the march. We'll have people watching from inside to see who puts on the most enthusiastic display. Bonuses for those that do."

The signs she was passing out? I only remember mine real well. It said, "Law and Order for Texas." I suppose I could agree with those sentiments;

though I didn't see it maybe quite the same way that woman did.

What the hell? I needed the money. Reckon those other folks in that line must have, too.

Western Currency Facility, Fort Worth, Texas

It was a tradition in Texas; that line, those voluntary steps. Ignore the tradition? Not Captain Williams; it would simply have felt wrong.

So, taking the A Company guidon—swords being in short supply these days, he used the metal ferule to draw an imaginary line across the front of the formation, beginning with the infantry company—its headquarters and three platoons standing toward the right, going across the oversized platoon of engineers, and then to the small detachment from battalion headquarters on the left.

The line he drew was essentially invisible. Only the displacement of some of the loose gravel on the parking lot marked it in scant places. Invisible . . . and yet it was clear enough, too.

"Boys," said Williams, "boys, you all have a decision to make today. The general said 'hold to the last.' But I'm not going to make anyone stay that doesn't want to. And you ought to be told, in fairness, that this place isn't all that important anymore to us; not since we shipped out about half of its printing capability.

"Before you make any hard and fast decisions, though, I want to read you something; something from our 'beloved President.' Well . . . she's behind it even if she didn't actually write it herself."

"Listen up, boys; this is from the *New York Times*: 'And as for the pitiful saboteurs and counterfeiters illegally occupying our Western Currency Facility, unless they surrender both themselves and the federal property in their hands the full rigor and justice of the law must be applied to them.'"

In the ranks, ranks themselves full of law enforcement men, one police desk sergeant turned and snorted to a highway patrolman, "Saboteur? Counterfeiter? Why, Sam, I would never have suspected. Consider yourself under arrest, you 'pitiful' bastard."

If the resulting laugh was slightly strained, it still contained real humor.

A hand shot up from one of the infantry platoons. "Sir, if this place isn't that important . . . well, then why stay?"

"Ah," answered Williams. "I said it wasn't all that important to us. I didn't say it wasn't important to them. To the Treasury Department? To Rottemeyer's Secret Service and her Presidential Guard? It is very important that they take this back. To them, the place where money is printed is about as sacred as a certain spot down in San Antonio is to us."

Another hand shot up, a bit hesitantly this time. "Okay, sir. Suppose we stay. Can we hold out here?"

"Don't see why not. We've got food for months, we're armed to the teeth, we're dug in like moles. No, what I see happening is they try to take us in a rush; we stop 'em cold, bleed 'em white. And then they sit down and *think* real seriously about how much they want to dig us out of here. While all that's going on the general and the governor will be making things happen elsewhere.

"But I won't lie to you. That's the way I think it's going to happen. There's no guarantee. We might all be dead by staying.

"Anybody else? Any more questions? All right then. Come on, make your decision. The officers have already agreed among themselves. We're staying put. The rest of you? If you're going to stay then cross over that line."

There was a shuffling of feet and no motion forward for several long moments as pride warred with fear in the breasts of the soldiers assembled. The men seemed to be trying to look anywhere but where Williams stood on the other side of his almost imaginary line. Finally, First Sergeant Pendergast cleared his throat, loudly so that all would know what he was about to do. Then, from his position to the rear of the formation he boldly stepped forth, rendered Williams a parade ground salute and said, "First Sergeant Pendergast reporting, sir."

Behind Pendergast, a few men straightened as if pushing away their fears. Then, off to the right, one lone man stepped forward and announced, "Private First Class Jerome Fontaine. I'm staying."

Pendergast suppressed a grateful smile as Williams smiled broadly, saying, "Well there's two men among us."

Yet even as Williams said those words another half dozen had crossed from across the formation. Then came two squads, to a man, followed by fifteen more crossing as individuals. Soon, there were only a half a dozen men still standing behind the line Williams had drawn. These, married men—every one, still hesitated.

Without being ordered to do so, Pendergast trooped the line. "You, Smitty? I would have figured you to want to hang on to this place."

Smitty—Sergeant Smithfield, shamefaced, crossed over.

"Just ask yourself how you'll feel if we lose this place because you weren't here to help us, Figueroa?"

With an audible sigh, Figueroa crossed as well.

"Just ask yourself how you'll feel if we hang on to this place *without* you, Petty?"

Petty snarled and answered, "Never happen, Top." He too crossed.

Pendergast looked over the last three. "Go home to your wife and your seven kids, Royce. No hard feelings. Robles? I know you've got an invalid mother who needs you. Go on."

Eyes closed, shaking his head, Royce crossed, as did Robles.

The last man, Staff Sergeant Melvin La Fleur, looked the first sergeant defiantly in the eye. Tossing his rifle to the pavement he shouted, "Fuck this shit! You're all crazy as loons. I'm out of here."

Pendergast shook his head in pity.

Santa Fe, New Mexico

Juanita felt a small surge of self-pity rush through her even smaller frame. *What did I ever do to deserve to live in times like these?*

But Jack had said that visiting Louisiana, Oklahoma and New Mexico was crucial, especially the latter. He had said that he had nothing adequate, either military or in the way of a natural obstacle, to stop either the Marine division or the armored cavalry regiment assembling at Las Cruces. He had told her that they simply could not afford a defeat or the symbol of one.

Lastly, he had insisted that cutting off the logistic pipeline from Mexico would doom them and that those troops at Las Cruces threatened to do just that. Texas was self-sufficient—"a whole other country," as the tourist ads claimed—in many respects. They had enough oil and gas. Most foodstuffs were home grown as well. But there were still things they needed.

"Juani," Schmidt had told her, "I don't *want* you sticking your head in the lion's mouth. But we don't have much of a choice. And I think you'll be safe; this once anyway. We can send somebody else to talk in Oklahoma and Louisiana, but New Mexico? That's got to be the biggest gun we have. And that's you."

And so, flying very low, escorted by a brace of fighters from her own Air National Guard, in Schmidt's own helicopter, with a couple of batteries of New Mexico's own—superlative—air defense artillery providing cover on the final approaches (for Schmidt had asked an old friend to help), Juani—bile rising and heart thumping, rereading her speech notes to take her mind off of gut-churning nap of the earth flying—approached the New Mexico state capitol.

With a stomach lurching drop the helicopter settled down by the simple brownish-pink stucco walls of the capitol building. Texas Rangers, among them Johnston Akers, scooted out and ran low to take up a perimeter around the governor. With a roar and a scream above, the fighters circled away to refuel, so they hoped, in Albuquerque.

New Mexico's Republican governor, John Garrison and *his* adjutant general, Francisco Garza, met Juani as she alighted from the aircraft. Garrison stuck out a hand. Garza saluted then asked, "And how's my old friend Jack holding up, Governor?"

"He's fine," answered Juani, breathlessly, while shaking Garrison's hand.

"We're all set for you Governor Seguin," said Garrison. "Nobody knows why you are here. Actually, nobody hardly knows that you even are here. I've got both houses assembled on the pretext of debating the present ... umm ... difficulties."

"Thank you, Governor," answered Juani, humbly. Jack had said it was arranged; she should have had faith.

The New Mexican legislature was, at first, shocked at the unexpected appearance. Thus, the applause that greeted Juani's entrance—once they began to overcome the shock of recognition—was much, much more subdued than one would have expected at, say, a political rally. Though subdued, yet it was sincere. She could see that from the faces of the men and women—most of them, anyway—applauding her as she walked uncertainly to the podium following Garrison's introduction, "Ladies and Gentlemen, the Governor of Texas!"

Briefly, Juanita outlined the history of the crisis, what Texas was doing, the reasons Texas was doing it, and what Rottemeyer and company were engaged in to thwart them.

She concluded that portion of her speech with, "And alone, we cannot resist them, not indefinitely.

"Need we stand alone?" Juani asked, not entirely rhetorically. "We are your brothers and your sisters, your uncles and your aunts, your neighbors and your friends. Our fight is your fight. Our success, your success.

"Our loss will be your loss.

"And what does New Mexico stand to lose? Ask your governor. Ask him what it is like to have to kowtow to a Washington appointee to beg back a few dollars from the billions the federal government has taken. Ask my brother and the nearly one hundred children—a quarter of them under age thirteen—murdered with him. Ask that quarter of kids no more than twelve years old about how it feels to be roasted alive. Ask your own newspaper editors how those muzzles wrapped around their jaws feel.

"You might even ask the soldiers and marines assembling on your soil how they feel about the question.

"But while you are asking them, let me ask you. Let me ask you for help: do not let pass the supplies those soldiers and marines need to invade us and break us to Rottemeyer's will. Let me ask you to—if not join us—at least not let your own state be used as a mill to grind us to dust. Let me ask you, if you are men and women of courage, to lead your people to help us.

"And now, before they can catch me, I must go see some other people," she concluded with a most unpolitical wink. "Thank you for hearing me. Thank you in advance for helping us."

The applause, as she left, was much less restrained than when she had arrived.

Washington, DC

Jesse Vega did not bother to replace the telephone on the receiver. Will a gleeful smile and a near cackle she disconnected then rang up the Oval Office.

"We've got that Texan bitch, Willi. She just finished speaking to the New Mexico Legislature and she's on her way back to Texas . . . yes . . . yes . . . okay . . . I want you to tell McCreavy to put two fighters at my command.

"We'll capture her little wetback ass or we'll splash it over twenty square miles of New Mexican Desert."

Southeast of Santa Fe, New Mexico

Juanita noticed that Johnston Akers looked worried. She enquired.

"Governor . . . ma'am . . . I'm worried about that escort. I don't like the idea of you . . . hell, of me flying up here all alone. Governor, you know that the White House has to know by now you were in New Mexico and how you got there and how you left."

McConnell Air Force Base, Wichita, Kansas

Jim Beason, Massachusetts, and Mike Sperry, Texas, were the Air Force's creme de la crème—fighter jocks. Fast, tough, hard, wiry, smart and not a little brave, too.

Even so, they visibly paled as Jesse Vega's nationally recognizable voice came over the loudspeaker in the base operations room to which they had been summoned at a run. It couldn't be said that they liked that voice . . . but they had to respect the power behind it.

"We've got a situation here," said Vega. "An Army National Guard helicopter has been stolen. We have reason to believe . . . good reason, gentlemen, that that helicopter is carrying a weapon of mass destruction— biological, we believe. We know it left Santa Fe, New Mexico, less than twenty minutes ago, heading toward Amarillo, Texas.

"You are to force it to land as soon as you intercept it. If-it-will-not-land . . . shoot it down before it reaches a city. FBI, EPA and the Centers for Disease Control will be following by helicopter to take charge of the weapon as soon as you force it down."

Air Force eyes widened in faces gone paler still. This sort of thing had happened in the past, though it was rarely discussed and never in a public way. "Yes, ma'am!" they shouted as they bolted toward their waiting aircraft. Already they were calculating heights and speeds and routes to come up with a likely intercept point. "Don't worry. We'll take it down. Goddamned RIF."

Unseen across the airways, Vega smiled happily. She had not herself mentioned anything like Radical Islamic Fundamentalists, though she had expected that the pilots would leap to that assumption. She had, of course, said "weapon of mass destruction" . . . but then was not Governor Seguin a weapon that promised mass destruction to Vega's party? Was she not biological?

Southeast of Santa Fe, New Mexico

Johnston Akers' creased ancient face relaxed visibly when he caught the first view of two F-16s screaming in from the direction of Albuquerque.

That relaxation disappeared with the first stream of tracers that passed just off the port side.

Juanita—startled from a doze—screamed once, crossed herself and began to pray, her lips moving fervently. Akers absurdly, and with utter futility, drew his pistol. The pilot cursed, veered sharply right and began punching buttons on his radio to come up on the general aviation frequency.

" . . . dentified helicopter; unidentified helicopter: this is Goshawk seven. Land. Land now, you fucking wogs. Land now or you will be shot down."

One jet streaked by as the other lined up for a shot. The turbulence caused the helicopter to buck like some unbroken mustang.

"Goshawk are you out of your fucking minds?" called the frantic chopper pilot. "This is Lone Star six carrying VIPs from New Mexico to Texas. You've got no call to shoot us down. You've got no call to even stop us." Of course, the pilot knew the fighters had a very good reason to shoot the helicopter down. But maybe, just maybe, they didn't know that reason.

There was silence in reply. The helicopter pilot imagined a brief conversation on the pilots' own push.

Then came the hoped for, "Maintain course, speed and altitude. One of us will approach."

Sperry glanced long and hard to the left as he passed the helicopter on its starboard side. *Christ, they don't look much like terrorists to me.*

"Jim . . . Jim, I think we've got us the wrong bird."

Beason radioed back to base ops for instructions and was somewhat surprised to hear Vega's voice come over the net.

"That is your target, Captain, that Texas National Guard helicopter. It is stolen United States' property and it is carrying a WMD. Force it to land or shoot it down."

"Ma'am, I can *see* into the helicopter when I pass it. There's nothing but some people aboard. No pods, no boxes; nothing but some people. It looks to be a legitimate Guard chopper."

"Those people *are* the weapon, Captain. Contaminated, every one of them. Now are you going to shoot it down or are you going to spend the next fifty years at Fort Leavenworth contemplating the tens of thousands of people you let die of a plague you could have prevented?"

Sperry was not fooled. He had seen the face of one of the occupants. It was a face more or less well known in some circles. Somehow, he thought that face had been praying.

He had a sudden thought . . . *What the hell, it might be worth a try. Maybe Vega is ignorant.*

"Jim, this is Mike, where the hell did the target go? I lost it in the weeds."

Beason, no fool, answered, "Damfino. I can't see it either."

Vega, *not* fooled, answered, "Listen carefully you morons. There's nothing below you but sand and rock and dust and a cactus every few miles. You haven't lost anything. Now get that helicopter," she nearly shrieked.

A voice previously unheard answered, "Before y'all do that you might maybe want to consult with us." This, too, was punctuated by a tracer stream, unaimed but plainly visible to Beason and Sperry. They automatically backtracked the flight of the tracers in their minds. Oh shit, another fighter.

"Ummm . . . and you would be?" asked Beason, wrenching around to eyeball another F-16 flying unerringly on his "six." *Double shit; there's two of them.*

Beason felt the inane urge to giggle over the old joke: *"Sir, it's a trap. There's* two *of them."*

"This is Lieutenant Colonel Paul Grayson—my friends call me 'Pablo,' 182 Fighter Squadron out o' Lackland. And—unless either or both you gentlemen want a Sidewinder up yo' ass—then, you suhs, are mah prisoners."

Beason and Sperry did some quick calculation, oh, very quick. They were fast, tough, hard, wiry, smart and not a little brave, too. The 182, however, was not only composed of instructor pilots—but its pilots were equally fast, tough, hard, wiry, smart and not a little brave . . . and experienced.

"Ah, what the hell, Mike," said Beason. "I'm a Yankee boy who's been claiming Texas as his state of residence for about eight years now. I think we have just been captured."

To Grayson he said, "And, Colonel, I appreciate your restraint."

Another previously unheard voice, this one from the helicopter, quite warmly female if a bit strained and shaky, said, "Welcome home, boys."

Denton, Texas

"What I want from you, Colonel, is a restrained response."

"Restrained, sir? We're a heavy battalion. That's not very 'restrained,' just in the nature of things."

"Nonetheless, that's what I want. At the first sign of a federal move near or behind you, drop the bridges and run back to the next set. Fight only as a last resort . . . though you can—and I want you to—make them think you are going to fight if you can figure out how to do that."

"Warning shots?"

"Maybe . . . with care . . . if they push too hard. But if you must fire, fire to frighten, not to kill or wound."

"That's one tall goddamned order, general, if you don't mind my saying so."

"There are people who are going to risk as much, colonel, and they won't have tanks to fall back on."

Las Cruces, New Mexico

The legislature had voted, the people had assembled, the busses had come and gone.

New Mexico was not quite yet ready to join Texas' protest in the way Texas was protesting. Neither was it ready to leave a neighbor in the lurch. "You just don't do that, in the American southwest; you pitch in and help." That was what Governor Garrison had told the Legislature before they voted.

What had they voted for, then? They voted to pay for transportation and food, to pay for their own national guard to set up tents for, and to provide food and water for anyone willing to go to the Army and Marine Corps assembly areas near Las Cruces to protest the coming invasion of Texas. They also cast a vote for the First Amendment, especially with regards to the news media. Lastly, New Mexico had voted to send the bulk of its own national guard, one very fine brigade—the "best by test" in any component of the U.S. Armed Services—of air defense artillery to join Texas' Forty-ninth Armored Division, along with the state's other combat support unit, a battalion of six-inch self-propelled guns.

And as the Air Defense Brigade and artillery had gone, so, answering a freed, and more than a little annoyed, news media, the people *had* come. Not so many, of course, in any objective sense; New Mexico was not a populous state. Yet there were enough. From Lordburg, from Deming, from Alamogordo and Albuquerque, from Socorro and Santa Fe, they came. They came in numbers enough to block the highways through Las Cruces; to block the flow of fuel and parts and ammunition to the cavalrymen and marines rotting in dusty tent cities between Las Cruces and El Paso.

And those people sat on the roads and would not move.

Normally, of course, the armed forces would have called on the local police authorities to disperse the protesters.

"That's not going to work here," muttered the commander of the Marines. "I don't even want to ask. Hell, the State Police are out there with the protesters, keeping order."

"We could clear them out ourselves, sir," answered an aide. "Or tell the Army to do it."

"No, Johnny. The cavalry colonel has already told me, in so many words, 'Don't ask.' And I don't know what we'll do if the police and the guard open fire. Then too, what will those Texas boys at El Paso do if it does turn nasty?"

"No," the marine sighed. "No. We'll buck this one up to higher."

Washington, DC

"It's spreading," said McCreavy, simply, to Rottemeyer.

"What's spreading?" asked the President.

"The 'Rebellion,' if you want to call it a rebellion."

Rottemeyer forced a calm into her voice she didn't quite feel, suppressing a shudder in her stomach she very much felt. "What now?"

"New Mexico. The Army and Marine force there is cut off from supply by protesters. The government down there is supporting the protesters, supporting them strongly."

"Define 'strongly.'"

"Transportation. Supply. Housing . . . of a sort. Police protection." McCreavy hesitated slightly, then added, "Military protection, too, though they have ordered most of what they had to Texas."

"And this means to us? To our plans?"

"It means that that force can go to El Paso and *maybe* a hundred miles beyond. Maybe less; the supply usage factors have hardly been updated since the Second World War and they are probably unrealistically conservative. In any case, when they run out they stop for lack of gas. Then they die for lack of water. The protesters . . . I should say the police . . . are letting enough water and food through now."

Carroll, ashen-faced, added, "It's . . . umm . . . worse than that, Willi. The state has ordered police protection for newspaper editors and other media types. Project Ogilvie is dead in New Mexico . . . dead for now anyway. We're having to beef up efforts in the adjoining states to keep them down."

Carroll gave a rueful and reluctant smile. "'Course, not all the reporters are being too very brave. The state can't protect all of them from us; only the major editors, really. So the reporters are, some of 'em, using bylines like 'Spartacus' and 'Frederick Douglass'—I'm pretty sure I know who that one is. He's black, the treacherous, short-sighted bastard."

"Shit. Can we switch some police down to New Mexico to disperse the protesters?"

Vega answered, after a fashion, "Can we? Surely. But what's available? What's available that could do the job? The Surgeon General's Riot Control Police would be . . . umm . . . let's say that faced with armed and organized opposition they would be overtasked.

The Presidential Guard could do it. But they're set for a different mission. Willi, I warned you we had to take control of all the law enforcement agencies in the country, to create a true national police. But no, you wouldn't listen."

"I listened, Jesse. But it wasn't yet time for that."

"Sure. Well, maybe that's so. But now it is too late. Do you want the PG's to pull off of the Fort Worth mission and go to New Mexico?"

Rottemeyer turned again to McCreavy. "How quickly can you turn them around once they take the currency facility?"

"And send them to New Mexico? Six hundred miles? A week . . . with luck. It will have to be planned."

"Okay," she told McCreavy. "Start planning."

To Vega she said, "They can take care of New Mexico after they take care of Fort Worth."

Pickup Zone (PZ) "Treasure," Oklahoma

They had armored vehicles. They had other heavy weapons. They had troops, mostly fairly well-trained for their usual missions. They had a logistic and administrative tail.

What the PGSS lacked was helicopters.

Oh, there were a few somewhat plush command and control jobs available . . . "for the brass," as they say. But as far as moving any substantial number of Treasury agents (for they carefully preserved the fiction that they were merely agents of the public fisc)?

None.

For this, they needed the Army. And the Army duly and dutifully complied by sending down nearly half the 101st aviation group out of Fort Campbell, Kentucky, that half being somewhat reinforced by the helicopters of the 160th Special Operations Aviation Regiment, at one time known as Task Force 160.

And yet using helicopters is not something that comes naturally to a military organization. True, some of the PGSS had previous military experience working with choppers. And yet many did not. As organizations, none of its battalions had any.

Austin, Texas

Juanita pointed to the helicopter idling on the pad beneath her office window. "And I told you, Jack, I will never get on one of those things again. No. Not. Ever. Never."

"Oh, Juani, be realistic, would you? You're expected in Fort Worth here shortly. The troops are standing by," Schmidt cajoled.

The governor answered with a grimace, "I know, I know. But, Jack I just can't. I . . . I wet myself when I saw those bullets—'tracers' you called them?—fly by. You have no idea . . ." Suddenly nonplussed, Juani stopped. She knew that Schmidt had a very good idea of what it was like to be in a helicopter someone was shooting at.

Still, no crybaby was Juanita. Even as her lip began to quiver, she admitted, "All right, all *right*. So you have an idea. But, Jack, I was never so terrified in my life."

Schmidt lifted one inquisitorial eyebrow. "You think those men in the currency facility aren't terrified, too, Juani? But they're there anyway doing what they have to. So now you, Governor, need to do what you have to. In this case that means following me downstairs, getting on that helicopter; closing your eyes and pissing yourself if you have to, to see those men who are going to die for you."

Juani's own eyes widened in horror. "Oh, no. Don't say that. Don't say they're going to die, let alone that they're going to die for me. I can't bear that idea."

"And it won't be any easier after you meet them, I know. But you have to. So come on. Now."

Finally, with reluctance bordering on terror, the governor agreed.

"And don't sweat it so much," said Schmidt. "Security here is pretty good, really. And I've already arranged for escorts going both ways. They may know where you are when we take off. They won't know, generally, where you're going. And on the way back we can take any old route we need to."

Fort Worth, Texas, Western Currency Facility

"And remember," said Williams, "we have got to pinch off any penetrations *before* . . ."

Even through the thick brick walls, deep in the bowels of the facility, the steady slashing of the helicopter's rotors could be heard and felt. "It seems the governor and General Schmidt are here, sir," commented Pendergast.

"Fine," answered Williams. "I'll keep the officers

here. Could you send a party out to escort them inside, Top?"

"Yessir," agreed Pendergast, turning immediately to leave. "No problem. In fact, I'll go myself."

At the exterior wall the first sergeant slipped through a mousehole broken through the bricks. All the normal doors had been sealed or, in some cases, sealed and booby trapped. Emerging into the pale afternoon daylight on hands and knees, Pendergast arose, brushed some dirt off of his uniform, and hurried to where Schmidt and Governor Seguin waited on the concrete.

Johnston Akers, ever suspicious where the governor's safety was concerned, took one look at the First Sergeant's slung rifle. He then immediately began to draw his pistol.

"None of that, Ranger," commanded Schmidt. "This one's on *our* side."

Akers considered. Yes, it must be so. He slid the pistol back into its holster and grinned an apology at the first sergeant.

"Indeed I am," answered Pendergast, ignoring the Ranger's previous moves. "And so are we all, here. Governor, General? Will you all be kind enough to follow me? You too, Ranger. You're welcome inside."

"Watch your head there Governor. It's low and crooked."

"Thank you, First Sergeant. Or can I call you 'Mike'?"

"Mike would do mighty fine, ma'am. Or "Top"; that's what the troops usually call me."

Stifling a small curse at scraped knees, Juanita

emerged into a rat maze. What's more, it seemed to her a rat maze designed by psychotic elves on LSD.

Whatever the Western Currency Facility had once looked like—no doubt a more or less regular printing plant with offices, hallways, open spaces—on the inside it resembled this no more. Eyes growing ever wider, Juanita swept the open hall into which the mouse hole led.

"Where are the doors?" she asked Pendergast, since the two leading out had been sealed with barbed wire.

"I'll show you, ma'am." Then Pendergast pushed aside a desk behind which was another mousehole. "We've sealed—blocked anyway—every normal door and crawlspace. Made our own, so to speak."

"But . . . but why?"

The first sergeant smiled. "Governor, it's routine. Even so, the people coming here are bound to have the floor plans for the place. They might even have rehearsed an attack based on those plans. Bound to fu— . . . err— . . . screw 'em up once they get in and find out the plans make no sense anymore."

The governor had a sudden image of a mouse caught in a maze. "Ohh. Yes, I could see that."

Behind Juanita, Schmidt suppressed a slight smile. *She's sooo innocent.*

"Now if you will follow me, Governor, General, I'll take you on the roundabout tour before we go see Captain Williams."

"I'm afraid you're going to have to crawl through this one, too, General . . . Governor."

Schmidt, unsurprised at the mass of barbed wire

hanging in midair in the corridor, simply got down on his belly and started to crawl. Juanita looked at the great wad of tangled up barbed wire very dubiously.

"No need to worry, ma'am," said Pendergast, pointing at some smooth and thin black wire. "See, it's held up there pretty well."

"But what good is it, Mike, if you can just crawl under it?"

"Well, Governor, we can crawl under it, sure. Then we cut the wires holding it and it drops down. A stone cold bit— . . . err . . . pain to move. Especially since we'll likely be shooting at anyone that tries."

Schmidt asked, "Shooting, grenading . . . hmm . . . Top, where are your claymores?"

Pendergast thought briefly, tapped a finger against his lower lip, then pointed up at the ceiling tiles. "Two up there, General, plus another at each end of the corridor, buried in the walls."

"Very good."

The party moved further upward, to one of the two large rectangular projections jutting up from the roof of the building.

"Can't take you onto the roof, ma'am. Nor even you, General Schmidt."

"Booby trapped, Top?"

"To a fine art, sir."

"What are you going to do once they clear the traps? The roof here doesn't look like you can hold it by fire from the inside."

Pendergast shook his head. "No, sir. Too thick. If they want to pay the price to clear a section of the roof we can't do much to stop 'em. We do have a few small holes cut that the guys can donate grenades through. But any kind of bunker we put up there would need a manhole and that would just be a way for the other fellows to break into our defenses. We've also cut some narrow half-moons in the roof to push through some claymores taped to poles." Pendergast gestured first at one such half-moon cut through the ceiling; then at a stack of poles—to which had been attached the claymores—standing in one corner.

"And then, once they do break in, we fight 'em for every inch; counterattack where we're able. We've been practicing for that every moment we weren't busy digging in. But the captain could tell you more about that than I could."

Pendergast led the way downward towards the command post for the defense. Reaching it at length he knocked and announced, "Governor Seguin and General Schmidt, sir."

Williams called, "Attention."

Schmidt let the men stand that way for only the barest fraction of a moment before commanding, "Captain Williams, gentlemen. Be at ease. The governor is an informal lady."

At Schmidt's order Williams, Davis, and James visibly relaxed. A stiff-backed Fontaine, detailed to bring up some snacks from the WCF cafeteria, however, didn't.

Juanita noticed. "You too, young man. I'm just the governor. You're a lot more important. You're a citizen."

Fontaine glanced a query at Pendergast who nodded, *Yes, you too, dummy.*

"You can leave, Fontaine," added Pendergast.

"First Sergeant . . . Mike . . . I wonder if you wouldn't

mind having this young man wait, either here or outside. I've seen nothing but senior people. I'd like to talk to him."

"You heard the governor, Fontaine. Wait outside."

"Yes, Top."

"And now, ma'am," began Williams, "let me tell you how we're going to hold this place. . . ."

An hour and a half later Schmidt thought, and not for the first time in his life, *Briefings suck*. Then he heard the engineer captain, Davis, say something that caught his attention. "Aces and eights? Dead man's hand? What do you mean, Captain?"

"Eleven tons of ANFO, General, down below. If they take this place, they're going to take a bunch of dust."

"What's he mean, Jack?"

Schmidt sighed. Juani was not going to like this. "In poker, 'Aces and Eights' are known as the 'dead man's hand,' Governor. And ANFO is Ammonium Nitrate–Fuel Oil explosive. He means that, as a last resort, they'll blow the place sky high."

The governor was horrified. "But what about the wounded?"

Davis explained. "Ma'am . . . after what we are going to do to them before they get even halfway through clearing us out? There aren't going to be any wounded; not of ours anyway. They'll kill everything. Anyone would."

"I see . . . well, we can't let that happen." She turned to Schmidt. "Jack, is there any way we can get these boys out after they've bought a little time for us?"

Schmidt and Williams exchanged knowing glances. *In your dreams, Governor, in your dreams.*

"Governor . . . Juani . . . it's possible I could do an end run around Third Corps when it rolls in, fight my way to this facility and extract the same way. Possible, but not likely."

Juani was adamant. "Whatever it takes, Jack. I will not leave these boys . . . men, rather, without some hope of rescue."

"You're the boss, Governor. I'll start planning it. Go on, Captain," ordered Schmidt. "Let's finish this up."

"Yes, sir. Well, the last thing I had to cover was auxiliary power. Seemed likely they'd cut off the electricity once they were ready, so we've set up three generators to take up the slack. It isn't enough for environmental control or anything but it should keep enough of the lights and the intercom working. Oh, and the security cameras . . ."

"Can you hold this place for us, Private Fontaine?" queried Juanita as she and Jack waited for Williams and Pendergast—involved briefly in a discussion with the other leaders—to join them and escort them out.

"We can surely try, ma'am. And we sure intend to try. No matter what."

Juanita thought about that "no matter what"— thought about "aces and eights," too—and felt her eyes begin to mist again. She averted her face while blinking a few times to clear them.

"Is there anything I can do?" Juani asked the young soldier.

Fontaine thought briefly. "I kinda hate to ask, ma'am . . . but there's one thing. I wonder . . . well,

I'd appreciate it if someone could look after my momma." Fontaine gave a smile somewhat rueful. "And, you know? Old Iron Mike? The first sergeant? He's harder than woodpecker lips, no mistake. But he's a mighty good first sergeant. I wonder if, maybe . . . someone could make him a sergeant major before it's . . . you know . . . too late. I think it would mean a lot to him."

Schmidt smiled and reached into his pocket, extracting two small cellophane wrapped packets. "Go get 'Major' Williams and 'Sergeant Major' Pendergast, would you, son."

"Send the car away, Jack. We'll go back by helicopter."

"Are you sure, Juani?"

"I'm sure. If those men in there can do what they seem determined to do then I'll be damned if those people in Washington are going to frighten me out of the air. We'll take the helicopter."

"That's my girl, Juani. . . ."

Governor's Mansion, Austin, Texas

Elpidia had thought she was alone in the house. Normally—every day, of late—the governor had gone to her office, the father of the family to his, and even the youngest boy, Mario, to school long before Elpi even awakened.

The girl was surprised, therefore, to hear the sounds of sobbing, quiet but distinct, coming from the governor's home office.

Also quietly, Elpi walked to the door. Shyly she knocked.

"Who is it?" asked the governor in a quavering voice.

"*Solo yo, Gubanadora* . . . just me, Governor, Elpi. I heard crying. Are you okay?"

Juani hastily dried her eyes on her sleeve and answered, "I'm fine Elpi," in a voice that gave the lie to the claim.

Elpi walked in, invited or not. "What's wrong?" she asked.

At the query Juani burst into fresh tears. She half bent and wrapped her arms around herself to try to control the trembling. Rocking back and forth she moaned over and over, "They're all going to die . . . they're all going to die . . ."

Elpi was literate in English, but freshly and barely so. She could make out the headlines from the newspaper laying on Juani's desk. "The Eyes of Texas are Upon You." She read a few lines, painfully slowly. It seemed to her that the state's free press was being a little irresponsible in putting any blame on the governor for the state of affairs. She came to the line, " . . . and the men who are about to die in Fort Worth . . ."

"Who is going to die?" the young girl asked.

It came out almost as a shriek, "All those men in the currency facility are going to die and who knows how many others? And it's all *my* fault . . . mine, *mine*, MINE! Oh why, oh *why* couldn't I just leave it alone? Why did I have to start this whole thing?"

Elpi walked over to Juanita and put a warm hand to her quaking back. When this did no good the girl bent her head down, resting a cheek upon the quivering shoulder of the Governor of Texas and whispered, "You didn't start anything. Neither did your brother. This was started by the people who throw riot police at people who protest killing little babies. It was started by people who attack churches and burn children alive."

"You didn't start it Governor . . . but you have to end it. You have to see us through this."

Twisting around, Juanita pulled the girl into her shoulder and sobbed, "I know."

State Legislature, Austin, Texas

Behind Juani, standing at the podium, a map of Texas and its surrounding states shone against a screen. News cameras panned across her, the screen, and on to the raptly listening legislators. This broadcast was going out live to Texans, and via continuous streaming on the Internet to the rest of the United States. A Chinese company had rented Texas the use of a satellite to bring the word to the rest of the world.

"This is what we know," began Juanita. Instantly, at Schmidt's direction, several dozen symbols appeared on the map behind her.

"To our west, just across the border with New Mexico, the bulk of the 1st Marine Division and the Army's 3rd Armored Cavalry Regiment stand poised to invade. To our north, in southern Oklahoma, is the Army's Third Corps. This force has in it the 1st Cavalry Division, the 1st Infantry Division, 4th Infantry Division, and about two thirds of the 101st Airborne Division, a helicopter heavy formation."

"East, in Louisiana, is the 18th Airborne Corps. This group has been reinforced by, again, about two thirds of the Second Marine Division. The rest consists of two brigades each from the 3rd Infantry Division, the 82nd Airborne Division, and the 10th Mountain Division.

"Southwards, the Navy and a brigade of Marines are blocking our coast and poised to descend upon it. We have reports—reliable reports—that a portion of the 1st Marine Division has boarded ship to pass through the Panama Canal to join the fleet assembling in the Gulf."

At this last bit of unpleasant news the legislators, those at least siding with Juanita, gave an audible groan.

Not everyone was on her side of course. Some were ambivalent, others hostile. Many were simply frightened and this news—though not unexpected in broad terms—made them more so.

Juani looked out, smiling, at a known opponent, Imogene Cochran, seated about center in the room. Imogene—pinch faced and severe—was of the rather rare far left variety of Texas Democrat. She returned Juani's smile with a sneer.

"We are prepared to fight them," Juanita announced baldly, voice ringing loud and clear through the hall. "On the Gulf Coast beaches, in the cities, in the towns, in the field . . . we are prepared to . . . but surely we do not want to," this last was spoken in a stage whisper.

"We will hold off from fighting until the very last extremity.

"Something else we know: officials named by the

White House have been integrated into the regular armed forces down to battalion level. These men . . . and a few women . . . are backed by federal police forces and appear to have the duty of insuring that the orders of the White House are enforced."

Juani gave a smile that was perhaps slightly out of place. "It seems that Washington does not trust its own army. Kind of makes you wonder whether, if Washington doesn't trust the armed forces, perhaps—just maybe—*we* can."

Most of the legislators joined Juani's smile at the jest. Imogene merely looked furious.

Juani took a deep breath, steeling herself. The next part was going to be difficult. She pushed a button on the podium. The symboled map disappeared leaving a blank screen in its wake.

"Did you ever notice how, when Somali kids are starving, the papers and television screens are full of pitiful pictures? Did you ever notice how, when Kurdish kids are driven from their homes you can hardly pick up a magazine without being bombarded with big, innocent eyes? A California girl gets kidnapped and murdered and the media pastes her picture across the nation.

"Why do you suppose we've never seen a single picture of any of the kids burned alive in Waco?" She tapped the button on the podium once again and the screen behind her lit with a portrait of a smiling little Mexican girl.

"That's Josefina Sanchez." Juani tapped the button again and the screen split. On the right side appeared the obscenely charred corpse of a very small person, curled into a fetal position and holding a smaller bit of once-human charcoal between arms and chest. The legislators groaned.

"That is also Josefina Sanchez. In her arms is a little baby . . . what is left of one . . . named Pedro."

A tap of the button and the picture zoomed in to focus on the little shriveled bundle that had been found wrapped in Josefina's arms. Another tap and it focused further onto Pedro's face, little carbonized teeth faintly visible inside a burned and distorted mouth, empty eye sockets staring from blackened face.

Again she tapped the button and a full color picture of Pedro at his first birthday party appeared on the right side of the screen. *Thank God I didn't let Elpi come to this and told Mario not to let her near a television or computer, thought Juani, fighting down her own gorge.*

Juani continued to tap, interspersing normal pictures with pictures of the recovered, charred bodies. At each she announced a name, "Maria Ramirez, aged nine . . . Pablo Trujillo, aged eleven . . . Peter Smith, aged eleven . . . Colleen Drysdale, aged ten . . . Katherine Collins, aged eleven . . . David Robles . . ." About halfway through there was the sound of someone wretching.

"You have no right," shouted Imogene. "You have no right to show us these things. It isn't decent."

Juanita scowled. "No right, Imogene? No one had a right to do to these kids what was done to them. And you don't have a right to bury your head in the sand and ignore what was done to them. Admit it, that's the real crime in your mind. Not the killings, but upsetting you." *Bitch.*

"Enough, anyway," Juani continued. "The rest of the pictures wouldn't show you all anything you don't know now.

"But you all needed to see why I decided to resist. It wasn't my brother and it wasn't even that . . . that . . . that bastard of a 'United States Commissioner for the State of Texas,' Forsythe, that Washington stuck me with. It wasn't the taxes and it wasn't the jobs and it wasn't even over the control they were taking in the schools.

"I just don't want to live, don't want any of our people to have to live, under a government that will do this; murder a bunch of kids then wrap itself in a shroud of sanctimonious hypocrisy and pretend nothing ever happened.

"One last thing before I go: we are about to be invaded. Washington will no doubt decide to call it something else . . . but an invasion is what it is. I am not going to ask every Texan to fight the invasion. In fact, except for those many thousands who have joined our National Guard and State Defense Force, I am going to ask the rest of the state not to fight.

"But I am going to ask, in fact I am going to beg of the people—here in Texas and elsewhere in the United States—do not fight . . . but do not cooperate. Block roads, interfere with supply columns, stop trains, swarm over airfields. In short, make this invasion impossible to supply and federal control impossible to maintain.

"If you will do this, I think we can win."

Matamoros, Mexico

Hanstadt never did quite buy in to the whole non-violent civil disobedience idea. It just wasn't in his nature. He measured things materially; so many guns, so many tons of rations, so many artillery shells . . . so much X . . . so many Y. That was what made him a prize as Schmidt's G-4 and something of a cipher for the governor's other plans.

"How many shells did you say came with those things?" he asked, pointing a finger at a passing CONEX on its way to Camp Bullis. He had to shout to be heard over the roar of massed diesels.

"Carl" answered, "Seven hundred fifty rounds, mixed high explosive, illumination and smoke, with each 85mm gun. two-fifty to three-fifty with the others. Plus you're getting a fair number of pure ammunition loads."

"And you say these things are self-propelled?"

"The SD-44s, the 85mm jobs, are *auxiliary*-propelled. That is, they have an engine, a steering wheel, a driver's seat and a small gas tank. For the 122s and 152 you're going to have to rig up something on your own and use civilian trucks."

"And the manuals are inside?"

"Every CONEX comes with a manual and firing table printed in Spanish. I figure you have enough Spanish speakers in Texas. Though, I've got to tell you, those manuals were translated from Chinese by people maybe none too good. You'll have some problems."

Hanstadt normally wouldn't look a gift horse in the mouth, but these guns were no gift. Texas had paid for them with the ships about to be seized while going through the Panama Canal. They had also forked over no small amount of cash for all the stock to Materiales de Seguridad, SA, the Mexican-incorporated, Panamanian-run arms company that had held these particular weapons.

He figured this entitled him to check the teeth. "Where and why did you get all of this? Why did you hide it?"

Carl hesitated before answering. Some of what Hanstadt was asking was very close-held. In the U.S. military and intelligence communities it would have been called "Special Compartmentalized Information." "We bought it from China, Russia and North Korea when this sort of thing was a glut on the market. We have kept almost two-thirds of it out of Panama expressly to avoid antagonizing the United States. And that is all I can say . . . except that some Panamanians have been in the surreptitious arms business for quite some time . . . TOW missiles to Iran in the 1980s . . . rifles and mortars for Croats in the 1990s . . . that sort of thing."

"Fair enough. Though I insist that it is *not* fair for you people to grab over five hundred newer and heavier guns we paid good money for and replace them with three hundred fifty lighter and older ones for even more money."

Carl shrugged. "General . . . if we didn't get them those arms were going to be seized anyway. We are also, as part of the deal, paying very good money to arrange a strike on the Panama Canal when that brigade from the 1st Marine Division is stuck in the middle of Gatun Lake between the locks. That strike is going to cost us money and cost us *big*. You are hardly paying any more than what this is going to cost us and I think you should stop bitching about it. You are getting some artillery and you ought to be happy with that. Me, personally, I think my boss is making a mistake."

"A mistake? My ass. You're screwing us plain and simple."

Carl shrugged again and began to walk towards the line of tractors hauling the flatbed trailers northwards.

"Where are you going?" demanded Hanstadt.

"Why, I'm going to turn these trucks around since you seem to think the deal is so bad."

"Now wait a minute . . ."

"Then stop bitching about it."

INTERLUDE:

From: *True Faith and Allegiance: the American Military in a Time of Constitutional Crisis,* Copyright 2067, Professor Samuel Horowitz, Harvard University Press.

It was well known. Indeed there had never been any doubt of the American military's sublime disgust with Wilhelmina Rottemeyer. No more had there been any doubt as to her distaste for her own armed forces. On the very day of her inauguration, an Air Force officer, one Colonel Douglas Farrell, apparently deliberately waiting for her to be sworn in in order to give his protest meaning, had pointedly and publicly voiced the opinion of nearly every serving officer and, it is widely believed, the bulk of the other ranks: "She's a rug-munching, acid-dropping, hippie-chick refugee from the '60s. I could live with all that. She's a national menace and *that* none of us should be willing to live with."

Colonel Farrell was of course duly court-martialed for violation of Article 88, UCMJ, "Contempt Towards Officials." This was one of two surprises. The first surprise was that he had not resigned from the Air Force to avoid that prosecution; this being the usual procedure. The second was that he was acquitted by a jury of his peers at that court-martial.

This acquittal did not save Colonel Farrell from a most unpleasant posting to Thule Air Force Base, Greenland, of course. . . .

Only once before had the American military, most especially its officer corps, been put to the test. And then, in 1861, fully a third had cast off their allegiance to the United States Constitution and joined their home states. These were joined, in some few cases, by officers of northern birth who were in political sympathy with the secessionists' aims.

That, however, was in a context of peculiar circumstances and widely differing interpretation of what was and was not constitutionally permissible and proper.

In the Rottemeyer presidency, on the other hand, there was little or no such difference of opinion among military officers. There was scarcely more among the rank and file . . . of any color, sex or religious persuasion. Almost openly spurned and despised by their commander in chief, the soldiers—officers and men, alike—heartily returned the feelings. Drawn themselves largely from the more rural—hence conservative—parts of the United States, they had little philosophical sympathy for her political and social goals, which were largely urban and liberal, shading over to Marxist. Their organizations twisted, warped and perverted by those goals, only long habits of obedience to civil authority, coupled with a lack of any clear alternatives, had kept these men and women to their duty.

And yet, what *was* that duty? These men and women had sworn an oath to support and defend the Constitution of the United States against all enemies, foreign and domestic. But a domestic force that flouted the first and second amendments, bought votes and influence through cash payments to the underclass, violated the doctrine of separation of powers, and persecuted their churches?

Increasingly, the habits of discipline, obedience, and subordination to civilian control found themselves warring with the deeper meaning of the military oath, "all enemies, foreign and domestic." Increasingly the military saw Rottemeyer and her movement as such. Increasingly, men and women in uniform resolved to—if not openly resist—at least damn by faint support whenever and wherever the opportunity might arise.

The first such instance during the crisis was, arguably, the departure of the heavy corps from Texas; leaving behind so much useful materiel. The second, almost open, rebellion came with the assault on the Western Currency Facility. The third, and sometimes this *was* open rebellion, was the refusal of the Air Force's pilots to participate.

Army and Marine companies and platoons could be led by their less politically astute or sensitive noncommissioned officers. Even ships could sail and maintain a blockade under their senior chiefs.

Planes do not fly without pilots, and to an extraordinary degree those men (and in a few cases, women) refused, openly or tacitly, to fly.

This was, of course, equally true of helicopters.

There were, of course, some pilots, experienced ones even, that could be bought. . . .

CHAPTER THIRTEEN

From the transcript at trial: Commonwealth of
Virginia v. Alvin Scheer

DIRECT EXAMINATION, CONTINUED
BY MR. STENNINGS:

Q. What did you find in Baltimore, besides a job,
   Alvin?
A. Well, I noticed posters going up all over town,
   eventually. They were kind of crudely done, if
   you know what I mean. Well ... maybe crude
   isn't quite the right word; the drawings were a
   good enough likeness, after all.

   You know the ones I mean? They showed
   Governor Seguin from a front view and from the
   side, just like she was a criminal or something.
   For a while there they were everywhere: "Wanted:
   Dead or Alive."

   Now, of course, nobody ever took any credit

for them. They weren't official. They didn't offer any reward or anything like that.

But it started me to thinking, which never did come too easy to me. I mean, I'm not stupid. I never read books much, but I'm not stupid.

Anyway, if the White House could pay people to march in parades, and I was pretty sure that's where that money I was handed did come from, why couldn't they make up—have someone make up—some posters like that?

Take it all together: the parades, the news that all seemed to come from one side only, the posters. What did it add up to?

To me? Well, I added one and one and one and came up with the White House. But I figure to a lot of folks, it probably seemed like it added up to real—what do you call it?—a tidal wave? Yeah, a tidal wave of support for doing whatever it took to knock Texas into the dirt.

Pickup Zone (PZ) "Treasure," Oklahoma

The faint nimbus of the rising sun was only just beginning to peek over the low Oklahoma hills to the east. A mild southern wind carried little dust on its breeze, and virtually none into the eyes of the Army teams overseeing the loading and departure of a battalion of PGSS "agents" towards Fort Worth.

The helicopters themselves, however, kicked up enough dust to be an annoyance. It was an annoyance to which the Army was long since used, however. The soldiers shrugged it off.

Not so the PGSS. Unused to helicopters at best—most of them, they snarled and choked as they neared the birds designated to take them by "chalk"—strange Army term meaning one load for one helicopter, so they had found out—to their landing zones.

The snarling was only about half due to the dust, however, or perhaps a bit less. Mostly they were frightened. They'd never been recruited, armed, organized or trained for this kind of mission. The last several weeks' intense training under qualified Army instructors had made good some of this lack—albeit not without some friction between the two. Still, the idea of close combat in buildings—the worst and deadliest kind of combat, so their instructors had told them—had not been high on their list of reasons for joining up.

With a circle of hands and a pointed finger the ground teams signaled their helicopters to take off into the wind.

Other battalions waited to load as soon as their transport returned.

Field Mess, 4th Battalion, 101st Aviation Regiment

Officers could not speak ill of the President of the United States. Noncoms and enlisted men could not insult officers but could say whatever they wanted about the President; no rule against it. At least there was no legal and official rule against it. The political officers—the troops had already taken to calling them "Zampolits"—might have different ideas.

Thus it was that, surrounded by officers and flight

warrants of the battalion, one lone, slightly chubby first sergeant by the name of Henry looked around, saw no Zampolits, then stood upon a folding mess table and announced, "Be proud, gentlemen, be proud. That sound you hear over toward the PZ? Why that's our own brave boys carrying the 'elite of the nation'— Rottenmuncher's Own, the arrogant cocksuckers—into battle. What an awesome and welcome mission. What a garland for our proud unit's history. Can't you just imagine it, imagine how you're all going to feel when we get that campaign streamer that says 'Western Currency Facility' to put on our standard right next to Ia Drang and Al Nasriyeh?

"Oh, yes . . . something for each of us to tell our children and our grandchildren. 'Why yes, Johnny, I was there pulling pitch . . . or turning a wrench . . . or running tests of the electronics when the Rotten-muncher hammered the last shackle on the United States. Yep . . . that was me, your old grandpappy, helping make the world unsafe for democracy."

Most present in the tent laughed; First Sergeant Henry was one of those characters a lucky unit has; treasured because of—not in spite of—his humor and cynicism.

One warrant pilot did not laugh. Chewing and swallowing his bite of "undifferentiated meat with dif-ferentiated sauce" quickly, this warrant officer, CWO2 Harrington, asked, "And what the hell are we supposed to do, Top? We get our orders. We follow them."

Henry's lip curled in a sneer, not at the warrant so much as at the world. "Do, sir? Why I didn't say we should 'do' anything. Why that would be mutiny, sir, and I would, of course, never counsel mutiny. Why

I would not even suggest to you gentlemen—oh, and ladies—that you remember your oaths to the country, because if I did then—who knows?—you might mutiny on your own.

"No sir, not me, never. No mutiny from this end.

"I might, though, ask the chaplain—oh, and you, too, sir," Henry indicated with a finger the battalion's JAG officer, "if it would be mutiny to ask God to help those men in the WCF that are going to be fighting there soon for our freedom."

Henry looked around for the unit chaplain. Finding him, and catching the chaplain's eye, the first sergeant shouted, "Hey 'Chap,' can we make this a *prayer* breakfast?"

In Flight

Sawyers shouted into the ear of the newsman assigned to follow him and his command into the Western Currency Facility. "They haven't got a prayer, those dumb bastards on the receiving end."

"Why's that, Commander," asked the newsman.

"We're trained professionals, son. Those guys are just part-timers."

"You or your men ever clear a fortified building before?"

"A building's not fortified unless it's well defended," countered Sawyers. "And I don't see those amateurs putting up much of a defense. Hope they had a decent breakfast. It's likely to be their last one that isn't behind bars."

Western Currency Facility, Fort Worth, Texas

"What's for breakfast, cookie?" asked Fontaine.

The mess sergeant sneered, not at Fontaine but at a battery of flat silver containers. "Same as usual, bubba: undifferentiated meat with differentiated sauce; accompanied by only mildly radioactive, notionally wholesome, 'potatoes-all-rotten'; optional fake ham omelet; and some half decent coffee. We're running short on sugar for the coffee, though, so go easy."

Cookie never had cared for being rendered half obsolete by modern T-rations.

"Sounds, umm, great, cookie. Let me have—"

Pendergast's voice thundered, "Breakfast in the mess is cancelled. Get your asses to your battle positions. NOW, people! Move, *move*, MOVE!"

Fontaine quickly added two and two, coming up with the mathematically perfect answer of, "Hungry, and soon." With a mumbled, "Thanks, cookie," he reached directly into the trays of food, extracting several slices of meat and a scooped palm-full of omelet.

Ignoring the cook's outraged look even as he did his successful best to avoid the cook's flailing spatula, Fontaine's heart began to beat quickly as he joined the arm-flailing, grunting, wall-slapping herd of guardsmen racing from the mess to join their comrades at the walls.

Outside and above the WCF, the bulk of the pilots were mildly surprised that there was no groundfire. That they were also somewhat pleased by the lack went almost without saying. Quick glances at the facility's roof showed no possible landing place. They'd known this in advance and had not even planned such. Instead, the choppers brought the PGSS to soft and safe landings well away from the target building.

Commander Sawyers—he had managed to escape from arrest at the mission where the problem had begun—grunted with satisfaction at seeing the brisk, orderly, and frankly military way his men dispersed from their helicopters, took the prone, then raced for their initial objectives.

All those objectives were, of course, at or just past the outside limit of effective small arms fire from the WCF.

As the last of his men reached those objectives, and the last of the ferrying helicopters departed, Sawyers advanced with one other man and a loud speaker.

"Attention. Attention, all you people inside the currency facility. In the name of the President of the United States and the Secretary of the Treasury I call upon you to surrender, now, while there is still time. You will be tried—at a minimum—for criminal trespass on Federal property in accordance with the laws of the United States. . . ."

It was only with difficulty that Williams was able to keep the stress and fear out of his voice. He'd never been in real action before, not unless one considered representing a client before the Tax Court could be considered "action." Williams somehow didn't think it was quite the same.

Still, feeling stress and fear or not, Williams' words were clear when he asked, "How do you answer something like that, Top—err, Sergeant Major?"

Pendergast thought briefly, spit some tobacco juice, then answered, "I think I'd answer it with Royce."

"Royce?" asked the newly promoted Major Williams.

"Yessir. Best goddamned shot in the unit, bar none. Royce."

"Royce," Williams mused. "Royce? Sure, why the hell not? Might as well add to our charges. And it'll be harder for anybody to back out after the shooting starts. Royce. Fontaine, go get me Sergeant Royce, would you please?"

Baffled as it was by the building and the slit through which Royce fired, from his distance Sawyers never heard the actual discharge of the shot. One moment he was speaking into a microphone, holding the loudspeaker in his left hand. The next the speaker was torn away, hissing, sparking, sputtering and crackling as it died. Only then did he hear the crack of the bullet as it left its shock wave behind.

Tossing the ruined thing to the pavement furiously, Sawyers muttered, "So you motherfuckers want to play it that way, do you? Assholes!"

To the accompanying newsman, Sawyers said, "Did you see that? Did you see? I offered them a chance to surrender peacefully and they shot at me. What's going to happen now is on their own heads."

I thought you said they'd surrender, thought the newsman. *Wonder what else you're wrong about.*

Sawyers turned on his heel, stomped off to his command post—sitting behind a nearby wall, and began to issue orders into a radio.

❖   ❖   ❖

The Guard didn't use their radios, too afraid of the transmissions being intercepted. Instead, they used the intercom system the WCF had had when they first occupied it.

"Major Williams, this is Davis down in the command post. Whatever you just did riled up a hornet's nest. I've got reports of troops advancing on all sides. I'm only catching glimpses of them on the security cams but I think they're serious."

Instead of answering directly, Williams flipped his intercom to make an announcement to the entire defending force. "Listen up, everybody. Hold your fire until I give the word. But keep me posted."

Using a periscope the engineers had jinned up for him from some broken bathroom mirrors and spare lumber (for a video camera similarly mounted would not only have been heavier, but might have needed hard-to-find batteries), Williams observed as small groups of black battledress-clad men advanced on the walls of his post using whatever cover—and that not much—was available.

When they reached the last of that sparse cover, though, those men stopped.

Williams called to all walls to report.

"Wall two: they've stopped advancing. . . . Wall three: looks like they've held up about where we cleared fields of fire to, but there aren't that many of them on this side. . . . Major, this is the rotunda. They've got a man behind nearly every one of those pylons by the walkway. And I think there's more in the deadspace past those."

Williams thought it curious that with combat so near his heartbeat had slowed, the nervousness had

evaporated and that sullen, sinking feeling he had
been carrying in the pit of his stomach had disappeared. He did not hesitate any longer. "Sergeant
Major, take the reserve platoon and all the machine
guns and reinforce the rotunda. You can fire if they
try to assault; don't wait for my command."

"Sir!"

Sawyers thought it would be a fine thing if he could
take the building even before the rest of the brigade
showed up. He mused, silently, *Not that anyone told
me to take it on my own. Then again, nobody said
not to and I was told to try to get them to surrender.
That would have been taking the building back too.
Seems like a simple extrapolation to me. . . . Besides,
I'd truly like to get the bastards that shot up my unit
at that old priest's mission.*

"Sir, the last company reports they're in position
on the other side of the building."

"Thanks, Ricky. Send to all companies: open fire. Tell
B Company they can begin their assault anytime."

Half frantic, Pendergast pushed, prodded and
physically shoved the machine gunners and the reserve
platoon into their positions. "Move it, damn it, move
it. We haven't got all fucking day. And remember,
hold your fire until *I* say to shoot. This might turn
out to be nothing."

Whatever Pendergast may have been feeling inside,
to the men pushed, prodded and shoved he merely
seemed very determined, perhaps even eager.

The positions themselves were set back some
few feet from the once glass-clad, now boarded and

sandbagged, floor-to-ceiling windows. The set back gave the positions, and the men inside them, a measure of protection from the concussion of shaped charges and demolitions that might be detonated against the walls. Most of these positions, made of wood and metal, sandbags and furniture, had but a single, narrow, slit of a firing port in those walls. This also made it all but impossible for an attacker to suppress those positions with rifle fire as the men inside were offset from the slits, their sectors of fire interlocking outside the building. There were also a few very strongly built bunkers that were right up against the walls. The men in these, machine gunners mostly, had much wider fields of fire.

With a grunt of satisfaction at seeing the last men slithering into their battle stations, Pendergast himself got down on his belly and crawled to a well-camouflaged observation post to watch developments.

At the OP, Pendergast selected two of four claymore clackers, one in each hand. These were wired, each to a different claymore mine, the mines themselves buried under broken glass from the windows and daisy chained together with explosive cord, called "det cord." Setting off either one would cause a chain reaction that would spill over ten thousand ball bearings outward from the rotunda.

From outside, rifle fire began to crack and splat against the walls.

"Hold your goddamned fire," the sergeant major shouted above the din, reminding the men. Even so, men snugged rifles closer to shoulders while others inspected linked machine-gun ammunition for kinks.

One near hit split a sand bag and drove sand and dust into Pendergast's eyes. By the time he had blinked away the grit and looked out again, a smoke screen was building.

"Top, I can't see shit," called one gunner.

"That's 'Sergeant Major' to you, son. Just hold your fire."

Pendergast raised his eyes to the view port. *Goddammit, can't see a damned thing. Can't hear much either. Wish I had one of those new thermal imaging rifle sights I was reading about a few months back. Then I could see through this damned smoke. Wish we all did. Might as well wish for the moon.*

Outside, there was a steady crackle of small arms fire from the men behind the pylons. Behind those, in the dead space—low ground protected from direct fire—grenadiers with 40mm grenade launchers popped up to fire small smoke shells before ducking back down to reload.

"Goddammit, I wish I had one lousy section of mortars to lay smoke," fumed the B Company commander as he watched his grenadiers load and fire, load and fire the little 40mm smoke grenades. "We'd have a screen then, a real one."

Even so, though, the grenades weren't doing a bad job. When he judged the time right, the screen adequate, he ordered forward two squads of men carrying much larger and more effective hexachloroethane, HC, smoke grenades. These they began to toss forward once they had crawled within throwing range of the screen laid by the grenadiers.

From both the forty-millimeter jobs, and the

hand-thrown grenades, a mild cross wind blew an impenetrable screen; impenetrable by sight, that is.

That was when the commander ordered his assault team forward.

"Oh, you stupid, stupid bastard," fumed Pendergast as he heard the shouts and scuffle of approaching men. "What the hell did your men ever do to deserve having an idiot like you in charge? Didn't anyone ever tell you the difference between cover and concealment?"

Pendergast flipped the safeties off of the two clackers he still held in his hand. As the temporary plywood wall resounded with the impact of one or more men slamming against it, he muttered, "Lord, for what they are about to receive . . ."

Then Pendergast squeezed the clackers.

Electricity, a mild charge actually, raced down the wires to two widely spaced claymores. At the mines, the charge nudged the otherwise fairly insensitive blasting caps into action. Deciding that the charge was sufficient, the caps did their job, exploding inside the pound-and-a-quarter of C-4 held by each of the two mines.

The Composition-4, a very high explosive, also shocked into awakeness, duly detonated, fragmenting both the case and the layer of seven-hundred-odd resinated ball bearings to its front. Those twin explosions likewise set off the det cord running from the fuse wells in the mines that had no fuses in them.

As fast as the ball bearings were moving, it was as nothing compared to the speed of detonation of the det cord. Before the projectiles had managed to travel much more than a foot, the second set of mines likewise detonated as the exploding det cord reached them. These in turn set off another strand of det cord each, which likewise set off another pair of mines.

In all, fifteen claymores, packing over ten thousand ball bearings, went off within approximately one one hundred and fiftieth of a second.

And that was not the worst of it.

This close to the blasts, the worst of it was the glass from the deliberately broken out windows that had served to cover and camouflage the claymores. This was no lightweight stuff; nothing but the best for the Treasury Department. The glass shattered under the blast, yes. But it shattered into fragments even more lethal than the ball bearings.

Those men nearest the wall, the one squad that had reached it first, were literally torn into fragments—chunks of bloody, disassociated meat. Farther away, where the glass had lost some of its initial velocity due to its relatively low density, it merely ripped and blinded.

The ball bearings were denser. They continued on unless stopped by something. In the case of twenty-seven "agents" of the PGSS, that something was human flesh. They went down as if scythed, arms flying and torsos hurled backwards.

Body armor stopped many of the glass and steel fragments, of course. Body armor did not cover arms, legs and faces.

Those ball bearings that did not impact on a body, which was—indeed—most of them, continued on.

Some of these went too high and were lost. Others buried themselves in the ground. In at least one case, however, a chunk of fourteen that had remained stuck fast together by the resin impacted on a grenadier who had neglectfully left his armored vest open. The chunk of steel and resin stayed together until it was halfway through his body. At that point, under the stress of rapid deceleration, the ball bearings said their goodbyes to each other and began to take somewhat different tracks out of the body.

And then, of course, came the glass—following the ball bearings dutifully. These slivers and splinters left a swath of screaming, face-tearing, blinded men in their wake.

Dutifully, the B Company commander had had his own head up, watching for signs of progress from his assault team. His eyes registered, indeed it was the last thing they ever registered, the sudden billowing of the smoke screen as the claymore on the far side of it detonated. Before another image could register, the man's face and eyes were hopelessly shredded by shards and splinters.

The commander felt nothing, at first; just the sudden shock of losing his vision. Then his ears were assaulted, first by the blast, then by the rising tide of horrified, anguished screams from the torn, bleeding remnants of his company.

Then came pain and, with the pain, realization. Following the realization of what had happened came the realization that it was to be permanent.

The commander added his screams to those of his men: "I'm bliiinnnddd!"

❖   ❖   ❖

Pendergast fought down the nausea that threatened to engulf him. *Ah, Jesus, you poor bastards.* Drawing in a deep breath he shouted to the half-stunned defenders, "Fire!"

Sawyers didn't need to be told to understand what had happened to his B Company. The ashen faced, trembling, vomiting and demoralized remnants that staggered out of the smoke, some dragging bodies and parts of bodies with them, told all that was needed.

One man—Sawyers didn't recognize him through the sheet of blood on his face and the strange, uncertain, staggering gait—walked right into the path of unseen tracers. The burst took him in the legs and spun him end over end.

It was a very long burst. Before it ended, and while the man was still flying, one bullet—at least one—passed into the man's body where the armor did not cover, at the juncture of neck and shoulder.

"Those murdering motherfuckers!" he hissed to the media type that followed him. "Did you see what they did to my man? Did you get it on film?"

Not waiting for an answer, Sawyers tore the microphone from Ricky's hand and screamed into it at the company facing the wall opposite the one B Company had tried, unsuccessfully, to breach. "A Company! Get me in! Get me a goddamned breach in that fucking wall!"

Down in an office labeled "Security," deep in the bowels of the WCF, Davis' eyes scanned the closed circuit cameras that ringed the building. Tapping the intercom, he announced, "They're going to try for Wall Four."

The B Company commander had been a not very bright treasury agent with a degree, transferred in for the chances of advancement. The A Company commander, a solid little fireplug of a man, was an ex-Marine infantryman with a combat action ribbon and a bronze star from the Second Gulf War. He had transferred in because he *liked* combat action and the PGSS had seemed like a good place for it.

The ex-Marine had heard the sound of the blasts, clearly—heard the screams, faintly—and had a very good idea of what the two added up to.

"Forget the *effing* smoke for now," he ordered his grenadiers. "I want HE grenades at every possible place along or in front of that wall."

Within seconds the dull crump of exploding 40mm high explosive could be heard hitting the base of Wall Four. The A Company commander had no certain idea of how effective they were. In truth, he hardly expected to set off a string of daisy-chained claymores by sympathetic detonation of the HE. He *did* expect to displace those claymores, to ruin their preset aim.

But, sometimes, one's expectations are exceeded. One round of 40mm HE, stray or random, managed to hit almost exactly dead center on almost the exactly most central claymore. The resulting small explosion resulted in a dozen larger ones.

Ball bearings, another ten thousand of them, arced out. Unfortunately for the defenders, they arced out where the PGSS should have been had they assaulted directly.

"Anyone hit?" queried the commander through his radio.

"Negative . . . Negative . . . Third platoon. I've got two minor wounded. . . . Negative."

"Ring team in!"

"The claymores went off prematurely," Williams heard Davis announce over the intercom. "I can't see a damned thing."

"Ah shit," the major muttered, then pressed the intercom button. "Pendergast? Sergeant Major? If you can hear this still, I'm taking what I can scrape together and heading for Wall Four. Join me as fast as you can or we're screwed. . . ."

"Fontaine? Go carry that message to the sergeant major. Run, boy!"

Williams turned to the half dozen men immediately nearest him. "The rest of you; follow me!"

Through blind, unaimed fire sprinted the half dozen men of the "ring team." Identified by and with their "ring"—a linear shaped charge twisted into a donut shape and used to blast a fairly precise circular hole in the wall of a building to be assaulted—the ring team duty was about as popular as carrying a flame thrower into fire had once been. Even so, they sprinted despite carrying the awkward charge. The men cursed the ring charge even as they cursed the nearby crackling fire that plucked at their fragile lives.

"Godammit. One fucking LAV, just *one*, to carry us up and give us a little supporting cannon fire . . ."

"Shut up, Corson. The LAVs will get here behind the Army's Third Corps," answered the squad leader.

And then they were at the wall. "Slap it up, slap it up." With practiced precision—this commander had spent more time training and rehearsing his men than he had on political lectures—the team affixed the charge to the wall.

Charge firmly in place, the leader pulled the friction igniter attached to the fuse that led to the blasting cap. Then the team sprinted back a half dozen meters, screaming, "Fire in the hole! Fire in the hole! Fire in the hole!"

Captain James happened to be standing, pistol in hand and shouting encouragement to his men, a scant few feet from where the entrance charge was set. When it detonated, a shower of disassociated bricks first pummeled him into unconsciousness, then half buried him in one corner of the room.

This was all that saved his life for in the next moment the ring team began deluging the wide-eyed, shocked and terrified defenders of the room with fragmentation grenades. Even where the light fragments did no harm, the concussion in that enclosed space was stunning, deadening—in the case of every other man in the room but James, deadly.

Into that confused, smoke-and-dust-filled maelstrom burst the ring team, bayonets fixed and blood in their eyes.

"That's the signal, boys," announced the fireplug at seeing the distinctly green smoke from the signal grenade popped by the ring team. "Now on your bellies . . . crawl up to the breach. But crawl *fast*."

❖   ❖   ❖

"Faster, dammit," Williams demanded of the men slithering under the mass of corridor blocking wire suspended above. "We've got one chance to kick their asses out of the building or it's room to room and we'll all be dead before nightfall."

Where the hell is Pendergast? he wondered.

"Firs— . . . I mean . . . Sergeant Major," Fontaine fought to make himself heard over the din of continuous machine-gun fire reverberating inside the rotunda.

"What the fuck is it, Fontaine?"

Huffing and puffing with the effort made to bring word to Pendergast, Fontaine briefly stopped trying to speak, drew a breath, then shouted, "Major Williams sent me to tell you . . . Wall Four is under attack and he's going to try to hold it. He said you were supposed to come, too. He ain't got too many men with him, Fir— . . . uh, Sergeant Major. Maybe half a dozen."

Pendergast rubbed the fingers of both hands along the side of his nose as he digested the news. *Williams will go right for the likely breach,* he thought. *That's okay, far as it goes . . . but it won't do more than hold a line inside the building. Soo . . .*

"Cease fire, cease *fire*."

As he waited for the word to spread and the noise to die down, Pendergast forced his mind to concentrate. *We've got a middling clear route, well . . . middling quick anyway, if we go upstairs. Then I can tell from the noise where the bad guys are. And then we come through the ceiling, right in behind them. Seal the breach and chop up any unfriendly intruders. Ought to work*, he told himself, skeptically. *Best chance, anyway*, he thought, hopefully.

"Okay, boys, now here's the plan. . . ."

"Don't you just love it when, fucking plan comes together?" muttered the fireplug as he pushed himself through the jagged hole made by the ring charge.

The dust had cleared enough for him to see the shot, hacked and blasted bodies of the defenders his men had left behind them as they advanced. The fireplug shook a fireplug-shaped head. *I'm sorry, guys. Truth be told, I'd rather be in here fighting* with *you than inside or outside fighting* against *you. But I had my orders.*

Ahead, firing broke out afresh. With a glance backwards at the two thirds of his command still crawling forward under fire, the commander marched to the sound of the guns.

"Smitty," called Williams loudly. At the order Smithfield stuck his M-16 out past the corner behind which he sheltered and fired a half dozen unaimed bursts. At the opposite corner, Corporal Petty armed a fragmentation grenade, released the spoon, and threw the grenade down the corridor between the corners.

Williams' party heard someone cry, "Grenade!" Williams himself was pretty sure he heard someone else yell, "Shit!" before human sounds were muffled by the grenade's blast.

"Figueroa," William called. From beneath Petty another rifle was thrust outward and another series of short bursts flew.

❖   ❖   ❖

"Did you hear that?" asked Pendergast.

"Hear what, Top . . . I mean Sergeant Major?"

"That explosion . . . wait . . . there went another one. Grenade, I think."

"Oh, that," admitted Fontaine. "Yeah, Sergeant Major. It did sort of sound like a grenade . . . near as I can remember."

"Okay . . . Fontaine, you take six men and put them on the firing ports we've got cut in the wall on this floor."

"Me, Top?" asked a wide eyed, disbelieving Fontaine.

"Yes, you, son. I want you to stop any more men from getting into whatever kind of hole they've knocked in the wall below us. Remember you've also got a couple of places cut you can roll hand grenades out. Use your judgment, son, but *stop them from getting through that breach.*

"Oh . . . any that are trying to leave? You just go ahead and let them. Got it?"

The young soldier's chest swelled. "You can count on me, Top . . . I mean Sergeant Major."

"I always knew *that*, Fontaine. The rest of you: there's a hatchway leading down four doors thataway. We're going down it and we're gonna hit them in the ass. Now—and *quietly*—follow me."

The fireplug risked a brief glance halfway around a corner. *Now isn't that a kick in the ass*, he thought as he glimpsed the mass of tangled up, gnarled barbed wire that blocked his men's forward progress. *Clever bastards, using that old World War One trench blocking idea here.*

The bodies of two of his men, gunned down while trying to move the wire, indicated that any further attempts would be futile ... futile and bloody.

Suddenly, without any warning whatsoever, the fireplug's attention was pulled away by the sound of explosions—more than a dozen, he thought—of automatic rifle fire, and the screams of struggling, dying men.

Pendergast held one finger to his lips before bending down to remove—oh, so quietly and carefully—the rubberized runner concealing the trap door. He made a motion to the belt of his combat harness while mouthing the word, "grenade." The dozen men nearest him each pulled one hand grenade from his own belt and flicked away the safety clip. Following the sergeant major's lead, a baker's dozen pins were pulled.

Pendergast motioned for two more men to stand ready with their rifles. Then he reached down and pulled up the trap door.

"Get out, get *out*!" ordered the fireplug. "We can't go forward, not with what we have and we need to hurry if we're not going to lose our only way out." Hand placed firmly between a young "agent's" shoulder blades, the fireplug gave a firm shove, and then turned around for the next. Soon, the ex-Marine turned to find no more men behind him and the sound of the Texans' advance growing closer.

There was a low moan followed by the sound of shifting bricks. The A Company commander looked to one corner and stared into the single beady eye of a 9mm pistol. His eyes followed the pistol to the wavering hand, the hand to the arm, and the arm to the bruised, bleeding man half buried by the bricks.

"What's your name?" asked James.

"Crenshaw," answered the fireplug.

"Well, go on, Crenshaw. I never could shoot a man whose name I knew."

CHAPTER FOURTEEN

From the transcript at trial: Commonwealth of
Virginia v. Alvin Scheer

DIRECT EXAMINATION, CONTINUED
BY MR. STENNINGS:

Q. So you did hear about the first attack on the
Western Currency Facility?

A. Oh, yes, sir. And I was tickled pink, too. It was a
scream, I tell you. I like to split my sides when I
heard. The feds tried to take that money printin'
plant at a rush and got their asses handed to 'em
by my home folks.

Not that it wasn't kind of sad, too, them boys
that got killed. But, I figured they took their money
and they took their chances, same as anyone.

Not that the papers hereabouts took my view
of it, mind you. Oh, no. I read every one I could
get my hands on. That included a couple from
what you might call the "lunatic fringe."

You know the kind I mean: *Save the Whales— Abort the Babies? Marxist-Leninist Times? The Anarchist?* Hey, I'm quoting here. I ain't smart enough to think up them titles.

Anyways, real far left stuff—chock full of all kinds of words I had never heard and couldn't even find in the dictionary. You know, the kind of thing that used to make a hobby of hatin' Washington and the President of the United States?

The mildest one of those, if I can recall correctly, called for turnin' Texas into a prairie.

Guess they didn't know we already mostly were a prairie.

Anyways, I didn't see—no one saw, far as I know—that incident on TV. Don't know whether that was because there weren't any news folks there or because the scene was just too damned nasty.

Besides, pretty soon there was lots of bigger news.

Washington, DC

If anyone noticed the scent of musk on the President as she entered the Oval Office followed by McCreavy, no one said anything. They were broad-minded men and women, all, and not a few of them had tastes similar to the President's.

"All right, what happened at the Western Currency Facility?" demanded Rottemeyer.

Vega gave the official story. "Our people there

called on the criminals inside to surrender. They lulled a large number of agents into the open then they opened fire. We attacked but were driven back by superior numbers and firepower."

McCreavy rolled her eyes. *Can't even make up a good lie, too damned ignorant.*

"How about this, Ms. Vega? You can't take a building like that, heavily fortified and defended, with less than ten to one odds. And then you can expect to lose almost everyone you throw at it."

"That's a military answer, Caroline," corrected the President. "It might even be a true one. But Jesse's answer serves our purposes better.

"There is a military answer I need, though. Are your forces ready to roll?"

"Everywhere but from New Mexico. The commander down there, a Marine," she added with a trace of disdain, "says he simply can't move anywhere much. No fuel beyond what his vehicles have in their tanks and a severe shortage of ammunition."

"Those goddamned sit-down strikers on the highway?"

"Yes," McCreavy answered. "Per your order we were waiting for the Presidential Guard to clear out the Currency Facility, before sending them to clear the highway. Obviously, they've been delayed."

"Do they have enough to get them to El Paso or a little beyond?"

"I asked the commander down there that question. He said he could."

"Have him do that then. All your forces. I want them to roll tomorrow morning."

McCreavy closed her eyes, holding in a wistful sigh.

I wish it had never come to this. Eyes still closed she silently nodded her acceptance.

Rottemeyer added, "We'll send the Surgeon General's riot control police down to New Mexico, instead of the Presidential Guard. They should be able to handle the problem."

Las Cruces, New Mexico

The Marine Corps Reserve truck driver—he was a California boy named Mendez—looked out at the sea of humanity blocking the highway before him. "Whew; I didn't think New Mexico had this many people in it."

"What you carrying, son?" asked the state trooper balancing on the truck's running board while hanging from its rearview mirror.

"I'm not sure I should say, sir." The driver looked down at the trooper's chest and read a name tag, "Peters."

The trooper—Peters—smiled grandly. "Well, you can say or we can just arrest you now; whatever's your preference."

The driver gave off a loud sigh. "Ammunition, mostly."

"Ah, I see. Well . . . come with me. Let's see if your truck is properly marked." The trooper stepped down.

The driver emitted another sigh as he opened his door to follow.

"It's always amazed me how often you guys hauling ammo fail to put up the signs required by federal law," commented the trooper as he ripped a "Danger-Peligro" sign from the side of the truck, folding it and tucking it in his shirt.

"But . . . but . . ."

"And another thing; you know how often you mix up incompatible loads of ammunition? Why, it's a national disgrace," he added while tearing off another bit of paper, this one stating in precise terms what kind of ammunition the truck was carrying.

The trooper looked the driver squarely in the eye and ordered, "Son, you are just gonna have to unload this here truck and let me inspect it."

"But, sir . . . it's over twenty tons of ammunition. I can't, I just *can't*; not in less than a week."

If possible the trooper's friendly smile grew broader and grander still. "I know."

La Union, New Mexico

The 1st Marine Division command post fairly crackled with energy. It crackled with radio transmissions as well.

The barrel-chested, iron-jawed major general in command, one Richard Fulton, stared with disgust at the charts hanging from the tent's frame along its walls. These showed all the pertinent information on the division, from personnel to logistics. It was the last which raised Fulton's disgust.

His unit's supply status merely raised the disgust, however. The voice coming from a radio's speaker gave it force. The Division's "Zampolit"—the Russian word had gained wide currency by now—sitting in a corner, amplified it even more.

He listened to, "And so, yes, despite your logistic inconveniences, you are ordered to proceed into Texas, commencing tomorrow morning at 0400, liberate El Paso, then proceed generally east along Interstate 10 to San Antonio. As you proceed, you are to drop off adequate forces southward along the Mexican border to seal that border as you go."

Fulton clenched frustration into a balled fist. "General McCreavy . . . you realize, do you not, that I have the fuel to get to approximately Van Horn, Texas, before my tanks are bone dry? And *that* is assuming I do not have to fight the Texans on the way. They can pull back, wait for me to run out of fuel, then beat the hell out of me. That's open country, great for tanks, not so great for infantry. And my force is mostly infantry . . . and the Texans—the ones facing me anyway—are mostly not."

"We are working on your logistic problems from this end, General Fulton. By the time you reach the eastern edge of El Paso, you can expect a clear supply route."

"I'll believe that when I see it. But fine then . . . fine. I'll start moving in the morning."

Marietta, Oklahoma

Nobody felt like singing "Garryowen" this morning.

It was a perfect time for it; the sun rising in the east, the smell of fresh diesel and motor oil on the gentle breeze, hundreds of thousands of tons of steel rolling in a long massive pike down the highway.

Still, nobody felt like singing.

Third Corps was coming back. They had left at command and now they were returning at command. They had left with reluctance and now they returned with much the same feeling.

Silent and sullen, the drivers and commanders scarcely risked a glance at the protesters lining either side of the highway. Yet they did glance from time to time and they did read some of the signs the protesters carried. "Don't mess with Texas," said some. "Thou shalt not kill," said some few others, a message pretty much lost on the professional killers of the Third Corps.

"The South shall rise again," "Lee surrendered; we didn't," and "Get Washington off our backs," were sentiments many, many of the officers and men of the largely southern and largely rural corps shared fully.

Moving at full speed, which is to say—roadmarch speed, the point of the Corps took little time in reaching the Texas-Oklahoma line. There it paused, briefly, waiting for federal police to come and clear away the eight or nine thousand Oklahoman protesters who put their own mortal bodies between Texas and harm.

These same federal law enforcement types had known of the protest and had stationed themselves fairly far forward in the long snaking column of medium armor. With truncheons and dogs, they set into the protesters quickly. Even so, since the protesters seemed willing to be beaten or bitten rather than simply leave, dispersing them took some time.

Curiously, though there were news reporters at the scene, not one report that day on national television showed the weeping women, the split and bleeding skulls, the canine chewed faces the federal police left in their wake.

Still, though the nation did not see, the men of Third Corps did. And this was not without significance.

North of Gainesville, Texas

"Mission accomplished, sir," the sergeant said to Bernoulli with a crisp salute. The "mission" had been to considerably reinforce the demolition charges previously set on the bridge to the north. From wherever it had come, General Schmidt had come through with enough—truth be told, more than enough—demolitions to bring down every bridge in the state, twice over.

Bernoulli returned the salute, then nodded solemnly. "Okay, Sergeant. Get the boys loaded up then take them to the next bridge down. I'll stay here until it's time to blow this one, then I'll join you later assuming I can get away."

"Sir . . ." the sergeant began to protest, but Bernoulli was having none of it.

"Don't argue," he said with an upraised palm. "Just go."

"Yes, sir," answered the sergeant, then, turning to the troops, he ordered, "All right, you dickheads, load 'em up. We're heading back."

Within minutes, Bernoulli was alone at his command post by the bridge complex spanning the Trinity River.

Not that he was entirely alone; nearby and ahead remained a mixed tank and mechanized infantry task force and a battery of superb New Mexican air defense artillery. But these were there for their threat value, to seem so dangerous that the federals would be prevented from grabbing the bridge with a helicopter insertion.

Yet, still, Bernoulli was alone with his mission and his thoughts.

Dark thoughts they were, full of the doubts that he never let anyone see. Am I doing the right thing? Is this the only way? Can I get by with saying "I am only following orders" when I have a choice of the orders I could follow?

A captain from the infantry interrupted Bernoulli's reveries. "I just got the word. The Corps is about ten miles out. Their point elements will be here in fifteen or twenty minutes; half an hour, tops. I told my people to get back here and over this bridge before there isn't any bridge to cross on."

"Just let me know when the last of them is across," reminded Bernoulli.

"You'll be able to see yourself; two tanks, four tracks, each with a big white star painted on front."

Ahead, from the north, came the sound of a 120mm cannon firing, distance and distortion making it seem more like natural thunder. The captain picked up a microphone and listened briefly.

To Bernoulli, he announced, "That was just a warning shot, nobody hit. My boys said the Corps was pushing them a little hard and they needed some breathing space. The point of the Corps is deploying now. We should get a few extra minutes."

"Just get them over the bridge before the Corps shows up, sir, preferably with a few minutes to spare in case something goes wrong."

After some short time had passed the pair heard, faintly, the roar of the Bradleys' diesels. They were still too far away to pick up the quiet whine of the tanks' turbines.

"There they are," announced the captain, pointing at the small column of six armored vehicles racing towards them.

Feeling a lump grow in his throat, Bernoulli nodded while affixing one wire to a post on his detonator. With hands trembling slightly he attached the second wire. *I guess this is really it.*

"Please tell your men to hurry, sir," Bernoulli advised.

"Yeah, I know, 'restrained response.' We don't want to have to blow up the bridge with a hundred guys from Third Corps on it when we do."

"No, sir. Though if I have to . . ." Bernoulli left the thought unspoken. *If I have to, I'm not sure I can.*

The small covering force reached the bridge then. They were close enough, and the engines racing fast enough, that Bernoulli could just make out the turbines' whining under the diesels' throbbing. Then he felt through his legs the slight tremors as three hundred tons of steel moved, and moved fast, across the bridge.

"It's on you, now, bubba," the captain announced as the last of his vehicles passed Bernoulli's command post. "Should we take cover?"

Distantly, Bernoulli answered, "Not necessary. The bridge will blow, mostly, down."

"Best do it then."

"Yes, sir." Bernoulli clutched both hands to his chest, the detonator between them. He clutched and then, unaccountably, froze.

"Lieutenant? Are you going to blow it or not?"

Bernoulli remained frozen. *Am I going to "blow it"?*

Across the river, a few miles away up the highway, the first of Third Corps LAVs, Light Armored Vehicles, made an abrupt appearance.

Ohh, shit. Bernoulli steeled himself. He set his jaw in a tight grimace. Then he closed his eyes and forced his hands together.

"Wow! Oh, my God! Holy fucking shit, that was fucking great!" The captain jumped up and down, in plain sight, shouting praise and waving two upright fingers in the general direction of the LAVs massing on the other side of the river. "Son, you done good," he continued, pounding Bernoulli on the back with exuberance.

"I went to college to learn to build bridges, sir, not to blow them up," answered Bernoulli, trying to retain his dignity under the pounding. With one hand he dusted from his uniform fine concrete from the shattered and sundered bridge.

With a last look at the Trinity River, now boasting a set of rapids it had never had before, Bernoulli recovered his detonator, got in his Hummer, and drove south.

Beaumont, Texas

The Trinity River flowed generally north to south, passing between Houston and Beaumont before spilling itself into the Gulf of Mexico. East of that river, east also of Beaumont, ran a series of creeks, rivers, and bayous. Most of these were too swift, too deep, too muddy, or had too insubstantial a set of banks for easy fording.

A LAV would float and even, after a fashion, swim. It took some preparation and, even so, water was not precisely the LAVs optimum environment. The Marines of the 2nd Division had LAVs, of course, as did the Army's 3rd Infantry Division, both moving quickly westward towards their final objective, Houston.

But the Marines had more than LAVs; they had AMTRACs, Amphibious Tractors. And the AMTRACs' optimum environment *was* the water.

Thus, while a mixed company of Texas Guard infantry and tanks, reinforced by some air defense, was enough to prevent a helicopter insertion to seize a bridge—as it had been up north—it was not enough to stop the reinforced battalion of Marines, swimming their AMTRACs, that crossed Cypress Creek between Deweyville and Orange, then fanned out to seize—without a shot being fired—not one but four bridges, along with their engineer defenders. The engineers, like the rest, had been under orders not to shoot.

In panic and despair, the covering force raced back toward Beaumont and even farther westward. Sadly, they did so without so much as a single detonator to blow the bridge over the Trinity River where it was crossed by I-10.

The road to Houston was open . . . and in less than a day.

Washington, DC

"Hah!" exclaimed a jubilant Wilhelmina Rottemeyer when she was given the news. "Hah!" she repeated, "Let's see that wetback wench stop us now! And her precious national guard is running like scared rabbits. Maybe we took all this too seriously."

"They're not running, Madam President," corrected McCreavy. "They're under orders not to shoot to kill; to warn and withdraw. I'm actually kind of amazed that they're following those orders, to tell the truth. It requires a level of discipline somewhat higher than one would expect in a reserve formation."

"Bah," answered Rottemeyer with a contemptuous snort. "They're folding, crumbling."

Exasperated, McCreavy ran fingers through close cropped hair. "I don't know how to make you see this . . . but they're really not. All my commanders report the same. Professionally prepared demolitions, in the hands of people willing to use them, covered by forces that buy them some time and then withdraw . . . rather well, too. And we took some prisoners from the Texans. . . ."

"I want those men to put on trial," insisted Vega.

McCreavy ignored her. "We took some prisoners," she repeated. "They—the ones who would talk anyway—insist that their orders not to shoot are temporary and that at some point Texas will fight. They likely would have fought along the Colorado River and the Balcones Escarpment. But with things having swung our way faster than they might have liked or anticipated, my guess is that they might fight to hold Houston. And that would eat the 2nd Marine and 3rd

Infantry Divisions alive. We need to approach that city *very* carefully."

Austin, Texas

"It's disaster," admitted Schmidt. "No other word will do."

"What can we do about it?" asked Juanita.

"Fight? I can move a brigade from the State Defense Force into the western parts of the city. I can reinforce them with a couple of battalions of mech infantry and even a few tanks."

"But you said the State Defense Force was mostly untrained."

"So they are, Governor, about half trained. But they're more like completely untrained for city fighting. They're not too badly trained—provided they have some help—in defending the fortifications we have thrown up. And the heavy troops aren't the most suitable for a city either. I asked if you wanted me to 'fight.' I didn't say I could 'win.' But this is so bad . . . Juani I have got to fight."

"You will *not* fight, General," insisted the governor.

Though old and waning in strength, Victor Charlesworth had become something of an unofficial member of the Governor's Cabinet. In his best patriarchal voice he said, "I will go. I will fight them . . . my way."

Schmidt didn't answer immediately. He took a long and very hard look at the old actor, seeking the strength, resolve and inner fire the man had once epitomized so well that even through the medium of cellulose it had shone across a million screens.

Deciding, Schmidt asked, "What will you need?"

Charlesworth considered. "Some way to tape a message before I leave. Maybe a helicopter to bring me into the city. A public address set and someone to man it. Some air time for you to send the message after I get there. Maybe a couple of policemen for escort so that when they take me it will be very noticeable. Can you do that?"

"Helicopter's no problem. You can use mine," Schmidt offered. "I think we can set up the PA set, taping and air time, too."

Nagy added, "I can spare a couple of my Rangers. Good men."

"I know," grinned Charlesworth. "I've played them."

"But Mr. Charlesworth," Schmidt cautioned, "this is not acting. If . . . no, when they take you the feds will not be playing roles. They're going to hurt you."

"I'm an old man, General. I've lived my life and—I tell you—it's been a good one. Now? What else do I have to look forward to? Hurt me? I'm counting on it, General." The old actor smiled with anticipation.

Juanita's stomach lurched as she realized there was one more person who needed to accompany Charlesworth. *Mario is going to be so unhappy. . . .*

Las Cruces, New Mexico

"Hurt 'em," insisted the white-uniformed, riot-armored leader of the Surgeon General's special police.

"That's the only thing these people will understand: physical pain. We'll probably be needed somewhere else soon enough. That pain will stick in their minds and keep them from blocking this road any more."

Grimly, the men and women around the speaker nodded their agreement. They didn't salute; that was for the military types. But they went back to their units with an approximately military determination to accomplish their mission, to inflict all the pain these demonstrators could handle.

A whistle blew. The first company of police began marching south down the highway towards the mass of wide-eyed, apparently very frightened people who awaited them. In time with half-stamped left feet came the steady thwap-thwap-thwap of riot batons striking the faces of polycarbonate riot shields. The growing sound added to the growing fright of the people in the crowd as they looked north at the mass descending on them.

At a distance of a few hundred meters, the leader of that first company began to speak into a microphone. His message was not directed towards the demonstrators, but to his own police officers. "Form skirmish line." With clocklike precision the SGRCP began fanning out at the double, forming a line that faced south as it stretched east and west across the north-south highway.

A uniformed Marine reservist, sitting dejectedly atop a pile of ammunition crates next to a large olive drab painted van, was astonished at the clockwork precision of the SGRCP as they formed a double line of club-and shield-bearing skirmishers, in front, rifle-carrying men and women behind.

"Motherfuckers must train *all* the time," he muttered.

From his pile of wooden crates, the reservist saw a recognized face emerge from the civilian crowd, Trooper Peters.

Peters, too, had a PA set. Without having been addressed he announced his name and informed the SGRCP that, "These people have a lawful permit to assemble. They are here at the behest of the Government of New Mexico. They have a right to be here and the New Mexico State Police will defend that right."

On line with Peters, and between the SGRCP and the crowd, a dozen troopers, about half and half armed with pistols and shotguns, began to form their own line.

This time the leader of the RCP did address somebody other than his own people. "I have instructions from the highest levels on dealing with unlawful interference by local authorities. I direct the New Mexico State Police, and any other agencies of the New Mexico State Government, likewise to disperse . . . or you will be fired upon."

The leader turned around, ordering, "Front rank; kneel. Rear rank; take aim."

Peters, and the troopers with him, merely stood grasping their own puny weapons the more tightly. He, really none of them, could quite believe that the SGRCP was serious. This was America, for Christ's sake; police didn't fire on police.

"Fire!"

Without any obvious hesitation, the second rank of the foremost SGRCP company scythed down Peters

and all those men with him. Some of their bullets went
past the troopers into the crowd. Men and women
screamed, children shrieked, as red blood began to
flow onto the black-topped highway before running
off to soak into the New Mexico sand.

"At the double time . . . forward." The RCP began to
wade into the crowd, adding to the flowing blood.

Nearby, a lone, uniformed and highly shocked
Marine reservist simply said, "Motherfuckers . . ."

Sanger, Texas

Clear Creek, just south of Sanger, was not so grand
as the Trinity, even though farther from its sources than
the Trinity had been. Two bridges—one highway, one
railway—spanned it within a few miles of each other.
Bernoulli's orders were to prepare both to be dropped
and, on the approach of federal forces, to drop them.

It had been thought that dropping the earlier
bridges, those spanning the Trinity, might delay the
feds by as much as ten days. In terms of logistics
capacity this had proven true; a mass of trucks had
been stalled on the Trinity's northern bank, along with
many combat vehicles. Others, however, whatever had
been supportable by army engineer ferry, crossed
quickly. And if the drivers kept a nervous eye on
their fuel gauges, still they drove.

Now, with more federals approaching the Clear
Creek bridges, Bernoulli didn't hesitate. A few quick
pumps of his detonator, a roll of artificial thunder
and a cloud of concrete dust, and the bridges settled
into ruin.

I suppose a new hooker would have felt that way, too, thought Bernoulli as he calmly unhooked the wires from the contact posts of his detonator. *The first one's the toughest.*

Governor's Mansion, Austin, Texas

Falling water gurgled in the fountain as Mario and Elpidia walked past. The girl's face seemed less stony, more animated, than usual. These walks had become something of a tradition. At first Elpi had walked alone. Later, Mario had merely sat nearby. Now they walked together, sometimes in silence, sometimes with talk. Today they talked.

"I hated it, Mario. From the first one to the last I just hated it."

"Then why . . ."

"Why did I do it?" asked Elpi. "You're so innocent," she told the older boy, a trace of wistful longing for her own lost innocence in her voice. "I had no education; I had no skills. I had a baby to support." The girl sighed, dreadfully. "It was all I had."

"Well, I won't judge you or anything you have done, Elpi," said Mario, almost—but not quite—reaching out a hand to stroke the girl's cheek. "And it is all past anyway."

"'All past,'" she echoed. "'All.' Even my baby is dead."

Sensing tears not far below the surface Mario started to turn towards Elpi; started and, as usual, stopped.

Elpi continued, "He brought me great difficulty, much hardship. And yet . . . and yet . . . He was my own, my very own, baby. Some people told me to abort him before he was born. But how could I do that? He was my very own flesh."

"You couldn't, Elpi." Mario considered, then asked, "Elpi, do you think you want to have more babies someday?"

"I do not know. Why bring more babies into a world that kills them? Why live in a world that will murder babies?"

"Is that why you agreed to go to Houston? I wish you would not."

She stopped and this time she reached out a hand to a cheek. "I know. And you're sweet, too, Mario. But your mother asked . . . and then, too . . . what would your uncle have wanted?"

Houston, Texas

It was a flashy city, in many ways; a warmer version of multicultural Toronto. Industry, automobiles, the sheer concentration of people there, all combined to foul the air and irritate the eyes and lungs. Tall glass and steel behemoths, the runaway imaginings of modern architecture, hung predatorily over more sedate structures from Houston's not-so-long past.

Ringed with highways that could not be demolished in time, Houston now found itself ringed in steel as well. Along the ring roads and the feeders, the Army's Third Infantry Division to the north, and the Second Marine Division to the south, swept out in long tentacles to embrace the city.

There had been incidents. Schmidt had attempted

to bring all those actually eager to fight under his control, mostly to keep them from doing so on their own initiative. This had been only partially successful; some groups and individuals were simply too paranoid even to trust their state authorities. Thus, on the outskirts of the town, there was some sniping and there were at least two, failed, ambushes.

The federal forces had barely noticed. Rather, they noticed barely enough to induce a bit of caution, to be ever so slightly slowed in their progress.

Thus, the west side of the city, in that area where the Texas National Guard still reigned, the federal forces had not yet taken.

In that hollow space in the federal net, a lone helicopter flew.

"Mr. Charlesworth? I am Colonel Minh. General Schmidt asked me to meet you, to assist, and to observe."

"What did you say? I can't hear a thing," said Charlesworth, cupping a hand to his right ear.

Minh made a "come with me" gesture to lead the old but still towering actor away from the helicopter and the sound and turbine-propelled stench it produced. As Charlesworth followed Minh, three un-uniformed National Guardsmen and two equally plainclothed Texas Rangers unloaded the public address system. A skinny, pretty, dark-skinned girl stood uncertainly nearby.

When they were far enough away for normal conversation to be heard, Minh repeated, "I am Colonel Minh. General Schmidt asked me to meet you, assist, and observe."

"Yes, thank you, Colonel. The General told me to expect you. Is everything ready?"

"'Ready' is an interesting concept, Mr. Charlesworth. You served in the army, I believe. You know, then, that nothing is ever entirely ready. We are ready for this much: after you and these people with you and those who come to hear you speak are utterly crushed, we will exact a price for that crushing. We are also ready to provide the crowd you will speak to and the video cameras that will film the crushing."

Minh's eyes narrowed as he bit his lower lip lightly. "It is a brave thing that you and these people with you are about to do. Unfortunately, that bravery would go unnoticed but for the cynicism of myself and my people who will amplify your bravery and self-sacrifice to a useful level."

"Just who *are* your people, Colonel?"

"Oh, we are a mix. A mix, that is, of former Vietcong and soldiers of the ARVN, the Army of the Republic of Vietnam. And their sons and daughters, too, of course."

"Old enemies, plotting together as friends?"

Minh cast a glance heavenward, wriggling fingers dismissively. "Well, so far from our first home such little political differences as we once had seem trivial now. And we do share certain skills."

Charlesworth knew the rule: "They'll talk to Martin because they don't want to talk to me." The skills of which Minh spoke were the skills of mayhem. And that was the purpose of this entire exercise: to get an overreaction from the federals for propaganda's sake; then to give them an almost equally nasty reaction in return. NonViolent Civil Disobedience depended on this mantra: Listen to us . . . or listen to the sound of the guns.

Anthony, Texas

It was a ballet; a noisy, stinky, dry, dusty, and miserable ballet. With Mexico on its right, a flank hanging in open air to the left, the Army's Third Armored Cavalry regiment—generally referred to as "the Cav" danced tentatively forward.

It *was* a dance; two unequal partners moving in time together. Ahead of the Cav, two task-organized battalions of the 49th Armored Division fired to miss, then fell back to the next set of sand dunes or strip development. Fire and fall back; fire, make the Cav *deploy*, and fall back. Miss just close enough to frighten. Hit the occasional landmark—building or sign post—often enough to let the Cav know that the misses were deliberate. Hit very close once the day's acceptable limits of retreat had been reached.

And the Cavalry danced forward in time with the pirouetting Guard.

McKinney, Texas

"I am getting as sick of this dance as I am of blowing bridges," murmured Bernoulli as the point of Third Corps approached the latest. One handed, with now very practiced ease, he squeezed and another multimillion-dollar structure shuddered, crumpled and began to collapse.

Bernoulli concentrated, no mean feat amidst the roar of thousands of tons of falling concrete, to pick out the sound of the western, Lewisville, bridge demolition. He listened for several minutes before uttering his first, "Oh, shit."

Even as he reached for his radio, the radio crackled into life. "Sir, the demo failed. I don't know why . . . maybe somebody crossed up a couple of pieces of det cord. But only about one in ten of the charges went off. That wasn't enough."

"Do you have time to reset them?" the lieutenant asked.

"Sir . . . Third Corps is already swarming the bridge. No way."

"Oh, shit." Bernoulli reached a quick decision. "Fall back."

Houston, Texas

There had been a day when Charlesworth might well have been able to speak to the crowd even without a PA set. Those days were fallen far behind him. Now, aged beyond anything he had ever expected to see outside of a biblical film role, his voice was weaker even though his heart—in the twin senses of both that which pumped blood and that which defined his spirit—was as strong as ever.

The crowd, about twenty thousand of Houston's more than four million, filled an area of not more than a couple of acres in the city's Galleria area. For this, the PA set was more than adequate.

Though weaker, Charlesworth's speaking voice had

lost none of its inner power. Electric amplifiers added whatever time had stolen.

"Almost two centuries ago, and just about two hundred and fifty miles from here, a group of Texans stood up for what was right at a little Spanish mission called the Alamo. Just as far away in space, but so recently that it still makes the headlines—makes them, that is, anywhere that headlines are permitted to speak the truth—another group of Texans stood up for the right at another mission, the Dei Gloria in Waco.

"In both cases, the defenders of the truth and the right paid with their lives. They fought a hopeless fight for principle. In the first case, whatever the short-term end, we know today that the defenders won after all. In the second case, the Dei Gloria Mission, boys and girls and an old Catholic priest lost their own fight . . . but they may just have arranged for us to win ours.

"There were several survivors of Santa Ana's tyrannical attack. There was but one from the Dei Gloria. Her name is Elpi—she is a very nice young lady—and she'd like to say a few words to you. . . ."

They'd had words before, the Commander of 18th Airborne Corps and the suited chief of the EPA's Environmental Protection Police—his personal "Zampolit." Much of this had been trivial. More had been hostile. The EPP simply abhorred roughing it and the Army and their attached Marines took a perverse glee in seeing that they had to do so. This was not the only point of disagreement, be it noted.

One of the more notable aspects of the many new

police which the Rottemeyer Administration had put on America's "streets" was the extremely "issue oriented" nature of those police. A precise breakdown would, of course, be impossible as some of these "police" fell into the secret variety.

But of those which were not secret? Their organizations, parent organizations and missions read as a litany of left leaning and outright leftist causes. Besides the Surgeon General's Riot Control Police—the mission of which was to make profits safe for abortionists—there were the Animal Rights Police, existing to make the world unsafe for purveyors of female cosmetics, the Internal Revenue Service's "Enforcement Arm"—for when the courts took a dim view of legalized extortion, and—notably—the "Raid Command" of the Bureau of Alcohol, Tobacco and Firearms—whose mission needed no restatement. Then there were the Environmental Protection Police which, within a couple of years of Rottemeyer's election, made it clear to would-be polluters that one could either follow the government's stringent environmental policies . . . or contribute heavily to the Democratic National Committee.

It went almost without saying that the PGSS, whose mission was the protection of Rottemeyer and the enforcement of her precise will, had a leftist cause all their own.

The one thing each of these agencies shared was that none of them were composed, strictly speaking, of police officers, of the simple constables of the peace that made civilized life possible. Snipers there were aplenty. Riot control trained thugs were in no shortage. But of men and women who could make a bad situation better, deal with people—sometimes angry ones—temper justice with a trace of mercy? These were vanishingly rare.

The people with whom they dealt generally despised them as police as much as the armed forces tended to despise them in their manifestation as soldiers.

"You people aren't soldiers and you aren't much as far as being cops goes. So stay the hell out of our people's way while we move into the city." Those were the last words the Commander of the 18th Airborne had given to the Chief of the EPP before his soldiers began to fan out into Houston.

Perhaps it was because a hooker had no time to be shy. Perhaps it was that her loss was too profound even for a shy girl to keep hidden. Whatever it was, the girl soon had the crowd eating out of her hand. She wept? Then they wept too. She showed her pain and her anger? The crowd growled with their own. She was such a success that Charlesworth was moved to whisper, "When this is over, Elpi, remind me to link you up with my agency."

Elpi had just finished speaking—Charlesworth had coached the untrained girl very thoroughly—when the first of the 3rd Infantry Divisions armored vehicles were spotted turning a corner into the Galleria. A thrill of anxious worry ran through the crowd.

As Charlesworth pulled Elpi to one side, the side where Minh stood by to help her escape when the time came, he said, "Be calm, my friends, be calm. These are just our soldiers. At heart, most of them are on our side. They feel about Washington as most of us do." A soldier—a sergeant with a nametag that read "Soult"—standing upright in a passing armored vehicle looked at Charlesworth and gave a soft thumbs up. He was not alone.

"Elpidia here has told you of what it was like from her point of view at the Dei Gloria. Now I want to remind you that there is yet another group, a third Alamo, if you will, making their stand up in Fort Worth. . . ."

Western Currency Facility, Fort Worth, Texas

The damage from the first fight had mostly been cleared; cleared, that is, to the extent it hadn't been added to in the interests of defense.

From one of the twin rectangular projections atop the main building, Major Williams gazed through binoculars eastward to Interstate 35.

"That's the First Cav passing through," he told Pendergast, standing next to him. "I think it is anyway. None of the tracks are flying Cav guidons. You suppose they are ashamed?"

"Dunno, sir. Might be."

Overhead another of the seemingly endless flights of Army helicopters passed by, bringing in another load of PGSS.

Williams looked upward. "How many is that now?" he asked.

Pendergast answered, "How many troops? About seven thousand would be my guess. I didn't know Rottenmuncher had that many in her private army."

"There's a lotta things about her people didn't know when she was running, Sergeant Major. Maybe more things she kept secret after she won."

Pendergast shrugged. *Well, too late to do anything about that now.*

A single shot rang out. To Pendergast it sounded like a .50 caliber. To a Guardsman standing just to Pendergast's left it didn't sound like anything at all . . . for it killed him instantaneously.

"Down! Goddammit, down!"

And so it begins again, Pendergast thought, as a steady spattering of rifle fire began to pelt the facility.

Houston, Texas

"Just come on, girl, forget the old man," Minh demanded of Elpi, he and a henchmen dragging her by each arm. The girl twisted and struggled to turn around and go back to stand beside Charlesworth in his hour of need, the hour which was possibly his final one. She struggled, but fruitlessly; for all his age and tiny stature the former Vietcong was still much stronger.

Even as they hustled Elpi through some merchant's doors, Minh looked behind him with a certain amount of satisfaction. Like some mindless colony of killer ants the EPP were wading into the crowd, beating, breaking, arresting in some cases. Photographers stationed by Minh in the overlooking windows would be catching all that, catching on film and tape the actions of the federals against a helpless, unresisting crowd. These images would appear everywhere soon; on television in unoccupied Texas and across the world, on the Internet in the still fully federated states; within the environs of Houston there would soon be no wall without its poster of bleeding women.

Minh gave Elpi a final push then turned around full and, with folded arms, watched the blue-clad horde chew its way closer to Charlesworth. *So it was not all just an act, you blue-eyed devil; all those heroes you played.*

Charlesworth, himself, kept to his microphone, speaking even until the club descended to shut his eyes and his mouth forever.

Bunker Hill, Texas

Once past Houston, proper, the point of the Marine's 2nd Division had split off southwest, towards Corpus Christi. The Army's 3rd Infantry Division continued almost due west towards San Antonio.

I don't know how long I can keep my eyes shut to what's happening, thought the grizzled, old sergeant major of the division. *The boss didn't see, he was too far to the front, what was left of poor Charlesworth. But I saw . . . and this is not what I signed up to do.*

The sergeant major was not alone. Almost two-thirds of the division had passed through or near the Galleria area on their way eastward. Many were too far away to tell much of anything. Still, a substantial number had seen the bodies, heard the screams.

The Army's Third Infantry was one very unhappy division.

El Paso, Texas

Smoke drifted on the breeze. Some of it was from the gasoline stations burnt and destroyed by the Guard on its retreat. As much came from wood cooking fires across the border in Juarez, Mexico. The Marines couldn't do much about Juarez. They were trying manfully to reduce the flames in and around El Paso.

But none of the locals will lift so much as a finger to help us, thought Fulton, unhappily. *You would think that at least some of them would want to save what could be saved.*

Fulton looked up as his G-4, his quartermaster, approached.

"Forget saving any of the diesel and gasoline, boss," announced the "Four," dejectedly. "It's all going up in smoke. I might be able to save some of the packaged POL"—Petroleum, Oil and Lubricants—"but we can't burn that in our engines."

"How far did you say we could go on what we have?" queried Fulton, though he knew the answer.

"Just like I told you, General—twenty miles past El Paso. By which point we are bone dry."

"Fine. Shit. Okay then, call a halt. Any word on clearing out our supply route back into and through New Mexico?"

The G-4 sighed deeply. "We've started getting what we don't need; ammunition, mainly. The fuel? Well, they cleared out the demonstrators at Las Cruces. So naturally, the State of New Mexico has declared all the roads closed and seized any trucks they can get their hands on of ours. But . . . General, sir? There's this driver, nice kid, a reservist who was at Las Cruces. Sir . . . you need to talk to this kid."

Fulton had a very strong feeling—nay, a certainty—that he was not going to like what the reservist had to tell him. Even so, never a coward—certainly not a moral coward—he agreed. "Send the kid to see me this evening, after chow."

Colorado River, Columbus, Texas

The sign by the highway said, "This far and no farther."

"You suppose that's directed to us?" Sergeant Soult asked his driver through the vehicle intercom.

Before the driver could answer, the Interstate 10 bridge spanning the river went up in a flurry of smoke and debris.

"Stop the LAV," Soult commanded. "Stop it now."

It was well he did so. Less than a minute after the bridge went down there came the sound of muffled freight trains. Soult instinctively ducked, pulling the hatch halfway closed above him. The driver merely hunched down a bit.

Ahead of them erupted a maelstrom of fire and flying shards as several dozen large-caliber artillery rounds went off more or less simultaneously at the near end of the bridge.

"Yeah, bubba," said Soult. "I think they mean it."

Northeast of El Campo, Texas

They *did* mean it.

AMTRACs and infantry—the bulk of 2nd Marine Division—moved slower than LAVs. And, though the Marine Corps had LAVs aplenty, they were to a large extent constrained by the speed of their slowest movers; in this case LPCs, or Leather Personnel Carriers.

Thus there was plenty of warning that the Guard was serious and that no more warning shots would be fired.

During the night, small parties of Marines went forward to recon the west bank of the river from the east bank. One and all they came back with the report, "Too hard." That is to say, they all came back with the report except for one patrol that was caught trying to cross the river. This patrol did not come back at all. In its way, this confirmed what the others had said.

CHAPTER FIFTEEN

From the transcript at trial: Commonwealth of Virginia v. Alvin Scheer

DIRECT EXAMINATION, CONTINUED
BY MR. STENNINGS:

Q. Did you think Texas was about to lose, Alvin?

A. Well, I'd like to think I had a little more faith than that. Thing was, though, I just couldn't see how we could win.

Q. And you kept close track of it on the news?

A. I tried, what there was of news. Things got really quiet once Houston went under. All you ever saw on the TV was more and more troops building up around that area of Texas the feds hadn't taken over yet.

They used to show us a lot of what had gone on, though. I swear, if I never again see some news type standin' by a wrecked bridge and lecturing about "criminal waste" or "lawless behavior" again . . . well, if I never do it will still be too soon.

There was one funny thing about them bridge shots. See, I knew the areas of a lot of them so it wasn't too hard to place where they were taken. And even when I couldn't place 'em, there was something always the same. Lots of trucks piled up on the north sides or the east sides of the rivers, waiting for a ferry to bring 'em across.

Now, I never did any time in the army, so I didn't know what those traffic jams were doing, not in any detail. But I figured, if they really needed all them trucks . . . and most of the trucks were stuck on the wrong side of some blown-up bridges, then they had to be short whatever it was them trucks was supposed to be carrying.

Wasn't just at the bridges, neither. Seems New Mexico decided . . . I didn't know why at the time . . . to throw in with Texas. Not that we got any details, naturally. But I did notice two things. One was that the "on location" newscasts suddenly switched from Las Cruces, New Mexico to Arizona and Colorado. The other? Well, when they started mentioning the governor of that state, Mr. Garrison, the same way they talked about Mrs. Seguin? I put two and two together and came up with . . . well, two. Two states, that is.

And I knew Texas wasn't alone anymore.

Austin, Texas

"New Mexico did it, Juani. We're not alone anymore," exulted Schmidt.

"Did what, Jack?"

"Adopted the full program. Nullified the income tax withholding within the state. Started rounding up federal agents and bureaucrats. Voted an expansion of their State Defense Force and National Guard. They've also ordered all highways and railways blocked. Though, you know, Juani, they don't really have a National Guard. They sent us damned near everything they had from air defense to medics."

Juani's face took on a worried expression. "I am not sure this is a good thing or a bad, Jack. What happened?"

"The feds opened fire on the people who were blocking the highway by Las Cruces. Killed a bunch of state police; some other people, too. Garrison called an emergency session of the legislature and they voted, almost unanimously, to join us."

An image of a disarmed and already occupied New Mexico flashed through her mind, followed by one of civilians and police shot down on the highway. Juani bit her lower lip and began to rock gently back and forth. *My fault, my fault, all my fault.*

Not one to hide an unpleasantness, even from an obviously stressed governor, Jack added, "But it isn't going all that well. We had some time to prepare. New Mexico really didn't. Didn't have the money either. And, like I said, what they had of National Guard they had already sent to us."

Jack concluded, "Garrison, the legislature, and about fifty cops are under siege in the State House. Their phone lines are cut but they obviously have some cell phones. And there's a local news team on site too. But there's not much food to speak of and the water has been cut too. Juani, they need our help."

My fault, too, if we don't help them. "What can we do? Give me some options."

"Out west I've got three battalions, one tank and two mechanized infantry, facing off against the 1st Marines and 3rd Armored Cav. It's a risk . . . I'm told that the supply status for the Marines and Cav is very low but I don't know it is. One of those battalions of ours was the one slated to go around 3rd Corps to extract our folks in Fort Worth. If you are willing to let them go under I can strip off that battalion and send it on an end run to Santa Fe. I think the other two would be enough to make the Marines and Cav dance around and burn up whatever fuel they might have left. I think."

"You'll have to break your promise to those boys in the WCF for me to do that."

Juani's rocking grew more pronounced before she settled back in her chair. "Don't ask me to go back on my word, Jack . . . please. I promised those boys we'd at least try to get them out."

Jack, here, was pitiless. "Maybe that was a promise you shouldn't have made, Governor."

Juani felt a wave of nausea wash over her. Dammit, she was a good politician . . . and a good politician keeps her word.

"Tell me what you think I should do," she forced out, painfully.

Relenting now, Jack reached a hand over and gave her shoulder a reassuring and comforting squeeze. "I'll tell the boys in Fort Worth they can surrender at discretion or try to break out and escape and evade. Then we'll send a battalion to Santa Fe . . . if we can."

"Can?" questioned the governor.

"Between where we have that battalion and Fort Worth there's some cover. There are first class roads. There are towns to hide in. The people are mostly *our* people or, at worst, neutral. Between where they are now and Santa Fe it's open and mostly flat and they can only *hope* to make any progress without being spotted and hammered from the air. The people there will probably support us just as our own would . . . but there are a lot fewer of them. No joke, Juani; it's going to be hard."

"Okay, then. It's a risk. But it's a risk we have to take, yes?"

"I don't know," answered Jack. "Garrison's too good a man to let go under. New Mexico's too good a state, too. They supported us—openly—when no one else would.

"But, Juani, the guys in the Currency Facility are good men, too. They're big boys now, all grown up. They know the deal and I'm sure they won't hold any hard feelings.

"Fundamentally, Governor, it's a political decision, not a military one. So it's up to you."

It's a political decision, Juani echoed in her mind. *My decision. No one else can make it for me.* "Do it, then. Tell the boys in Fort Worth I'm so sorry." *And leave me with my guilt.*

Washington, DC

It is so very much too late for guilt, and I am not big enough for all the guilt I have. I miss old Goldsmith, mused Representative Harry Feldman. Redneck New Mexican or not. He wouldn't have rolled like I have. Maybe I wouldn't have rolled—frame job or not—if he were here to buck me up.

A great wave of self-loathing washed over the New Yorker; a wave compounded of disillusionment, disgust, and despair . . . along with a heavy admixture of serious personal guilt. *I have no excuse. I should have known. Ross was right all along, right about the important things anyway.*

Feldman gave out a sigh that would have been audible had there been anyone else to hear it. There was not. He had found that he preferred to be alone these days; a rarity in a career politician. It was bad enough that he had to live with his own guilt and grief. Having to hide it from others, to "put on a happy face," while he was seething inside? That would have been impossible.

How did we let it get so out of hand? Everything Willi said she wanted to do for this country was right, *dammit.*

Feldman turned back to his speech notes. Later today he was to put on a speech in the House condemning Texas and New Mexico in no uncertain terms. Those were his orders from the White House.

Maybe—just maybe—I would rather go to prison . . . or would . . . if I weren't a coward.

Santa Fe, New Mexico

Governor Garrison pulled back from the narrow window from which he had briefly glanced at the ring of federal agents surrounding the State House. His eyes wandered around the walls of the assembly to where his state police confidently manned positions to repel any assault. The thought, *no cowards here*, made his chest swell with pride.

He patted the shoulder of the nearest trooper, even now returning to the position he had vacated to give Garrison a quick look. *No cowards.*

Not only were the men manning the state house not cowards; any fear they felt was utterly subsumed in sheer fury; fury and hot hatred. In the seventy-eight year history of the New Mexico State Police, thirty-one troopers had fallen in line of duty by murder or accident. In the thirty-odd minutes between the arrival of the SGRCP at Las Cruces that number had been more than doubled.

Garrison overheard the shotgun-gripping trooper who had resumed his place at the window mutter, *sotto voce*, "Come on, you bastards, you miserable murdering fucks. Come on and try us."

Pecos, Texas

The commander of the westernmost brigade of the forty-ninth Armored Division, plus both its tank and infantry battalion commanders, looked Schmidt square in the eye, hooked a thumb over his shoulder, and said, "All Tripp, here,"—he indicated the short and stout infantry battalion commander with the pointing thumb—"can do is try. It's over three hundred and fifty miles to Santa Fe, most of that by U.S. highways, not interstates. Between the company of tanks and

the two companies of mech infantry—which is all
he has left anyway with one company sitting in Fort
Worth—he'll be lucky to arrive with more than about
two companies. The rest will be strung out behind
him and might or might not join him later. At that
it will take him about a day to get there. And that
assumes that we don't meet any opposition on the
ground or from the air."

The colonel continued, "We've had a couple of guys
from the Marines and the Third ACR come over to
us. They indicate that the supply status is still pretty
poor. But they could rape the rest of their formation
to field a force big enough to stop us and they can
move faster in their LAVs, across a shorter distance,
to block us. If they use helicopters, there's no question
they can beat us there. If they beat us there, there's
no question they can stop us before we get to New
Mexico's state house."

"There's a way . . ." The brigade commander hesitated.

"Go on," encouraged Schmidt.

"General, I know you do not want this. I know
we've bent over backwards to keep from killing any
regulars. I even, maybe, understand and I may even,
generally, approve. But if you want me to send one
of my three battalions to Santa Fe I need to use the
other two to tie the people facing me down where
they are. This would not have been true if we had
gone to Fort Worth instead.

"I need to attack—even at the crappy odds
I'm facing—attack to buy time, attack to draw
attention."

"Otherwise?" Schmidt asked.

"Otherwise, it's a gallant gesture but no more than that. Sorry, sir, but that's how I see it."

"I see. Hmmm. You said, 'a day.' Tell me exactly what you mean by that and how you arrived at it."

"Well, we can only move as fast as our slowest movers. Those are the Infantry Fighting Vehicles. Top speed is about forty-five miles an hour. At that speed figure on beating the crews half to death even on a good road. Figure on more breakdowns, too . . . a lot more. So I am planning no more than thirty miles an hour. Twelve driving hours for the trip, minimum. Call it fourteen to be safe. Add in rest and food breaks . . . oh, and at least one refueling, and we're talking more like seventeen hours.

"Speaking of refueling, we had a cache hidden near Abilene for the Fort Worth foray. There's no cache between here and Santa Fe."

Schmidt understood. "Can you send enough fuel trucks to make up the difference?"

"Barely, sir, but yes. In any case, continuing on, add a couple of hours to plan the final relief once we get close to the state house and we're up to nineteen hours. Once we're up to nineteen hours of continuous operations then we need to talk about some sleep before the actual relief."

"So, yes, General; a full day. If Tripp moves tactically rather than just doing a 'balls to the wall' road march it will be more like three days. I figure it's important enough to sacrifice security to speed though . . . so we'll call it a day."

Schmidt thought he had an answer, rather, a part of one. "How disciplined are your troops, Colonel?"

"Normal. Nothing special. Nothing awful, either. Why?"

Schmidt answered slowly, "Well, I am willing to let you make an 'attack' . . . but you can't actually kill any federal troops doing it."

The colonel shuddered. "No . . . we're not *that* disciplined. If the Marines shoot to kill, my boys will shoot back."

"Then attack without ammunition or make a mere demonstration. But do it this evening."

Tripp spoke up for the first time. "Then we're really going to leave my boys in the Currency Facility in the lurch, are we?"

"They're big boys, aren't they, Colonel?"

Western Currency Facility, Fort Worth, Texas

Deep in the bowels of the facility's security room, four men, a major, two captains, and a sergeant major met to discuss their predicament. The lights were dimmed, the better to see the television screens lining one wall. Many of those screens were blank, however. PGSS snipers had made a point of disabling any camera they could identify.

Rubbing the left side of his face, Williams said in a low voice, "And those are our choices, gentlemen: hold fast and hope the problem gets solved elsewhere, hold fast and be destroyed, or try to escape on our own . . . or we could surrender."

Williams' face set with a determined grimace. "Me, I plan on staying. And with New Mexico throwing in with us I think our chances of holding the feds off long enough went way up."

"That much is true," said James. "I don't think I would surrender anyway. If they don't hang us we'll spend the rest of our lives behind bars. But we probably don't need to worry about prison because they *will* hang us all."

Davis added, "I don't see how we can escape either. There are seven thousand PGSS troopers—and now they've got their armored vehicles with them—surrounding this place. We would be lucky to get two steps from any of the doors. Sure wish we'd kept our Bradleys."

"They were needed elsewhere," Williams answered. "And we weren't planning on escaping when we took this place over."

Pendergast summed it up. "I've been talking with the boys, Major Williams. Sir, they know the score. And they want to stay and fight it out. Hell, we sent the bad guys packing once already. Who says we can't do it again? At least, that's what the boys are thinking."

"You mean none of them want to surrender, Sergeant Major?"

"No, sir. They know—just like Captain James said—surrender is either a quick ticket to prison or a quick ticket to a rope. They'd rather fight it out, sir. All of them willing to talk about it, anyway.

"And sir, I know you would rather let any go that want to . . . but you can't. Every man here knows just about every booby trap and trick we've laid on. Don't think for a minute the feds won't get it out of them either. And every man knows that every other one knows. They'd shoot anyone that tried to desert themselves."

Williams began massaging both his temples. "So be it, then. We hold. Sergeant Major, send a message to Austin. . . ."

Austin, Texas

Schmidt read aloud, "'To the people of Texas and to all Americans: We are besieged by over seven thousand federal troops; none of them, so far as we can tell, of the United States Army or Marine Corps. We are under continuous sniper and machine-gun fire, though casualties—so far—have been light.

"'We will never surrender or retreat. If there are neither reinforcements nor relief to come to our aid we will still never surrender or retreat. If the enemy assault us, we will still never surrender or retreat and will, by God's grace, exact a terrible price for every forward step they may attempt. Hurrah for Texas and hurrah for Governor Seguin.'"

"I *told* you they understood, Juani . . . though I surely do wish we could get them out. They're too good a group of men to let die."

Western Currency Facility, Fort Worth, Texas

Every time Sawyers looked at the building he liked what he saw less and less. Open, no cover, clear fields of fire from positions inside he couldn't see much less hope to effectively engage. He had a battalion's worth of armored vehicles now—and didn't the army bitch over the costs in fuel of getting them here? But as to whether that would help or just give the guardsmen inside more profitable targets for the antitank weapons he was certain that they had . . . well, he just didn't know.

All in all he had misjudged the defenders very badly to date. Worse, he knew he had. He had never imagined that the Texans would attack to relieve that miserable old priest's mission. He had assumed that—faced with the prospect of a real attack to take back the Western Currency Facility—respect for the law would cause them to fold. Even when they had answered his demand for surrender with a defiant, and remarkably well-placed shot, he had still assumed that a real attack would break them.

He'd been so very wrong. And his men had paid the price for it.

Sawyers, it was fair to say, had suffered something of a crisis of confidence.

He had asked for air support; a couple of fighters to drop a couple of large bombs each. He'd asked and been told, in no uncertain terms, "No."

His superior at Treasury had explained, a bit. "No, the President has outright refused to drop bombs on American soil. Bad PR, you know."

Sawyers didn't buy it. He'd gone over her head to her boss. Similar story.

He'd pressed. Finally, it came out. "Commander, you can't have any air support because we do not trust them not to drop the bombs on you before flying off to San Antonio to join the Texans. It's not on the news but there have been a couple of cases of that; pilots stealing their planes and defecting. More of the bastards are faking sick to avoid flying, and the President is furious about that too. Unfortunately, she can't do much. So you're on your own."

El Paso, Texas

The fires were out at least. That much Fulton could be thankful for. There was still a godawful stench from Juarez, when the wind was just right, or just wrong. But over that the Marine Corps had no control.

Fulton made his headquarters in a now abandoned restaurant just off of Interstate 10. There, at least, he didn't have to see the sullen bitter looks the people of El Paso cast at him and his Marines.

There came a knock on his door that Fulton answered with, "Enter."

"Sir, Corporal Mendez reports."

Fulton, the commander of the 1st Marine Division returned the corporal's salute and then spent a few seconds studying him. He saw the beginnings of a paunch, but that was nothing unusual in a reservist. The salute had been snappy. The driver's uniform was as clean as circumstances allowed. In all, the kid made a favorable impression.

"Relax, son. The G-4 told me I ought to see you; that you had something important to say. So spill it."

Mendez didn't relax, not quite. Instead he assumed a stiff parade rest, eyes focused somewhere above and about one thousand yards past the general's back. He kept that position, and that focus, while relating every detail he could recall about the actions of the Surgeon General's police at Las Cruces, New Mexico.

Fulton's face kept a neutral expression throughout. When Mendez finished he asked a few questions, made a few notes on a yellow pad.

Finally he asked, "So what do you think we should do about it, Corporal?"

Mendez looked directly at Fulton for the first time since entering his office. "Sir, I wouldn't presume to tell the General . . ."

Fulton wriggled his fingers, dismissing the difference in rank. Still Mendez remained silent.

Ohh, thought the general, suddenly understanding. *He's afraid to tell me because if he told me what he was thinking it could be construed as mutiny.*

"Let me rephrase that question, Corporal. Are you happy to be here, with us, on this operation."

"No, sir," Mendez answered without a moment's hesitation.

"I see. Let me ask another one. Who do you hope wins this little confrontation?"

Mendez did hesitate over answering that one. He didn't know much about military law and wasn't certain he should answer it.

"Scout's honor, Corporal. Nothing you say is going out of this room."

"Okay, then, sir. I think we ought to ask the Texans for some gas, turn around, and march back through New Mexico arresting or shooting every federal agent we can find on the way. But that's just me. . . ."

Wardroom, USS *Peleliu*, Gatun Lake, Republic of Panama

"Is it just me or does anyone here agree we never should have given this place back?"

The speaker's comments were greeted with snorts of assent and louder snorts of derision at the local "hosts." No one in the Navy, and few if any in the other services, had thought that giving the Panama Canal Zone back to Panama had been a very good idea. The knowledge was made all the more bitter, especially among the more senior officers and chiefs that the return of the Zone had never been necessary. Rather, so they perceived it, it had been the mistaken decision of a past—be it noted, Democratic—President also widely considered within the military to have been a national mistake. It had been carried through fruition by a man convinced beyond contradiction of his convictions and ignorant beyond ignorance of his limitations.

Now the price had to be paid, ironically by another Democrat President. Three amphibious warfare ships, carrying the better part of a brigade of Marines, had entered the Canal from the Pacific. Other ships—some carrying troops and others carrying equipment and supplies—had assembled off of Venado Beach and in the bay of Panama on Panama's Pacific side in anticipation of making the passage.

Then, with the bulk of the force sitting in the fresh water of Gatun Lake the Canal had experienced its first stoppage since 1989 and only the second one in its history as thousands of Canal workers went on strike simultaneously.

The strike was as spontaneous as a man named Patricio could make it.

The Marines were not going anywhere soon.

In the warm blue waters of the Pacific, and the steamy brown waters of Gatun Lake, mixed in among the Marines' transports were merchant ships registered around the world. Among these were several registered with and owned by the People's Republic of China.

Those ships carried arms once destined for Texas and now traded to an international arms dealer . . . but of those the Marines and Navy knew little and cared less.

The captain of the *Peleliu* likewise knew little of the Chinese arms. He did, however, know better than any one else in his marooned ship just how stuck they were. Even if he attempted to use the Marines his ship carried, not one of them had the first clue about operating the Canal.

The Marines were not going to be able to break this foreign strike.

Colorado River, Texas

A military organization—and, while the Marines were a part of the naval service, none had ever suggested they were not in every important particular a military organization—might be likened to a bizarre sort of snake. At its point there were teeth and eyes and venom. Somewhere in the middle was the fresh meal it needed and was digesting to continue on its way. What made the snake bizarre is that its tail was an enormous conglomeration of fat and flesh, muscle and machine stretching out for anywhere from tens to hundreds of miles behind it.

And the point of the beast could move little if at all faster than that fat, bloated, dragging tail.

The point of Second Marine Division (minus that brigade roasting on ships in the Gulf of Mexico) might be at the Colorado River. Its gargantuan tail was still anchored somewhere east of Houston.

In Houston itself that recent and future meal—rather, its passage point—was being squeezed.

Houston, Texas

From his vantage point overlooking the intersection of Interstate 10 and U.S. 59 Colonel Minh smiled happily at the vista spread below him.

It hadn't even been too very hard. Before they were shut down by federal authorities, the newspapers had waxed lyrical about the martyrdom of Victor Charlesworth and those who had gone to see him speak. Immediately following the shut down, posters had gone up on walls, flyers had been anonymously delivered. Speakers at a dozen platforms appeared, aroused a crowd, announced a rally and then disappeared.

The local police—before they, too, went on strike—seemed quite indifferent to the impromptu rallies.

Now Minh had the results he wanted at this stage. Thousands of cars blocked the intersection. Thousands more people demonstrated around the cars. Not that more than some hundreds of these intended a demonstration. Many, many more had been caught up in the blockage and simply had no good way to leave.

And mixed in with those demonstrators and unwitting demonstrators? A hundred or more of his own "troops" . . . his own "armed and dangerous" troops.

To either side of the blockage military convoys had been building for hours, helpless to push on either to deliver the goods or to return for more goods to deliver. This, too, was part of Minh's plan. He intended that the very people who needed federal help to clear the road block should themselves help congest that road to delay federal help.

Still, he hoped—truthfully, he completely expected—that the feds would show up eventually.

"Ah, there they are," he whispered. A mile away, plainly visible from his vantage point, the ragged lines of the Environmental Protection Police snaked around herringbone parked military trucks. "Shouldn't be long now."

Elpi watched with Minh. For the most part, and per Schmidt's instructions, he kept her in one or another of the safe houses that dotted the city. Even so, and even with some clever makeup, she would never pass scrutiny if one of the federal agents dominating the city took a careful look. For one thing, the safe houses were often in Vietnamese neighborhoods. For another, her face had become rather well known as a result of the speech she had made by Charlesworth's side.

Mostly Minh kept her off the streets. Still, for reasons more instinctive than articulable, he occasionally risked bringing her out as a witness to events.

The military vehicles had stopped well shy of the blockage, of course; soldiers were not stupid, Marines no more so, and neither soldiers nor Marines wanted to be anywhere near a potentially unruly crowd.

As the first agents of the EPP debouched into the open space Minh's people began a chant, "Charlesworth! Charlesworth! Charlesworth!" Others picked it up, even among those who had only been inadvertently stuck at the rally. Soon, the volume had grown to the point where most of the demonstrators could not hear, let alone obey, the EPPs perfunctory order to disperse.

The police formed a skirmish line. Brandishing batons, they advanced. This the crowd had to notice and many shied away, shuffling backwards around the mass of misparked automobiles and further from the threatening clubs.

Not all did so, however. Minh's people, for example, did not shy away. Of course they were for the most part in cars which they could not leave. Most especially could they not leave with the rifles those cars hid.

A command rang out in Vietnamese over a loud-speaker. A hundred rifles came out of hiding. The EPP recoiled in shock as soon as these were recognized.

The shock was short lived.

Columbus, Texas

The 3rd Infantry Division had made its forward headquarters in this small town overlooking the Colorado River. Having just finished his daily tour of selected units, the Division Sergeant Major entered the command post, pulling off uncomfortable helmet and sweaty field gear as he did so.

The first thing the sergeant major noticed was an air of shock among the denizens of the command post. He stopped a passing sergeant and inquired.

"It's Houston, sergeant major; the MSR, our main supply route. It's erupted into fighting . . . low scale as near as we can tell and they're avoiding our people and the jarheads . . . but it's enough that we are effectively cut off here."

"Shit," muttered the sergeant major. "Does the old man know?"

"He's been closeted with the G-4 since we got word."

"We should have talked to Martin," said the sergeant major, under his breath.

"Huh?"

"Never mind, son. Before your time."

Waco, Texas

Not far from the ruins of the Mission Dei Gloria a very worried and a very dejected Army lieutenant general likewise sat in conference with his G-2 (Intelligence), his G-4 (Logistics) and his Provost Marshall (Military Police).

"It's just not enough, sir," announced the G-4. "Between the wrecked bridges, the sit down strikes in and around Dallas, the limits on the engineers' ferries . . . well, I can take you to Austin. But if we have to actually fight for the place there's no way I can provide the ammunition you'll need; not for weeks at best."

The provost marshal interjected, "That presumes that the federal police behind us can keep the lines open at least most of the time. I'm not too sure. . . ."

"They won't be able to," confided the G-2. "Sir, I've

sent my people back a number of times to observe. The bulk of the PGSS . . ."

"Why not just call 'em what they are?" demanded the provost. "Either 'Rottenmuncher's Own' or just plain old 'SS'?"

The Corps commander unconsciously glanced around to ensure that his Zampolit was not in earshot. "We can continue to call them the PGSS," he ordered. "We all know what we mean by it."

"Sir," continued the G-2. "The PGSS and FBI are keeping the supply lines clear through and around Fort Worth and Dallas . . . but—except for the FBI, in Dallas—the way they're doing it, the way every federal agency has been doing it, is just so damned heavy-handed that they're driving even neutral folks into Governor Seguin's arms. And what's been going on in Houston? It's obvious; the Texans have a plan, a good one, and they're following it."

"What plan?" asked the Corps commander. "I see a plan to defend the rump of Texas."

"No, sir. The plan's deeper than that. The defense of that rump is intended to hold *us* up, to take us out of the main theater. The plan is to eat up the main theater, our rear. While we're stuck forward leaving those . . ."

"Those sloppy, miserable, bloodthirsty excuses for police officers," muttered the provost.

"Yes, them. Seguin intends to make it very difficult for us to move supplies forward. Then, when the federal police suppress that, the rear breaks out in something very like a revolution. Houston tells us that the forces for a revolution are probably in place everywhere behind us."

"Leaving us stuck at the end of a nonexistent supply line?"

"Yes, sir. I think there's more to it than that, but that—from our point of view—will be enough. If the PGSS lose control of Dallas and Fort Worth we will die on the vine here."

Western Currency Facility, Fort Worth, Texas

We could just leave them to die on the vine, thought Sawyers. *They're not blocking anything. The facility is not that important really, not anymore. It's just a symbol. They can't have food for more than a few more weeks.*

But, though Sawyers had tried to have the assault called off, he had been refused at the very highest levels just as he had been refused air support. He *had* managed to browbeat the Regular Army into giving him a half battery of self-propelled artillery.

He really didn't trust them though.

Thus it was that, with heavy heart, Sawyers greeted his subordinates as they filed into his command post for their final orders; orders certain to be final for many of them.

Pecos, Texas

Tripp asked, simply, "Any final questions?" Seeing that there might be, he added, "And no, I don't mean questions like, 'Why aren't we going to rescue

Major Williams and B Company?' That subject is already closed."

In the greasy and soiled garage turned into an ad hoc command post, Tripps' officers and his sergeant major shifted uncomfortably. They were no happier about leaving Williams and company in the lurch than Tripp was. They had no better answer, no better than Tripp, than to follow their orders and leave the guilt—if guilt it was—to others.

The silence, not so much sullen as sorrowful, built for a full minute before one of the staff captains, the quartermaster, asked, "Am I to be allowed to commandeer any supplies we might need on the way? Could help, sir."

"Take what you need. Give them a receipt."

"Yes, sir."

Tripp had a platoon of air defense artillery attached to his battalion. "Sir, can we get any easing of 'Weapons Tight'? My Rolands are good systems, but they need *some* time—at least to engage."

"No, son. Higher authority thinks the Air Force won't engage and the brigade commander thinks he can suck up the Marine's air onto the rest of the brigade. 'Weapons Tight,' it stays."

The lieutenant raised his eyebrows, lowered his eyes and made a small, annoyed symbol of his mouth. But he answered only, "Sir."

Western Currency Facility, Fort Worth, Texas

"And the condemned ate a hearty last meal," joked Davis as he and the other officers feasted on such rare

and costly delicacies as packaged bread, undifferentiated meat, nuked potatoes, and squeezie cheese.

Almost all chuckled though the humor was plainly
forced. James alone did not chuckle. He was sick; the
doc had diagnosed pneumonia brought on by damage
to his lungs during the first attack. James picked at
the food with little interest or appetite. His color was
pale and he seemed to have lost weight.

Suddenly, seized by a fit of coughing, James put
down his plastic fork.

"You okay, bubba?" asked Davis.

"I'll be fine," he answered, without conviction.

Davis exchanged a look with Williams. *No, he
won't be fine.*

"Captain James, I think maybe you ought to exchange
places with the engineer; take over the command post
and let him handle the south wall."

Recovering with difficulty from the fit of coughing, James could only nod his head reluctantly. "If
you say so, boss."

"I'll leave a good engineer with him," volunteered
Davis.

"He ought to be in the aid station," insisted the
doctor. "But then again . . ."

"Doesn't make a whole helluva lot of difference,
does it, Doc?" countered James.

CHAPTER SIXTEEN

From the transcript at trial: Commonwealth of
Virginia v. Alvin Scheer

DIRECT EXAMINATION, CONTINUED
BY MR. STENNINGS:

Q. So it pleased you, did it, Alvin, that Texas wasn't
alone anymore?

A. Oh, yessir. Not that I thought New Mexico added
much. But I figured it might be important that
the governor didn't look so much like some sort
of lone wolf like they was trying to paint her.

Q. Sure. I understand how that might be so. So what
did you see next, Alvin?

A. Next? Well, next on the TV was the assault on the
currency facility. And those poor bastards . . . pardon
my language . . . they were sure enough alone. I
didn't have no TV, like I said before, so I watched
it on the TV at a bar near where I was staying.
Well, that is I got to see the outside of it anyway.

I had to buy more beer, a lot more, than I really like to drink to stay and watch it through to the end.

Western Currency Facility, Fort Worth, Texas

From the heavily sandbagged lookout position on the roof, the sun had not yet begun to peek over the horizon. Down below, to an even greater degree, all was plunged in gloom.

The sentry on duty, Fontaine, heard the sound of diesel engines roaring in the darkness. This was nothing new; since the PGSS had been linked up with their LAVs they had made a habit of moving them frequently at night.

The sound Fontaine heard was a little different though; deeper and fuller. He decided to risk a look. Straining his eyes to make out the indistinct silhouettes he concentrated . . .

"Holy shit!"

In a flash Fontaine had ripped the field telephone from its cradle. He began frantically twisting the crank that caused a buzzer on a similar phone deep within the building to come to life.

"Major Williams, here."

Fontaine exclaimed, with panic straining his voice, "Holy fucking shit, sir, the PGSS have a battery of self-propelled artillery and they're taking up firing positions across from the south wall now!"

Even as Fontaine replaced the handset on the cradle a blossom of fire erupted from the centermost gun.

Austin, Texas

As it turned out it was Jack who lost his nerve when the word came. It surprised him; he had never even contemplated the possibility that the impending deaths of not quite a couple of hundred of his men could affect him so. But, with Williams' frantic voice relaying the brick by brick reduction of the Currency Facility—each sentence spoken mis-punctuated by the muffled blasts of artillery, Schmidt had found that political considerations meant less and less.

"It's not too late, Governor," he'd insisted. "I can still reroute that battalion to Fort Worth. They might make it in time."

"'Might'," echoed the governor. "And if we did? If we did leave New Mexico in the lurch?"

"Well . . . they'll definitely go under," the general admitted, his face and tone of voice showing great unwillingness to so admit. "Probably within a few days. But if we don't save the boys in the Currency Facility they have at most forty-eight hours. I think not that long."

Juani sat stone-faced, unanswering.

"Or I could send a half dozen sorties of air . . ."

"No," she cut him off.

Juani looked down at her cluttered desk, deep in thought. When she raised her head it was to explain, "Jack . . . we have gotten away with as much as we have, in part, because the Air Force is sitting this one out. But if we use our planes they'll feel they have to get involved. And they'll beat us."

Seeing that Jack was still ready to argue that point she drove it home. "How many planes do we have?

Not enough, yes? How much of an . . . What's that term you use? . . . umbrella? How much of an umbrella can you put over us? Not enough, yes? How much of the supplies and equipment you need will you be able to get through Mexico when the Air Force gets involved and is shooting up every convoy that tries to cross the border? Not enough, yes?

"And how, Jack, *how* are we going to win on our own? If New Mexico goes under then no one, no one, *no one* else is going to join us.

"And then we lose.

"Now think about what 'lose' means here, Jack. It means that the people who killed my brother, killed your best friend and burnt alive a couple of dozen kids under age twelve get off scot-free. It means that we'll have Wilhelmina Rottemeyer's little spiked heels on our necks forever."

Juani paused briefly. "No, I take that back. 'We' won't because 'we' will be dead."

"'Lose,'" she continued, "means that the constitution as we know it will also be dead, dead, dead beyond hope of recovery. It means that our kids and grandkids will grow up learning the party line and nothing else. It means that our economy is going to be trashed by a cabal of people least well suited to running an economy."

"'Lose' means the end of the fucking world, Jack."

If he was shocked by the vulgarity, Schmidt didn't show a sign of it. He said, "Then I guess we had better not lose, Governor."

U.S. Highway 285, New Mexico

Tripp coughed a little as he was enveloped by a cloud of dust from a rolling, blacked-out tank. He thought abstractly about perhaps ducking down and buttoning up his own armored vehicle. It would save him from the dust, somewhat, but—dammit—he wanted to see his battalion as it launched itself forward.

Not that he could see much. Not only were the vehicles blacked out but he had spaced them over a very long line of march. He was taking a chance and he knew it, both from the probability of a major accident and the frightful possibility that the Marines to the south would detect his march and beat him to Santa Fe; meeting, fighting and defeating his battalion in detail.

El Paso, Texas

The word had been passed quietly. The hour was set for the time when the command and staff of 1st Marine Division could be most certain not to be interrupted by any of the division's Zampolits.

The Political Officers liked their sleep.

Quietly, too, the colonels and generals assembled in the division command post. Quietly they entered. Quietly they took their seats.

Fulton, the general commanding, entered accompanied by a pudgy, nondescript corporal named Mendez. He made a small hushing motion. *Do not call "attention." Do not stand. Just listen.*

"Ladies, gentlemen . . . oh and you, too, Colonel Stilton," the general lightly pointed a finger at the commander of the Army's 3rd Cavalry. "Corporal Mendez here has come through Las Cruces recently with a load of ammunition for us. I want you to listen to what he saw there. Go ahead, Mendez."

Obviously somewhat unnerved by the presence of so much brass, Mendez began haltingly. As he saw anger growing on the dimly lit faces, an anger that matched his own, he became more eloquent. As he finished speaking he heard two colonels mutter, "Motherfuckers."

"Yes, sir . . . sirs. They were motherfuckers."

"Motherfuckers," General Fulton repeated, definitively. "Now the question is, what do we do about it? Mendez, go take a walk. What we're going to discuss . . . I won't say it isn't your business. I will say that I don't see any good reason to put your neck in a noose, too."

The general waited for the corporal to leave and close the door before continuing.

The Cavalry commander interrupted as soon as he heard the door ease closed. "Me, personally, I'm sorely tempted to beg whatever diesel you guys have, turn around, and head north shooting up federal cops all the way," said Stilton. There was a muted murmur of broad agreement.

"A worthy ambition, young Colonel. Now how do you square that with your oath of office?"

"You don't have to anyway," piped in Fulton's intelligence officer. He pointed a thumb in a roughly northward direction and announced, "The Texas Guard is already sending what looks to be a heavy battalion to

Santa Fe, though I don't think they know that we know. The general knows," he continued, defensively.

"Yes, I knew. And I decided we all needed to chat before we decided what to do about it."

"What do *you* want to do about it, sir?" asked Stilton.

"Do about that battalion? About the federales that shot down American citizens in cold blood? Or do you mean about our general—and unfortunate—circumstances?"

"Yes, sir. About that."

Fulton flashed the briefest and smallest of smiles. "They say that a council of war never fights. Even so, that's what I'm calling here, a council of war. There are some decisions I can't make for you. I wouldn't, in any case. This is one such.

"We have three questions and three choices. The questions I have already asked. The choices are these. We can continue to do what we've been doing; moving painfully forward to try to knock the Texans to their knees as part of the federal armed forces. Alternatively, we can join the Texans and try to knock the federal government to its knees. Lastly, we can decide to just sit things out right here, call a truce, and ask the Texans for some goddamned gas and water just to survive.

"Note that the last two choices mean we will have to round up the Zampolits we've been saddled with." Fulton looked over at his provost.

"We're ready when you give the order, sir," that worthy answered, not without an undertone of happy anticipation in his voice.

Fulton nodded before continuing, "Note, here,

gentlemen, that once I called this council my personal options became quite limited. I am in favor of one of those last two choices and by so stating I have effectively counseled a mutiny.

"And that's all I am going to say about it. Speak, argue . . . decide."

"Get up, you pudgy little fuck," harshly demanded the Marine holding a rifle to the nose of the division's political officer. Two more Marines, large men both, came, one to either side of the Zampolit's rather luxurious bunk in his rather expensive and air-conditioned RV.

"You're coming with us, asshole."

Washington, DC

"Willi? Willi, wake up. We've got a problem, a bad one."

Rottemeyer sat up instantly, unconsciously brushing McCreavy's hand from her shoulder. "What is it, Caroline?"

"First Marine Division—well, the two thirds of it that is in Texas anyway—has mutinied. They've arrested their political officers and I have unconfirmed reports that they have sent parlementaires to the Texans."

"Oh, my God. What's this going to do to us? And what's a 'parlementaire'?"

"A *parlementaire* is someone sent to negotiate with the enemy. I think the Texans are either going to gain the better part of 1st Marine Division or, as a minimum, the Marines are going to bow out and release the Texans that are facing them to facing somewhere else . . . like against the rest of our force."

Open-mouthed and wide-eyed, Rottemeyer exhaled forcefully. "Why?"

"I don't know. There're nothing but rumors. But it might be because of the way the Surgeon General's police freed up the supply lines to the Marines that ran through Las Cruces. They were pretty heavy-handed, Willi."

"Well they had to be," the President retorted. "The Marines themselves needed that highway opened."

"Yes, the Marines needed the roads opened. And maybe the SGRCP did have to play rough," McCreavy admitted. "But the effect has not been good. Willi, I am worried about 2nd Marine Division now. And even the Army . . ."

"Yes?"

"There was an armored cavalry regiment with the 1st Marine Division. They mutinied, too. I don't know who you can trust anymore."

Tossing away the bedclothes, Rottemeyer arose to throw on a bathrobe. "Get me my cabinet."

Dallas, Texas

It was almost a northern city, in many ways. Like Atlanta and a few other places in the old south, the old Confederacy, Dallas was filled with northerners and flush with northern, and urban, attitudes and values. While a Texas—or Georgia—Democrat was likely to be more to the right than a Massachusetts—or New York—Republican, a Texan or Georgian Democrat from Atlanta or Dallas was equally likely to be only somewhat to the right of Marx or Engels. That was, of course, considerably to the right of a Massachusetts Democrat, many of whom stood considerably to the left of Marx and Engels.

Support, therefore, for Governor Seguin was far more muted in Dallas than it was in, say, neighboring Fort Worth. Indeed, that support was sometimes hardly in evidence at all.

And, however much federal law enforcement agencies had expanded and rotted under the Rottemeyer administration, some had done so less than others.

The premier agency, in fact, had—excepting some newer and much expanded sub-groups like the Hostage Rescue Team—hardly rotted at all. Although in the shadow of a pile of filth, and affected by the stench of it, the FBI—the core of a fine old organization—still retained some measure of its old dignity, restraint and purpose.

So, although there had been some incidents in Dallas—the FBI's area of responsibility for rear area security, those incidents had been few and not one had escalated into the type of random viciousness which were making the name of the United States government a stench in the nostrils of Texans, and others, elsewhere.

In Fort Worth, however, things were different.

Western Currency Facility, Fort Worth, Texas

"Well, this is certainly fucking different," muttered Pendergast into his protective mask. Another incoming shell slammed into the brick, causing him to duck behind the sand bags of the interior bunker he occupied. Bits of shattered brick and the odd piece of razor-sharp shell casing pattered the sand bags and bounced off of the concrete floor. Distantly and from behind him Pendergast heard someone cry out, "I'm hit, goddamit, I'm hit."

Pendergast turned around. Already a team of medics was carrying off the wounded trooper, leaking a trail of blood onto the concrete floor. He nodded approvingly.

A body flopped into the bunker next to Pendergast.

"Afternoon, SMaj," said Williams through his mask's "voicemitter."

"Sir."

"Have you noticed if the shelling has lightened up on this end?"

"They're firing a low rate, sir. Hard to tell if it's four guns firing really slow or two guns firing a bit faster. Why?"

"They've started blowing holes in two of the other walls, too."

"Casualties?" asked Pendergast.

"Not bad. Couple dead, half dozen wounded."

"Damn good thing we let the engineers talk us into these interior bunkers, no?"

"Oh, yes," Williams agreed.

"What's your guess, sir? Think they're going to try to hit all four walls at once?"

"Dunno. But that's what we have to prepare for."

✤   ✤   ✤

Sawyers grunted with a grim satisfaction as a shower of displaced brick fell in a semicircle about the point of impact.

"How much longer are we supposed to prep the walls, sir?" asked his driver.

"Well, technically, Ricky, we are not supposed to prep them at all. But I'll be damned if I'll let my boys fall into another trap . . . and all it took to get this half battery of guns was throwing my weight around a bit. The Army types weren't happy with it but . . . so what? Anyway, we'll pound them until I am sure there are no working claymores on the outside and that, on the inside, the Guard is reeling with bleeding ears and noses."

"Sir, if we're not supposed to prep them . . ."

"So? Let the secretary relieve me *after* the building is taken. For now I am not going to get any more of my boys killed than I can avoid."

"Sounds good to me, boss."

Pendergast shrugged uncertainly. "So what are we going to do if we haven't a clue where they'll attack from or if they go after all four walls at once, sir?"

"Well . . . casualties have not been that bad so far. Even so I want to pull back as much as we can from the inner perimeter and have a big reserve for when they actually decide to go for it," answered Williams.

"Makes sense," Pendergast agreed. "But we are still going to have to keep a screen on the inner perimeter and wall and that is going to cost."

"I know," said Williams, "but there's nothing else to do for it. So select an initial guard from this area then pull the rest back to the interior."

"Wilco, sir."

Another blast shook the exterior of the building as it shook the interior of Williams' and Pendergast's bodies.

"I'll move like the wind, sir."

Highway 285, New Mexico

I wish I knew whether this wind was helping or hurting, thought Tripp, breathing with difficulty the dust-laden air kicked up by churning tracks and carried on the stiff breeze. He dropped below to the commander's position in the turret and swept the thing in a medium speed three hundred and sixty degree scan. Nothing much in the thermals. I think it must be helping.

Tripp had run his battalion spaced out along the highway for as long as darkness permitted. With the rising of the sun, however, he'd felt compelled to order his men off the road and into the New Mexican desert. There they had had to slow their breakneck pace considerably. Even so, the tanks and tracks still kicked up a massive amount of dust.

Not for the first time since receiving his orders, Tripp felt an iciness gripping his stomach. *I wish to hell I knew what the Marines were doing.*

Washington, DC

Though the ambient temperature was normal and comfortable, the Oval Office held a chill to make fat men shiver. Rottemeyer was in a rage so icy and yet so forceful that her Cabinet and staff—most of them—cowered in her presence. "What the fuck . . . I say 'what the *fuck!*' . . . do those goddamned Marine Corps morons think they are up to? Who the fuck do they think they are? Who do they think they are fucking with?"

She paced the Oval Office in a furious snit. Up went a hand to a bookcase; down went a shelf of books to the floor. Out went both hands to a globe; out went the glass of a antique book cabinet as the globe sailed through it. The President worked her way from artifact to antique, from file to phone, destroying everything her strength allowed. Finally she gave out an inarticulate scream of pure frustration and pounded her broad desk with both hands before collapsing back into her chair.

"Willi, they haven't joined the other side, at least. They've just said they're going to sit this one out. That's worth something, isn't it?"

Rottemeyer shot McCreavy a venomous glare. "Not too much, it isn't. Didn't you yourself tell me that this fucked up everything."

"It makes it harder," McCreavy admitted. "With the west flank no longer threatened the Texans can shift forces to the north and east. And . . . well . . . being honest, no matter what the Marines and the Third Armored Cav have said, there's no guarantee they won't join Texas at some time. And that means that our west flank is open and threatened, potentially."

Carroll had sat silently through Rottemeyer's tirade. He spoke now in a voice full with wickedness. "Take their families hostage, Willi. Send a force to Camp Pendleton, California and grab the wives and kids."

McCreavy's eyes opened very wide in stunned disbelief. "You are out of your mind to even suggest such a thing," she said, turning them onto Carroll. "Are you going to grab the families of 2nd Marine Division too? How about all of the Army's? The Air Force's? The Navy's?"

Shifting her focus back to Rottemeyer, she exclaimed, "Willi that is the one thing I can guarantee will turn the entire armed forces against us! If we so much as start to move in that direction we'll be destroyed."

Looking at the President's face McCreavy's eyes opened wider still, if possible. "Willi, you just *can't* be seriously thinking about this."

"Why not?" Rottemeyer snapped. "What the hell do I owe those people *or* their families?"

"Remember what Machiavelli said, Willi," added Carroll. "You know; about people who do not know how to be forceful or wicked *enough* to survive turmoil?"

He stood and began to pace among the scattered books and broken bits. Wickedness disappeared from his voice, being replaced by a more reasonable, even intellectual, tone. "We have come so far, so fast Willi . . . we are so near to completion of the . . . the . . . the *revolution*—and that's what it is—to which we all pledged ourselves so many years ago that it would be nothing less than criminal to let anything stand in our way now."

Carroll leaned forward, resting his hands on the President's desk and staring her straight in the eye. "If we lose this contest, everything for which we have worked for so long and so hard will disappear. This government will be pared down to impotence. Every federal program we believe in will be dismantled. Control of the economy will go back to an unelected cabal of the rich. The environment will be trashed in the interests of greater and greater profits for fewer and fewer financial aristocrats."

He turned around to speak more generally to the Cabinet. "I don't even claim that Texas and this Seguin bitch even want that. She was, after all, a Democrat of sorts. But that's still the logic of what will happen if we lose. Not even Seguin will have the moral authority to keep this marvelous machine—this wonderful federal government we have created through the sweat and blood and sacrifice of millions—from being largely dismantled.

"If we fall, Madame President, the nuts will come out of the closet. And the momentum of events will be with them. The federal budget? Watch it pared to a fraction, a *small* fraction, of what it is now. Civil rights? Women's rights? Minority rights? Watch every progressive Supreme Court ruling made over the last seventy-five years legislatively disappear as if they had never been. Multiculturalism? Gone. Group rights? Gone.

"Everything we believe in . . . gone."

Carroll turned back to Rottemeyer. "You cannot let that happen."

Rottemeyer turned to Jesse Vega, in effective control for the nonce of the PGSS. "Tell my personal guard they are to reduce the Western Currency Facility before midday tomorrow—regardless of cost—and then move sufficient force, post haste, to California to ... mmm ... 'secure' the persons of the military dependants in and around Camp Pendleton."

Looking up at an obviously distraught McCreavy, the President added, "Those are my orders, Caroline. Do not balk me on this."

McCreavy sat heavily, putting her head in her hands, incredulous that it could have come to this.

Carroll added, "We need to put some kind of spin on this. People won't like the idea of us taking hostages. Might I suggest instead that we arrange some sort of incident with some of the locals around Pendleton. A demonstration, maybe, that gets out of hand. Perhaps a couple of rapes and a murder or two. Our party organization in California is strong, Willi. I can arrange the incidents within a few hours."

"And then we bring the families in for ... ummm ... 'protective custody'?" Rottemeyer grinned.

"Yeah," said Carroll slowly. "Yeah ... 'protective custody' ... that's the ticket."

Carroll stopped for a moment before continuing. When he did continue it was with a hesitation unusual in someone of such forceful character. "There's one other thing I think we need to do, Willi."

Rottemeyer raised an eyebrow.

"I checked with CIA. They can provide any required number of Predator Remote Piloted Aircraft."

"So?"

"The Air Force won't play." He turned an inquisitorial eye toward McCreavy who shrugged in agreement.

"So I think we need to bomb that cunt Seguin out of the equation."

"That's going to cost us . . ." began the President.

"Damn the cost," shouted Carroll. "Madame President we are fighting for our political *lives* here."

Western Currency Facility, Fort Worth, Texas

Regardless of cost, Sawyers read for approximately the fortieth time. *Reduce the Western Currency Facility before mid-day tomorrow, regardless of cost.*

Sawyers heard and felt the tremendous roar of one of the guns he had commandeered to reduce the WCF. The flash from the big gun's muzzle lit the landscape, forming it briefly into surreal shadows. Another flash and roar followed almost instantaneously as the shell impacted on a new section of exterior wall.

Oh, well, thought Sawyers, resignedly. *It could be worse. After all, we've got a minimum of half a dozen practicable breaches in each of three exterior walls; two more in the fourth. And I can be certain now that all their exterior claymores are either gone or at least deranged or disconnected. Since we pounded the roof it's likely as not there won't be any more mines there either. So there'll be no repeat of the goddamned fiasco we had the first day we arrived . . . my fault, my fault, all my fault.*

Once we break inside though . . . that is going to be pretty horrible.

"It's pretty awful up there, ain't it, Top . . . I mean Sergeant Major?"

Pendergast, just returned to relative safety from

a mind-numbing tour of the ruins the big guns had made of much of the edifice could only nod his head dumbly at first. It was bad away from the safer, inner perimeter, no doubt about it.

After a moment Pendergast gasped out, "Fontaine, go tell the major that Captain Davis's been hit. Well . . . shit . . . tell him he's dead . . . I mean really fucking dead. Tell him I put Royce in charge of that sector." Pendergast trembled slightly with the vivid memory of a man ripped into two pieces and screaming his lungs out—begging, pleading—for someone, anyone, to kill him and put him out of his agony.

Though Pendergast didn't mention that part; could not, in fact. The memory of his own rifle's muzzle pressed against Davis' head . . . the squeeze of the trigger . . . the flash that burned even through his closed eyes . . . no, that he could not mention, nor even quite bring himself to think about . . .

"Sergeant Major? Sergeant Major, wake up."

Pendergast's eyes opened immediately from the rough shoving. It took him several moments to place the voice. "Major Williams? Sorry, sir, I just . . ."

"Never mind. You needed the sleep. But sleep time is over. The guards say there's movement outside, a lot of it. All the walls."

"Figure they're coming?"

"Yes . . . BMNT comes in about forty minutes. I figure they'll hit us simultaneously from every direction."

Pendergast forced a smile with a confidence he did not truly feel. "We'll hold 'em, sir, never worry."

Outskirts of Santa Fe, New Mexico

Tripp really could not quite believe his good luck, if it was luck. Still, against his own expectation here he was, he and his battalion, sheltered under cover in a small town south of the city.

Though the people were friendly and cooperative, Tripp had had the phone lines and cellular repeater tower knocked down just in case. Now, with a small party dressed in civilian clothes forward to recon the state house and the routes leading towards it, the battalion—minus a small local security element, himself, the company commanders and the staff—caught up on rest. Even those still awake had had some chance to eat; Tripp vaguely remembered reading an Israeli study that said troops recently rested, fed and watered were much more effective than those without that consideration. Not that it would have mattered what any study said; to Tripp it just seemed plain common sense.

CHAPTER SEVENTEEN

From the transcript at trial: Commonwealth of Virginia v. Alvin Scheer

DIRECT EXAMINATION, CONTINUED
BY MR. STENNINGS:

Q. You watched the entire battle on television, Alvin?

A. No, sir. I didn't see when it started, wasn't even awake yet. Though the TV did give some flashbacks. But I did see everything that went on from about ten o'clock that morning until late that afternoon. That took a lot of beer, like I said.

The beer was maybe a mistake because I starting cheering when they showed some of the killed and wounded being brought out on stretchers. Some folks in the bar weren't too happy about that and I shut right up.

Didn't stop me from smiling a whole lot, though.

Western Currency Facility, Fort Worth, Texas

"Think of it as an opportunity," Major Williams had suggested, once the artillery pounding had begun. "Sure, they will make some holes in the walls. Likely they'll get some of us, too. But see, we will know where those holes are . . . and we'll be able to prepare a very warm reception for anyone trying to come through one."

And so it had been. Working like beavers whenever there was a lull in the incoming fire, sometimes even when there was not, the defenders of the WCF had shifted firing positions, moving entire bunkers to take advantage of the routes in that they now knew the PGSS must use.

Unseen in one such midnight-dark bunker, Fontaine forced a smile to his face. He had perhaps hoped that the smile would give him confidence, even help him to slow his rapidly beating heart. It did not; his heart continued to pound in his chest, breath coming short and hard.

This was worse, far worse, than the first day's action had been. Then, following Pendergast around and simply doing what he was told, the young enlisted man had barely had time to think; he could only react. Now, with weeks of pondering and fretting behind him—weeks of tension, days of frightful bombardment and hours of chest-pounding fear . . . the boy was simply terrified half out of his wits.

He heard the scraping of something metallic on the concrete floor behind his bunker. A friend, he was sure; there had been no break in as of yet.

"Fontaine, that you?"

"Yes, Top . . . I mean, Sergeant Major. Me and Silva on the machine gun."

Pendergast noticed the strain in the boy's voice. "You okay, boys?"

"I'll be fine, Sergeant Major. It's just the waiting . . ." Silva grunted agreement.

"Not much waiting to go. They're massing all around."

"I know. Sometimes you can hear the diesels," answered Fontaine. "They're close. . . ."

Under the dim red overhead light, Sawyers crouched in the back of one of the LAVs, looking over the sketch of the objective, looking for flaws in his plan. Occasionally, the light of one of the radios mounted forward, behind the driver, would illuminate his face with an orange glow.

Four times had the radio's light flashed as his assault columns reported having taken up their positions. Now Sawyers heard the fifth, expected, transmission.

The transmission warbling, broken; the "fifth column"—two companies of PGSS aboard Army helicopters—reported, "five minutes out."

Sawyers keyed his own micophone, "Black this is Black Six. Five minutes."

A chorus of "Rogers" made the radio light flicker like a strobe.

It had just become light enough for the pilots to dispense with their night vision goggles. Warrant Officer Harrington announced, "Co-pilot's ship," then released his stick as he felt the other warrant take over. He could have simply left the goggles attached to his helmet, flipping them up and out of the way. But he'd never liked the weight of the things so he opened the plastic case, removed the goggles and placed them in the case.

He looked around and behind him at the thirteen PGSS "agents" littering his passenger area. His eyes rested momentarily on the two thick, coiled ropes on the floor to either side of the helicopter. *I have a big surprise for you boys*, he thought, darkly. "Pilot's ship."

"Here they cooommme!" shouted the man, Smithfield, bearing the antitank weapon up near the hole in the wall.

Fontaine's heart began to pound even harder than before. Even so, he gripped his rifle, steadying it on the sandbags of the bunker and taking a general aim at the seven-foot-wide hole blown in the wall that was his firing sector, his and the machine gunner's.

"You ready, Silva?" he asked.

As if to punctuate and agree in one, Fontaine heard a machine-gun bolt slam home.

"Be careful you don't hit the antitank man up by the hole," Fontaine cautioned.

"No sweat, Fontaine. We done worked it out. Smitty's going to fire one round, two if he can get away with it . . . and ain't that going to ring our chimes, back here? . . . then crawl left and back to us while I cover. No problem."

"'Ring our chimes'? You sure Smitty worked out the backblast problem?"

"Oh yeah . . . we got just enough ventilation . . . just enough to live through it, that is."

The roaring diesels of the PGSS suddenly grew louder. Fontaine heard, distinctly, "Backblast area clear!"

Then it seemed like the world blew up.

It was overkill, really. The rocket Smithfield was using was an AT-4. Brutally, even impractically, heavy for a one-man weapon, it had been designed to defeat heavy armor, armor much heavier than any LAV boasted.

Thus, within less than a second after Smithfield had fired, the warhead had reached its target. The cone shape began to deform on striking, crushing a piezo-electric crystal within. This created a momentary surge of electricity that raced down to the warhead detonator. This exploded, causing the rest of the explosive in the warhead to likewise detonate.

That explosive was also shaped into a cone, but in a mirror of the ballistic cone to the front, this cone was recessed. Most of the explosion was, in effect, lost in every direction. Yet a portion was not. In the hollow cone hot gasses collected. These were held and focused by the surrounding explosion. The collected gasses then formed a plasma jet, moving at phenomenal speeds ... straight towards and right through the armor of the PGSS LAV.

If the defenders of the facility had been partially and momentarily stunned by the serious backblast emanating from the AT-4, the recipients of that fire were more than stunned. One unfortunate, the one right in the path of the shaped charge's blast, felt only a momentary flash of agonized burning before the hot gasses forced into his body caused his torso to literally explode.

Being covered with bits of flesh and slime was the least of the occupants' problems, however. The sudden overpressure, pressure which could not escape the sealed armored vehicle, burst the eardrums of every man trapped inside. Most were knocked out, outright. Several took serious interior damage to vital organs from the concussive blast.

And then the vehicle began to burn. . . .

"The bitch is burning!" shouted an exultant Smithfield as he began to prep his second AT-4 for firing. "Hah, hah . . . look at it. . . ."

The burst of machine gun fire coming from another of the approaching LAVs brought the soldier's celebration up very short.

"Oh fuck . . . oh, fuck," whispered the sergeant, looking down at red ruin and spurting blood. Drilled through a thousand repetitions for operation of the antitank weapon, the man's hands continued to go through the motions even as his life leaked away. But the hands moved so slowly . . . so slowly.

Smithfield looked up to seek a new target. He did not need to look very far or very hard as the bulk of a LAV loomed above, a scant 15 feet from the hole.

What the fuck? I'm dead anyway. He raised the weapon, took a hasty aim and . . .

"My God!" exclaimed Silva as Smith's inert body came to rest a few feet to his right where the force of the blast had blown it. One glance was enough to confirm; Smithfield was very dead, his blasted and shot-up body actually smoking. A faint glow outside the smoke-filled hole in the wall suggested very strongly that Smith's final shot had been as true as his first.

Silva poked a finger in one ear, rooted around briefly, then settled back onto his machine gun and began to hammer out a staccato concert for the benefit of the PGSS men just beginning to ooze through the hole.

Harrington eased back on his stick as the helicopter arrived over one corner of the WCF's roof. He took a quick glance below, then turned to his crew chief with a nod.

The crew chief on one side and the door gunner on the other tossed the thick coiled cables out of the troop doors. The cables' free ends descended rapidly to the roof below. Above, great black nylon loops affixed to pipelike projections jutting from either side held the ropes in easy reach of the PGSS men. The crew chief, mirrored by the door gunner, took positive control of the PGSS troopers, easing them to where they could easily grasp the ropes. Those men grasped the ropes, looking straight ahead into the distance.

At the command, "Go!" one man to either side began the slide downward.

Ahead, in the pilot's seat, Harrington eased his stick ever so slightly to port. The helicopter responded, sliding to the left unnoticed.

Below, the first pair of descenders touched down without incident about fourteen feet from the edge of the roof. The second pair were closer to that edge, much closer.

The third and subsequent pairs . . .

"Arrrgh! Jessssuuus!"

❖   ❖   ❖

"That motherfucker did it on purpose!" screamed one of the four, only four, men of the chalk who had landed safely. The other nine had, much to their surprise and chagrin, discovered that the rope ran out about seventy feet above the ground. Both surprise and chagrin had been brief phenomena, rapidly replaced by panic-stricken shrieks. The shrieks, too, had subsided very quickly as the men, by twos, had slammed into the hard-packed ground. These now lay in crumpled heaps—dead or very badly injured.

The angry survivor raised a rifle as if to fire at the helicopter. Only the door gun, pointed unerringly at his chest by the door gunner, dissuaded him from firing.

That gun never wavered as a chuckling Warrant Officer Harrington pulled pitch to go back for another load.

It was funny how he had named the only man who could save him now . . . snickered Harrington, silently. *Just wait til Top Henry hears about this. Now how the hell do I explain my way out of this one? Oh, I know . . .*

Harrington keyed a microphone on the general frequency. "All flights inbound the objective area, be advised, we have some high winds gusting over the roof. My bird was blown off position about fifteen or twenty feet while I was fast-roping some people in . . . it was pretty ugly." He looked back at the target building and smiled.

"Motherfuckers," repeated the PGSS man as he watched the helicopter recede into the distance.

"Never mind that," insisted his leader. "We'll fix that asshole after we take the building. Now, help me carry this breaching charge."

With that those four survivors, plus the others landed nearby, raced for a place believed to be sheltered from any explosives the defenders might push through the roof. There, they began to lay out a doughnut ring full of shaped plastic explosive.

Bullets caromed off walls with malevolent cracking sounds before continuing on their half-spent way farther into the building. From a sandbagged shelter Pendergast fired nine short bursts from his rifle before pressing the magazine release and seating a new magazine. Farther back and below, a bloody hand snaked out to grab the spent magazine as it bounced. Empty magazine retrieved, the wounded guardsman who had grabbed it attached a small device and frantically force-fed more rounds, in ten round clips, into it.

From behind, a man with a blood-streaked face crawled into the bunker with Pendergast and the other. He reached a distracting hand to Pendergast's shoulder. "Sergeant Major . . ." the troop gasped out. "They're on the roof . . . I mean through the roof . . . all over . . . we ain't gonna hold 'em. . . ."

Pendergast looked from the newly arrived troop to the other. *Both wounded pretty bad. And I can't leave here.*

"Can you make it to Major Williams, son?"

The newly arrived soldier gulped unconsciously and nodded.

"Go then. Tell him. Tell him we're holding okay here too . . . but I don't know for how long."

New-filled magazine seated in the rifle, the sergeant major turned back to the serious business of discouraging unwanted guests.

Williams helped ease the bleeding and exhausted soldier to a chair as he digested the news. Reaching a sudden decision he looked around the command post. *One junior lieutenant, a sergeant, James . . . and a number of people whose eyes just became much wider in their heads.*

"Jimbo . . . take over here. I'm going to go try to seal the breach in the roof."

Captain James nodded weakly, then began to pull himself to a sitting position. Ordinarily he should have stayed in the makeshift infirmary . . . yet he had insisted his place of duty was here in the CP. His eyes wandered to a curious device with four playing cards, blue pattern printed, attached to it.

"I can do this. Go," he half whispered.

Williams saw where James' eyes had come to rest. He drew his pistol from its holster with his right hand, grabbed the company guidon with his left, then ordered, quietly, "Do it then. Take over. The rest of you"—a hand swept in the other eighteen or so men in the room—"fix bayonets and follow me."

Smoke filled the air in the upper half of the unblocked corridor, causing the necessarily tight little knot of troopers following Williams to have to crouch half bent over. *Somewhere, some portion of the building must have caught fire*, mused the major. *Might help; might hurt. No telling.*

From nowhere, seemingly, a rifle-bearing man

in the black battle dress and helmet of the PGSS
appeared. The agent appeared confused as much as
anything. Possibly he was in shock, as sometimes
happens with soldiers in sustained, close and vicious
combat.

Williams raised his pistol, took two steps towards the
disoriented agent, aimed and fired. The bullet entered
the victim's head having passed squarely through the
bridge of his nose. Both eyes were forced out of the
man's head even as his brains scattered across the light
green painted wall behind him.

Waving his pistol forward, Williams repeated the
refrain, "Come on; follow me."

The smoke grew worse, chokingly worse, as the
group ascended a broad flight of stairs. "Don masks,"
Williams ordered, though he knew this would not
help if the fire—wherever it was—had sucked all the
oxygen from the air. "Forward."

From chokingly thick with smoke the air soon
became a gaseous morass of blinding fumes and sooty
embers. Williams could see precisely nothing. He felt
the tension and fear of uncertainty emanating from
the men following him.

"Nothing is good," he whispered to himself.

"Sir?"

"We can't see, right?"

"No, sir . . . not a goddamned thing."

"That means they can't see either, right?"

"Yes, sir . . . ohhh."

"Right. We've been here before. They haven't. Let's
go . . . quietly. And remember; we have this corridor
booby trapped about fifty yards ahead."

Onward they crept, silently. Ahead were shouts and

orders. None sounded quite like Army standard. Nor were the accents, in general, quite right.

"Bayonets only," ordered Williams, wishing he had one himself; that or a good sword. *Oh, well, the guidon will do for a spear.* "Come on . . . and once we hit 'em? 'Keep up the skeer.'"

Williams holstered his pistol and reversed the guidon, gripping it firmly in both hands. Then, with a fierce toothy grin, sharklike, he advanced.

The first PGSS man was taken from the rear. Concentrating on some problem up ahead, that man never heard the stealthy approach of the Texans.

Williams' eyes registered neck-to-buttocks Kevlar and decided that the only way in was right through the aramid fibers. He drew the guidon back a bit, then with an open mouthed, predatory glare he drove it forward, all of his bodily weight and strength behind it. The sharp point of the ferule touched the tightly woven fibers and slid slightly until reaching a small space where two of them met. The point parted these, parting likewise the next several layers. A small flange on the ferule hung up on the fibers. No matter, the point only penetrated three inches into the PGSS man's back—missing his spine by several inches—but the force of the thrust, along with the surprise, knocked the wind from his body. He went down, gasping for air.

Williams, on the point, pressed onward. Behind, another of his men tore the helmet from the fallen PGSS man, half strangling him in the process. That guardsman then proceeded to beat his victim's skull in with his own helmet.

Bayonets slashed; rifle butts crashed. In moments

the corridor had turned into a swirling orgy of struggling, screaming, cursing and fighting men.

And then it was over. Williams saw the last actively resisting enemy physically picked up by a bayonet point thrust under his armor and into his groin and then tossed, screaming, upon the tangled and matted up wad of barbed wire that had been blocking the corridor. He released the corpse of the man he had strangled and looked around. The guidon was broken in two, though the smoke was too thick to see more than the kindled upper half of it. To his right another guardsman was rhythmically cursing as he raised his rifle over and over to smash it downward into the red paste face of what might have been a PGSS *woman*. All the others were gasping for breath except for two who had had their own masks torn off in the fight and were choking and vomiting as they frantically attempted to reseat their masks.

A headcount revealed there were four Texans dead or so badly wounded that they could not go on. No one bothered with a headcount for the PGSS as they were very dead indeed.

Williams grasped the remnant of the guidon in his left hand, redrew his pistol with his right, and ordered, "Forward," while pointing the pistol up a broad stairwell.

They met the enemy—the next wave of the enemy— as they were coming down the very stairs the Texans were going up. This time, with fresh men facing worn ones, with momentum on the side of the PGSS, and worst of all without the surprise that had made the previous encounter such a relatively easy victory, the Texans could not win.

Yet they died hard. Williams met the first of the PGSS' thrusting bayonets with a sweeping block from the guidon. Then he plunged his pistol forcefully into the soft spot under the jaw of the bayonet wielder and pulled the trigger to create a shower of brains, blood and red-speckled bone.

To Williams' right a Texan went down to a bayonet thrust that just cleared the man's Kevlar collar before plunging seven inches into his neck. Williams swept his pistol rightward but a rifle-smash from the PGSS blocked his arm, hurling the pistol away.

Undeterred, Williams plunged in. Dropping to one knee, he used the dullish spearpoint of the guidon to pierce the thigh of one likely target. He heard a dull, muffled curse then lunged through the forest of flailing legs to come to grips with his foe.

Crenshaw felt the piercing point as a wedge of fire burning rather than cutting into his leg. It did not slice the muscle so much as it tore it asunder. The pain was so great that he could barely mutter a curse before losing control of his body. With an unintelligible, agonized gasp he fell to the stairs.

His eyes rapidly lost focus as his brain tried to deal with the pain. His fuzzy near view was blocked by a tangle of legs as his far view was by the smoke, and the ex-Marine could not truly see the clawing hyena that tore its way up his body in a desperate effort to reach his throat.

"Hh . . . Help," he barely squeezed out. "Help me."

No need; as the Texan clawed his way upward four PGSS bayonets drove downward. Crenshaw breathed

a sigh of what would have been relief had his thigh
not been so horribly gored.

As he began to pass out, he heard someone . . . His
XO? He wasn't sure . . . yet someone shouted for a
medic and to "get the captain the hell out of here.
And no quarter!"

Williams barely noticed as his life's blood drained
away, barely noticed the dozens of booted feet tramp-
ling him on their way past. Behind and below him
he could, dimly, make out the sounds of his soldiers
going down with a bitterly hard fight.

He thought, *We needed more men . . . we could
have held if we'd had more men . . . the rest of the
battalion . . .*

Then, without a whimper, he died.

Santa Fe, New Mexico

His breath coming short and harsh, Tripp felt the
exhilaration and the terror of impending combat.
Around him, ahead of him . . . but mostly behind him,
his battalion's tracks began to turn over, one after
another. The soft whine of the tanks' engines was lost
amidst the thunderous roar of the Bradleys' diesels.

Just ahead of Tripp stood a lone police car from
the Santa Fe Police Department. The officer standing beside the patrol car looked expectantly upward.
Tripp nodded, slowly and deeply. The officer jumped
in, started his sirens, and began to lead the battalion
forward at a fast clip.

Useful that that cop decided to attach himself to

us, thought Tripp. *No telling what accidents we might have had with civilian autos crossing our path at every intersection.*

Civilian bystanders, drawn by the sirens, came out to watch the battalion's progress. A few, understanding, cheered.

The column raced on, the leading police vehicle changing the lights by remote control at each intersection.

Tripp's mind wandered to that portion of his men cut off in Fort Worth. He thought that it would go hard on them when the PGSS assault finally went in, very hard . . . terminally hard.

This isn't really war, is it? Tripp asked himself. *Do the rules even apply? To people that gunned down helpless civilians and outgunned state troopers. Fuck it; today they don't.*

His eyes steel cold and determined, Tripp keyed the radio by flicking a switch on the right side of his helmet. "Battalion, this is Black Six. The rules do not apply to these murderers. No quarter."

Western Currency Facility, Fort Worth, Texas

Crenshaw found himself sliding in and out of consciousness with neither pattern nor control. He remembered sharp pains, at times. At others he could recall only a dim foggy ache. He managed to turn his head to one side.

More broken toys like me, he thought. There seemed to be a lot of pain going around, much moaning, many screams. *Why don't we have enough medics to treat the wounded? Didn't they know we would have wounded. Where are the helicopters, the dust-offs?*

Turning to the other side, Crenshaw saw black-clad men, more and more of them, ascending what had to be flexible ladders anchored on the roof and dropped over the sides of the building. Unable to turn his head very well, he lost track of those men as they cleared his field of vision.

His vision blurred, dimmed. Crenshaw passed out.

Santa Fe, New Mexico

The Surgeon General's Riot Control Police had plenty of warning, both immediate, from the siren, and more long range, from a few sympathetic reports.

So they did what they could. They got behind their cars and busses; loaded their shotguns, pistols and submachine guns. And then they waited for a short time.

The tracks hit the police cordon from two directions. Tanks led, but they led with their machine guns and their bulk, scorning to use their cannon on such trivial targets.

Ahead of Tripp, his lead tank, A-24—nicknamed "Abdan," stitched a row of half-inch holes across the waiting line of SGRCP vehicles. The turret traversed slowly . . . leaving holes in the metal much too close together for there to be many survivors behind that metal.

Abdan swept onward, reaching, cresting and—in

the process—crushing the pitifully thin-walled civilian vehicles. Its crew did not hear the mournful cries that came from crushed federal riot control agents as it pressed their lives out like juice from grapes.

The turret turned, fast—so fast, and began chattering out a new chorus at panicking thugs in armor fleeing from the hastily formed line of police cars. The bullets, heavy .50-caliber rounds—one in five a tracer, danced among the routing RCPs, each bullet giving off a flat, heavy crack as it tore the air.

Behind the terrorized federales more armored vehicles reached and battered their way across or through the barrier. These, too, joined the chorus, lighter machine guns adding the sound of giant sailcloths ripped asunder by giants. More police fell in tumbles and shrieks.

"No quarter," repeated Tripp, over the radio and the men of his command took it as gospel.

Western Currency Facility, Fort Worth, Texas

Crenshaw awoke as a crew of Army medics bustled his stretcher aboard a "dust off" bird. His shock was so great that he could not speak, could not acknowledge the softly spoken, confident, "You'll be fine. It isn't a bad one," the medic reassured him with as he gave the wounded ex-Marine a shot of much needed morphine.

Even with the morphia, Crenshaw screamed, once, as a medic accidentally jostled the barbed spear sticking into and from his leg.

"I'm sorry, Captain. Sorry. I couldn't help it."

Crenshaw tried to reassure the man that he understood, that it was all right. Tried, but lacked the strength.

In any case, the medic was gone to the other side of the bird before he had a chance to do so. And then Crenshaw felt the sudden surge of the helicopter lifting with its burden of broken parts.

Maybe I'll make it. . . .

The helicopter flew away a distance to the northeast and then turned, heading west to a Fort Worth hospital. The PGSS man watched the smoking building recede. Everything went suddenly dark and he knew his vision was blacking out again.

It was dark down in the subterranean levels of the Currency Facility; dark with smoke but also simply dark from the electricity having been cut off. The only lights were the usual red-filtered emergency ones. These were enough to show a dirt- and blood-begrimed Pendergast the last dozen worn out survivors of the defense force. One man, Fontaine, held the only entrance in or out.

Well . . . this is about the end, thought the sergeant major. *There might be a few of us still kicking and gouging, here and there, but this is about it.* A faint chatter of rifle fire, followed up by two grenadelike explosions, confirmed his judgment.

He glanced at the weakened Captain James, barely keeping his head up. He looked at the shocked and dazed few that remained. He looked to the small device with playing cards wired to it.

Doesn't seem right, somehow, to just blow these guys up. "Suicide's a sin," the nuns always taught.

Pendergast shook his head, ruefully, and walked over to James and the device. He shook the captain to a semblance of alertness. "Sir, we're gonna charge. I'm gonna hand you the 'aces and eights.' You hang on as long as you can, then just let go, okay?"

James forced a hollow smile. "Okay, Top . . . I me . . ."

"Top's just fine for this, sir." He handed the captain a device that looked like nothing so much as the torsional steel hand-grip exerciser from which it had been created. "Get a good grip, sir," he advised. Seeing that James had as good a grip—though, in truth, it wasn't all that good—as he was capable of, Pendergast removed the steel oval that had held the device safe. He laid the cards down on a desk—aces and eights.

"All right, you apes," he shouted loud enough even to wake the zombies under his command. "The captain is live. We're gonna charge now. On three . . . one . . . two . . . THRR—"

James lost his grip and eleven tons of Ammonium Nitrate-Fuel Oil finished the job the PGSS had begun. Along with eight hundred and forty seven of the PGSS that had been in the building.

CHAPTER EIGHTEEN

From the transcript at trial: Commonwealth of
Virginia v. Alvin Scheer

DIRECT EXAMINATION, CONTINUED
BY MR. STENNINGS:

Q. I saw the same thing, Alvin. What did you think
   had happened?

A. No question about what happened, sir. Not even
   then. See, you can't even grow up in Texas without
   learning about the Alamo, even if you grow up
   kind of dumb like me. Those folks knew the
   story as well as I did. Maybe better. They blew
   themselves up, there at the end. I knew it as sure
   as I knew the beer I was drinking had gone warm
   and a little flat.

Q. And the other people . . . just your own impressions,
   Alvin?

A. They was shocked. Maybe stunned is a better word.
   I'd guess they just didn't realize, up to then, how
   damned serious Texas, and the Governor, were.

Austin, Texas

"It's over, Juani."

The governor's head rested on folded arms on her desk. Eyes puffed and reddened with lack of sleep, she looked up from the papers, reports and files littering the wood to gaze blearily upon Schmidt. "The Currency Facility?" she asked.

Schmidt nodded. "Yes. Gone. At the end they blew the whole thing up, just like they said they would. There won't be any survivors. Even televised, I've never seen anything like it. No survivors."

Juani spoke dully, "My fault, too, I suppose."

Schmidt shook his head, then walked around the large desk to take Juanita's face firmly in both hands. "No, Juani. Not your fault. You did what you had to."

He moved a hand from her left cheek to the top of her head, tussling her hair as he had not since the day he had left Texas for a war few wanted to remember. "I was so proud of you, my Juanita. Always, but never so much as the day you made the only decision you could have under the circumstances; the decision to lose the Currency Facility and save New Mexico."

Juani found speech difficult. Nonetheless, she choked back her feelings and nodded brisky. "Thank you, Jack. Now what?"

Schmidt drew a hesitant breath. "What happens? Well, Third Corps continues to come south to Austin, the Marines and 18th Airborne Corps to our east continue to get ready to hammer us . . . and eventually they do."

"Out west?"

Schmidt took a deep breath before answering. "Fact is, Juani, I don't know. Their commander wants them to openly side with us, I think. But politically, he just doesn't have the horses inside his own organization for that."

"Politically? In a military organization?" Juani looked extremely skeptical.

"Yes, 'politically.' Oh, I know people look at the military and see a dictatorship. But it just isn't so. Every military organization is a very delicate—and to a large degree democratic—political entity. A commander is more than a rabble-rouser and cheerleader, true. But if he didn't have some political skills, to persuade his own troops, he'd be hopeless."

"You've never explained this to me before."

"You never needed to know," Schmidt answered.

Schmidt paused momentarily, then said, "There is something you need to know though and it also has to do with our friends around El Paso."

Juani turned her hand palm up and made a "come on, give" gesture.

"The Marine part of it is based out of San Diego. There have been a couple of incidents involving, apparently, the families of some of the Marines."

"Incidents?"

Schmidt gave a disgusted sigh. "A speech that turned into a demonstration. A demonstration that turned nasty. Several break-ins. One rape. One murder. One other rape that ended in a murder. My people are trying to confirm some rumors that the PGSS," he showed a wicked smile, "or what's left of them anyway, are being sent there to take the Marines' families into protective custody."

"Hostages," announced the governor.

"Hostages," agreed Schmidt.

"What will that do to us? If they take the Marines' families hostage I mean?"

"Juani, I haven't a clue. It could mean that suddenly our western flank is open and vulnerable again. It could mean that the Marines march right back to San Diego picking up as much rope on the way as they can get their hands on. If the White House handles it just right it could mean nothing more than that the Marines stay out of play. If the White House can do it, or thinks it can do it, it could mean the Marines start to march on us again. But I can't tell you which."

"I can tell you that if the PGSS lost as many men as I think they did at Fort Worth there are going to be some pissed-off honchos . . . the kind that are not too likely to handle a delicate mission well."

"How many do you think were killed, Jack?"

"Over a thousand. Maybe over two thousand. They are going to be really, *really* pissed, Juani."

El Paso, Texas

"Motherfuckers haven't seen what pissed means, yet," murmured the Marine, Fulton, as he read his intelligence officer's reports of the incidents happening to his people's families back in California. "Funny how the Presidential Guard was ready to move in to 'secure things' so quickly. Yes . . . funny."

Fulton lifted his eyes from the report to shout to his driver, sitting at a makeshift desk just outside the door. "Get me the quartermaster, the division recon battalion commander, and the trans officer. Now!"

Then, very softly so that none but he might hear yet, Fulton said, "And I'll need lines to Austin and Camp Pendleton."

Camp Pendleton, California

Mrs. Fulton spoke calmly over the phone. She was certain that, whatever problems she and the other dependents at and around the camp had, her husband's problems were much, much worse. She spoke calmly, but also very carefully. The Presidential Guard officer seated opposite her seemed much too unstable—a boiling mix of anger, pain, fear, regret and something the general's wife could not quite put her finger on—to risk his displeasure.

"Yes, dear, it looked like a spontaneous thing. Someone started speaking downtown and the next thing we knew there was a crowd marching on the camp gates. Some of the crowd didn't come here, though. They fanned out over some of the nearby residential areas . . . looking for the wives, I guess. It was pretty bad . . . yes, dear, you do know some of the women that were caught up in it. You remember Captain Diaz' wife—cute little thing? She's in the hospital and it doesn't look good.

"Yes, dear, we're all safe enough now. The Presidential Guard has taken over our security and is evacuating all the dependents they can find from off the installation. Everyone is kicking in to put them up in our quarters, doubling up. The overflow is going to gyms, the theaters, anyplace we can get a roof over their heads.

"Yes, dear . . . I'm sure we'll all be fine," she lied. "You just take care of yourself and the division."

El Paso, Texas

Hanstadt had been closest. Alone, clad in civilian clothes, he had driven a commandeered rental car from San Antonio west, down the Balcones Escarpment, past the thin, amorphous Texan "front" line and to the forward trace of the 1st Marine Division.

There, at a nondescript segment of Interstate 10, he had been met by Fulton's sergeant major. After saluting and looking over Hanstadt's bona fides, the sergeant major had escorted him through the lines and onward to Division Headquarters.

At the headquarters were a number of tour busses, each with a full or nearly full load of men clad in civilian clothes. The men were so obviously Marines that Hanstadt wondered why they even bothered. Entering the headquarters, Hanstadt was unsurprised to see both the accompanying sergeant major as well as the uniformed guards at the entrance "present arms" to another civilian clad man who looked about the right age to be a somewhat youngish battalion commander.

Seeing Hanstadt's raised eyebrow the sergeant major merely said, "General Fulton will brief you on that, I imagine, sir."

"I can hardly wait, Sergeant Major."

Hanstadt was startled as a long rattle of musketry,

seemingly from some miles away, shook the windows of the headquarters.

Austin, Texas

Juani stared from her office window at the gathering clouds. So many problems pressed upon her that it could not be said she was concentrating, or was even able to think clearly, upon any one of them. In a few days, she knew, the main body of the force to the north would arrive in the vicinity of Austin; the point of that dagger had long since come. To the east, Houston, cut off from open communication, was rumored to be in a state of violent anarchy. South the Navy stood poised to descend upon the coast. Further south, from Panama, she had been informed that the ruse was wearing pretty thin and that soon the gates of the Canal must be opened to pass the Marines through.

Far to the west? New Mexico was beginning, late and slowly, to imitate Texas. Nearer though, in the vicinity of El Paso, the Marines were forming up for something. Possibly to march east again. Jack had told her, though, that their supply status was said still to be terrible so perhaps if they marched, they would do so slowly. Even so, combat could not be far away; not on any front.

Besides New Mexico, not a single governor or legislature had thrown in with Texas, despite her pleas. They were sympathetic, yes. They wished her and Texas well, yes. They were "concerned" about the direction the country would take after Texas went under, yes.

They were afraid of the same treatment . . . also, yes. *"Governor, if you somehow manage to survive what's coming for you then maybe we can talk."*

So deep in her thoughts was she, yes—and her bitterness, that Juani didn't notice as Schmidt entered and quietly closed her office door behind him.

He cleared his throat to announce his arrival.

"Yes, Jack?" she answered, without moving her eyes from the cold gray sky.

"Hanstadt's back."

"And?"

"He says the Marines are going to take care of their own problems with the PGSS. For now, they are under a threat and they know it. The White House has been too canny to try to force them to do anything . . . but the message was clear: if the Marines decide to side with us their families will suffer for it."

"That means that the Marine—Fulton was his name?—is going to have to turn back control to the political people that were watching him before they were arrested."

"Ummm . . . no. Hanstadt said that Fulton had the less important half all shot and is holding the rest as hostages of his own."

Wide eyed, Juanita's hand flew to her mouth. "Oh, *my*."

"I confess, I like the man's sincerely . . . oh . . . forthright attitude. Can't get much more sincere than shooting seventy-one federal agents and mid-ranking members of the incumbent party out of hand. I am pulling back the people we have facing him by about twenty miles and moving their supply dumps back thirty. We just can't know what is going to happen with

1st Marine Division and, if it turns to shit, I'd rather have them walking forward at maybe three miles an hour than rolling forward—using our gas—at forty."

"If things work out the way they are supposed to in California, Fulton is going to need gas though. He says that the second his people's dependents are safe then the 1st Marine Division and 3rd Armored Cavalry regiment will declare for Texas."

"And the other side of that," observed Juani, "is that if they can't rescue their families, and if those families continue to be held hostage, and if it looks like the Presidential Guard is bloody minded then the Marines might have to attack us."

Interstate 10, Arizona

Miles and miles of fuck all, thought Diaz as the bus carrying him and the bulk of his company continued on a seemingly endless track through desert and scrub.

Seated at the front, he was in position to see, or rather not to see, the other busses returning 1st Recon Battalion to its home. He could not see any of the others because they were strung out over more than one hundred miles and many were not even using the Interstate.

Not for the first time Diaz felt an almost overpowering urge to call home. He could not, he knew. The operation was a potential intelligence sieve already and, should the people "guarding" the Marine's families find out they were coming, there was no telling what might happen.

Not that it was home, precisely, that Diaz wanted to call. His wife would not be there, he knew. She was comatose in the hospital. But a friend? A comrade's wife? Anybody who could assure him that she would be fine.

Even if the assurance were a lie, still he wanted it.

Before leaving Texas, Diaz's initial anger had been directed toward the unknown, unnamed, likely never-to-be-caught assailants. Then his division commander had sat him down and asked him to consider a few questions; questions like, "Whose good did this all accrue to; what happened to your wife and the others?" Questions like, "And isn't it funny that the PGSS was ready to move at a moment's notice after coming out of one of the bloodiest battles ever to take place in this hemisphere?" And, "Do you suppose it's a coincidence that we voted to bow out of the current troubles and then our families were attacked?" And, "Isn't it funny how the demonstration that got out of hand started with a speaker from the party in power? The same party that controls the PGSS? The same PGSS that was ever so ready to take our families hostage?"

And so, after reflection, Diaz had added up one plus one plus one plus one plus one and come up with the mathematically suspect but morally perfectly precise answer, "Rottemeyer."

"Bright boy," Fulton had beamed. "And I assure you we are going to get even . . . if not a bit ahead."

Diaz wanted assurance of, oh, many things. And, knowing he could not have it, he turned his thoughts, along with his eyes, to a map of Camp Pendleton and thought about the one form of assurance he thought he could have.

Austin, Texas

"Time to leave, Juani," announced Schmidt. "They'll be here in a few hours. And you can't let them catch you."

"I'm not leaving the Capital, Jack. Just forget it. It's not going to happen."

Schmidt answered, "Governor, the federals will be here in a couple of hours. They may stop and wait a bit if they think we are going to fight. And," Schmidt held up a quieting palm, "we are going to fight. But the end result is all the same. Now you have to leave. Before the bullets start to fly.

"Juani, if you don't go quietly I'll have you carried out."

Juani set her face grimly, plainly determined to argue. Jack was having none of it, equally plainly.

She relented. "I have a few hours, don't I?"

Seeing his nod she continued, "Then I want to make a televised address before I go."

"Okay, Governor. We have time for that."

"You've never approved entirely of nonviolent civil disobedience I know, Jack. But I am going to give it one more try. Can your quartermaster come up with a great deal of transportation in a hurry?"

Camp Pendleton, California

Marines can be very practical folk. Faced with a lockdown of a fenced camp, said lockdown conflicting with either the desire not to be on the camp or the fact that one is on the other side of a fence—perhaps without permission—and wanting to be on the camp, a Marine will usually find a practical solution.

Nine times out of ten, he'll cut the fence.

The fence around Camp Pendleton had been cut so many times, by so many Marines, for so many excellent reasons, that more than one 1st Division commander had contemplated simply leaving the holes there.

Others had spent precious installation maintenance funds keeping the fence in constant repair.

Fulton had adopted a different approach. He had, true, repaired the fence upon his arrival. But then, somewhat unusually, he had had the likely cutting points guarded and ambushed.

For some weeks after his arrival, as a Marine cut the fence and was duly caught, Fulton had called out the battalion of the offender for a no-notice and rather strenuous roadmarch with full—rather overfull, actually—packs. The march was invariably followed by one or more weeks of pulling guard in full battle uniform, by companies, at the breach.

This worked at least to the extent that a) the Marines' breaching grew craftier and b) they tended to repair the cuts they made behind them.

The cuts were still there, of course, but harder to see, find, and use.

The PGSS knew nothing about the breaches, though Crenshaw might have told them had he not been in a hospital somewhere in Kansas.

The First Marine Division Reconnaissance Battalion knew *everything* there was to know about the breaches.

❖   ❖   ❖

Captain Emanuel Diaz, 1st Recon Battalion, lying in a shallow drainage ditch that led through the fence and into the camp understood all about the breaches. He understood full well, also, why he could not go to see his wife's shattered body where she lay in the hospital. Her mind wasn't there anyway, not for the nonce . . . not, perhaps, in the future.

She'd been beaten—badly—by thugs, before being raped.

Diaz twisted his neck, pulled down a shoulder and risked a single brown eyeball to look over the lip of the ditch. Standing to either side of a side entrance door, facing the ditch, stood—rather, slouched, and slouched in a manner that seemed tired unto exhaustion—two apparent members of the Presidential Guard.

The moon fell behind a cloud, darkening the landscape and, especially, the gymnasium that was the target for Diaz's crew. He tapped two men with a very softly whispered, "Go."

Sudden grins were as suddenly suppressed. Faces blackened, browned and greened; knives in hand, the men slithered from the drainage ditch that had run under the chain-link fence surrounding the camp.

"Swift, silent, deadly," whispered—prayed—Diaz. Celer, Silens, Mortalis—the motto of Marine Recon.

Diaz could neither see nor hear the snakelike approach or the action, in itself a good sign. But less than a dozen minutes later the glowing red of an issue filtered flashlight shone three times.

"Pass it on; follow me," he whispered before slithering out himself to join his point men.

From other places, along other avenues, the Marines

of 1st Recon slipped onto Camp Pendleton . . . swiftly, silently and—based on the number of black battle-dressed, bleeding, bashed, strangled, dismembered and throat-slashed corpses they left behind them—in a fashion *most* deadly.

El Paso, Texas

"1st Battalion reports Pendleton is secure, General," announced Fulton's flush-faced Public Affairs Officer, or PAO, bursting into the general's office. The PAO's voice grew somber. "Six of ours killed, seventeen wounded."

"The dependents?"

"Some are missing. The recon battalion is looking."

"The PGSS?"

The PAO gave an evil smile; he had not always been a paper pusher, had started in the Corps as a rifleman, in fact. "Surprisingly few prisoners."

Fulton grunted. "*You* may be surprised. I'm not."

The PAO lifted an eyebrow as much as to say, *that's an official notation of surprise, General, not a personal one.*

Fulton noted the raised eyebrow and correctly interpreted it—*no damned surprise at all.*

"Assemble the officers in one hour."

10,000 feet over Austin, Texas

The Air Force wouldn't play; that had been made clear enough. Whether pilots insisted they were too sick to fly or ground crews insisted that the planes were too sick to be flown, virtually nothing in the Air Force inventory had taken any part in the troubles. Nothing had taken any truly aggressive part.

But there were planes . . . and then there were planes. There were air forces hidden within a number of nonmilitary entities.

The CIA was one such.

Unburdened with a fighter pilot mafia, equally unburdened with a close-air-support mafia, the Central Intelligence Agency had taken to Remote Piloted Vehicles, RPVs for short, with a vengeance.

The Predator III RPV was one such. Descended from earlier models which had, over and over, proven their value both for reconnaissance and attack in foreign and hostile places, the III model was larger, faster, carried more of a bomb load, and carried a greater variety of ordnance as well.

Two of these models, remotely controlled via secure satellite link from the CIA's main headquarters in Langley, Virginia, circled high above Austin, Texas. The pilots, sitting in a dimly lit control room many leagues away from Austin, watched their screens and waited for the word to engage.

Austin, Texas

It wasn't that she had lived there all that long. Still, leaving the Governor's Mansion for what was quite possibly the very last time hurt in a way Juani had never expected.

The mansion was brightly lit. In anticipation of the

federal onslaught some of her assistants were boxing up state memorabilia to move south to San Antonio. Her husband was doing the same for family mementos. And Mario, who had still not forgiven his mother for sending Elpidia into danger in Houston, was busy, Juani knew, packing up Elpidia's meager possessions.

Juani turned to look briefly at her former home, then, at Jack Schmidt's insistence, boarded his Hummer for the long drive to the south.

Langley, Virginia

"We've got a vehicle pulling away from the target area," announced one of the Predator III pilots, hunching over a view screen. "Given that the house is lit up like Christmas, I don't like it."

"Can you identify the vehicle?" asked the mission chief.

The pilot snorted. Ten thousand feet was no obstacle with the television system he was using. "It's a Hummer. I can't make out the identity from this angle, but it's a Hummer."

The mission chief just wasn't sure. The Predators were carrying rather large bombs, suitable for demolishing a rather large house. But there were only the two of them. If they wasted one on the vehicle the other might not be enough to ensure the complete destruction of the target.

"Hold fire while I make a call," he announced.

"Hold up the car, Jack," Juani demanded.

The driver looked at Schmidt for confirmation.

Seeing the general's reluctant and heavy nod he applied the brake gently and pulled to a stop near the mansion ground's main gate. Juani fiddled with the plastic handle, pushed the light door open, and stepped out.

Jack and the driver, likewise, emerged from the vehicle. The driver left the Hummer running. Feet again on the asphalt, he walked a short distance away and caused a sound indistinguishable from water hitting a rock. Muttering something about discipline, Jack went to stand by Juanita.

Seeing Juani leaning against a stone pillar, her head hanging and tears streaming down her face, Jack threw an arm around her shoulder to lead her back to the Hummer.

"No," she insisted, voice breaking. "Not yet." Then, completely breaking down, she cried, "It's all over. . . ."

The mission chief said, "Yes, ma'am," into the telephone receiver. Then, hanging up the phone and turning to the pilots, he said, "Ignore the Hummer. More important to make sure nothing survives inside the mansion. But we have authority to attack now. Do it."

Without a word from either of them the two pilots began manipulating the controls that would bring their Predators into optimal attack position to ensure the Global Positioning System–guided bombs hit precisely where they were intended.

Schmidt had begun turning Juanita back to the Hummer by main force when something caught his eye. Reacting entirely by instinct, once finely honed and still at least good enough, he screamed "Down!" and forced her to the asphalt, covering her body with his own.

The driver, somewhat distracted by other concerns, never saw the smashed roofing material that flew up where two two-thousand pound bombs penetrated. He didn't see the walls and windows suddenly billow out, even as the roof, or rather pieces of it, began to ascend. He felt a remarkably sudden build-up of pressure.

And then he felt a very large piece of masonry smash his torso.

"Jesus," murmured one of the two pilots, watching the mansion disintegrate in his screen. "Jesus." The other pilot merely gave off a soft whistle. Neither had ever seen such complete demolition, done so suddenly, from their aircrafts' perspective.

The mission chief gave a grunt of approval, then picked up the telephone again to make his report.

"Nooo!" shrieked Juani once Jack had gotten off of her and helped her to her feet. "Nooo! Mario!" she wept for her son. "Emilio . . ." she murmured through tears for a lost husband.

She began to try to tear herself away from Schmidt's grip.

"No," he shouted, enfolding her in a bear's embrace. "They may not be done and you are too valuable to lose."

Juanita fought to escape but Jack was having none of it. Transferring his hold to grasp her in one arm he reopened the Hummer door with one hand, then used two to forcefully throw her into the front seat, slamming shut the door behind her.

Juani's head struck the steering wheel hard enough to stun her into submission while Schmidt ran frantically to the driver's side. He spared one glance at the unconscious driver, even now breathing his last through bloody-frothed lungs.

"Sorry, son . . . I can't help you," Schmidt muttered.

Throwing himself into the driver's seat, Schmidt took a fierce grasp of Juani's hair and pushed her from the steering wheel, keeping the grip to avoid the risk of her escaping.

With his left hand Schmidt fumbled with the parking brake, then awkwardly put the Hummer into gear and drove off as fast as the vehicle would move.

In the distance he could hear sirens, police and emergency vehicles, converging on the flaming wreck of the mansion.

CHAPTER NINETEEN

From the transcript at trial: Commonwealth of Virginia v. Alvin Scheer

DIRECT EXAMINATION, CONTINUED
BY MR. STENNINGS:

Q. Of course the Feds, they were pretty serious too, right Alvin?

A. Oh my yes. Blow up the governor's house? Kill her husband and her kid? Kill a whole bunch of folks that just worked there? That was about as serious as you could get, wasn't it?

Q. What did you think had happened?

A. I wasn't rightly sure. The papers and TV said, at the time, that it was some locals what done it, protesting the rebellion. I remember seeing the head of the Air Force saying on the TV that there was no way any of his people or planes had bombed Austin. Seemed real serious. I kind of believed him, too.

Austin, Texas

The Corps entered the state capital without incident. Expecting a bloodbath, the commander had waited until he had enough artillery, most importantly enough weight of shell, to be certain of crushing all opposition, along with enough fuel and small arms ammunition to be certain of being able to clear the town and exploit the breakthrough.

This had not been easy in the face of demolished bridges and roads, burned stocks at every town they entered, and a populace gone generally sullen, hostile and very uncooperative.

Yet, the evening before the assault on Texan lines was to begin, the Texans abandoned those lines, retreating hastily but in fairly good order some miles south.

Standing beside one such, a well-excavated and revetted trench, the commander of 3rd Corps and his sergeant major watched the stately procession of armored vehicles and accompanying infantry disappear into the suburban streets north of the town.

"Sir, I'm having a hard time believing the Texans aren't going to fight for their capital," commented the 3rd Corps sergeant major to his chief.

The general removed his helmet and scratched his head, a bit worriedly. "I know, Top . . . but that's what we're hearing from all along the front. The Texas Guard and State Defense Force have pulled out to the outskirts, the southern outskirts, of the city."

"They've still got defenses dug south of town, sir."

"Yes, I know. I expect they'll be occupying them right now."

"You heard what happened to Governor Seguin's place?"

"I heard, Sergeant Major. I'm not sure I heard the truth though. Do you think she's really dead?"

"Dunno, boss. There were no survivors reported at the house. And her husband and son were killed. That time of the morning? I figure she was in there too and they just haven't found a body yet."

"Shame, isn't it? She was a great woman, in so many ways."

The sergeant major merely grunted a warning as none other than Harold Forsythe, Political Officer for the 3rd Corps since losing his job as Federal Commissioner for Texas, approached on foot.

"Mr. Forsythe," noticed the general, without offering a hand.

"General," Forsythe returned, a minor note of exultation creeping into his voice. "Sergeant Major."

The sergeant major just nodded, not even offering so faint a greeting as had his boss.

"You'll be wanting to resume your duties in the capital directly," offered the general.

"Yes. How soon will the area be cleared?"

"If progress keeps up, we should be past the state house by tomorrow, about midmorning."

Forsythe smiled in anticipation of paying back some scores. The only dark spot on his future horizon was the fact that the Seguin bitch was dead. He had been looking forward to her execution with shivering anticipation.

❖   ❖   ❖

"It's time to leave Juani. Time to leave here, to leave the state, to leave the country. We've lost."

Juanita, unanswering, just swung her head minutely from side to side. She had cried herself out hours since and seemed to have no emotion left to her, no feeling at all.

"You'll go by car. I've got an unmarked civilian sedan. There's a trunkful of money in it. It'll take you to Brownsville where one of Hanstadt's people will see you across into Matamoros. 'Patricio' told me off line that he'll arrange to give you a refuge in Panama."

Juani just continued her minuscule headshaking.

"Come on." Schmidt reached for the woman's arm.

"No!" she shouted fiercely, pulling her arm away from Schmidt's grasp. "No," she repeated, more calmly.

"Stop being silly, Governor. It's time to go . . . and past time."

"I'm not being silly," Juani retorted. "But I am not leaving until I have tried every last thing."

"We have," commented Jack. "Nothing worked in the long run. Now we have to fight. That's all that's left. I intend to do it. And you are going, first to San Antonio and then to someplace safe."

Schmidt might never have admitted it, even to himself, but the thought of his best friend's sister, who was also his governor, and even also the woman who might have, in a different and better world, become his wife, being hurt or killed had in part unhinged him.

"No . . . there's one more thing we can do."

"What?"

"Can you still get me on television, one last time?"

"Why? What good would it do?"

"I want to talk to our people."

"You want to go into the breach one more time?" asked Schmidt, somewhat incredulously.

"Jack, I have to. You say we've lost. I tell you I haven't even *begun* to fight."

Washington, DC

"Do you suppose the bitch is really dead, Caroline? God I hope so."

The general felt a small quiver of disgust, not an emotion she had ever before associated with Wilhelmina Rottemeyer. She answered, coldly, "I don't know. No one knows."

Willi looked at her number one military advisor suspiciously. "What's your problem?"

"I can't go on with this, Madame President," McCreavy said with reluctance.

"With what?" demanded Rottemeyer. "It's almost over. A few more days, a week at most, and all of Texas will be back under control. Another few days and New Mexico will be broken, too."

"You don't understand, do you?"

"Understand what? I understand that they've abandoned their capital, that their troops are pulling back. That Houston is being brought back under control."

McCreavy sighed. "Nothing is under control. The hostages you made of the Marines' families? I just found out this morning. They've been freed. Apparently the Marines who took the base back kept up appearances for a bit while they worked out some details. Now you can expect the Marines there by El Paso to join the Texans. And word has gotten out. The Second Marine Division has sent emissaries to the Texan forces facing them and declared a truce. Those two Marine brigades at sea in the Gulf of Mexico? Same deal. And the 18th Airborne Corps has said to hell with you too."

"I'll have them all shot!"

Again, McCreavy sighed. "Then you'll have to give the orders yourself, Willi. I'm through." With that McCreavy reached into a jacket pocket and removed a letter which she presented to Rottemeyer. "That's my resignation."

Before going on, McCreavy forced away the beginnings of a sob. When she continued, it was to say, "And I'll be moving out today, Willi. All my things will be gone by this afternoon."

Rottemeyer's eyes opened wide in shock and horror. "Caroline, you can't be serious. You can't leave me."

Tenderly, for she still felt some tenderness toward her President and now former lover, McCreavy reached out a hand to stroke a face. "I must, Willi."

Austin, Texas

Juanita sat patiently while the studio makeup man applied a few finishing touches. Holding very still, she attempted to make some order out of the chaos of jumbled thoughts and psychic agonies running through her mind.

The word had gone out over the airwaves, via telephone, and on the Internet, that there would be a major address by the governor. Of course, that word had gone out before her house was bombed and before she was listed as missing and presumed dead.

I'll just have to hope for the best, she thought as the makeup man stepped back, inspected, and turned and departed.

In moments, the studio chief began a verbal countdown, ending with, "You're live, Governor."

Across Austin, across Texas, and even across the world, people watched their screens and monitors as the olive skinned-woman lifted her face to the camera.

"Rumors of my death," she began, wearing a somewhat strained and forced smile, "have been greatly exaggerated."

Washington, DC

"The bitch is still alive," fumed Carroll, using a remote control to turn on the television in Willi's office and bring up the right channel.

"That's not *possible*. You assured me she was dead."

"Yeah, well," drawled Carroll, "I was misinformed."

All present turned their eyes to the television screen where Juanita Seguin was just finishing up her speech.

"She's assembling a mass of people to march against 3rd Corps," announced Carroll for those present who had missed that part. "And we don't have any law enforcement people right with that Corps."

"None?" asked Rottemeyer.

"None. The force we would have had there, the Presidential Guard, is scattered to the winds. One group, the one we sent to Camp Pendleton in California is effectively destroyed. The others are in bad shape after taking back the currency facility. Most of the rest are tied down policing the supply routes and controlling the major cities. The Environmental Protection Police are knee-deep in alligators in Houston. The SGRPC are for the most part incarcerated and awaiting trial in New Mexico. The FBI was stretched just to provide a force for Dallas.

"Third Corps is on its own. And, given events, I don't know if you can trust them."

Rottemeyer pushed a button on her desk intercom. "I need to speak with Harold Forsythe."

State House, Austin, Texas

"The President for you, sir," announced a flunky.

Forsythe took the cell phone, answering happily, "Forsythe here, Madam President . . . ah, yes, we've heard rumors to that effect . . . no, Willi, I haven't seen a television lately . . . Yes, yes . . . I'll certainly talk to the military commander here, Madam President. . . ."

Handing the cell phone back to his flunky, Forsythe pondered the information he had just received from Rottemeyer. A mass march? Here? Against the Army's guns? What could they hope to prove by it?

❖   ❖   ❖

The Texas Rangers had been the first to arrive at the rally point, an intersection of First Street, SW, and Oltorf. They first cleared the immediate neighboring buildings and then radioed for the Public Address people to bring in the microphones and loudspeakers. Juanita and Jack showed up just as the last connection was being made between microphone, amplifiers, and speakers.

The people began to assemble to hear the governor moments later. Businesses had closed in anticipation of the coming occupation. There were many people available, from all stations and walks of life. Of those available, many came. They came from poor barrios where spoken English was a rarity. They came from upper-crust mansions along the river. They came from everywhere in between as well.

Juanita had never said what she wanted them for. All that her recent TV and radio broadcast had conveyed was that she wanted to speak to them. Many assumed it was to lay down her mantle as governor. Some came, indeed, as a last gesture of respect for what Juanita had tried to do, even if she had, as she apparently had, failed.

The crowd was solemn. Solemnly, the recently widowed Juanita Seguin mounted some steps to address them.

Before beginning to speak, Juanita looked to the north, trying vainly to discern the thin pillar of smoke that she knew arose above the ashes of her husband, her son and many of her friends, aides and co-workers. The crowd followed the governor's gaze as if they knew what she was thinking and for what she was looking. Some of them may have known what she was thinking. All knew, in their hearts, what she was feeling.

"My husband is up there," Juanita began, pointing north across Town Lake. "My son, Mario, as well. I intend to go there now, whatever or whoever bars my way, and see to their bodies."

"The Rangers are coming with me." Juanita glanced over at Nagy, who nodded a firm agreement. "The Forty-ninth Division is coming with me." Schmidt scowled but ultimately agreed.

"I'd like you all here to come with me, too.

"You think we have lost? I've lost the larger and better part of my family but I haven't 'lost.' Texas seems better than half occupied but we haven't lost either.

"Even as I stand here speaking to you now the Marines between here and El Paso are trading cigarettes and stories with our own National Guard troops that were facing them. General Schmidt tells me that as soon as we can refuel the Marines and the soldiers with them, we will have three new brigades to defend ourselves with.

"Houston is still fighting. And the soldiers and marines between here and Houston have said 'enough.' They will not act against us on behalf of that woman in the White House any longer.

"All that remains is the force to our north, the force that is sitting on the bodies of my family. Do you think they are sitting on those bodies because they want to? Because they believe in and support a government that kills helpless people without reason or even warning?

"No. Those uniformed men and women up there

are our friends. They do not want to be here. They
do not want to support our enemies or the enemies
of the country and Constitution that were ours.

"Now come with me; come with me to recover the
bodies of my family; come with me so I can show you
that—while we have enemies, enemies of liberty—we
have friends too."

And with that, Juani offered her right arm to
Schmidt, her left to Nagy, and stepped off into the
street.

It was the second largest-capitol building in the
United States, second only to the national capitol in
Washington, as a matter of fact. Even more, Texas'
legislative building was the taller of the two by fifteen feet.

From the front steps Forsythe looked down the
central walkway, the walkway flanked by greenery
and monuments, the greenery being flanked in turn
by a driveway to each side. To his right front arose
a faint trace of smoke from the charred ruins of the
Governor's Mansion.

Pity, he thought. *I had hoped to move in there
myself.*

The driveways in front of Forsythe linked just before
the main gate, a wrought iron screen held up by red-
dish stone pillars. On the other side of the gate, and
the low stone wall that surrounded the capitol area
and fronted on Eleventh Street, soldiers armed and
with bayonets fixed stood in unwavering lines.

Rangers and guardsmen joined the arm-linked,
walking wall as Juanita passed. Some, lacking faith in

the result, did so only because they had faith in her. Schmidt had faith in neither, but was determined to see things through with Juani, wherever events might lead them.

Behind the line of arm-linked men and women, civilians, some with children, fell in behind.

Inevitably, an old black woman, certainly spurred by memories of an earlier struggle, began to sing in a high, weak voice. The words were simple and well known. In seconds, so it seemed, the crowd had drowned out the older woman.

The lyrics, when he first sensed—more than heard—them, touched a note with Forsythe. He, too, had once been young and idealistic. He, too, had once sung the simple song.

He pushed the feeling away, brutally.

Juani and her leading rank turned half right on Barton Springs. Keeping to a slow and stately pace, they crossed Riverside. At South Congress the point turned north again to cross the bridge over Town Lake. With each turn and each passing step a few more people, sometimes a few hundred more, added their weight to the procession.

By the time the lead reached Tenth Street the crowd had swollen to nearly 100,000 people.

The song had grown to be very loud by that point.

The Capitol was where the action was, where the threat was, and perhaps most importantly where his Zampolit, Forsythe, was. Thus, accompanied by his sergeant major, the commander of Third Corps made sure it was also where *he* was.

The troops along Eleventh Street had their faces turned away from him toward the approaching crowd. It didn't matter; the faces of his officers told the general everything he needed to know.

The boys just do not want to be here; do not want to be doing what they're doing.

This was followed by a more ominous thought: *And they can't be relied on to do it, either.*

Forsythe approached. "What are you going to do about this riot, General?" he asked, a trace of personal fear in his voice.

"What riot?"

"That riot; that unruly mob headed this way."

The general sneered. "I don't see any unruly mob. I see a peaceful procession of citizens coming to their state capitol in peaceable assembly."

"You idiot!" Forsythe exclaimed. "When I tell the President you'll be lucky to stay out of a cell at Leavenworth. You have one chance to avoid that and that is to disperse that mob."

The sneer never left the soldier's face. "That's what you want, eh, Mr. Forsythe? You should be careful what you ask for."

Turning to the sergeant major the general ordered, "Top, bring me a loudspeaker, would you?"

Even over the singing coming from behind her, Juani's heart skipped a beat when she heard the order coming over the loudspeaker, "First Squadron, Seventh Cavalry: one magazine, lock." The general was careful not to use the word "load."

❖   ❖   ❖

Schmidt and Nagy both began to pull her back, even as the crowd behind them recoiled from the threat.

"No," she said with a calm she did not feel. "No, we go on," with determination.

Exchanging glances, Schmidt and Nagy tacitly agreed: *If she's got the balls to go on . . . then so do we.*

The sergeant major watched, horrified, as the general gave commands over the loudspeaker. *Boss, this isn't balls. This is bullshit.*

Unperturbed, the general continued, "Now I want you to aim for the women and the children first, boys. Extra points and a four day pass for drilling a mother carrying a baby. Don't sweat it, boys. Mr. Forsythe here, from the White House, says it's just 'okay.' He says if we don't shoot down these 'rioters,' we'll all go to Leavenworth for the long course."

Tilting his head to one side, the sergeant major asked silently, *Are you trying to start a mutiny?* The old soldier's eyes widened, *By God, you are.*

Spec Four Franklin Washington had seen and heard enough. He'd also had just about enough, too. Standing there on Eleventh Street, with a rifle in his hands, a bayonet on the end of it, a magazine seated firmly in the well; facing a crowd that looked no different and no more threatening than a crowd at a beach; for a government and a cause he neither understood nor very much liked—Washington had indeed had just about enough.

The crowd had reached the intersection and begun

to spread out and around the street-wide line of arm-linked men and women. They were close enough for Washington to make out faces easily. There was a familiar one, right there in the center; the Texan Governor.

But that face wasn't the problem. It was all the others—those many, many others—that looked no different from folks back home.

How could he, Franklin Washington, ever go home to Alabama and tell his folks that he had shot at people that seemed so much the same? Bayoneted and clubbed them?

The simple answer was: he couldn't.

So while better than half the officers and men on that line were thinking much the same thing, it was left to a young black man of no great station in life to state the popular feeling first.

"Fuck this shit," said Franklin Washington, tossing his rifle on the ground. "I ain't a-gonna play anymore."

At the sound of not one, but hundreds of rifles being dropped and thrown to the ground, the general turned a beaming smile on Forsythe. "Did you hear that, sir? That sound? Why here I have given orders for my men to put down this 'riot' . . . and guess what? They didn't listen.

"The sound you've just heard, Mr. Forsythe, was the breaking of your government in Washington. I suggest you run, sir. To Canada, perhaps, because no place in the United—or even perhaps disunited—States is going to be quite safe for you.

"And—to quote that young man down on the street—'We ain't a-gonna play anymore.'"

The general turned from a shocked Commissioner Forsythe and said into the microphone for his loud-speaker, "First Squadron, Seventh Cavalry: on your feet and face this way. Pick up your rifles, boys. Now let's escort the Governor of Texas back to her job."

INTERLUDE:

From: *The End of the Dream: Reconstruction in Post-Rottemeyer America* by Patrick T. Hamilton Copyright 2051, Baen Historical Publishing

The end, when it came, came suddenly.

With the Marines and soldiers to the west in rebellion against federal authority, with the main force, the Army's Third Corps having turned, it was a matter of hours before the Eighteenth Airborne Corps and 2nd Marine Division likewise pointed poignant fingers in Washington's direction. Even the Navy, shadowing the Texas coast, refused to continue the blockade imposed by President Rottemeyer.

At that point the federals could count on nothing but their own law enforcement agencies, already badly depleted and demoralized, and the states' National Guards.

The states' National Guards were, of course, under the authority first and foremost of the state governors.

These came from states of two different classes: northern and western urbanized states where the National Guards suffered a considerable degree of both unpopularity and benign neglect, and southern and rural states where the guard remained rather popular.

Thus, when California mobilized its National Guard in response to a presidential demand, Arizona, Nevada, Wyoming, Utah, and Colorado did the same in response to California. Unlike California, however—which merely sat there, once those other National Guards were reinforced by the 1st Marine Division, they advanced and California's Guard simply melted away.

In the deep southern states, aggressive action was also contemplated. That no fighting took place was largely the result of more moderate, even centrist, states like Pennsylvania, Maryland, and Virginia whose collective reaction to both sides might well be summed up as, "Oh, no, you don't. Not again."

The first peacekeeping call is reported to have come from Utah to Governor Garrison of New Mexico and Governor Seguin of Texas. The substance of that conversation has never been reported. Yet, the very next day Utah's legislature—at her governor's behest—adopted what had come to be called "the Texas Program." The governor also called for a constitutional convention, a request heartily endorsed by his legislature.

Within the week that call for a convention had become general. From Alaska to Alabama, Mississippi to Maryland, New Hampshire to New Mexico—forty-one states demanded a new Constitution or at least substantial revisions to the old one. Only four of the six New England states, plus New York, Minnesota, California, Oregon and Hawaii, refused to join it.

Elsewhere, the sentiment—or the scent of blood in the water—became overwhelming.

The popular reaction was more severe. Federal agents and bureaucrats were hounded, burned in effigy . . . sometimes beaten and in a few cases killed. Nor would local authorities protect them. The media, that group—ever so "ready to feed the masses on the carrion of events"—the same group for whom Rottemeyer had once been as near a goddess as one might hope to find on Earth, turned—if anything—more rabidly anti-federal than the national norm for the day. "Project Ogilvie" had soured more than a few in the industry on the federal goverment.

It was said, possibly truthfully, that—in any one day of the next three weeks after the defection of 3rd Corps and its beginning to fan out to the north—more Americans sought refuge in Canada than had done so during the entire Vietnam war.

It was whispered too, perhaps unkindly if not entirely untruthfully, that some fleeing the fall of the Rottemeyer presidency had also fled the call to Vietnam.

These numbers picked up noticeably when states' troops began assembling along the political and philosophical boundaries between north and south, urban and rural, conservative and liberal.

When the Marine expeditionary forces in the Gulf of Mexico steamed back through the Panama Canal, this time without any strikes by Canal workers, even Hawaii decided to send a representative to the constitutional convention . . . even as that state's population began to drop from the many, many chartered flights to Vancouver, British Columbia.

The City of Washington would have come under siege, one suspects, except that the 3rd Infantry Regiment seized the Pentagon, all of the notable public places, and all of the roads leading into and from the city.

Rottemeyer herself, along with key staff, left via a Marine helicopter for New York City.

It was perhaps significant that the crew of that helicopter refused to fly until cleared to do so by the Commandant of the Corps. Possibly of greater significance, the commandant, signally, failed to consult with—allegedly refused to consult with—General McCreavy's replacement.

But if anyone believed that a constitutional convention was going to solve all of the problems of the United States, those persons were to be sorely disappointed. . . .

CHAPTER TWENTY

From the transcript at trial: Commonwealth of
Virginia v. Alvin Scheer

DIRECT EXAMINATION, CONTINUED
BY MR. STENNINGS:

Q. So, Alvin, were you taken by surprise when things
turned around so fast?

A. Oh, yes, sir, Mr. Stennings. I never thought for a
second that the whole . . . well, nearly the whole, I
reckon . . . of the military would turn on Washington
the way they did.

Q. And you saw your chance then, exactly when,
Alvin?

A. Well . . . with them soldiers in the blue dress
uniforms guarding Washington, I was no better off
than I was before . . . not so far as getting close
to my target went, anyhow. But I heard that all
the governors were getting together in Virginia
Beach and I figured, under the circumstances,

that eventually the President would have to go there too. So I packed my bag and my rifle and I headed south. . . .

Washington, DC

A cynic might have scoffed at smoke-filled back rooms. The cynic would, of course, have been years—decades—out of date. There was no smoke.

Other than that, though, the back room was much the same. In it assembled the real movers and shakers on the national political scene. One party's worth, anyway.

"Ladies and gentlemen," began Carroll, "our fortunes have definitely headed south."

"Is there no hope then, James?" asked the party chairman.

"None with Willi, no, sir. She's burned more bridges than the Texans blew up. Worse, she tied a whole bunch of the rest of us to railings on those bridges and . . . man . . . I tell you . . . the fire's gettin' hot."

The chairman lifted an eyebrow, inquisitorially. "All of us?"

"Yes, sir. I mean, we know her close confidants are going down. Vega . . . well, hell . . . the whole Cabinet. Maybe that cunt McCreavy might have gotten out in time. And don't think for a minute McCreavy won't be testifyin' against us, too. The rest'll be singin' like birds inside half a month."

"Willi can't control them, then?"

Carroll shook his head emphatically. "No way. She's going to be spillin' her guts, too . . . and likely it won't

take her as long. She's a lot smarter than most; more
ruthless, too."

"Does she know about this meeting, James?" asked
one of the two women present.

"Ma'am, I don't think so. She's, for the minute, in
such a blue funk about everything that's happened
that I don't think she's listenin' to much of anybody
about much of anything."

"Useless, then . . . or harmful."

"Harmful is the only way to read it, Mr. Chairman,"
piped in Walter Madison Howe, Rottemeyer's always-
kept-in-the-background Vice-President.

Sadly, reluctantly, the chairman nodded his head.
Looking around the room's important occupants he
saw . . . some regret, yes. But little opposition; none,
in fact.

The chairman looked pointedly at Howe. "Can
you handle your responsibilities to the party, Walter?
Rebuild everything we've lost or are about to lose? I
know it will be hard, very hard."

Howe exhaled. "I can set us on the right road, sir.
But rebuilding seventy years of effort? And that was
seventy years in a world already more or less under our
thumbs? We'd be doing well if we did it in forty. And
that's a big 'if.' That miserable Seguin woman is going
to be an awful impediment to our purposes as well."

The group discussed Juanita, Willi, a host of
problems—Republican, Democrat and Independent—
before reaching any firm conclusion.

Again nodding the dignified old head, the chairman turned to Carroll. "Can you fix the problem for
us, James?"

"I've already taken the liberty, sir. . . ."

Houston, Texas

After so long without it, liberty felt strange to the senses of Jose Bernoulli. Indeed, based on the shocked, stunned expressions on half the faces emerging into liberty's light, Bernoulli was by no means alone.

Not that the sight of liberty, confronting people emerging at last from a long dark, was so very pleasing. That sight, in this case, in this city, was as often as not one of wrecked and burned cars, trashed buildings, and bloodstains.

At least they've taken the bodies down from the lampposts, thought Bernoulli.

Underneath a nearby lamppost, under guard by the engineer's platoon, some dozens of former federal agents labored at cleaning up the mess, shoveling broken glass, prepping wrecked automobiles for towing . . . cleaning up unsightly stains.

"God in Heaven," muttered the short Tejano, "I hope we never have to do anything like this again."

Convention Center, Virginia Beach, Virginia

"Please don't ask me to do anything like this again, Juani," pleaded Jack as he walked by her side down the long aisle between cheering—and a few scowling—attendees at the convention.

It was the off season; hotel space was plentiful, the convention center unbooked. Transportation by air and ground was easy. Moreover, the U.S. Army's own "Transportation Center," at Fort Eustis, was nearby to assist and coordinate, as was Oceana Naval Air Station and Norfolk Navy Base. And, given how much the Armed Forces were looking forward to the expected changes from the convention, that support was cordial indeed.

And Virginia Beach was a great place for a convention, in any case. Though off season, the weather was unseasonably warm. The area reeked of history, of sights to be seen and restaurants to be sampled.

It was a place and time of the greatest excitement.

It was also bedlam, nothing less. Schmidt followed Juanita through the mass of cheering . . . cheering what? Nuts, was Schmidt's opinion. And, though he tried to hide it from everyone, Juanita knew that opinion, even shared it to a degree.

A quick glance confirmed Juani's suspicions. "Smile, Goddamit, Jack. You're the man of the hour. Act like a politician for once in your life, will you? It won't kill you, you know."

Schmidt nodded, forced a smile to his face and then leaned over to whisper in Juani's ear, "These people are insane, Governor."

Juani shifted her eyes, glancing quickly at a bearded man in a confederate uniform with a pole bearing the Battle Flag of the Army of Northern Virginia grasped tightly in his hands. The man wore gray clothes with a double set of brass buttons topped by a broad brimmed gray felt hat.

She smiled, warmly, and tore her widened eyes away. "I know, Jack, but what can you do?"

"Run to the insane asylum?" he asked, rhetorically.

"It should be safe enough since all the real nuts are here."

"Jaaack . . ."

"Okay, Governor, okay. I'll be good."

Juanita, followed by Jack, began to climb the steps to the stage on which stood the podium. She really didn't feel quite at home. Worse, she felt a horrible itching between her shoulder blades, as if someone had set cross hairs on her back.

At the top of the stairs, once again standing by the governor's side, Jack whispered, "I've heard Willi herself is going to show up."

New York, New York

Wilhelmina Rottemeyer looked grimly at the message bearer, not more than half listening to the message. She thought, *Feldman seems to have lost that useful obsequiousness for which he had once been so notable. Ah, well . . . why should he be any different from any of a hundred others of the "four f's" that have turned their backs on me? Even Caroline . . .* but that thought, that wish, that reminiscence, she let go as being too painful to consider.

Feldman was far less groveling than she had become used to over the term of her administration. But there was a nervous quality to his voice and manner that raised Willi's hackles.

"So, yes, Madame President, the party is insistent that you must go and address this convention, to save what you can. The chairman says you owe him this much."

"My ass," snorted Rottemeyer. "I wouldn't trust my safety in Virginia now to a division of tanks. I sure as hell won't trust it to anything less."

"You'll be safe enough," answered Feldman, his doubtful tone belying his words.

"Even you don't believe that."

"You'll be safe from arrest, then. Will that do?"

"No."

Momentarily nonplussed, Feldman considered his next move. A slight smile crossed his face. He checked his wristwatch and said, "Governor Seguin is due to address the convention in about three minutes, Madame President. Why don't you watch that and then consider?"

Convention Center, Virginia Beach, Virginia

Juani took the podium, took a deep breath, and lastly took in her audience. *They're not all nuts, Jack, no matter what you think, nor even most of them.*

And Juani was right, as she had been right about limiting the violence, about resting her cause on the backs of the people. As she had been right and Jack had, often enough, been wrong. There were nuts in the audience and nuts at the convention. But there were also governors, legislators, academics. There were people of note and people unknown. Most of them were definitely not "nuts."

The governor, who was the chairwoman for this convention, looked out again over the sea of faces. Most seemed friendly, pleased, and supportive. The ones who were not? *Well . . . there are a number of states that are hostile.*

Juani began, "I would like to think that most of us know why we are here at this historic event. Nonetheless, for clarity's sake, we ought to restate it now. We are here, constitutionally assembled, to write or rewrite a Constitution for the United States of America. Perhaps it might be better to say that we are here to amend our existing constitution. I say 'amend' because everything I have learned since this convention assembled and everything I am told by the people of my own state says that few people, if any at all, really want to get rid of the Constitution that we have lived under and cherished for more than two centuries.

"I don't want to dispose of it myself. And I will, for whatever my own vote is worth here, vote and argue and filibuster and do whatever I can to keep from losing that magnificent law of our land."

Juani gazed out over the crowd. *No real reaction to that. Does that mean they agree with me? Disagree? Aren't sure yet? Well . . . on we go . . .*

"What I propose then is that we, as our first order of business, go over the current constitution and vote yea or nay on each line and passage, that we then do the same with the existing amendments, and only then should we open up debate on further amendments and changes."

Juani's face turned determined. "And we must be so very careful that we do not throw out the good with the bad, the baby with the bathwater.

"Because not everything the federal government has done is bad. Much of it has been so completely necessary that we could not exist as a country without it."

They didn't like hearing that too very much, did they? she observed. *Well, they have to hear it.*

"Let me explain.

"You do not like, most of you, some of the things the federal government has done with . . . oh . . . say . . . the commerce clause to the Constitution. Fine, I agree with you; I don't like some of them either. So let's say we get rid of the commerce clause at this convention. How long will it be before Louisiana enacts tariffs on Midwest food coming down the Mississippi? I give it a year. Maybe less.

"You don't like federal taxation? Fine, I agree with you. Do you like having a secure supply of oil? Well, how do we get that without an army to secure the Middle Eastern oil fields? How do we pay for that army without taxation?

"How do we build and maintain highways? Control flooding? Coordinate legitimate anticrime efforts that cross state borders? Keep up the railroads? Keep the ports dredged?"

"Ah, but 'The feds interfere too much,' I hear you say. Fine. I agree with that, too. But while Louisiana is enacting those tariffs, once we dispense with the commerce clause, how long before every state north of there dumps every kind of trash and pollutant into that same taxed Mississippi River . . . because there's no higher authority to keep them from doing that?"

Casting her eyes to the left center of the assembly, Juani caught sight of what she assumed, from their signs, was the National Rifle Association contingent.

"You do not like the Bureau of Alcohol, Tobacco

and Firearms, many of you. And I agree wholeheartedly that it was a branch of government that went completely out of control along with most of the Treasury Department. But consider just what you do want. Do you want anyone, anywhere, to be able to have any kind of weapon they want, no matter how destructive? Chemical weapons? Nuclear weapons?

"Of course, you don't want that. Nobody does. How are you going to draw a sensible line, though? These are the kinds of questions this convention must answer."

Juani tapped delicate brown fingers on the podium, keeping time with her next words, "And it must answer them, as did the original Constitution, *for the ages!*"

She paused, reached for a glass and took a sip of water before continuing.

"The last thing I want to address to you is how we got to this point. No, I don't mean the slow steady growth in federal power that overwhelmed the states and individual citizens in time. No, I also don't mean the cultural changes in the United States.

"I mean the worst mistake. The one that made it impossible for a political party in power to accept losing. The one that former President Tavern made when he let his predecessor, Thomas Gates, be prosecuted for his malfeasances in office.

"Was Gates a swine, a rapist, a panderer and philanderer? He was all those things and worse. Did he deserve jail? Oh, yes.

"But was anything he did worth what prosecuting him did to us, eventually? It was not.

"For this reason, and though it pains me to the core,

and even though I hold her responsible for the deaths of my brother, my husband and my son . . . and even though she brought rack and ruin to my home state, I am going to ask you for one special amendment to the new—hopefully also the old—Constitution. I am, in fact, asking you now for an amendment that will prevent a former President from being found criminally liable for political acts committed while in office.

"Fine her, if you wish. Exile her, if you wish. But do not let anyone send Wilhelmina Rottemeyer to jail lest you build at the same time, as President Tavern did, a jail for us all."

She closed shyly, "Thank you."

New York, New York

Rottemeyer glared at the television, furious. "That bitch! That cunt! That miserable wetback twat! How *dare* she be magnanimous to me? How *dare* she?"

Feldman merely shrugged. It seemed like a pretty good deal to him.

The President stood and began to pace the room. "Killed her brother," she mimicked. "Killed her son. Killed her illiterate fucking husband, did I? When I think about what that *bitch* cost *me* . . ."

She turned a cold, harsh gaze onto Feldman, one so cold and harsh he actually shivered. "Fine. Tell the chairman I'll go speak to this . . . damned . . . treacherous . . . convention."

Once again, Rottemeyer glared at the television screen where Juanita was receiving the ovation that in her world was rightfully due only to herself.

Houston, Texas

Elpi had been staying at a house of some friends of Minh. She was comfortable there, physically. Emotionally though it had never seemed quite right to her. The house was arranged differently. The furniture was different from what she was used to. The smells of cooking were—yes—pleasant, but also different, and a little unsettling.

The owners and her hosts, Madame and Monsieur Truong, certainly tried to make her comfortable. But their Spanish was poor and Elpi's French nonexistent. Communication in English was a trial for all concerned.

The girl found herself watching a lot of television. That also helped her refrain from worrying about her future.

For the governor had never sent for her. Or even communicated. Elpi was certain that Juanita was overwhelmed by events; she attached no blame. Elpi also had a sneaking suspicion that, whether the governor actually thought that way or not, the association with loss—Father Jorge, Mario, and Mr. Seguin—just might have caused Juanita to push the girl as far from her consciousness as possible.

On the television Juanita was speaking in English to the crowd. Naturally, Houston being Houston and the cable channels reflecting that, the speech was subtitled in Spanish.

The Governor looks so worn and tired on the TV, thought the girl. *She looks so sad, too.*

Elpi resolved to have a talk with Colonel Minh.

Kansas City, Missouri

Mr. Smythe was a simple man, in his way; an undistinguished one, also, to all appearances. Medium short, with a slight paunch, crowned by thinning blond hair tinged with unremarkable gray.

He lived simply enough, alone, in a two-bedroom condo between the city and nearby Leavenworth, Kansas. His needs were few and his job, though he was rarely called upon, more than met them.

Carroll had met Smythe before, once. As he had then, Smythe pushed across the table a piece of paper with a number, a rather large number, written on it.

Unnecessarily, Smythe added, "My fee is not negotiable."

"I understand that," Carroll answered. "You will be needing credentials?"

"Yes. I will list my requirements later."

Though a cold man, Smythe couldn't help a warm shiver of anticipation. He had his own standards of achievement. Two major figures in one lifetime. No one has ever gotten two in one lifetime.

CHAPTER TWENTY-ONE

From the transcript at trial: Commonwealth of
Virginia v. Alvin Scheer

DIRECT EXAMINATION, CONTINUED
BY MR. STENNINGS:

Q. So you went to Virginia Beach, Alvin?
A. Yes, sir. I already said so, didn't I? But, Lord, it
was a nightmare. I couldn't find a cheap room
and I couldn't afford a good one if'n I could have
found it. I ended up sleeping in my old truck.
Moving from one rest area to another. And the
nights were pretty chilly, too. Cold . . . and that
wet breeze off the ocean? Well, it was bad.

I drove around a lot during the day. Wasn't
too hard to figure out where everything was going
on. And, too, I listened to my radio. That's how I
found out where the President was staying. . . .

Hotel Cavalier (Hilltop), Virginia Beach, Virginia

There was not, technically, a presidential suite at the Cavalier, though there was one in the nearby, and much newer, Cavalier Oceanfront. Normally. In fact, the old building, the Hotel Cavalier, was not usually open after the end of the normal season. These however, were not normal times. Sensing vast profits accompanying the convention, management had moved Heaven and Earth, calling back seasonally laid off employees, rushing to hire fillers, and even calling back some retired personnel to fill the remaining gaps.

Even in the Oceanfront, the Presidential Suite was nothing more than an ad hoc joining of four normally independent suites. Absent a President, these had already been rented individually.

The next best thing, and even Wilhelmina Rottemeyer had to confess that next best was very good indeed, was the Cavalier Suite in the old hotel. Not that it pleased her, precisely. Nothing could really please her but a long, peaceful contemplation of Juanita Seguin's corpse, well embalmed and neatly laid out.

But, sigh, that was not to be. Or, if it was, it was not going to happen as a result of anything Wilhelmina Rottemeyer could do, one way or the other.

If she believed in a God she would ask for that one little boon. Since she didn't believe . . .

The Secret Service, the real Secret Service, not the bastardized political army Rottemeyer had created and now lost, still took its duties seriously. They didn't like her, they could hardly wait for her disappearance from office, but they had—by God—a duty to defend her and they would meet that duty come hell or high water.

Among the precautions that the Secret Service had taken were the posting of countersnipers on the roofs of both parts of the Cavalier—Hilltop and Oceanfront, plus on the roof of the Ocean Tower, a different hotel south of the Oceanfront and southwest of the Hilltop. These were not on duty twenty-four hours a day, but they would be on duty at anytime the President was in or around her hotel.

Smythe noticed this, of course, and wrote them off. The Secret Service was essentially irrelevant to his plans.

Alvin was having a difficult time of it. He drove the length of road fronting the beach over and over. He simply could not see any way to do what he intended to do. Dressed as he was, with a rifle that he could not very well hide, with little money and no expectation of actually getting inside of one of the hotels without being noticed . . . well, the task seemed hopeless.

Finally, the tall steeple of a red brick church caught his attention as he drove past the Cavalier for the fourth time. He read the sign: Galilee Episcopal Church.

Would the good Lord above forgive me for using a church for what I intend to do?

Then he considered his late wife, killed by the system. He thought of his state, now free but recently attacked.

Would the Lord forgive me for not using a church, if that's all I have?

✧   ✧   ✧

Willi gave the church a short glance as her limousine pulled away from the main entrance to the Cavalier on its way to the convention center. She gave a much longer glance to the southwest lawn of the hotel where Carroll, so she presumed, was busy overseeing those themselves overseeing the setup for her post speech press conference. Trusting Carroll and his abilities implicitly, she turned her mind and thoughts back to the speech she was on her way to give.

Alvin's hands were trembling slightly as he left his truck to walk around the church. He noticed the setup of speakers, podium and chairs on the lawn between the big old hotel and the church. *Was the President going to give a press conference?* He couldn't know for sure, but it seemed to him that was the way to bet it.

He walked back to his truck and drove up right next to a more or less hidden side entrance. Again leaving the truck, he tested the door, only to find it locked from the inside.

Alvin then walked around, once again, to the front. This door was unlocked. He entered the church openly. Once inside, it was no great feat to find the door by which he had parked his truck. Opening it from the inside, he went to the truck and retrieved the rifle he had rolled up in a tarp in the bed.

Convention Center, Virginia Beach, Virginia

Willi had never before in her life faced so hostile an audience. They didn't boo, hiss, or throw things of course; it was a well-behaved hostile audience. But the sheer psychic venom emanating from the visages of well over half the convention attendees would have been enough to overwhelm a lesser woman.

She was not a lesser woman, however. Surrounded by her Secret Service agents, she boldly strode the aisle-way and on up to the podium. She spared a few smiles for the delegations she was certain were friendly: Massachusetts, California, New York and a few others. For the rest she projected nothing warmer than an icy glare.

Standing behind the podium, that icy glare turned, if anything, more frigid still.

"So you think you can change things," Rottemeyer sneered. "You have come here to make up a new set of rules, have you?

"You're pathetic. You're also hopelessly beneath the challenge. I can see that by the silly amendments you are already proposing. Let's look at some of them, shall we?

"You want to repeal the income tax and the social security tax? Let me assure you; it is too late. This country's economy would collapse almost overnight from the disruption or cancellation of all those federal procurement contracts and the loss of spending power on the part of those working in the federal bureaucracy. What's more, I see very few young faces out in the crowd, mostly older people. What are you going to do when you get older and find you haven't saved enough for your retirement? And find further that your kids, like yourselves, don't want to be bothered taking care of their parents? I'll tell you what you'll do; you'll vote yourselves federal relief that might not be called social security, but will be the same thing, perhaps not half so well organized and run, under a different name.

"And who takes care of the people already retired? Their social security savings? Nonsense. They don't exist, not in the sense that the money exists in such a way that it can be paid back in full."

Rottemeyer shook her head as if scolding naughty schoolchildren. "At least one of the lunatics here has, apparently, some legal training. This idiot wants to re-create the old nondelegation doctrine the Supreme Court repudiated in the 1930s. Not a chance. There's simply too much, too many of you want—or will want—the federal government to do for you that which Congress cannot hope to do."

"And speaking of the Supreme Court, are you all *really* so enthusiastic about castrating it? Creating some governor's council that can overturn its decisions? Hmmm. So, when Alabama decides to reenact some Jim Crow laws and the rest of the South follows right along, you really don't want anybody who can say 'no'? I don't believe it for a minute."

Rottemeyer paused briefly, scanning her audience with boundless contempt. "And you want term limits? Well, you've always had them. All you had to do was not vote for someone for another term.

"No federal interference with religion? Oh sure . . . and when Utah decides on polygamy again?

"Now let me tell you why none of this will work. You—all of you—want the federal government to do things for you. The things you want done may vary, but you *all* want something. And so you, and people just like you, will demand that the government give you those things you want. And so, no matter what you do now, you'll be racing each other beginning about two weeks after this convention closes to give the government back whatever power it needs to give you what you want."

She summed up in a voice dripping scorn and contempt, "And that is why this . . . movement . . . is doomed. Have a nice day, suckers."

With that comment Wilhelmina Rottemeyer simply turned and, accompanied by her guard detail and a thunder of boos, left.

Juanita didn't boo. Neither did Schmidt. The former merely looked thoughtful while the latter's face was shrouded in something akin to anger . . . or perhaps worry.

"The bitch is right, Juani. Nothing is going to work, to turn back the clock. Rebuilding the federal machine is going to begin the second we stop tearing it down."

Juanita shook her head in negation. "No, Jack, she wasn't right, or not entirely anyway. That comment about term limits and people not voting in career politicians for multiple terms? Typical. She skipped over the fact that with one state competing against another for benefits from Washington it made sense for a state to keep electing the same man or woman over and over. But when we reduce the amount of benefit to be gained by cropping the federales, and put all states on an even footing so no one of them can gain an advantage by keeping career politicians in office, the term-limits provisions will make sense . . . and they'll work, too."

"Hmm. Maybe," Schmidt grumbled.

"But the biggest thing she was wrong about was this: sure, the federal government will grow again . . . or the state governments will get so powerful that they'll become as obnoxious as Willi's ultimately did. But so?"

Jack shrugged. "So?"

"So we do this again. And again. And again. As often as necessary. But, you know, that may not be all that often. And we're a great country, Jack. Even now. We can afford a revolution every now and again to shake things up and put us back on the right track. I just hope . . ."

"Yes?" Jack encouraged.

"Well . . . I just hope we can always do it without resorting to a real civil war."

"Me, too, Governor. But I doubt we can. So where do you think the danger of government growth will come from next?"

The governor considered before answering. "Well . . . I doubt it will be a foreign threat anytime soon. And, given that the states are pretty capable of controlling crime on their own without much federal interference, I don't think it will be crime control." Juani the far-seeing politician closed her eyes to see into the future.

"The environmental movement."

"Huh?" snorted Schmidt, disbelieving.

"Yes, the environmental movement. It's maybe the one thing the states really can't do, won't do anyway, on their own. Or, rather, they won't do it very well. It's also tailor-made for intrusion on private property and property rights. And, since everything has some environmental impact, it's as well made for taking control of the economy, eventually. And that is what people like Wilhelmina Rottemeyer want, you know: a state where the government runs the economy, a socialist state, so that it can then run everything else."

CHAPTER TWENTY-TWO

From the transcript at trial: Commonwealth of Virginia v. Alvin Scheer

CROSS EXAMINATION
BY MS. CAPUTO:

Q. So you found yourself up in that steeple, did you, Alvin?

A. No, ma'am. I didn't "find" myself there. I put myself there. Like I already done told you, I went up there to shoot the President. I ain't ashamed of it and I ain't trying to hide it. The thing is though . . .

Galilee Episcopal Church, Virginia Beach, Virginia

Alvin did the best he knew how. A hunter most of his life, he kept to the shadows. Shivering, for the weather had turned for the worse, he unrolled the rifle from the tarp and then rolled the tarp into a rest for the rifle. This he placed on the corner of the interior bar encircling the church's bell. Then, getting behind the bar, he checked for his line of sight to the podium. Satisfied, he placed the rifle, a scoped military .30-06 of a very old design, on the rest and waited.

Cavalier Oceanfront Hotel, Seventh Floor, Virginia Beach, Virginia

Smythe had actually checked into the hotel twice on the prior day. The first time, to a room away from the land and toward the ocean, he had done so under his own face and credentials. The second time, checking into a room facing the Hilltop Cavalier's eastern side, he had used the press credentials provided by Carroll, a bit of makeup, and a false mustache.

He had also taken up two loads of baggage on those different occasions. On the first, it was the normal couple of bags anyone might have brought in, though what was in one of those bags was not precisely normal. The second load was not much of a load at all, just an overnight shoulder bag.

From the first load he produced a rifle. Not just any rifle, this was a custom–made 7mm Remington magnum, mounting a superb scope and modified to be dis- and re-assembled. It lay in its case, along with a small tripod, inside one of Smythe's bags. The case and its contents Smythe took to the room facing the Cavalier Hilltop.

❖   ❖   ❖

Inside, and safe from prying eyes, Smythe put on a pair of gloves and a shower cap. Then he adjusted the blinds, moved a table and a chair, and set up the tripod. The rifle he removed in its two major pieces. These he joined together with the flick of a couple of latches and the easy tightening of a single screw.

The reassembled rifle then went into its custom cradle on the tripod.

Smythe went back and forth between the blinds and the scope, adjusting both fixtures and rifle until he had a clear sight picture of podium from which, he knew from Carroll, Rottemeyer was to address the press.

Smythe knew the range to the podium to within a meter and a half. Even so, he checked and rechecked that range with a small, hand-held range finder. Then he rechecked the scope adjustment to confirm it was properly set for the range.

The window was fixed, immobile, as Smythe had assumed it would be. This presented no obstacle. He placed a small, handmade wooden implement on a stand on the sill by the window. With two more trips back to the scope Smythe was able to place the implement precisely where he needed to cut away a small section of the hotel window's glass.

The attachment of a suction cup and the deft swirl of a glasscutter preceded the removal of a small piece of the window. This Smythe put gently aside.

Lastly, Smythe removed from the smaller bag, the one already in the land-facing room, a plastic body garment which he donned before settling down behind his rifle to wait.

Galilee Episcopal Church, Virginia Beach, Virginia

Alvin had noticed one of the counter-snipers, the one on the roof of the Cavalier Hilltop. As he said later, he was uneducated, but not exactly stupid. *Where there's one, there's liable to be more than one.*

He promptly removed himself from view, trying to look as innocent as possible as he did so. From a window lower in the steeple, blending into the shadows at the far side, he kept a watch of the podium where he believed the President was going to stand during the press conference.

Alvin knew little of the personal security measures taken by the Secret Service where the life of a President of the United States was concerned. And he was a hunter. A center of mass shot was natural to his experience, though he had taken head shots when everything was perfectly suited to them. Yet the more he looked at that podium, the more he tried to picture the not very tall woman who was going to stand behind it, the more he realized that a center of mass shot just might not be possible.

Damn, damn, damn. I'm a good shot, Daddy always said so. But a head shot? At this range? I dunno. And, then too, I don't know if'n I can go through with it: looking a human bein' in the face while I shoot her. I dunno.

Alvin shook his head, uncertain. Then he reached into his back pocket and pulled out his wallet. There was a little money in it, but, he thought, *Ain't gonna have no use for money where I'm goin'.*

He pulled out an old picture of his wife. Even

at the best of times, she had been no more than slightly pretty. Yet Alvin had loved her with all his heart. To him, she had always been beautiful, inside and out.

He gazed at the picture, longingly, for some appreciable time. His mind went back to a time he had been happy, to a time when he'd had a decent job, a normal family, a wife. He didn't so much think about as feel the indignation of being subjected to the whims of a doctrinaire and arrogant social worker, of being forced onto charity, of being threatened with the loss of his children.

Alvin closed his eyes, shutting off the image of his wife as she had been when he had first seen her and replacing it with the shrunken, pale, husk of a woman in a cheap hospital bed, with needles and tubes stuck into her as she had been when he had last seen her.

Finally, he was sure. *Nope, these people, and especially that damned president, have got to take responsibility for what they done. They had all the power; they're responsible for what happened to me and my woman. I can do this.*

Satisfied, he turned his eyes back to the podium.

Presidential Limousine, Atlantic Avenue, Virginia Beach, Virginia

Her feelings were all spilled out, from her speech to the convention, leaving the President to feel little but emptiness inside. Even the thought of going to her own, formal, political seppuku did not move her.

For Wilhelmina Rottemeyer's impending press conference was for no other purpose than to announce her resignation from the office of President of the United States.

Though her body felt empty, her mind was full, full of thoughts and questions and wonderings. What went wrong? How did it all go so wrong, so quickly? I was at the top, the pinnacle. Not only at the top, but with more real power than anyone, even Roosevelt and Lincoln, had ever had.

Did I move too fast, as Carroll said once? Or did I move too slowly, as Vega insisted? One thing I know I did wrong; I underestimated that damned wetback from Texas. But who would have guessed that that little no-account, who wasn't even independent enough to keep her own name when she married, would have had the will to move her state almost to independence? Breaking me in the bargain.

Should I have left that old priest alone? Left the anti-abortion nuts alone? How could I? I had a constituency, not the least important part of it, my own federal law enforcement chiefs. How much hold over them would I have lost if I had caved in on the priest? Too much, I think.

And I had plans, I had dreams, for this country and for the world. Sure I was ambitious for myself, but who ever got anything worthwhile done that wasn't ambitious? I saw a world at peace, because why should anyone fight when everyone has enough? I saw a world where the environment was protected and cherished. I saw a world where everyone was equal . . . well, maybe women a little more equal than men. What was so wrong with that?

I wish sometimes that there really were a God so that I could ask him what I should have done.

Galilee Episcopal Church, Virginia Beach, Virginia

Alvin saw the President's limousine as it turned west off of the main road and onto the hotel driveway. He watched as the President emerged from the vehicle and two men helped her on with an overcoat that seemed somehow very heavy.

He walked, calmly enough, to the rifle, getting behind it and letting the tarp on the bar serve as a rest for his nonfiring hand even as the pedestal holding up the bar served as a rest and brace for his body. Still unseen in the shadows, Alvin took up a solid firing position, looked in the scope, and rested his cross hairs first on Rottemeyer's torso. Then, that view being frequently interrupted by the movement of the security agents, he shifted his aiming point to the President's head. Then he waited, forcing himself to breathe calmly, the breathing itself serving to calm him.

Cavalier Oceanfront Hotel, Seventh Floor, Virginia Beach, Virginia

Calm, still, silent—like a praying mantis in ambush, or a Shao Lin monk in training, Smythe had not so much as twitched a muscle since assuming his firing position. He had, in a real sense, become one with the rifle and the view in his scope.

That view changed. On the right side of the field of view a woman, easily recognizable as Wilhelmina Rottemeyer, entered it. Smythe remained still, however. If there were any minimal adjustments to be made, they would be made when Rottemeyer stopped at the podium.

There were none. Smythe had known her height in advance and placed his cross hairs at precisely the right place. Wilhelmina Rottemeyer, President of the United States, placed herself directly on them.

Smythe took a deep breath, let a quarter of it out, moved his finger to the trigger and began to apply a gentle pressure.

Galilee Episcopal Church, Virginia Beach, Virginia

Alvin was no artist, no assassin, no highly trained oriental spiritualist. He was not even a predatory insect, however buglike a social worker had once made him feel. He was simply an angry man with a job he felt he had to do.

As soon as Rottemeyer reached the podium, he—as had Smythe—took a single deep breath, let much of it out, and began to squeeze the trigger on his rifle. Not so highly trained as the professional was, Alvin's trigger moved more quickly.

Hotel Cavalier (Hilltop), Virginia Beach, Virginia

The only man or woman present at the scene who had cause to expect a shot, Carroll had placed himself well behind Willi and slightly to her right. He had less than no desire to be either in the way, or immediately behind.

Unlike the others present, Carroll also knew exactly why Rottemeyer had called this press conference—to resign. Thus, as a memorial to the ages he forced his face into a regretful, somber mask as he watched Willi open the folder containing her resignation speech. It was either force the mask, or risk showing the nervousness that threatened to take him over.

Willi had just looked up from her notes when three things happened: the top of her head flew off in a shower of blood and brains, there was the report seemingly of a single rifle shot, and the entire scene immediately and instantaneously devolved into bedlam.

Carroll especially noticed the fourth thing that happened. A bullet, unspent, passed—only slightly deformed—through Rottemeyer's head, through the intervening space, and right through Carroll's stomach. Only the fact that the air was knocked from his lungs kept him from screaming in agony.

With the next breath he drew, the screams began.

Cavalier Oceanfront Hotel, Seventh Floor, Virginia Beach, Virginia

Smythe's finger stopped tightening as soon as he felt the recoil and saw the top of his intended target's head fly off. Off to the right side of his scope he saw a man he recognized easily as James Carroll go down flopping like a dying fish.

"What the . . . ?"

Immediately realizing from the obvious angle of the other shot that he must have had an unknown competitor, Smythe grumbled something about "amateurs." Although his original plan had been to leave the rifle in the room and make his escape, he knew that that might be a mistake now. There was always a chance that the weapon, however "underground" it may have been, could be traced to him. Therefore, while insanity erupted below, and while he knew all eyes would have to be focused on the true assassin, he reversed the steps he had taken in preparation for his shot.

Off came the rifle from its cradle. Quickly it was broken down into its constituent parts. These were stowed in the case, to be followed by the tripod as soon as it was collapsed. The case was then closed.

Tearing off the shower cap and the plastic garment, Smythe stuffed these into the overnight bag. There was nothing inherently suspicious about them anyway, so he determined to leave them in the room, at least for now. The rifle case he slid under a bed. He could return for it later, if possible.

Smythe went to the door and opened it, looking down the hall. *Good. No excitement here yet.*

Lastly, as calmly as may be imagined, Smythe opened the door, stepped into the hallway, and began to walk to his own room.

Galilee Episcopal Church, Virginia Beach, Virginia

Alvin had no desire to kill anyone but the President. In fact, he expressly did not *want* any truly innocent blood on his hands. Thus, when a fusillade of shots from what he thought might be three different vantage points began to impact on the church steeple, instead of returning fire, he crawled to the steps and began to slither down them to the main church. Already he could hear sirens, both police and ambulance, converging on the area.

They'll be along for me soon. I wonder if they'll arrest me or just shoot me. Guess it don't much matter, no how. I ain't afraid.

Washington, DC

Caroline McCreavy could not at first believe the news reports. Over the next several hours after the shooting, she might be said to have been in a state of denial. Finally, the reports became too consistent, as well as too insistent.

At that point, McCreavy went to her desk drawer, removed a pistol from it, and with a sobbed, "Oh, Willi, I never stopped loving you," placed the pistol to her own head.

Convention Center, Virginia Beach, Virginia

The news traveled around the floor like wildfire. Juani could not at first believe it. She came to believe it, though, when a representative from Massachusetts, a woman, walked up to her and, first spitting on Juani's face, announced, "So it wasn't enough to drive her from office and ruin everything she's done for the people. You Texan bastards had to kill her, too, just like you did JFK."

Putting a restraining hand up to prevent Jack from flattening the Yankee, woman or not, Juani just shook her head in negation.

"It's all over the news. The President is dead and one of you Texas rednecks killed her."

Juani didn't, couldn't, make a verbal answer. She turned to Jack and pleaded, "Please take me to my hotel room."

EPILOGUE:

I

"Well, what did you expect to come out of the convention, Juani? Some utopian dream of truth and justice?"

The governor glared at Schmidt, at her side as he had been every day since the attack on her family. She glared, and then relented.

"I don't know what I expected, Jack. Something better. Something that had a better *chance* to last. Maybe if Rottemeyer hadn't been killed. . . ."

"If she'd lived she would have been a thorn in our side, true, Juani. Dead, the bitch is a dagger. Frankly it has me worried. The new President is likely to win reelection by hanging on to Willi's spiritual coattails. And he is, if anything, even less principled than she was. He might be smarter, too. Worries me."

Changing the subject, Juanita asked, "Is there any word from Elpidia?"

Schmidt hesitated before answering. Finally, reluctantly, he said, "She made it through all right, I know that much. But she's not coming back here. She can't face you. She won't."

"Poor girl," muttered Juani. "As if I would blame her for anything that's happened."

"You don't have to blame her, Juani. She blames herself enough."

II

Elpi had never flown before, other than that once in the helicopter with Charlesworth. She was looking forward to the experience no more than she had wanted to fly with Charlesworth; which is to say, not at all.

But what choice do I have? Go back to Austin? Stand around a constant reminder of everything my actions cost the governor? No . . . I don't think so.

She'd had no money of her own, but Minh had loaned her a fair amount. Well, he'd called it a loan to preserve the girl's meager self-respect. It had been intended as a gift, though, one Minh was pleased to make.

Minh had also made a phone call to a friend in a different country, asking for someone to meet her at the other end of the trip, see to setting her up, show her the ropes.

Minh understood that sometimes one just had to leave and start afresh.

Elpi wanted that, a fresh start someplace new. There were too many memories, too many harsh memories, in Texas for her ever to hope to be able to stay there. *The Padre, young Miguel and Mario . . .* at the thought of the governor's son, *what a sweet boy he was*, Elpidia forced back a little sob.

Minh's ears caught the tiny sound. He squeezed her shoulder once, for assurance, and then again, for luck. "You'll do fine, girl. A fresh start somewhere new is all you need."

Elpi smiled her thanks and relaxed slightly. "You'll tell the governor?"

"Yes, surely. She'll understand but I think she may be hurt you didn't come back."

"Maybe," answered the girl. "But she'd be hurt worse if I did come back."

"You might be right," said Minh. "In any case, that door will stay open, I think."

"Yes . . . I hope maybe someday . . ."

An unseen speaker interrupted Elpidia's sentence. "Continental Airlines Flight 888, nonstop Hobby Field to Tocumen airport, Panama is now boarding. . . ."

Elpi turned to the even smaller Vietnamese man. "Good-bye, Colonel. And thank you."

Minh merely smiled in his subtle Asian way. "Never mind, young lady. Just make a better life for yourself."

III

Same script, different players, thought the convalescent Carroll, initially. Then he amended the thought, *Well, no, a slightly different script after all. Now, while we've lost Willi, she's entered the ranks of martyrs to*

*the cause. And while we've lost quite a bit of power,
Willi's "martyrdom" also gave us back some.*

*I wonder if she knew and understood how important
it was to the cause that she become a martyr?*

The new president, Rottemeyer's previous Vice—
Walter Madison Howe, had seemed nearly a political
nonentity to Carroll, a mere adornment to the ticket.
Indeed, other than a widely suspected penchant for
females young enough to be his daughters, and a
widely held contempt for the new President's extremely
poor taste in women—those tending to the fat and
insecure—there had seemed to Carroll nothing to
recommend the man.

Politically, Howe was regarded as being somewhat
moderate, or—as many had said to Rottemeyer in her
heyday, "Compared to you, Willi, the man's practically
a right wing Fascist."

But Howe was no such thing. He was, in fact, possibly the least politically committed President since
Calvin Coolidge.

This was not to say, however, that Howe was uncommitted to politics. From his earliest boyhood, one
thought had dominated his heart and mind. *I will be
President someday.*

Running successfully and successively as a populist,
Howe had served as representative, governor, and
senator for his home state. Never once had he ever
shown the slightest tendency to let principle interfere
with expedience. "I'm against the death penalty," so
had Candidate Howe told more than a few cheering crowds at fundraisers. "I'll support the will of
the people," so had Governor Howe said in signing
an almost unequalled number of death warrants. "I

believe in protecting the environment." So had said candidate Howe. "A few million towards my next campaign and I think I can find ways to rein in those environmentalist people who want to shut you down." So had Governor Howe told a major contributor, the second largest pork producer in the nation.

A man utterly without political or moral principle, thought Carroll. *Perhaps that's just what we need.*

"So what's left?" asked Howe of his assembled Cabinet.

"That's a shorter list than what's gone," answered Carroll.

"Meaning?"

Carroll drawled back, "Well . . . we've managed to save some of the federal law enforcement capability, Customs, the INS and a part of the IRS. The Army's not been cut, as a practical matter, and won't be anytime soon if we can find a use for them. The Environmental Protection Agency still stands, though it's lost most of its direct enforcement powers . . . and I think that's going to be important . . ."

"It is," answered Howe. "But what we really need is to get our tax base back, am I right?"

"Yes, Mr. President. But they've stripped us of most of the responsibilities we need to have in order to tax. 'Promote the general welfare' lost most of its meaning and use to us."

"We still have 'provide for the common defense,' don't we?"

"Yessir, we do."

"Okay then, what's the problem? We got the government we had through foreign wars, didn't we? We just need to have some more of them."

Carroll considered. It was true, he knew. "But where, Mr. President? The Arabs are still reeling from the drubbing we gave them a few years back. The Europeans? Nah. The Balkans? A quagmire. And we don't have much reason to go in there anymore, anyway."

"Oh, I agree, Mr. Carroll. But I was thinking maybe somewhere closer to home."

Carroll inclined his head in deep thought. "Mexico? Maybe. 'Stop illegal immigration.' South Africa's going to hell, so there's another place. Colombia or Panama in another drug war might be possible. The Chinese can always be relied on to threaten Taiwan, I suppose. Iran? Well, it's no big deal to drum up popular feelings against Iran; that's become something of a national habit. The press won't roll for us as readily as they used to."

"I am thinking, Mr. Carroll, that one of those might do just fine. . . ."

IV
Greensville Correctional Center, Jarratt, Virginia

For once the Warden regretted a death penalty case the feds had not insisted on taking over themselves when they had a chance to. But in the current political enviroment, and with Virginia having no noticeable squeamishness about putting convicted murderers to death, the feds had simply stood aside.

Still, thought the warden. *I wish I didn't have to go through with this one.*

"It's time, Alvin."

Scheer looked up at the warden, and the two burly guards accompanying and nodded, calmly and with great dignity. "Yes, sir. I figured it would be."

"The governor—"

Alvin held up his hand to cut off the warden's words. "I never asked anybody for clemency, Warden. All those appeals? Well-meaning folks, most of 'em, I'm sure. But I never asked."

"I know," answered the warden.

Looking over at the tray of half-eaten food, the warden queried, "The meal, Alvin? It was cooked okay?"

"Yes, sir. It was just fine. Only thing is I weren't all that hungry. You understand." The condemned man smiled.

"Sure, sure. I understand."

Another man walked into the cell, more or less stiffly. "Alvin," said the warden, "this is Dr. Randall. He's going to give you a shot to relax you."

Scheer looked suspiciously from the warden to the doctor. "This isn't the one that's gonna kill me, is it?"

The warden shook his head. "No, son. But it will relax you some so you aren't so afraid."

Scheer felt his hackles begin to rise. He started to say, "I ain't—" Then he laughed at himself and said, "Thanks, Warden . . . Doctor."

"What's the shot, doc?"

"Just thorazine, Mr. Scheer. Nothing to harm you. Now if you would roll up your sleeve?"

Alvin bared his arm. "You know," he observed, "if'n you folks really wanted to be kind to me, that there thorazine stuff would kill me so quick I wouldn't even know."

To this the warden said nothing, though he privately agreed. A fair number of the condemned had come through this facility after being housed for some years up on death row in the Mecklenburg prison. Most of them the warden considered to deserve to die, and in many cases to die more painfully than they did. Alvin, though, had been a model prisoner in Mecklenburg—so it was reported, and quite easy to deal with for his necessarily short stay in Greensville.

Alvin tried not to flinch as the doctor's needle entered his arm.

The walk from the cell to the execution chamber was a short one. Alvin noticed a partition that had been set up, then let his eyes rest on the gurney on which he would begin his final sleep. Though drugged, he understood that much clearly.

Alvin could not see, because the partition shielded it from view, the electric chair that remained an option and was still, occasionally, used.

In the chamber, the warden invited Alvin to make a last statement. He just shook his head in negation and said, "I've never been a man of many words, sir."

Also in the chamber was, among the other witnesses, a tall, gray-haired man in a military uniform. The warden nodded at that man who then arose and walked to Alvin's side.

"Alvin, I'm General Schmidt, from Texas. I just want you to know two things. One, you did what I wanted to. Two, your kids are going to be cared for. My word on it."

"Good enough for me, sir. Thank you."

Schmidt grasped a shoulder and gave a comforting squeeze before returning to his seat.

The two guards assisted Alvin onto the gurney, then began strapping him down, arms, torso and waist. Alvin lay quietly, cooperating when asked. The strapping finished, the guards stepped back. One of them made a small head signal for the medical technician to come forward.

Expertly, the technician found Alvin's veins and tapped them. A saline drip was started to keep the veins open while the tubes that would carry the lethal drugs were connected.

Alvin closed his eyes and made himself think of his wife as she had been. He imagined her scolding him, *Alvin Sheer, you've got to take responsibility for your actions.* Even the scolding brought a smile to his face, unaccountable, perhaps, to the witnesses.

The warden's head nodded a last time. From behind the partition two men began to force the drugs through the tubing and into Scheer's veins. First came a heavy dose of sodium pentathol. It rendered Alvin unconscious, though not necessarily incapable of dreaming . . . the smile remained, after all.

The sodium pentathol would have killed Alvin eventually on its own, so high was the dose. But no chances were taken with such matters. It was immediately followed with a lethal dose of pancuronium bromide. Alvin's diaphragm and lungs were instantly paralyzed. This, too, would have killed him, eventually.

Lastly was administered a killing solution of potassium chloride. Alvin's heart stopped. Perhaps his dream remained, for a few minutes.

Huntsville Prison, Texas

Friedberg cursed and twisted and shrieked abuse at her guards, at the warden, at Juanita Seguin, and at Texas in general.

"Let me go, you fucking assholes. Let me go! Don't you realize who I am? I'm the fucking head of the fucking FBI. You don't strap me onto a gurney. I put you on one."

Ignoring her protests, her guards hauled her to the gurney and strapped her down roughly. The entire time, Friedberg hurled abuse at them, abuse they ignored.

She began to scream and twist, upsetting the technician's aim and causing him to have to make multiple strikes with the needle. At each failed penetration Friedberg screamed anew. Finally, weakened, she began to sob and to beg. The needles went in.

Juanita took the place of the warden for the next phase, something of an unusual deviation. "Louise Friedberg, you have been found guilty by a jury of your peers of the murders of Josefina Sanchez, Maria Ramirez, Pablo Trujillo . . . Father Jorge Montoya," she concluded.

At the conclusion of Juanita's list of nearly one hundred murders, the warden took over again.

Friedberg screamed until the sodium pentathol reached her brain.

APPENDIX

Various amendments to the United States Constitution proposed at the Virginia Beach, Virginia, Constitutional Convention:

Amendment—The Sixteenth Amendment is hereby repealed. No direct taxes shall be levied upon living persons, real or artificial.

Amendment—Federal expenditures shall not exceed ten percent of Gross Domestic Product. An estate tax, not exceeding fifty percent may be levied on estates over ten million dollars in current dollars upon portions of those estates exceeding that amount. The figure of ten million dollars shall be adjusted annually in accordance with the rise in cost of living as determined by the Consumer Price Index.

Amendment—The Social Security and Medicare tax is repealed. Current interest holders in the Social

Security system shall have their money repaid within ten years at an interest rate of nine percent.

Amendment—Within ten years from the date of enactment of this amendment the Congress shall not have the right to delegate its authority under the constitution. The Congress shall reduce the manpower of currently existing agencies to which it has delegated its authority by ten percent per year.

Amendment—No one shall be elected to any office of the federal government more than twice in succession, three times in life, or twelve years total.

Amendment—Every four years, in conjunction with the election for the presidency of the United States, each ballot shall list all the members of the United States Supreme Court. That justice of that court whose name garners the greatest number of votes in that election shall be forever disbarred from a seat on the Supreme Court or any federal elective office.

Amendment—At any time when a majority of the governors of the states shall vote, in joint session, to overturn any decision of the Supreme Court impacting upon the rights of the sovereign states under this Constitution, that decision shall be overturned. Thirty such governors shall constitute a quorum.

Amendment—The Second Amendment is hereby repealed. The federal government shall insure that no private individuals keep or possess nuclear, chemical or biological weapons of mass destruction. All other forms of weapons may be owned, borne and possessed by the citizens of the United States without restriction or registration. Such weapons may not be taxed.

Amendment—No suit against the United States, or any of its states, for any grievance which accrued more than twenty years prior to the enactment of this Amendment, shall be maintained or sustained.

Amendment—The Regular Armed Forces of the United States shall be no greater in manpower than half of one percent of the population of adult citizens of the United States. In the event of war requiring greater levels of manpower, the states are required to provide further troops, up to six percent of the state's population as determined by the most recent census.

Amendment—Neither the federal government, nor any of its branches, shall make any rule limiting or interfering with the free exercise of religion on the part of any of the lesser polities of the United States or the citizens of those polities.

Amendment—A human being shall be defined as an implanted, fertilized ovum of the human species, or any later stage of development of that implanted ovum. All human beings within the United States shall be entitled to the full protection of the law.

Amendment—It shall be the right of citizens and lawful residents of the United States to speak in plain, standard and traditional English. It shall be illegal and actionable against any citizen, resident, business entity, educational institution or government to make any attempt to limit that right on the part of a citizen.

Amendment—Federal law enforcement personnel are restricted to not more than one twentieth of one percent of the adult population of the United States.

Amendment—Whereas responsibility and authority must be equal, and whereas it has been demonstrated that abuse of authority is inevitable at some point for some responsibilities, so the United States Government is relieved of the following responsibilities: to ensure the economic well being of individuals of any class or by any means or for any period of time, to regulate commerce except that no state shall be permitted to set up tariffs against any other state or states, to conduct economic planning, to ensure the rights or presumed rights of any group as a group, to engage in social engineering, to interfere with or aid education at any level.

About the Author

In 1974, at age seventeen, **Tom Kratman** became a political refugee and defector from the PRM (People's Republic of Massachusetts) by virtue of joining the Regular Army. He stayed a Regular Army infantryman most of his adult life, returning to Massachusetts as an unofficial dissident while attending Boston College after his first hitch. Back in the Army, he managed to do just about everything there was to do, at one time or another. After the Gulf War, and with the bottom dropping completely out of the anti-communism market, Tom decided to become a lawyer. (Big mistake, way big. Chilluns, don't do it.) Every now and again, when the frustrations of legal life and having to deal with *other* lawyers got to be too much, Tom would rejoin the Army (or a somewhat similar group, say) for fun and frolic in other climes. His family, muttering darkly, still puts up with this. Tom is currently an attorney practicing in southwest Virginia. *A State of Disobedience* is his first novel.

• BOLO: The Future of War •

. . . .

What is a Bolo? The symbol of brute force, intransigent defiance, and adamantine will. But on a deeper level, the Bolo is the Lancelot of the future, the perfect knight, sans peur et sans reproche. With plated armor, a laser canon, an electronic brain, and wheels.

. . . .

Ranks and files of caskets, twenty-six of them undersized, stretched across an open area that was part of the Mission's old Spanish cemetery. The priest had finished and the time had come for the governor to have her say. Tired, and with fatigue and stress showing on her face, she walked steadily to a podium, followed by the cameras that fed to Stone's Internet node and from there to the world.

Juanita began calmly, "The people who did this, who committed this horrible crime, believe that they have accounted for everything, that with their guns they have frightened half of us into submission . . . and with their taxes bribed the rest of us into acquiescence. They think they can get away with anything—murder, mayhem, massacre."

Among the crowd, many began softly to weep.

Bitterness fell away before rage. "Oh, the fools, the fools, the stupid and utterly contemptible fools." She stopped for breath before continuing and put her hand on her brother's casket. "They have left us our sacred Texan dead. And while Texas under their yoke, holds these dead, Texas will never be at peace.

"For I have had a vision. And with this vision, I speak to those who think themselves my people's master, and I speak to them in my people's name. Beware, you tyrants in Washington. Beware of the day that is coming. Beware you sanctimonious hypocrites. Beware of the risen people. Do you think, you tyrants, that law is stronger than life? Do you think, you hypocrites, that your fascist propaganda can outweigh mankind's desire to be free?"

Looking directly into the camera now, face grown red even through her olive complexion, Juanita pronounced the future. "We will take back what you have stolen. We will be free."

Baen Books by Tom Kratman

A State of Disobedience
Watch on the Rhine (with John Ringo)